SIGNAL

Signal

Tony Peak

Signal

They were sent to investigate the first extraterrestrial signal. What they found was beyond anything they could have imagined—or feared.

On a voyage to a mysterious moon in the Alpha Centauri system, the UEA Centaurus meets with disaster. Only the quick thinking of the flight engineer, Rachel Terman, saves some of the crew. Crash-landing on the moon, trillions of kilometers from Earth, they struggle to carry out their mission and try to survive.

But nothing has prepared them for what they will face. False readings on sensors. Bizarre nightmares. Crew members vanishing.

Then Rachel discovers a blue, glassy lake.

And everything changes. If the signal abides—will humankind fall?

Books by Tony Peak

Beethoven's Tenth
Inherit the Stars
Prophet of Pathways
Signal
Wages of Cinn

To anyone who has ever felt lost.

Table of Contents

ACKNOWLEDGEMENTS

A big thank you to my agent Ethan Ellenberg, who found a publisher willing to give this story life; to Steve Farber at Audible, who believed in SIGNAL from the start and stood by it through thick and thin. A special thanks to the audiobook cast, particularly Natasha Soudek for taking on so many roles and providing my characters with such a good voice. Chris McGrath deserves a shout-out for his beautiful cover art; that image is like something stolen from my greatest sci-fi dreams. Many thanks to my beta readers: Ian Welke, Meredith Morgenstern Lopez, and Juliette Wade—you kept me honest when it came time to revise. Last but not least, thanks to all of my family for standing by me when I too felt lost out there in the darkness.

1

CMD Granger: Okay, everyone's suit link is showing online. Report in.

CMP Eaton: Eaton here, Commander Granger. Flight path is steady.

CFE Terman: This is Terman, cabin is good.

CMP Worrel: Worrel reporting for *Maray*. No worries.

MS Khandaar: Khandaar reporting, sir.

CFE Moore: Yes, sir, Moore reporting.

CFE Terman: Proxima Centauri C on scanners. Equatorial radius of 2,578 kilometers. Inclination at 18.2 degrees. Other data not coming through, sir.

CMP Eaton: Signal noise?

CMD Granger: It should clear up once we get closer. *Seeker*, you copy?

(static)

CMD Granger: *Seeker*, over?

CSO Kovac: Sorry about that. This is Kovac, *Seeker* is good.

MS Sakurai: Sakurai here, cabin is good.

MS Burgess: Burgess reporting, *le commandant*.

MS Li: Li here, sir.

CMP Eaton: Final approach to Proxima Centauri C, Commander.

(various whoops, cheers, laughter)

CMD Granger: (laughs) Calm down, everyone. *Luzinia*, report in.

CEO Paredo: Paredo here, sir. We are all a "go."

MS Richter: Richter reporting.

MS Jemutai: Jemutai reporting in. Cabin is good.

CFE Terman: Commander, I'm having difficulty getting Centrifuge B online.

CMD Granger: Keep trying, Terman. Eaton, how are we?

CMP Eaton: We should be in orbit within two minutes, sir.

CMD Granger: Good. I'll give the mission briefing then. *Aloha*, report.

CMO Bakir: Bakir reporting for *Aloha*, Commander. Monitoring everyone's suit links—we are one healthy crew. Except for Larsen, your pulse is up.

(laughter)

MS Larsen: Larsen here. Cabin is very good. Controlling my excitement, Doctor.

MS Santos: Santos reporting—

(several voices cry out)

CMD Granger: What the hell was that?

CFE Terman: Centrifuge B is still not responding.

CMP Eaton: Sir, I've got caution lights for Centrifuge B.

CMD Granger: Terman, get it under control before we make orbit.

CFE Terman: I'm trying, sir, but—

CMT Stevenson: There's a fire in Centrifuge B!

CMD Granger: What? Can you confirm?

CMT Stevenson: I can see it from *Vivaldi*'s viewport.

MS Santos: Confirm that visual from *Aloha*!

CMD Granger: Terman, get on it!

Rachel Terman swiveled her seat to the onboard systems terminal. This wasn't what she needed while helping Eaton pilot *Centaurus* into orbit. They were already entering the moon's exosphere. Another thirty seconds and they'd experience reentry.

Crammed into the cockpit with Commander Granger on her forward right, and Eaton on her forward left, Rachel tried not to panic. She'd been trained for this. Everyone was outfitted in tight blue IVA suits, complete with helmet and air supply. The hull was well-shielded against cosmic radiation. They would make it.

Ahead, the orange-brown sphere of Promixa Centauri C hovered barely within reach of its parent star. A ghost she and her comrades had been chasing for four years. She forced herself not to stare at the moon. Duty first, not tourism.

"Automatic extinguishers not responding," Rachel said into her headset mic. "Trying the manual ones."

"I want that thing out ASAP," Granger said. "All hands, stand by."

"Encountering atmospheric drag," Eaton said. "Pitch is two hundred degrees, yaw is 110."

"Activate forward thrusters." Granger glanced at Rachel with worry. "Terman?"

"I've got it under control."

They'd woken from stasis two hours ago—the first time Rachel had moved in four years. All had suited up and strapped into their respective modules, prepared for any event that might endanger their mission.

Except for a fire right in the middle of the ship.

"The blaze is spreading," Stevenson said.

"Damn it," Granger said. "Open the service hatch. That should suffocate it."

"Why is there air inside it to begin with?" Stevenson asked.

"Someone must have forgotten to purge it," Granger said.

Rachel swiveled back to her main console. Gloved hands flicked the proper switches, anxious eyes tallied the numbers on the screen. *Centaurus* vibrated as the thrusters fired. Rachel's teeth shook along with it.

"We're at 4 g's, holding steady," Eaton said. "Roll at thirty degrees."

"Terman, talk to me," Granger said.

"The hatch won't open," Rachel said. "It's not working."

"Terman, I need that fire out!"

Rachel mashed button after button. "Sir, it won't—"

Centaurus quaked. Alarms burst from the cockpit speakers. Warnings flashed across various screens in glowing, terminal red.

The lighted diagram of *Centaurus* on the main screen, showing each individual module and system, darkened in the middle. The exact location of both centrifuges.

Granger blanched. "Everyone, report in!"

Centaurus shook again. Crew modules *Maray* and *Olduvai* went off-line.

"Shit!" someone cried over the radio.

"I've lost control!" Eaton wrestled with the manuals. "Pitch is 240!"

Several people shouted simultaneously over the comm.

"Hull breach in—"

"He went right through the hole, oh my God, he went right through—"

"We're at 7 g's!" Eaton yelled. "8 g's!"

More voices clogged the channel. Granger yelled something, but Rachel ripped open the emergency module release, under the main console. Eighteen buttons for eighteen modules. Forty crew. Some had to be dead already.

Still, Rachel punched each button in rapid succession.

The screen displayed one module after another detaching as *Centaurus* streaked toward the moon. The cockpit blew away from the main ship but something tossed it into a spiral dive. Rachel gripped her restraints as the radio faded from screams to static.

Sparks flew as the hull on her right was punctured. Decompression followed in violent fury. A jagged bulkhead zipped past her and sheared through Eaton. Both halves of him darted out the breach, along with a scattering of crimson globules.

Granger reached out for Rachel, face twisted with fright.

A jolt of gravitational force struck her, crushing her into the chair. It hurt to breathe. A second later, she couldn't breathe. She feared a blackout or even a G-LOC, losing consciousness because of hazardous g-forces. The glowing screens, the blinking alarms, Granger's limp, flailing form, Eaton's floating blood—it all created a barrage of madness without sound, the only noise her dry lips trying to suck in air.

Her fingers kept mashing the ejection buttons, little entities with minds of their own, attached to her consciousness only by skin and bone. A wobble in her gut developed into full nausea. Tried to fill her lungs with air. Tried to say something, anything, into the mic, before she met her end out there, trillions of kilometers from Earth.

The memory came unbidden and proceeded through her mind with an awful slowness. Each second was an agonizing span of torture.

"You can't keep jerking yourself around like this," Dad said. *"Earth's not so bad. Your mother and I, we came here for you. I don't know what else you want from us."*

"I've made my decision."

She didn't remember saying it with such finality.

Dad gazed skyward, then faced her. "Think you'll be able to start all over out there? Forget all this? It's not going to get any better. You know that."

She'd hated him for not understanding. Hated herself for not inviting him and Mom to *Centaurus*'s launch.

"Maybe." Rachel shifted, uncomfortable under Earth's gravity. Under his stare.

"The star, planet, whatever, might change, but not you. But we'll always love you, Rachel." He reached for her hand but she drew back. Finally, he left the apartment.

A bang against the hull yanked Rachel's attention back to her impending death.

The cockpit module spun through the moon's atmosphere, which was thicker than what they had expected. A satellite of Centauri B, no more than a speck visible from UEA's best telescope that orbited Mars. Reentry turned the view from starry field to burning orange wrath through the viewports. Rachel couldn't raise her hands to shield her eyes, but the faceplate auto-tinted, sparing her eyesight.

Color drained from everything. A dark tunnel filled her vision. Fingers twitched. Eyelids stuck together, then fluttered. Still no breath to scream.

Turbulence flipped the cockpit to and fro, finally knocking the ability to breathe back into Rachel. Each inhalation came as a ragged, painful gulp of her suit's air reserve. Granger sat slumped in his chair, the interior of his faceplate covered in blood. New alarms sounded, though in tinny whines, since the speakers were singed or busted. The screens showed the ship's altitude at 2,500 meters. Just 2 g's of force now.

But the descent pitch was at a suicidal 260-degree angle.

Sucking in the next breath too hard, Rachel coughed. The quasi–rigor mortis holding her in place relented and she fumbled for the console controls. The autopilot functioned, but because of the damage from the explosion, some sensors indicated the computer thought it was landing with the benefit of Module One's thrusters.

Thirty-seven seconds to impact.

She accessed the autopilot, then switched it off. Flew the cockpit module manually. The joystick, made more for psychological benefit than pragmatic application, filled her hand like a petrified snake. Screens flashed, suggested, warned. She assimilated the data with quick glances while lowering the module's angle of descent.

Twenty seconds to impact.

Her thrusters fired too late. She would crash.

"*Centaurus*..." She swallowed, didn't look at Granger.

Ten seconds.

"This is Chief Flight Engineer Rachel Terman, making a distressed landing on Promixa Centauri C, satellite—"

Impact.

The module creaked and whined as the hull buckled in places. Hoses and wires snapped, enfilading her with burning gases and vicious blue sparks. One restraint ripped free, bruising her right shoulder. She rocked back and forth from the crash, even though the parachute had deployed. Granger's body now lay on the floor, held by one shredded restraint. A fine red stream leaked from his busted helmet. She realized the shrapnel that had killed Eaton had also struck him. How he must have suffered, bleeding out—

"This is Flight…Engineer…oh shit." Rachel fought back a sob. "Fucking shit."

Remnants of Eaton's blood had mottled the cabin walls in scarlet blotches. The breach had been sealed by other debris lodging itself there, welded in place during the first seconds of reentry. If not for that, Rachel would have been incinerated.

"This is Flight Engineer Rachel Terman. Does anyone read me?"

The static-filled reply chilled her. Like a million dying flies buzzing in her ears.

Rachel found a sharp piece of hull and used it to saw through her last restraint belt. The taut fabric gave way, loosing her onto the cracked, smoking deck. Light shone through the fractured viewports—maybe sunlight, maybe the burning vessel itself.

Taking calmer breaths, Rachel steadied against her chair. Gravity wasn't intolerable, perhaps a few tenths of a percent less than Earth's. Still a burden for her Martian body, though. Living for years on Earth, she had never acclimated to its harsh pull.

The cockpit had depressurized, and Rachel already felt dizzy; the moon's atmosphere must be a lower pressure. She needed her EMU suit.

Objects inside the module's walk-in locker had been shaken up but all was intact. Leaving her IVA suit on—it was slim enough—Rachel tugged herself into an extravehicular mobility unit. It was brand-new, tailored specifically for this mission. She avoided looking at the empty suits bearing Granger's and Eaton's name patches.

Once online, her suit's sensors indicated the outside temperature and atmosphere weren't forgiving: 375 Kelvin, hot enough to boil water. The air was 56 percent nitrogen, 32 percent hydrogen, 9 percent oxygen, and 5 percent methane. A very odd mixture, since that much hydrogen, being a light gas, should have already escaped into space. Plus, her dosimeter showed radiation content at 100 millisieverts—though that might be caused by *Centaurus*'s explosion. Still, one dose of that much radiation could give her cancer in a matter of years, or less.

That level of exposure, daily, would do much worse. Her EMU blocked some radiation but not all. With the cockpit module compromised, she needed to find shelter.

First came the immediate concern of Granger's body. After tugging his corpse a dozen different ways, she sealed him in a body bag to avoid contaminating the planet. That left Eaton's dried, scorched blood all over the cabin walls, but those cells were dead.

A moment passed as she studied the abattoir that had once been a cockpit. Stilled herself against the horrors within, and what horrors she might discover without.

There were no prayers or last words. The living needed her now.

She pressed on the exit hatch. It fell away, having blown its sealed hinges. Another second of reentry and she'd have been fried. Twice she'd cheated death so far. The sheer nonsense of her luck made Rachel laugh, but it came out as a barking cough.

"Who is that?" a voice asked over the radio.

2

Rachel stumbled from the cockpit module onto a ridge of sand and stone. The compunction, even the need, to answer another human voice after such an ordeal was forgotten. The vista ahead demanded her attention.

A plain hemmed in by dunes stretched to the horizon. Rocky pillars and arches had assembled in forlorn groups, eroded to skeletal shapes. Their exposed layers were a dull collection of reds and greens. Occasional mineral veins gleamed blue in the sunlight. It was all scalloped and smooth as if crafted by hand rather than the elements.

Proxima Centauri shone overhead like a light bulb viewed through dirty cellophane. A yellow-brown haze languished despite a recurring breeze, carrying sand with it. Her suit's sensors indicated atmospheric pressure was at 52 kilopascals—half of Earth's. At least it wasn't low enough to boil the water in her body, unlike her Martian home.

The compass app on her HUD indicated that north was behind her. At least this moon had a magnetosphere, which would block cosmic radiation.

Distant ridges and plateaus, pocked by the occasional crater, were cast in shadow. Was it sunset or sunrise? Sweat rolled down her face as she stared at the landscape she'd sacrificed so much to see. Her family, her home world, even her pre-cybernetic body were no longer hers, but wraiths in another star system—all for this.

Her suit's astronav app indicated which point in the sky was Sol. The glowing ball that had once burned her sensitive skin, nourished Mom's orchids, and blinded her on those late-evening drives to Shalbatana Valley, was now a dim, unremarkable dot.

"Please, answer me!"

The voice shook Rachel from her interstellar reverie. She tuned her suit's antenna for a better signal. "This is Flight Engineer Rachel Terman. I've landed on the moon, but Granger and Eaton are both dead. The cockpit module is beyond repair."

"Terman, this is Chief Medical Officer Adnan Bakir. I'm standing outside *Aloha*. We just touched down on a mesa eight degrees from what we think is your crash site. *Vivaldi* and Supply Module Thirteen landed nearby, but our situation…"

Rachel scanned the horizon until she spotted a column of smoke. "I think I see you, Bakir. Any contact with the rest of the crew?"

Seconds passed. Empowered by the need to know, Rachel walked up and down the ridge, seeking signs of any other crashed modules. None.

"Bakir?" She checked the frequency on her faceplate HUD. "You copy?"

The connection buzzed. "Sorry, Terman. Communications keeps dropping in and out. That's a negative on contact. There's still debris raining down."

He was right. Thousands of tiny embers streaked across the sky. Her eyes watered, her guts churned. Some of those glowing ashes had been her teammates.

"How many survivors can you confirm in your location?" she asked.

"Five so far," Bakir said. "One is wounded and requires immediate care. The others remain in a state of shock. There are…two bodies still inside *Vivaldi*."

"Are their suits compromised?"

"No. There's no risk of contamination. Not yet. Terman?"

She trudged down the embankment, keeping the smoke in sight. "Yes?"

"If Granger and Eaton are gone, that places you in charge."

The statement filled her with a new horror. Concentrating on a hundred other things, she'd not given the command structure any thought.

"Do you have any idea what Granger was going to brief us about?" Bakir asked. "There's nothing in the UEA logs that indicate extra information for our expedition."

"I...I don't know," Rachel said.

"Can you cope with this?" Bakir's tone was neutral but the innuendo was there.

"That's why the UEA selected me." Rachel felt a familiar throb in her chest. The chill in the small of her back whenever people expected more of her for being Martian.

"I'm simply asking as a physician," Bakir said.

"Yes. Gather everyone and build a shelter. Double the walls up if you can, the radiation readings are pretty brutal. Deploy your drones for a scan, if they survived."

"Should I send a rover to find you?" Bakir asked. The connection faded out for a minute before he came back online. "Terman?"

"No." Rachel plodded across the sandy regolith below the ridge. With each step she sank past her ankles. "Save all resources. I'm heading in the direction of the smoke. I'll reach you within the hour. This gravity isn't so bad."

She didn't bother checking the cockpit module for salvageable supplies. Later she'd return with a rover and someone to help with that. Right now she had to deal with being the sole commander of the expedition. What remained of it.

And what an expedition it was. Forty of the brightest, hardiest people Earth—and in her case, Mars—could offer. Forty people who weren't afraid to risk everything to reach this touchstone for humanity. At least, that was the romantic version fed to the public. Out here, there was no place for such idealistic notions, no time to ponder fatuous matters like destiny or the double-edged sword her species called progress.

Out here, it was just her and what remained of the crew. Her responsibility.

Four years ago, Earth had received a signal from the very moon on which she now walked. It'd been a mishmash of audio and images. Most of it had been indecipherable, and all of it controversial, since the images displayed the moon's surface and chemical content. This was viewed as an invitation by many, though some expressed doubts. All nations and states agreed the signal had to be investigated. Many declared it could be a "first-contact" scenario. United Earth Aeronautics—UEA—sent its latest, fastest vessel, *Centaurus*, to the trinary system, Alpha Centauri. Wayfarers in search of tomorrow.

Their mandate was to make contact with whoever sent the message, as well as establish a temporary colony—the soil information contained in the signal had excited scientists. After six months of study and assumed contact, they were to return home.

No one would be returning now.

A distant *thud* and a slight quake told her another module had either landed or crashed. Rachel didn't quicken her step. No need exhausting herself, for then she'd be of little use to anyone. She had three hours of oxygen, and the calorie block/insulin growth factor kit she'd consumed after waking from stasis still fed her body with eager power.

Though her bowels were sealed in capsular segments, enhancing digestion in variable gravities, there was nothing on this new world that would allow her to survive. Then there were her bones. Augmented with the latest nano-osteology, with all joints consisting of solid, light polymers far stronger than human bone, she was hardier than any previous explorer. She was the first human to set foot on a planet outside of their solar system. The first Martian. The weight of that achievement wasn't lost on her.

The weight of other concerns was far heavier.

So much she'd given up, just to see this horizon. Where even the concept of god lost all meaning, even on pitiful human terms.

There was nothing on Earth for her, never would be. She'd hated Dad for it, even though he'd ultimately been right. As a second-generation Martian, she'd received offers to serve as a surrogate mother for Martian, Lunar, and even Ganymedean families—people who wanted a child native to low-G. But she refused to be a uterus-for-hire, and the risk was still substantial, given her delicate Martian physiology. Then there were the UEA scholarships. She barely got one, and then promotions went to other astronauts with less experience and training, since Earthlings enjoyed favoritism in the selection process.

But she refused to let them beat her. She was stronger where it counted.

How she'd longed to leave the dry, lifeless prison that was Mars. Staring at the new canals built across Shalbatana. Staring with loathing. After leaving the red planet, though, Earth—and the UEA—had been a different prison. Both were beautiful cages. Crushing her body with merciless, cumulative gravitational side effects.

Crushing her heart because they thought her frail and inferior.

But the publicity of a Martian going to Promixa Centauri gave her the promotion. A chance to mold herself, rather than be satisfied with what her parents, her homeworld, or even Earth, deemed acceptable. Twenty-seven years old, and she had survived getting her heart broken by a few women, survived Earth's bigotry, survived its gravity.

The new world she sought wasn't extraterrestrial, but one of her own making.

She'd slept four years on *Centaurus*, in stasis, her body enhanced to survive nature's blackest reaches. Fortified against the wasting of bone from gravity, and cellular death from cancerous radiation, she remained mortal in all the ways that counted.

All the ways that could still destroy her.

Over the next ridge, the smoke appeared closer, originating from atop a mesa. Her boots sank a few more centimeters in the sand, no doubt built up from the constant winds. Though possessing a thin atmosphere, the moon didn't lack for aerial drama. The cockpit module might be covered over in a few days unless it was cleaned off.

Which again prompted thoughts of a rescue mission.

Four years from Earth, with no relief coming. Any SOS message would take four years to reach Earth since radio waves moved at the same speed as light.

She recalled her first meeting with Commander Granger.

"There's no need to worry." Granger smiled as Rachel studied the technicians assembling Centaurus, *module by module, on the stardock outside. "We'll have everything we need in those eighteen self-contained worlds. Each one will be like a little Earth we take with us."*

"I've had enough of Earth." Rachel flexed her hand, feeling no difference between her new, titanium-laced knuckles and her old, biological ones. The surgeons had not even made her double-jointed or ambidextrous. Never give a cyborg more advantages than the government was willing to pay for.

"I just want to say I admire what you're doing," Granger said. "My sister married a second-generation Martian. She says they all look up to you over there."

"Really? Where's your sister's spouse from?" Rachel asked.

"New Paris." Granger smiled. "You know, well away from the rest."

She looked away before he saw her anger. The "rest" were the native-born Martians not wealthy enough to live in the new metropolis. Like her.

"Can I name a module?"

"Sure, why not?" Granger reclined at his desk. "Your own slice of heaven."

Rachel formed a fist with her new fingers. "Bimini."

After saving up for years, Mom and Dad had taken her there for their first Earth vacation. The tiny island in the Bahamas was the loveliest paradise, all that crystalline water scintillating under a sun that felt larger, more dominant. All had seemed possible then—her hopes of becoming a UEA pilot, finding an Earthling woman to settle down with, maybe even children afterward. Only after submerging in those waters, frightened by the painful pressures of greater and greater depths, had she realized her folly.

Her movements to Bakir's mesa stirred up dust. The particles remained airborne a split second longer than they would have on Earth. As if they, too, sought escape from this strange prison world. For now, she and the rest were its prisoners.

She paused upon sighting a shriveled, ropy object. Like a length of sinew, left to dry after the kill. Kneeling down, she surmised it was dried vegetation. Lacking the proper instruments in her sensor suite, she couldn't identify it. She hated to leave it, but surely there would be more. Plus, she needed to rendezvous with Bakir before he got skittish and sent the rover after her anyway. The fear in his voice had been palpable.

Few crew members really knew each other that well. They'd been assembled in a hurry, gathering at the UEA station in Earth orbit. They were all under the agency's employ beforehand or had applied for the mission. Briefings for a week, refresher training for a month, then entering stasis on *Centaurus* for the voyage. The UEA depended on test results, statistics, and probabilities for crew cohesion. Everyone knew their duty.

Granger had apparently known a little more.

She'd never understood what the rush was, to get them here so quickly. Whatever had sent the signal would still be present, if it expected a reply. But she'd come anyway. Entered that dark cocoon in the ship, slept away while *Centaurus* traversed more than thirty-seven trillion kilometers. While Mom and the Dad grew older, lived their lives, maybe even died, she dreamed of the life she really wanted, so far out here where there was nothing but her reflection in a dusty faceplate.

"My own slice of heaven," she murmured, climbing up the mesa's western face. Despite her slight frame Rachel ascended the rocky butte like a mountain goat. Growing up at Pathfinder Base, she'd climbed up from many canyons and ravines, carved in her homeworld eons ago. Her deltoids and trapezius burned, her triceps weakened, her lats quivered, but she was used to battling gravity. Pulling herself up the slope, she grinned. A victory, no matter how small, was still a victory.

The plain atop the mesa extended a few kilometers. She discerned the distant shapes of modules, mere specks on the skyline. The smoke rose higher. Darker.

"Bakir?" She looked around. On her left the mesa fell off into a canyon, winding north across the moon's surface. On her right, the mesa sloped south into cratered flatlands. A graveyard of previous meteorite visitations.

"Bakir, you read me? This is Terman, over." Her strides, powered by desperation and more than a little worry, devoured the landscape one boot print at a time.

Static teased her ear.

Her boots scraped past debris. Blackened bits of hull. Someone's physical diary, an anachronism missing four years' worth of entries. Wires. Slivers of smoldering metal.

A charred hand, with half a glove still melded to the flesh.

"Bakir!" Rachel broke into a run as a large shower of debris flew over the sky, headed for where Bakir and—as far as she knew—the only survivors had made camp.

Flight Recorder – *Maray* Crew Module
Sol 1 – 1405 hours
Orbiting Proxima Centauri C

CMP Worrel: We have separated from *Centaurus*! Repeat, we have separated from *Centaurus*!

CFE Moore: Captain Granger, we've lost signal, do you copy?

(unknown response from unidentified module)

CFE Moore: Captain Granger, do you copy? This is—

CMP Worrel: We can't help them, Moore. Damage report?

MS Khandaar: The sensors are scrambled, I can't—

CFE Moore: Pitch is 270!

CMP Worrel: Son of a bitch. Fire thrusters.

MS Khandaar: Thrusters deployed.

CMP Worrel: Status?

CFE Moore: *Maray*'s intact. All systems online.

MS Khandaar: No, thrusters A and B aren't working.

CFE Moore: Jivika, honey, the readout shows—

MS Khandaar: Damn it, they aren't working!

(break in transcript due to power failure)

CFE Moore: The auxiliary generator kicked in. Cabin's good.

MS Khandaar: (sighs) All thrusters active.

CMP Worrel: Why the bloody hell are we still dropping toward the planet?

MS Khandaar: Guidance system is correcting, sir. One moment.

CMP Worrel: Don't use the auto guidance, it's a cactus with all the electrical noise around us. Use your training.

MS Khandaar: Sorry, sir. I have it under control.

CFE Moore: *Maray*'s now orbiting the moon like a good little boy. Pitch is 190.

MS Khandaar: Oh, my God. Debris visible from the portside viewport.

CMP Worrel: Khandaar, stay focused.

MS Khandaar: Yes, sir.

CMP Worrel: Any data on the other modules? Transponder signals, radio traffic—anything?

CFE Moore: System's doing a check.

MS Khandaar: Thrusters off. We are holding perigee at 170 kilometers altitude.

CMP Worrel: That's too low. We're a day, maybe two from reentry. We'll have to risk a burn and rack off. Moore, how's that check coming? Get me stoked.

CFE Moore: System task's at 85 percent. Keep your pants on.

MS Khandaar: Sir, you don't plan to land on the surface?

CMP Worrel: Not until we establish communication with the rest of our mates. Especially the captain.

CFE Moore: I've got visual on some hellacious debris out the starboard viewport.

MS Khandaar: It's heading straight for us! Impact in twenty seconds!

CMP Worrel: Starboard thrusters, Khandaar. Now!

CFE Moore: (gasps) Holy shit that's a lot of wreckage…

MS Khandaar: (sobs) Oh my God…Oh my dear God…there's a body…

CMP Worrel: (clears throat) We must continue the mission. They were all brave people. Khandaar, try the radio again.

MS Khandaar: This is Mission Specialist Jivika Khandaar aboard *Maray* crew module. We have been separated from UEA *Centaurus.* Does anyone read me?

CFE Moore: Check's done, sir. Our scanner and antenna were banged up during the explosion and separation.

CMP Worrel: (grunts) This moon's not giving us a fair go, is it?

MS Khandaar: With all due respect, sir…most of *Centaurus* is gone. Our communications are out. We should attempt a landing.

CMP Worrel: Not yet. Not with all that debris raining down on the surface. We'll have to remain up here at least a day for all of the…all of the larger sections to either burn up in reentry or crash on the surface.

CFE Moore: Those're our people you're talking about.

CMP Worrel: And we'll not honor them by lairing it up and getting killed. The success of this mission is up to us now.

MS Khandaar: How can we even accomplish anything now that—

CMP Worrel: We discover what we can about the alien signal and find a way to relay that back to Earth. We're still responsible for this mission. Let's give it a go.

CFE Moore: Sounds good to me.

MS Khandaar: Me, too. Apologies, sir. I'm just… (sniffs)

CMP Worrel: No worries. My heart's broken, too. (sighs) We owe it to those we've lost to continue on. Maintain orbit, record video and still images. And keep trying that scanner, Moore. It might come back online.

This is the personal journal of Adnan Bakir, Chief Medical Officer, UEA Centaurus. Mission date: Sol 1.

My first day on this awful moon was akin to entering fiery Jahannam itself.

All I can remember, after we heard the alarm in Aloha, was a bright flash. Then the sides of the craft shuddered, and rivets popped from the bulkheads. One flew right through Larsen's hand, but she didn't even scream. I don't know how she managed not to. The rest of us, buckled down, could only stare as the ship came apart. Each module detached from Centaurus—a sight I'd rather not have witnessed. The very hull split, and flames ate their way up into Aloha. We screamed and tried hailing Granger on the radio, but all seemed lost. I glimpsed stars, the curvature of a new world, and shrapnel hurtling through space as we tumbled down into nothingness. After that I must have blacked out, for I recall nothing of the descent, nor of the landing itself.

Allah granted me that small mercy.

When I finally came to, it was Stevenson tugging at my shoulder. He had already dragged Larsen and Santos from Aloha and Vivaldi. Through the open hull, I spotted Zentsov standing outside in a sandy waste, gaping at our surroundings in shock. Santos wailed in anguish. I felt neither, for my own instincts kicked in at last. Thanking Stevenson, I hurried outside to care for my friends and fellow crew.

The first thing I noticed was the gravity. Slightly less than Earth's. Everyone seemed to be dealing with it fine. The next thing was the atmosphere. Poisonous in the extreme. I double-checked my suit's oxygen supply, then everyone else's via my HUD. As CMO, I had apps displaying everyone's vital signs in real time through their suit links.

Too many were absent in my feed.

Other than Stevenson and myself, only three had made it so far. Zentsov kept saying he couldn't breathe and tried removing his helmet. It took me, Stevenson, and Larsen to prevent him from such a suicidal action. His eyes were filled with shock and his blood pressure was up. Though I had no sedative, I convinced Zentsov to calm down.

Larsen kept her right fist closed, barely sealing her IVA suit where the debris had burned through her hand. She was more concerned with getting the others into EMUs, and I could not argue with that. The moon's heat was oppressive.

The worst was Santos. Shrapnel had punctured his left pectoral below the collarbone. Blood had coagulated around the rip in his suit and flesh, possibly the only thing saving his life. We dared not remove the shrapnel, as it would depressurize his suit and expose him to the moon's atmosphere, with no way to stem the bleeding once the object came free. I ignored the burning debris around the supply module, Thirteen, and rushed into Vivaldi for something to alleviate my companions' suffering.

The imagery of that horror will remain with me the rest of my days.

One half of Officer Jeong was spread across Vivaldi's deck. The other half was missing. Nagel was still screaming in her chair, the restraints holding her in place as fires melted her right inside her suit. Stevenson and I tried putting out the blaze but it was too late. Nagel's shrieks finally stopped when the heat made her faceplate pop off. I stumbled from that charnel house, still bereft of medical supplies. The others gathered, asking questions, demanding that I do something. Some shouted at Granger or Eaton over the radio. Larsen pointed at the debris still falling from the sky—as if there was something I could do about it.

Zentsov stared at me with a blank look and reached for his helmet release again.

I have no idea why I tackled him so hard. I don't know why I screamed in his face, faceplate to faceplate, holding down his arms with all my strength. All I know was that I wanted no more death. I wanted him to live.

The others pulled us apart and secured Zentsov to Aloha with a few surviving seat restraints. Tears of frustration and impotence stung my cheeks.

My friends certainly deserved better. I was no captain, I wasn't going to lead them on a trek of senseless hope in this wilderness. I am a healer, and I grant hope only after I know I have succeeded in surgery or in a correct diagnosis. Praise to Allah for granting me such gifts. Still I felt guilty for it as the others watched me, wanting me to do something, willing me to get up and tell them what to do. Yet cowardice harms the brave. I tried to think of things to say that would make them feel better, but after witnessing Nagel's horrible end...I had nothing to offer.

That's when laughter sounded over my radio.

As I slowly rose to my knees, I listened to that mocking, desperate, terrified jollity. It angered me. I demanded to know who it was. The others gathered around me. Even Zentsov snapped back to cognizance. We were all interested in the identity of one who could find humor in such a place.

It was a female voice that answered. Barely discernible over the static-filled connection. But it was as if a heavenly malak *now spoke to us. I felt a grin spread over my face, saw it on the visages of my comrades. It was Chief Flight Engineer Rachel Terman.*

We now had hope that others had survived as well.

A new energy overcame us, and we set about creating the semblance of a base camp. Though Vivaldi continued burning, we ascertained we were in no danger, so we brought out the drones from Aloha and Thirteen. Both flew above our site, scanning and making contact attempts with the rest of the crew. We donned EMU suits, save for Santos.

Now outfitted with better sensors, the moon's habitability—or lack thereof—concerned me greatly: 100 mSv of radiation was a large dose. And while the EMU suits shielded us for now, Santos was still in his IVA, which provided little protection. All agreed we had to do something about him. Vivaldi was aflame, plus Aloha and Thirteen had both decompressed in our evac. Santos needed stabilizing immediately, and I didn't have time to wait for Aloha to repressurize. We had to use the shelters.

I was in my element. It is not something I seek praise for, nor wish to engage in, but I am at my best when others' lives hang by a very ragged thread.

The shelters are prefab, hexagonal affairs crafted from polyethylene that can be attached to each other for resilience and support. We followed Terman's suggestion of "doubling up" by overlapping one set of walls over another. Though Stevenson grumbled, I understood her concern; our dosimeters were registering in the triple digits. Our EMU suits couldn't safely handle that much radiation for more than a few hours at a time. As soon as we got the first one up, I had them bring Santos to me. He lay on a cot, squirming in pain, as we filled the shelter with breathable air. There was no time to worry if we were using supplies needlessly. A life was in danger and I would act. Once the shelter was sealed, and the temperature normalized, I unsuited and set to work on Santos.

That was when a thud *rumbled our chests, shaking cot and shelter. More debris.*

Yet I was focused. Santos's life was now in my hands. I continued, cleaning the area around the wound with chlorhexidine. I could only hope the antiseptic would deal with any pathogens or bacteria this moon harbored. Eyes rolling back into his head, Santos mumbled in Portuguese, a language with which I am unfamiliar. There is a universal language, however, between those who are caretakers, and those who are their wounded charges. It was this language I spoke, those words I enunciated as I prepped him for surgery. I asked a question in English, Urdu, even Punjabi, and Santos nodded each time. The content didn't matter: We had forged that patient-doctor connection, and if my voice helped him maintain that tenuous connection, then I would babble forever, if necessary.

After Stevenson helped put the anesthesia mask on Santos, I used a scalpel to remove flesh from around the shrapnel, stemming bleeding as needed. I gently removed the foreign, invasive object from his delicate system. A grotesque trophy.

After stabilizing Santos, I tended Larsen's right hand. The injury was a small cavity burned through the center of the palm, bypassing the metacarpal bones. So she still had full use of her hand and fingers. Then she joked about needing all of her fingers in the event the "aliens" we came to find only communicated in sign language.

I admonished her and then regretted my negativity. She simply smiled and said something about "from harm, one gets wise." Then she winked at me. As if she hadn't almost died from depressurization. Still, her widening grin was a welcome respite.

I joked that her sign language might have to remain monosyllabic for now. Mainly, I just wanted to express myself in some fashion without breaking down again.

Most of our suits had suffered superficial burn damage, though none, as far as we could ascertain, had been compromised. The drones, having better sensors, indicated the moon's atmosphere would kill a human within one to two minutes after exposure. The surface temperature was far too warm, and there remained concerns of stronger radiation if the clouds proved too thin to block ultraviolet rays.

I watched over Santos, the only sounds the wind outside and the beep of his life monitor. Like a radar signal seeking signs of hope in this wasteland.

Recording personal journal, Mission Specialist Li Tian, UEA Centaurus.
Mission date: Sol 1.

As soon as my module Seeker *landed on the moon, I realized that Milo Kovac, Chief Science Officer—and my immediate superior on this mission— wouldn't allow even something as crazy as the mother ship exploding to stop him from exploring.*

You see, Kovac was the only crew member I met before the UEA briefing back on Earth. I liked him instantly. He looked more like a sports celebrity with that swept-back blond hair, easy smile, and an attitude that said he'd let nothing beat him, no matter the challenge. We even had a few beers before the briefing. When I originally asked him about this mission, he simply smiled and said we'll win the next Nobel Prize.

When the alarms went off right before the fires and explosion, Kovac was trying to locate the problem and stop it. He was on the radio with Stevenson before they contacted Terman. Whose response, I have to say, was pretty fucking lackadaisical. I expected as much, since the UEA lumped her with us for the publicity. Guess the protests on Mars can stop now that we finally gave in to them.

That pandering might kill us.

Instead of cutting all power to both centrifuges, Terman waited until she had no choice but to eject all of the modules. That almost doomed us all. Kovac and Stevenson might have fixed it, right? I mean, was this her first mission?

But once we were on the moon's surface, I didn't bother bringing it up. One thing science can't do is change the past. I know. I majored in archaeology. But we can *change the future. So Kovac immediately set about checking our supplies, the environmental conditions, and, of course, the health of all crew members in* Seeker.

I won't lie: I was scared shitless. But Kovac, he has this strange immunity to fear. Like it's not even a variable in his universe. He was making wisecracks, flirting with Burgess and Sakurai, talking about having rakija and figs in some bar in Dubrovnik, and how we'd all love it. It took our minds off of the reality, you know? Made us smile, even laugh. Kovac, like the discipline of science itself, is all about generating hope.

I'm just glad I crashed with him and none of the others.

Seeker was pressurized and stable, so we changed from those tight-ass IVA suits into the EMUs. I felt like a giant robot about to fight a kaiju, they're so bulky.

Once outside, we goofed for a few seconds in the lower G until the smoke coming off Seeker doused our enthusiasm. Kovac tried the radio, but there was so much static we gave up for the moment. Burgess checked the inventory. Her report shattered our spirits.

We only had two weeks' worth of air, food, and water on Seeker, and all of that was survival-grade, bland stuff. I say it like that because not all of us had undergone bowel augmentation like the rest of the CYBs, or cyborgs—shit, Terman's Martian and a CYB—and would need to cook some of the supplies before eating them. The IGF shot felt good after stasis, though. Huh. Taking insulin growth factor made me feel like one of those old-fashioned bodybuilders before that shit was finally outlawed. The more mass you have, the worse space travel is for you. Me, I'm just a tall, skinny bastard.

And without Centaurus, there was no way out of here.

But you know what Kovac did? He packed some supplies, sent out our drone, and fired up the rover. Flashing that smile, he asked if we wanted to start exploring.

Yeah, we all thought he'd taken a knock on the head, too. Explore, without even knowing the fate of the rest of the crew, while smoke from other crashes rose in the distance, and debris still lit up the atmosphere? It was the craziest suggestion.

Kovac explained that our mission was still of prime importance. That the people back home would want to know about this moon and the alien signal. That any rescue was unlikely, and we might as well learn as much as we can and transmit it back to Earth, while we still drew breath.

I have to say, that sentiment sobered us really damn quick. I'm not a religious nut, but the mission suddenly seemed like a sacred duty. One where we couldn't fail if we but applied ourselves. We wanted to learn as much as we could before dying, and if we could manage that, while gifting it and our lives to posterity, then so be it.

Kovac was ready to die, ready to make that sacrifice. You could see it, right?

Maybe it was the desperation. The fear of snuffing it on this world. Or just something to take our minds off of our horrible circumstance, all the death.

I'm proud to say I was the first to volunteer. And the grin Kovac gave me…I would brave anything for such a man. The type who will spearhead humanity into a prosperous future. To be around like-minded people made me giddy with excitement.

The first order of the day was to take soil samples. That was Sakurai's duty, being the expedition's geologist. She enjoyed getting her hands dirty, digging through the sand, crushing stones apart. Each grain of sand was like a diamond to her, but she preferred to work alone, so I rode out with Kovac and Burgess a few hundred yards from the crash site. A botanist, Burgess seemed out of luck until she discovered what she ascertained to be some sort of decayed vine. Kovac placed it into our first sample jar. He joked that this might be the garden of those who sent that signal to Earth.

Burgess muttered something in French, but I cautiously agreed. There was no other sign of vegetation on the moon so far. Reports from UEA observation indicated that Centauri B and its moon were bereft of the chemicals required for life. That planet was a lava and basalt wasteland, and its moon, a desert caught in perpetual twilight.

But someone—or something—had contacted our species from this sandy satellite, Centauri C. Before the signal reached Earth, no one knew Centauri C even existed.

Kovac was hoping to find some subterranean settlement, if those who contacted us did, indeed, dwell here. I agreed. The surface wasn't shielded enough from solar radiation—my dosimeter was driving me mad with all its updates across my HUD—and given its relative flatness, would be victim to violent dust storms, with no natural barriers to lessen their onslaught. But the vine, or whatever it had been, suggested otherwise. This sparked a conversation about our favorite sci-fi cinemorgs. Burgess, playing the artsy intellectual, claimed to prefer the two dimensional movies my grandfather thrilled to. Yeah, weird.

Talk of home brought silence, and even Kovac was at a loss to make us smile. I activated my suit's astronav app, staring up while the program told me the name and distance of any star I pointed at. Given the dim quality of the moon's parent sun, it was easy to spot many twinkling lights up there. When I found Earth, I gestured to catch Kovac and Burgess's attention. They knew what that little dot was without my saying so.

We kept driving in the rover, kicking up a dust cloud that never seemed to drift back down due to the lower gravity. Kovac kept flirting with Burgess, though I sensed he was more worried about her deepening frown than any actual interplay later.

Not me. I absorbed the vista before me. To some it would appear lifeless, barren. A place our leaders had sent us to die. But that shit's all wrong. This new world was an addition to human knowledge, the first real extension of our ambitions as a species. It thrilled me, frightened me. Taunted me with its secrets, teased me with its treasures.

Riding along with them, I couldn't have been more comfortable if I'd had a beer in one hand and a joint in the other. Like we were college students— stupid enough to try anything but smart enough to survive it. We weren't doomed. We were ascendant.

3

Three modules—one of them burning—lay at odd angles on the mesa's surface.

Breaking into a run, Rachel felt nauseous again. There was no one about, no rovers moving. No breaks in the radio silence.

"Bakir?"

Surely something else hadn't gone wrong. Electric noise still hampered radio communication. By the time she found the source of interruption it might be too late.

The possibility that she might be the sole survivor chilled Rachel inside her suit. It wasn't just that she'd be alone on a strange world, four light-years from Earth, without hope of rescue. It would mean she had let down her crew.

Like she'd let her mother down that day.

Mom crossed her arms and gave her that look. "I don't want you to go."

Rachel continued unpacking groceries in the apartment provided by the UEA. "I'm too delicate for Earth. Too alien for my last two girlfriends. Not that you cared."

"You're weren't a person to them," Mom said. "You were simply a Martian."

"Think I don't know that?" She slammed the canned goods into the cupboard.

"I know you're better than those other pilots, but the UEA wants you because it makes them look good," Mom said. "With a Martian on board, they hope to mask their treatment of the rest of us. Their bigotry. You're giving them what they want."

Trying not to wince, Rachel loaded the water jugs into the fridge. Still too heavy.

"You don't have to unload all this yourself. Use the harness I bought you."

Harness. Like she was an animal. But she'd cope. No matter how much it hurt.

"You're still the Other to them," Mom said. "I've read some of those nasty jokes on the Internet. That you're simply an alien taking humans to meet another alien."

"None of it will matter out there," Rachel muttered.

"It still matters to your father and me. It sure as hell matters to other Martians. That's why we came to Earth with you, to prove to them that we're not monsters—"

She flung the coffee bags onto the counter. One burst open, scattering the grains.

"Listen, stop being so selfish—"

Rachel glared. "'Selfish'? You wanted me to marry that creep from Chasma City, even though you knew I'm gay. You still wanted grandkids, so you nagged me to undergo insemination despite the doctor's warnings. When I refused, you disowned—"

"I was wrong!" Mom shuddered as tears streamed down her face. "But this…"

"You and Dad told me Earth would be different. That I could get whatever I wanted if I worked hard enough. And now that I get promoted to the most famous expedition in history, you fucking want me to back out? How does that help Martians?"

"Because you still aren't one of them. You've been included for entertainment value, to boost ratings, to ease the worker tensions on Mars. Your father said you even agreed to become a CYB. A goddamn cyborg. Is that who you are? Changing and twisting yourself until you are finally acceptable to them?"

"Like you tried?" Hot tears slid down Rachel's cheek. "How many times have you tried to convince me to be who you want me to be?"

"I did it because I love you," Mom said. "They will never love you."

"I've never felt loved," Rachel said. "So nothing will be different."

"That's a lie, we're your family." Resentment burned in Mom's eyes. "Isn't that the most important thing? The only thing?"

Rachel wiped her cheeks. "Not anymore."

The memories had made her cry at first. Now they were phantasms of the person she used to be. Selfish? Yet here she was, placing someone else above her own welfare.

"Bakir, you read me? This is Terman. I have visual on your crash site. Bakir, do you copy?"

Still nothing. She ran on, trying to forget herself, forget her past, in the wastelands now devouring her. So far she'd not seen any more of the vines, but there were plenty of sinkholes on the mesa and across the flatlands below. They collapsed whenever she came near, puffs of dust and pebbles leading into dark, earthy maws.

She slowed to a jog, pacing her breathing and energy expenditure like a machine. Back on Mars she'd won the Tharsis Marathon twice. That had been the catalyst that granted her the confidence to attempt a life on Earth. She'd placed last in that race.

Rachel spotted the emergency shelters near *Aloha* and Thirteen. *Vivaldi* was a burning wreck. She stopped jogging and drank deep breaths. "Bakir?"

A second passed, then a laugh sounded.

"Terman? How close are you?"

"Close enough to see that whoever put those shelters together did a pretty good job." She walked into the makeshift camp as two figures hurried from the shelter.

It was Bakir and Larsen, grins visible through slightly tinted faceplates. Larsen's right glove was bulky, stuffed with something.

"A rivet went through it." Larsen's Norwegian accent lent her voice a singsong cadence. She pronounced the *v* in *rivet* with a *w* sound. "I am fine."

Rachel hugged them both. "You don't know how glad I am to see you two. Who else…Who else made it?"

As Bakir recited the short list, Rachel made herself not glance at *Vivaldi.* Jeong and Nagel would get some sort of memorial, along with Granger and Eaton. Along with all the others who had died just to answer the question everyone one Earth was asking.

"Did you feel a distant quake, like another module crashed nearby?" she asked.

Bakir nodded. "Yes, but we haven't investigated yet. There is still a lot of debris raining down west of us. I have one wounded, critically. We did dispatch a drone."

"You were right to remain here," Rachel said. "Granger…I need to collect his body from the cockpit module, plus the supplies on board."

"And Eaton?" Bakir asked in a low voice.

Rachel shook her head. "He…"

"Is gone." Larsen gave a solemn nod.

"We belong to Allah, and to Him we shall return," Bakir whispered.

Moments later, Rachel stood with the others in the shelter. She welcomed the chance to remove her helmet. Her short hair itched from sweat after running. Santos lay on a cot in the center, asleep and stable. Stevenson and Zentsov reached across him and shook her hand. Smiles were brief but polite.

"What's your drone got so far?" Rachel asked.

Stevenson held the control tablet. "I've got the one from *Aloha* flying at a hundred meters. It's spotted several smoke plumes west of here. There's no way of telling how much of that could be wreckage, or intact modules. I've already set up its wireless network but the range only covers this site. There's too much signal noise otherwise."

"Judging from all the sand and apparent saltation, this moon must have regular dust storms," Zentsov said. "One big one, and *bom!* There goes our drone."

"And what about your supplies? Could anything be salvaged from *Vivaldi*?" Rachel's heart sank when the others shook their heads. "What about Thirteen?"

"Each crew module came with a rover, a drone, a 3-D printer, plus two weeks' consumables—food, water, air—for four people," Stevenson said. "The odd-numbered supply modules each has a spare rover, a drone, and a month's worth of consumables."

"What about each module's transponder?" Rachel asked. "Or our suit links?"

"The signal noise is canceling them out, if they're operating at all," Bakir said.

"Maybe we are the only ones who made it." Zentsov's shoulders slumped.

"We don't know that." Rachel accepted a water flask from Larsen and sipped. "Anyone work out the trajectory of debris in relation to *Centaurus*'s explosion?"

"Not possible yet," Stevenson said. "We still don't have much information, and long-range scanners aren't reliable. It's the interference again."

"We'll have to search for survivors somehow," Rachel said. "I want a volunteer. We'll take *Aloha*'s rover, salvage what we can from the cockpit module, collect Granger's body, then return here. Maybe other survivors will find or contact us by then."

"How much experience do you have with rovers?" Zentsov asked.

Rachel gave him a quizzical look. "Plenty. Why?"

"Those rovers aren't hot rods," Stevenson said. "You'll have to pace yourself to conserve battery power. Those things sat unused on *Centaurus* for four years."

"The terrain out there, as well as the gravity, matches my homeworld," Rachel said. "I assure you, I know what I'm doing."

Stevenson and Zentsov shared a look. Rachel's jaw tightened.

Bakir cleared his throat. "The radiation out there makes me uncomfortable. I'd like to suggest that we limit all excursions, even in the rover."

"Right now we have to gather our people," Rachel said. "I'll risk it."

Stevenson set aside the drone pad. "Then I'll go with you."

"We'll be back within the hour," Rachel said. "Try to keep all channels open."

"We must be cautious about using so much battery power," Bakir said. "Until we get Thirteen's solar station online, we'll have no way to replenish our stores. I need those batteries for my medical equipment. Santos needs them."

"I know." Rachel put on her helmet. "But if there's any chance we might find the others, we have to take it. Hopefully we can salvage the cockpit's power cell."

Bakir's frown made her feel coldhearted. She wondered if he would do the same.

Stevenson offered to drive and she acceded, planting herself in the passenger seat. The six-wheeled vehicle was lighter than a car but stronger than a tank because of its nanite-alloy shell. Not much different than her bone and joint replacements.

The rover sped over the mesa and down onto the western flatlands. Its fat tires rolled over rocks and sand with ease. Stevenson didn't speak much, just focused on the landscape ahead. Rachel wasn't sure if he disagreed with her plan, or was simply concerned for their comrades. Maybe she was being paranoid. They were all under stress.

They reached the cockpit module in much faster time than it had taken her to reach the mesa on foot. Nevertheless, the red dwarf sun looked ready to set in a couple of hours. Already the world grew dimmer and the sinkholes deadlier.

"Temperature's starting to drop," Rachel said, trying to make conversation.

Seconds stretched into years before Stevenson replied.

"I almost had the fire out in Centrifuge B." He drove past a collection of half-buried salt pillars. "I rerouted power to that hatch. It was about to open."

Rachel fidgeted with her seat restraint. "It all happened so fast."

"All I needed was another second or two." His mouth set in a grim line. Like he was driving to a funeral.

"I had no way of knowing. We all might have blown apart in the blast if—"

"Did Granger order it?" Stevenson slowed as they approached a smoke plume.

"No."

"I was the second person assigned to *Centaurus*," he said. "I helped design its module system. I knew that ship better than anyone. It shouldn't have been your call."

"Like I said—"

"You were the last added to our roster."

"What's that got to do with anything?"

"Look, it's not you." He sighed. "Forget that I said it."

Rachel glared through the windshield. Of all places, she hadn't expected to deal with that here. There was no escape from Mars, no matter how hard she tried.

Stevenson exited the rover as soon as they stopped. While he checked the cockpit module's supply cache, Rachel walked right up to him.

"I wish things had happened differently, but they didn't. Right now we need to have each other's back. If not for each other, then for the rest of the crew."

He looked at her, nodded, and removed the cache's cover.

She crept into the cockpit. Rankled by Stevenson's words, she took deep breaths to relax. She'd passed all of the UEA's tests. But was he right? Had she acted too soon?

Eaton's dried blood, Granger's body bag…reminders that she would never know.

Some display screens were still on. One showed *Aloha*'s transponder signal for a second, then noise interrupted the reception. Rachel tried the other channels. They were dead. Perhaps the cockpit antenna had been damaged. Next she studied the flight recorder, trying to ascertain what had caused the explosion. Sensors indicated a fire in Centrifuge B, then a chain reaction as the fire became an explosion tearing through the middle of *Centaurus*. Modules Nine and Eleven—bookending the centrifuges—had been destroyed instantly.

Swallowing, she had to pause. That meant four people had perished before she'd ejected all of the modules. There was nothing she could have done, but her shoulders felt the weight nonetheless. She read their names on the manifest, viewed their UEA portraits. All smiling faces in maroon uniforms. Cast to oblivion.

Minutes later, after collecting the computer's portable drives, she spotted Stevenson loading a supply crate into the rover. The vehicle's robotic pulleys—plus the moon's low gravity—aided him. The whole time, though, he stared across the flatlands.

"What were you able to salvage?" she asked.

"Another prefab shelter, two days of rations, and three tool kits."

"Good. If you'll help me with Granger?" Rachel placed the drives into the rover.

As they loaded Granger's body, Rachel's boot crunched over something.

It was another vine. Coated in a dun-colored, nodular substance.

Stevenson frowned at it, then at her.

"What is that?"

Rachel looked around, but spotted nothing resembling it.

He handed her a storage carton and she carefully brushed the remains into it with her fingers. At least he remembered the proper procedures. They hurried to the rover.

No sooner had she buckled in, than Stevenson sped away from the crash site. He was quiet on the return drive and she didn't bother initiating conversation. Rather than let him get to her, she spent the time thinking about the other modules. If their transponders still worked, that meant the modules themselves might be whole. Their crews, alive.

Upon returning, Rachel found Bakir and Larsen outside. They were arguing about the spare rover. The discussion was so heated they didn't even notice her walk up.

"What's this all about?"

Bakir shook his head. "Larsen saw a dust cloud to the southeast. She thinks it is another rover and wants to investigate."

"I am not chasing trolls from a bedtime story," Larsen said.

"I wanted to wait until you and Stevenson returned before we start splitting up on the basis of a whim." Bakir looked to Rachel, expecting support.

"Did you make radio contact with anyone?" Rachel asked.

"Negative." Larsen frowned at Stevenson as he unloaded the rover. "*Dritt.* That's all you found? Was the cockpit module that damaged?"

"It's all we could bring back for now." Rachel didn't look at Stevenson but felt his eyes on her. "Where did you see that dust cloud?"

After Larsen told her, Rachel led them inside the shelter and accessed the drone's control tablet. She zoomed in on the coordinates with the drone's scanner suite and searched multiple wavelengths—visible light, infrared, even X-rays.

Sure enough, she caught heat traces. They were scant but nothing else in the drone's scanner range came up. The signature had to be a rover or something mechanical. As she set aside the tablet, she mentioned the transponders on the other modules.

"That is a possibility," Bakir said. "Perhaps I was wrong, Larsen."

"No," Rachel said absently, staring at the scanner readings. "You're right, we must stay together as much as possible. But I hate not looking."

"We can do a wider search tomorrow," Bakir said.

Larsen placed hands on hips. "Our friends might not last until tomorrow."

"What if *we* don't?" Stevenson asked.

"That isn't helping," Bakir said.

"What if it is the aliens?" Larsen asked.

"We can worry about that after we've accounted for everyone," Rachel said.

"It's almost night," Stevenson said. "Not a good idea to search in the dark."

"*Aloha* is repressurized," Zentsov radioed from outside. "Cabin is good."

Bakir walked around Santos, still unconscious on the cot. "Now we can all leave this shelter. I'll need everyone's help moving Santos. His cot, these machines—"

A voice came over the radio. "...right beneath the sediment. Though there's not much else...three storage cartons' worth..."

Everyone gaped.

Rachel activated her mic. "Hello, this is Flight Engineer Rachel Terman. Do you read me? Please respond, over."

Static and pops garbled the reply. But there was a reply.

"You see?" Larsen said.

They all waited while Stevenson tracked the radio signal with the drone. "Maybe thirty kilometers southeast of us. Interference could be coloring the readings, though."

"I'll take a rover to those coordinates," Rachel said. "Larsen, you're our communications officer, so come with me. You'll work the radio while I drive."

"What about Santos?" Bakir asked.

"We won't be gone long," Rachel said. "Stevenson, I need you and Zentsov to prepare Thirteen for habitation in case we find more crew members. Then we'll send a message back to Earth. They deserve to know what's happened, even if it'll take four years to reach them."

A moment passed before Stevenson finally nodded. Rachel gave Bakir a meaningful look, then got into the other rover with Larsen. Once they'd ridden a short distance from camp she hailed Bakir's private frequency.

Seconds dragged by before Bakir answered. "Yes?"

"It's Stevenson. He seems to blame me for our situation."

"How so?" Bakir's tone was neutral yet curious.

"He thinks he could have saved *Centaurus.*" Rachel drove down an embankment on the mesa's eastern end. The vehicle's robust suspension made her and Larsen bounce up and down in their seats. "He thinks I acted too quickly."

"We are all in a delicate predicament, Terman. We have no hope of immediate rescue, or returning home, and the supplies won't last. Until we get hydroponics online, and assure the viability of the remaining stasis pods, everyone will be on edge."

"My addition to the crew seems to have already done that," Rachel said.

"That is presumptive," Bakir said. "I know the situation between Earth and Mars was…delicate when we left, to say the least, but we need to set that aside."

"I'd love to," Rachel said. "Try to convince Stevenson to do the same."

"I am Chief Medical Officer, not the thought police."

Rachel hit the throttle, the rover bouncing over the flatlands. "I'm trying to maintain order, foster hope. That's all. I need your help with that. Can I count on it?"

"Certainly."

"Good." Rachel sighed. "Terman out."

Larsen was watching her, head cocked to one side.

"Well?" Rachel asked.

"I am a simple linguist." Larsen's demeanor was neutral. "Not a judge."

"Okay, then," Rachel said. "Any tips for communicating in a clearer way?"

"Use sign language the next time anyone doubts you."

Rachel snorted. "Like what?"

Larsen raised her middle finger.

Grateful for the humor, Rachel laughed. "Works for me."

"Thank you for agreeing with me back there." Larsen gave a shy smile.

"I believe that you did see dust from another rover," Rachel said. "There's nothing else it could be."

Larsen became impartial again. "Unless it is those we came here to find."

"Yes." Rachel gripped the wheel tighter. "There's always that."

Etana exits *Olduvai* only when she is sure the others are dead.

She feels cold in the EMU suit, the former military-grade panoply she'd trained in during her pre-UEA stint with that contractor group. But cold is something she doesn't fear. Cold is something, like emotion, she has control over.

Her first steps on the moon's surface do not impress her as they might actual explorers. Rather than feel awe, she seeks signs. Hints. Opportunities.

For she is a being of opportunity. Ones carefully constructed, and ones stolen. She gazes over the arid landscape, blanketed with rising night, knowing there is nothing this world can give her.

Knowing there is only one thing she can give it.

Hands loose at her sides, Etana walks around *Olduvai*. It has suffered no damage from the explosion in Centrifuge B. The generator of their gravity en route to this world, shattered just like the crew's center of gravity. Yet hers remains strong.

Certainty is the one thing they could never take away.

Etana opens the module's storage berth, makes a mental note of its contents. After killing the rest of the crew in *Olduvai*, she has four months of air. Four months of water, of hard-packed foodstuffs with all the appeal of sweetened dog food.

Four months before her window of opportunity is snuffed out by mortality.

Growing up in Abuja, Nigeria, Etana had had no worries about survival. The streets, then the factories, then the high-rises, had been her territory. Survival is more than fast reflexes, a comely face, or the ability to keep a secret. Survival is the ability to adapt until one does not require such things.

Her homeland, a latecomer among Earth's spacefaring nations, is already among its most robust. Building an economy on fossil fuels, exploiting its workforce in the name of progress, wringing every possible resource from the environment—her country has learned well from other nations. Turning misery and disenfranchisement into a profit model—the final irony of colonialism.

Out here, she will not allow colonialism to take root. She will kill it first.

After packing extra oxygen canisters and water, Etana walks away from *Olduvai*. There is no need to bury the dead. Time and sand will provide tomb enough for them all.

But the module hasn't caught flame, as she suspects some of the others have, judging from the horizon an hour ago in better daylight. If other survivors do locate *Olduvai*, it will be via transponder or dumb luck—neither of which she is prepared to trust. For Etana trusts nothing, and no one. Only herself.

Heading north, she studies the stars as the red dwarf finally crawls back into its lair. Of all the systems the signal could have reached, it had contacted Sol. And of all the people they could have chosen, they'd selected her.

The answer, then as now, is a simple one. One who has lived and done as she no longer has questions. Only baseless acts that can be construed as answers.

4

"I see them," Rachel said as Larsen pointed at the faint light ahead. In the moon's near-total darkness, the source was as subtle as a spotlight in a cave. She tensed, wondering what awaited them. More wreckage? More bodies?

"There is nothing so bad that it cannot be worse," Larsen said.

"Huh?"

"My grandmamma often said it," Larsen said. "We will overcome this."

"You sound pretty confident." Rachel adjusted the rover's scanners, but they were going haywire like all their other equipment. The wireless link to *Aloha*'s drone had been lost minutes after departing camp. They'd been unable to hail anyone on the radio.

The dosimeter still worked. Still reading in the triple digits.

"I left all doubts on Earth." Fervor made Larsen's blue eyes even more striking.

"Then let me loan you some of mine." Reducing speed, Rachel pulled alongside another UEA rover, its headlights focused on three crew members kneeling around a sinkhole. All wore EMUs. They looked up as she stopped the engine.

Anxiety gave way to relieved excitement. Rachel leapt from the rover and hurried toward them. "Are you all okay? What module did you land in?"

Milo Kovac, *Centaurus*'s chief science officer, stood. "Yes, we're fine. We landed in *Seeker*." His Croatian speech was translated by her language app.

Rachel grinned with relief. "We've been trying to reach you on the radio—"

"One moment," Kovac said. "We are conducting an important experiment. Please do not interrupt." He knelt back down by the sinkhole.

Rachel shared a frustrated glance with Larsen. What could be more important than finding each other after such a disaster?

The others—Mission Specialists Burgess and Li—squatted beside Kovac, engrossed by the hole. Sand slid into its confines like light vanishing into a black hole.

Despite their indifference, Rachel found herself intrigued. Li was typing data into a field lab while Burgess read off numbers from her HUD. Kovac remained focused on the sinkhole, as if he expected the most wonderful thing in the universe to rise from it.

Finally, something did. A drone. Holding a shriveled object in its tiny claws.

It was another vine-like specimen, similar to the one Rachel had discovered.

"Amazing," Kovac whispered.

"Now we have three." Li took the vine, rolled it up, and placed it in an airtight storage carton. Two more cartons hung from his belt.

Rachel remembered the nodular growth on the vine she'd stepped on earlier. She retrieved the carton from the rover and presented it to them. "What do you make of this?"

"Perhaps a chemical buildup?" Kovac handed it to Burgess.

"It's too bad you stomped it to dust." Burgess sighed. "I will examine it."

"What about these vines?" Larsen asked.

"It is the craziest anomaly." Kovac rose and smiled. "There should be no possible way for any vegetation, under all of this radiation, to survive on this world. Yet we have these samples. All of them have been procured from these sinkholes."

"I found one, too," Rachel said. "Where I crashed in the cockpit module."

Grinning, Kovac patted her shoulder, but Rachel drew back. "First, I want a full report. Every minute we waste, our comrades might be dying."

"Every moment we waste talking, we lose another discovery." Kovac spread his arms, palms up. "This is why we are here. Let someone else helm the rescue efforts."

Rachel fought to keep her voice calm. "Granger and Eaton are dead. So far, only *Aloha*, *Vivaldi*, and now *Seeker* have been accounted for. That leaves me in command."

Li and Burgess halted their work and watched with interest.

"I am sorry to hear that," Kovac said. "But with all due respect, their demise, and your promotion, does not alter my mission."

"We all have the same mission." Rachel gave him a hard stare.

"That is not true." Kovac gave an apologetic smile. "The UEA specified that the science team, under me, will operate under Protocol Three. The search for the signal's source comes before all else. We will spend our time doing what the UEA expects of us."

"We're still a team." Rachel couldn't believe his arrogance, but Kovac was right. Protocol Three stated as much. But she'd never thought she would be placed in charge, or that the mission would meet with disaster, or for the directive to hamper the expedition.

"I am simply obeying orders," Kovac said. "Granger would have agreed."

"A lot of people died today," Rachel said in a low voice. "Our survival depends—"

"On us doing our jobs," Kovac said. "This isn't personal, Terman."

"Okay, then." Rachel stared him down. "Report your findings."

Though he spoke with reluctant irritation, Kovac told her all that had transpired since *Seeker* landed on the moon. She was thankful to hear Sakurai was alive, and that their module was intact. But Kovac kept looking at the sinkhole and his HUD readings.

"Let me know the results when you get back to *Seeker*," Rachel said after it was obvious Kovac had finished his report. "Tomorrow, we'll link both camps and divvy up supplies. We're all in this together, let's not lose sight of that."

"Tomorrow, then." Kovac and the others loaded into *Seeker*'s rover. Dust blew over Rachel and Larsen as the vehicle sped off.

"See?" Larsen smiled. "It could have been worse."

"It should have gone better." Rachel kicked pebbles into the sinkhole. "Come on. We need sleep, and if my apps are correct, the sun will rise in a few hours."

While Rachel got back into the driver's seat, Larsen took her time, continually looking over her shoulder.

"What's wrong?" Rachel asked.

"I thought I saw a bluish gleam near that sinkhole. They left in a hurry, so I wonder if they left a tool behind."

Rachel wished Kovac had left his ego behind. But she kept silent. The survivors needed a leader, not someone who couldn't control her temper. She tried not to think of what she would have to do tomorrow, which was convince everyone they could still survive. But for how long, and to what end, she had no real answer.

Driving back to *Aloha*, Rachel tried to sound nonchalant. "What do you really think is out there? Aliens? Or some unmanned probe that we finally detected?"

"You always talk this much?" Larsen asked.

Rachel's eyebrows rose. "Well…not really. It's not like there's another woman to talk to around here at the moment and—just never mind."

"You are not bothering me." Larsen offered a heartfelt smile.

"I'm, um, glad." Rachel hoped she didn't look as embarrassed as she felt.

Larsen stared out her window. "You know when your favorite song pops into your head, and you must hum it?"

"Yes…?" Rachel kept driving.

"This place is like that." Larsen leaned back in the seat. "Like the waters of Nærøyfjord. I grew up beside it in Gudvangen. My grandmamma said that grandpapa haunted it. That he enjoyed my visits. I never believed her, but I liked the story."

"That's the most I've heard you speak in two hours. I'm a little scared."

Larsen scrutinized Rachel for several moments, then loosed that shy grin again. "*Uf da*, you are joking with me?" Her cool veneer melted.

Rachel chuckled. "Of course. Please, tell me more."

"Voyaging out here, we're coming into contact with a true 'Other,'" Larsen said. "That is this moon. You cannot feel it?"

The words of Rachel's mother came back, about how Earthlings regarded Martians. As an "Other." She had recognized that in Li's and Burgess's stares.

"No," Rachel swallowed. "Not yet. Maybe I just need to adjust to this place first."

"I felt it as soon as we landed," Larsen's eyes assumed a dreamy look. "Like being in love or the first time I had sex. You cannot feel anything?"

"Nope, not feeling it." When she got back to *Aloha*, Rachel planned on asking Bakir for everyone's psych evaluations. Especially Larsen's. "Why don't you rest a little? It's been a hard day for all of us."

As she glanced at Larsen, the Norwegian was already asleep.

The rest of the drive was anything but peaceful for Rachel. She swerved twice to avoid sinkholes despite the rover's excellent guidance system. Larsen never stirred. Adding to her worries was the occasional meteor. Rachel wondered if they were remnants of *Centaurus*, still caught in terminal orbit.

Tomorrow she'd try to find those transponder signals. Reassert herself, make sure these people survived as long as possible. Better yet, maybe the aliens who'd contacted Earth would appear. They'd help Rachel and her comrades, they'd make good on the promise that their signal entailed. Rachel was a realist, but so much had happened, in so short a time, that she was willing to entertain such folly if it helped her to endure their situation. That was something her parents had never understood or refused to admit.

She was a survivor.

Chief Medical Officer's journal. Mission date: Sol 2.

Though I miss facing east to pray, using the astronav app to find Earth—and thus Mecca—reminds me of how grand Allah's creation is. I can almost forget our situation.

My first morning on this new world has not been pleasant. Though seeing the red dwarf sun climb over the horizon is a truly stupendous sight, any joy it brings is sobered by our situation. Santos had a very difficult night, screaming in his sleep several times. I had to rebandage his wound since it loosened during his nocturnal terrors. I gave him more antibiotics and fluids, and a sedative to keep him still. An hour later I changed his MAG, his maximum absorbency garment, and put a clean one on him.

I am thankful to Stevenson and Zentsov for helping me move Santos into Aloha last night. When Terman and Larsen returned, they helped as well, while informing us that they'd found four other crew members: Kovac, Sakurai, Li, and Burgess. That is great news, and we had a small celebration. Yet Terman remained aloof, her mind elsewhere, I suppose. There is still tension between her and Stevenson, but I don't think he desires her position as leader. Perhaps he doubts her abilities.

Stevenson is a good man, and as Chief Mechanical Technician, has brought everything online in the modules. He calls it the ECLSS, or environmental control and life support system. It monitors and cleans our air, water usage, CO_2 levels, even methane if someone passes gas. He and Zentsov made jokes about that for more than an hour, but I understand it alleviates the horrors of yesterday's catastrophe.

We all pitched in to stake tethers around the camp, to aid anyone caught outside during a whiteout. Given our suit scanners and apps, this normally would not be an issue. The moon's signal noise, however, has made such devices unreliable at best. Larsen played a game while we worked, guessing everyone's origins based solely on our accents. To our amazement, her deductions were never incorrect, and were always made with good-natured humor.

That was how Nasreen dealt with pain and disaster. One reason I loved her.

She was my wife for three years, before the earthquake took her life and the lives of sixty-two others. I thought that was something only my grandparents had been forced to live through, in the decades before Pakistan's seismic retrofitting programs.

That was a year before we learned of the alien signal from this solar system, originating on this very moon. I had just been accepted onto the UEA's medical staff, on my twenty-ninth birthday. Nasreen, herself a neurosurgeon, wanted to celebrate by making some of her delicious rabri, *my favorite dessert. She went to the marketplace in person to purchase the ingredients rather than call a delivery drone—she had an affinity for little traditions like that. Another reason I loved her.*

The marketplace was at the quake's epicenter. It was two days before I discovered she had perished, due to the state of the bodies and the wreckage that had to be cleared. Those were the two most terrifying days of my life as I called her phone, sent texts, whatever I could to contact her. Hoping and praying she yet lived.

Nasreen always believed in what I was doing—what we were doing—to make the world a better place. I healed bodies; she healed minds. She always said she could pick my brain without having to operate on it. So many reasons that I loved her.

When the UEA offered me the position of chief medical officer on Centaurus, I accepted immediately. It was Allah's will.

I would show these "aliens"—no; I despise that term—the goodness in humanity. I would show them that, even after Nasreen's death, I could still forgive and retain hope. It is what Nasreen would have done. I came to show them the beauty and love I saw in her.

It reminds me of a favorite passage from Rumi:

**I honor those who try
to rid themselves of any lying,
who empty the self
and have only clear being there.**

Later today, we are to meet with the other survivors. I'm looking forward to meeting Kovac and his team. I hope that, with their help, we might have a chance.

Flight Recorder – *Maray* Crew Module
Sol 2 – 0700 hours
Orbiting Proxima Centauri C

CMP Worrel: Moore, how many orbits have we completed so far?

CFE Moore: Forty-two big ones. Looks like that'll be the daily average.

CMP Worrel: Khandaar, any more data on those crash site photos?

MS Khandaar: Yes, sir. I have ascertained that at least one of the sites features survivors, judging from probable rover activity. There are three modules close together. One was on fire. There are dust storms due to hit the area within the next eight hours, though, so the data may change every day.

CMP Worrel: What about the cockpit module?

MS Khandaar: No activity that I can detect around that crash site, sir. Sorry.

CMP Worrel: No worries. Good work, and keep looking. Moore, any progress with that scanner?

CFE Moore: Nothing the diagnostics app can help us with. How about a physical check? A spacewalk could fix it. One hour EVA, tops.

CMP Worrel: I don't want to risk that with so much debris still in orbit.

CFE Moore: C'mon, Worrel. Once we orbit to the other side of the moon, we should be out of the debris field's range. I could give it a shot in two, three hours tops.

MS Khandaar: It sounds crazy.

CFE Moore: That's my middle name, honey.

MS Khandaar: And "honey" isn't my first one.

CFE Moore: (laughs) Touché!

CMP Worrel: Not yet, Moore. I'm still hoping for some communication from those who made it to the surface. They should be able to detect our radio chatter by now.

MS Khandaar: Unless their equipment was also damaged, sir.

CMP Worrel: Then Moore can take a walkabout in the black and check the scanner. But let's be patient. We still don't know how many made it down there.

CFE Moore: Fingers crossed, people.

CMP Worrel: Too right. Fingers crossed.

5

The first morning on Proxima Centauri C, Rachel slept in, since she and Larsen had returned right before dawn. The night foray to meet Kovac still stung her and she'd not rested well. Dreams of getting lost out in the wastes, of being surrounded by sinkholes, robbed her of decent slumber. She rubbed her temples and rose from the cot.

They were all crammed into *Aloha*. Meant to house four crew members, they'd had to double-up after filling one cabin with supplies from Thirteen. Rachel and Larsen shared a room while Stevenson and Zentsov had their own. Bakir slept by Santos's cot in the main chamber, refusing to leave his patient.

Bakir's voice came over the radio: "You talk in your sleep."

Rachel grimaced and adjusted her earbud. "Good morning to you, too."

"I didn't sleep well, either." Bakir yawned. "How's Larsen? Her channel is off."

Larsen was already awake on the other cot, humming, trying to comb her tangled blond hair. They both still wore the blue IVA suits; Bakir remained concerned about the moon's radiation despite *Aloha*'s shielding.

"She's the smart one." Rachel groaned and stretched. The moon's gravity was already affecting her nerves. "What's for breakfast?"

Larsen tossed an NF ration packet at her. "Cashews, peanuts, granola."

"Great." Rachel opened the natural form food wrapper and munched on the contents. Sweet and salty, but dry. "A veggie calorie block would've been fine."

"You are one of the CYBs and vegetarian?" Larsen asked. "You lived on Earth? Is that why you accepted the surgeries? Or was that after joining the UEA?"

The peanuts lost their taste. "After."

Larsen ceased combing and frowned. "I apologize. I should not have—"

"It's okay." Rachel finished the packet and tried to straighten her own short brown locks. "Earth was hard to deal with, but not impossible. I wanted to be prepared for whatever we encountered out here, and the UEA was paying. So I became a cyborg."

"I could not tell. If that helps." Larsen's smile was warmer than their current sun.

"Thanks." Rachel's cheeks burned.

They shared a tube of edible toothpaste and brushed. Its banana flavor was awful.

"Breakfast is over," Bakir said over the radio. "Kovac and his team are here."

"I'll be right out," Rachel said. "Have everyone gather in *Aloha*'s main chamber."

Larsen put away the comb and waited by the hatch. "Assholes and elbows."

"It'll be cramped, but I'm hoping for less assholes."

Rachel and Larsen left the room and joined the others in the chamber. Bakir stood in the center beside Santos, who still lay unconscious on the cot. The others—Stevenson, Zentsov, Kovac, Sakurai, Li, and Burgess—waited in a circle. Kovac and his team wore their EMUs, helmets off. Larsen stood behind Rachel, chewing the last of her granola.

"Thank you for coming," Rachel said. The others mumbled or nodded.

Her thin Martian physique made her self-conscious. It always did around so many Earthlings. At least there were no whispers or pointing fingers. Kovac leaned against the wall with his arms crossed, looking bored. Stevenson stood the farthest from her, disdain in his eyes. Li kept looking at his datapad, Sakurai drummed fingers on her helmet, and Burgess raised her brows in annoyed expectation.

At least Bakir gave a slight nod of encouragement.

"Our main priority is to find survivors," Rachel said. "I'll be taking *Aloha*'s rover out every day, trying to track the other modules' transponders and investigating any wreckage. I'd appreciate a volunteer to go with me. Stevenson, I'd like you to get Thirteen's rover and shuttle supplies back and forth between our camp and *Seeker* as needed. Bakir has his hands full with Santos, but I know he'll be monitoring everyone's suit links remotely, especially your dosimeters."

Kovac cleared his throat. "The science team will obey Protocol Three, as we discussed last night. Zentsov can help us by studying whatever samples you find out here. Sakurai, Li, and Burgess will continue their experiments with me."

"Keep us updated." Rachel tried to gauge their reactions as her cheeks warmed.

"Is that all?" Li didn't look up from his datapad.

"No." Rachel's cheeks grew hotter. "As soon as we can get a clear signal, I want a report sent back to UEA. I don't want anyone exploring alone, nor leaving either camp without notifying the rest. Any supplies recovered from *Centaurus* wreckage need to be accounted for and divided among both camps."

"Where do we bury our dead?" Stevenson's gaze was iron. "Our commander?"

"All remains must be bagged to avoid contaminating this planet," Rachel said. "As for a burial site…we'll use this mesa, if possible, to keep them all in one place."

"Speaking of Granger…" Bakir glanced at Rachel. "What about the briefing he was going to give us right before the accident happened?"

"I haven't found anything about it in the surviving data drives," Rachel said.

"No one knows?" Larsen asked.

Kovac cleared his throat. "Granger was going to follow a UEA suggestion to only allow one or two modules to be present on the moon at a time."

"Why?" Rachel asked. "That isn't typical UEA procedure."

"The UEA thought it best to approach a possible first-contact scenario in a…patient manner," Kovac said.

"How come you know this and we don't?" Stevenson asked.

"Let me guess," Rachel said. "Protocol Three."

Kovac smiled.

"What about the stasis pods on each module?" Burgess asked with a heavy French accent. "Can we still use them?"

"You mean, go back into stasis?" Zentsov tugged at his trimmed beard.

"Why not?" Sakurai asked. "We could pilot each module back into orbit, enter stasis, and wait for a rescue mission."

The others spoke for or against until Rachel raised her hand. "The pods received most of their power from *Centaurus*'s engine, which is gone. Plus, each crew module had only enough fuel for one liftoff. Lacking *Centaurus*, there's no way to refuel, no artificial gravity. And after what happened up there? We're safer down here."

"Each module could still power one or two pods for several years," Burgess said.

"That would preserve supplies," Bakir said. "But I advise it only in desperation."

Kovac shrugged. "Or, Terman, you and the rest could enter stasis while I and my team proceed. The supplies would last much longer. Hard decisions must be made."

Rachel slowly paced around the chamber until she neared Kovac. "Such as?"

He glanced at Santos.

"No," Bakir said. "Santos isn't beyond hope."

"How can you suggest something so awful?" Larsen tossed her empty NF packet at Kovac. "Santos is our IT specialist. Our best chance of contacting UEA."

"Let us face the facts," Kovac said. "If some of us enter stasis, and we get a message to the UEA, then a few might live until a relief mission arrives. If everyone remains active, then we will all surely die on this moon. I'm willing to do what we came here for, even if it costs my life. I will not ask that of others. Can you, Terman?"

"There's no guarantee that the crew modules can power even one pod for that long," Bakir said. "You're talking eight years until rescue, at least."

"The deuterium core inside each module could power one pod for two dozen years," Sakurai said. "And more modules might be found."

Li rolled his eyes. "C'mon, this isn't hard to figure out."

Rachel shook her head. "We have only two intact crew modules so far: *Aloha* and *Seeker*. That's two of us in stasis."

"No, that's two who can live," Li said.

"We need to know who else might have survived before coming to that kind of decision," Rachel said. "I know it all looks bad, but our situation isn't that desperate yet. The equipment modules have all we need to make a colony here, per UEA's orders."

"You all saw that debris," Li said. "Like a meteor shower last night. There's no way in hell enough can be salvaged to help us live here, much less build a colony."

"The UEA's training was pretty comprehensive about this," Stevenson said. "Oh, that's right, Terman. You were added at the last moment. I guess you missed all that."

Li nodded. Burgess stared a hole through Rachel. Larsen and Bakir frowned.

The familiar unease of having shorter Earthlings look up to Rachel returned. The fear of being manhandled by those with greater body mass, greater strength. Even though her fellow crew members were adults and expert professionals, the fear lingered. Once experienced, it could never be forgotten. Only controlled.

She walked over to Stevenson. "My commitment to ensure that everyone here survives is just as comprehensive."

"Good." Stevenson didn't look away.

"Anything else?" Rachel turned her gaze on the others.

The others shared glances or stared at the floor. Kovac continued exuding confidence. Stevenson's scorn hung over the proceedings like a dark cloud.

Bakir cleared his throat. "How long will you look for survivors, then?"

"A week," Rachel said. "After that—"

"Then it's settled." Kovac made for *Aloha*'s inner air lock.

"*Bonne chance*, Commander," Burgess said.

Moments later, Kovac, Burgess, Sakurai, and Li were gone. The echoes of the outer air lock's decompression hatch shutting filled the chamber.

"I can't believe how cavalier he is," Rachel said. "Kovac has used Protocol Three as an excuse twice now, in as many days. Like he's the only one permitted to know."

"I cannot argue with his logic," Zentsov said. "You have plenty to worry about, taking Granger's place. I do, however, take umbrage with placing the mission over the crew. No one came here to die for anything."

"But some have," Stevenson said.

"Or others should have?" Larsen asked. "Is that what you mean?"

Bakir sighed and raised his hands. "Jared, Vanja, enough."

Rachel wanted to rub her temples again, sigh, or just sit down, but she couldn't let her stress show. "I'm suiting up for a drive in the rover. Who's coming with me?"

"Me," Larsen said. "Maybe we will find elves out there."

"This is no joking matter," Zentsov said.

Larsen regarded him with humorous contempt. "Who says I am joking? Kovac looks for aliens but I am best suited to communicate with them."

Bakir checked their dosimeters and monitored their blood pressure on his datapad. "This moon has a twelve-hour day, give or take a few minutes. You have four hours until sunset, so don't stay out after dark. Even the rover can't detect all of those sinkholes."

"Found that out last night." Rachel suited up in an EMU and paused at the air lock. "We'll be back soon. With others, I hope."

Bakir murmured a prayer in Arabic. Zentsov waved.

Stevenson grunted and started inventorying their supplies again.

Once outside, Rachel tuned in to Larsen's personal frequency. "Hey…thanks."

"You are the only Martian I have met. You look like you will not mind a discussion about rongorongo while we drive." Larsen made for the rover.

"What?" Rachel opened the door and climbed into the driver's seat.

"I am saying you are more interesting than the others." Larsen closed the passenger door. "Rongorongo was an alphabet used by Easter Island natives. It is in the UEA's opening course for xeno-linguistics and epigraphy. I once imagined those characters told a grand saga, and we moderns were too complicated to decipher it."

"So now you're going to talk my ear off?" Rachel asked.

"You have two of them." Larsen smiled. "Growing up in Gudvangen I met many tourists. I loved their words and accents."

"That's why you became a linguist?"

"*Ja,*" Larsen said. "It opened me up to the world. Afterward, grandmamma said I talked more than a busload of schoolgirls."

The sad undertone in Larsen's voice was familiar to Rachel. She knew what it meant. "Is that why you joined the UEA?"

A rosy blush filled Larsen's cheeks. "I am proud of my heritage. I follow the Law of Jante. Everything is for the group and not myself."

"That's not what I asked."

"She raised me after mother and father died." Larsen sounded defensive.

"You didn't become an astronaut for that reason."

Larsen shifted in her seat. "You joined UEA to leave Mars?"

A flicker of anger rose in her heart, then Rachel sighed. "Partly. So many Martians didn't understand it at first. They thought I should stay and work against the unfair trade practices, try to improve life there rather than go on space voyages. I'm proud of my heritage, too, but I'm more than that. I...need to be more than just that."

The empathy in Larsen's face was sublime. "Yes," she whispered. "Yes."

Rachel spoke very little during the rest of their excursion, allowing Larsen to talk of possible alien dialects, alphabets, and even the genitive singulars of the Lule Sami language. She sensed Larsen needed it. Her passion made Rachel smile often, reducing some of her own stress.

But not all of it. Mom and Dad had been right. Wherever she went, people would judge her simply for her heritage, her body, her accent. They could accept the diversity of stars and planets, of a universe free of metaphysical agency. Even death itself, the great existential test all humans must face. But not her. They'd never accept her.

Every kilometer they planted a waypoint beacon on ridges or large boulders. The rover's nav app could pinpoint each, forming a virtual highway the vehicle could follow.

Sixteen kilometers out they found burned debris and a still-smoldering crater where a large object had crashed. So little remained that Rachel couldn't determine what part of *Centaurus* it might have been. A dust storm ripped toward them from the west, so they had to turn back. She did glimpse something gray, or even blue, to the south, but it would have to wait. By the time she drove back into camp the sun was disappearing.

Like her hopes.

Personal journal, Mission Specialist Li. Mission date: Sol 2.

What a bullshit meeting. I mean, I see what Terman's trying to do. If this expedition were some cinemorg, where you know the heroes win in the end, then sure, let's spend all our time looking for survivors. But what Kovac said—being willing to die, so that the others might have a chance— that moved me. I could tell it made an impact on Burgess, too. She even fist-bumped me afterward. But Sakurai still acts like we're all doomed. On the way back, though, Kovac did get her to smile at one of his corny jokes.

We're committed to this. If finding the truth kills us, then bring it.

Back at Seeker, *we mapped out the local area using our drone. Damn thing keeps losing signal and power. We were lucky it didn't crash outright. It even soft-landed a couple of hundred meters from the module. While it was still airborne, it managed to give us a serviceable map to go by. Just basic radar imaging, but the results blew us away.*

Seeker is east of the mesa where Aloha *and* Vivaldi *crashed, out in some desert region Sakurai likes to call an arid biome. South of us is a lot of stony reg, craters, and flatlands bordered by crazy-high dunes. The dust storms will change the landscape on a regular basis, too. Which means: If there was an alien civilization on this moon, digging it up will test even my patience. West of us is what appears to be patches of* Centaurus *wreckage. Guess Terman will be combing over that for the next week, wasting time.*

I'm not heartless, but we need to move on.

Can't believe Zentsov didn't speak up more in favor of Kovac. He's an astrobiologist, one of us. Kovac's even worked with him before, back on Earth. We did email him what data we have on the "vines," and the thing Terman stepped on, though the network shared between our drones is worse than the internet I had as a kid.

This alien desert isn't so unfamiliar. Having grown up in Dunhuang, I'm used to waking up to sand and dunes. While my dad helped build the third solar grid in the Gobi, and my mom worked as a business consultant for a biotech firm, I watched my uncle excavate the Han Dynasty sites. Many a day after school, I played around that ruined tower outside of town. On the drive home my excited uncle always told me what he'd found. Soon I was helping him sift artifacts, learned not to overcut a dig site, and how the eyes were still an archaeologist's best tools, despite modern tech.

By my teens, I had more field experience than those wannabe college kids who came up from the south every dig season. I never fucked anything up like they did. Mom and Dad were disappointed at first—they'd hoped I would get a job keeping China the world tech leader into the twenty-second century, instead of studying the past—but when I aced semester after semester at the university, they were extremely proud. When they found out I was going on this mission, they wept with joy. I wish my uncle had lived to see it. He passed away at the dig site a few years prior, an excavation brush still in his hand.

I remember when the UEA approached me. Though I'd applied to be an astronaut two years before, they passed me over for the big name candidates from Hong Kong and Beijing. They ignored a rural person like me—until I excavated some of those old twenty-first-century rovers on Mars, like Curiosity. That got me on the news, and the job.

Yeah, I've been to Mars. I've seen the shit the UEA and Earth governments do to the locals there. Crap workers' rights, and only the rich get the domes with the best radiation shielding. But sticking Terman on this mission won't solve any of that. You want to end inequality and poverty across the Inner System? You fund more expeditions like this one. Not place a rookie on the best ship because it'll make good press.

The chance to study another sentient civilization was something I couldn't pass up. I mean, if you look at the signal's footage and images, it's clear that they come from some old alien probe. I bet its creator is either long dead or light-years distant. So, in a way, I've got one of the most important jobs on this expedition. Larsen might be trying to decode the message, but it's up to me to dig up who sent it.

After we studied the moon's surface data, we ordered the drone to take a GPR scan. I told Kovac not to expect much—ground penetrating radar never yielded a lot in China's deserts, where the electromagnetic waves rarely penetrated deeper than fifteen meters in something as loose and nonconductive as sand. Sure enough, the drone's data averaged ten meters, though I think the electrical interference screwing with our radios and networks may be partly responsible.

But, holy shit, those ten meters showed some strange things.

We detected buried, angular structures thirty kilometers southeast of our camp. There was little logic to their placement—like somebody had dumped a bucket of Legos in a sandbox—but I told Kovac that a field study of the stratification would help us make sense of it all. We could be seeing several layers of sediment, built atop one another over time. I felt like Yang Zhifa must have when he found the first soldier of the Terracotta Army, or Schliemann uncovering Hissarlik. But those discoveries don't compare to something as awesome as this. Sakurai's spirits lifted, too. She wanted to test the soil and rock samples if we dug there.

Kovac agreed, and we set out. Burgess stayed behind in Seeker to run labs on the vines. She was happily singing some French song about la mer *as we left. We were all thrilled. Let Terman and her camp wallow in depression. We're going to make history.*

6

On the third morning Rachel woke herself by crying out.
Larsen was at her side, wiping sweaty bangs from Rachel's face. "Lie still. I have you. Lie still now."

As she cleaned sweat and sleep scum from her eyes, Rachel recalled her nightmare. "I was lost out there, in the desert. There was nothing but sinkholes all around. My helmet was off and I couldn't breathe. Something shiny and blue was just over the next dune."

A knock at the hatch. "Terman? Are you okay? Your blood pressure is spiking, and your insulin—"

Rachel gently pushed Larsen away and sat up on the cot. "I'm fine, Bakir."

"Not according to my apps," Bakir said. "Come see me when you are ready."

Larsen grunted. "'Ready'? He thinks we sleep in pajamas?"

"I hate pajamas." Rachel mopped her face and sighed. "Shit."

"Me, too." Larsen handed her a water bottle. "I also had weird dreams."

"Like what?" Rachel needed to make conversation, anything to take her mind off the nightmare.

"I was communicating with people who understood me. I could not understand them. The subconscious plays strange games while we sleep."

"Then mine must have gone into overtime and lost." Rachel stood and reached for the hatch, then paused. "Want to ride with me again today?"

Larsen smiled. "*Ja.* I will tell why I disagree with Foucault on semiotics. Oh, and fascination with your Martian accent. Pathfinder Base?"

Rachel had to laugh. "It's that obvious?"

"No one else puts such emphasis on bilabial sounds," Larsen said.

"Umm…okay."

In *Aloha*'s main chamber, Bakir waited with his whole app suite ready. He offered a smile and gestured for Rachel to sit at his make-shift medical station. The 3-D printer was set up nearby, along with a live video feed from the drone, which was hovering a hundred meters above the camp. Lines of static occasionally ran down the screen.

"Zentsov said that Kovac and his team found buried ruins to the south." Bakir swiped around her chest and back without touching her, using a stethoscope app and ergo sensors. "Deep breath. Release. Deep breath…and release."

"That's incredible," Rachel said. "Did he say anything else?"

Bakir's knowing frown said it all. Protocol Three again.

"Where is Zentsov?" Larsen slipped on her EMU's leggings.

"In his room, poring over that 'vine' data Burgess emailed him."

"And Stevenson?" Rachel glanced at the screen on Bakir's wrist pad. Her blood pressure had lowered to 118 over 80, and her insulin drop was more likely due to needing breakfast, instead of her nightmare. Not that she would say that aloud.

"He's packing all of our supplies into Thirteen." Bakir tapped the pad a few times, the examination finished. "A slight fever, some periorbital puffiness, and your cortisol levels are higher than yesterday."

"So I'm tired and I have bags under my eyes." Rachel put on the rest of the suit.

"The radiation?" Larsen grimaced as Bakir changed the bandage on her hand.

"It still averages 100 mSv outside," Bakir said. "I'll need blood samples soon, for a deeper look at everyone's cellular health. Especially Santos. He's been in his IVA suit since we arrived, receiving less protection than the rest of us. That much exposure…"

"We'll try not to be out as long today," Rachel said. "Has our drone worked out any debris trajectories? Stevenson's had it in the air long enough to try."

"A few spotty leads to the southwest, but the noise might be contaminating every piece of data it picks up." Bakir glanced at Santos. "If he were awake, he might help us solve that problem. Unless this entire moon emits an electrical disturbance."

"We'll see what the rover's apps can detect," Rachel said. "Hold down the fort."

"Commander?" Bakir lowered his voice. "I want to apologize for yesterday."

Larsen excused herself and left them alone in *Aloha*.

"Why?" Rachel tensed. Talking about it weighed her down all over again.

Bakir tried to smile but it became a grimace. "Stevenson is a good person. I'm sure his views may come across as—"

"I need to hear this from him. Not you."

"He did not ask me to intercede on his behalf." Bakir frowned.

"Then what you were about to say doesn't matter." Rachel put on her helmet, then patted Bakir's shoulder. "I appreciate it, but the apology isn't yours to make. It's his."

They shared a tired smile.

"Then I won't keep you." Bakir went to check Santos's vital signs.

Rachel followed Larsen outside, already wishing she could start the day over.

An overnight storm had piled up centimeters of dust against the modules and a thin coating over the rover. While Larsen cleaned the windshield, Rachel's faceplate auto-tinted as she gazed at the horizon. The view still took her breath, with visibility extending for at least twenty kilometers. The distant green and red pillars shimmered in the morning heat. Tendrils of sand jumped from dune to dune, stirred by the breeze.

Rectangular tracks led from *Aloha* to Thirteen. Stevenson must be moving entire supply crates, then. At least it created more space inside *Aloha*. Should they find other survivors, they'd need it.

Minutes later, inside the rover, Rachel drove with her helmet off. She nibbled yet another granola-and-nut breakfast. "So tell me how you plan on talking to these aliens."

Larsen removed her gloves and rubbed her hands together. "Now that both camps are on the network, and the drones have taken aerial snapshots, I was able to decode one frame from the signal's video component."

Rachel choked on a nut and sipped water from her suit's collar, which was connected to an internal reservoir. "What? And you didn't share this with the group because...?"

"I need confirmation. Better know rightly than hope wrongly."

"Larsen—"

"Call me Vanja."

"Vanja, you can't keep things like that from the crew." Rachel cleared the ridges and boulders at the foot of the mesa and increased speed. "That sounds like Kovac."

"I will tell all once I am sure. The signal sent to Earth was interlaced with video and audio content. The aerial photos resemble some of those frames. I was up for an hour before you woke, comparing them on my tab."

Rachel chewed her lip. "Like...this is where the aliens, or whatever, this is where they wanted us to land?"

"I cannot say without further proof."

"I don't like it," Rachel said.

Larsen smirked. "That frightens you?"

"Hell yes it does."

"Terman, we—"

"Rachel." Speaking her own name—asking another to start using it—made her ease her grip on the wheel. "Please. Call me Rachel. But only here in the rover."

Larsen grinned. "Rachel." Her accent made it sound like *Rashel.*

"No, it's 'Rachel.'"

Larsen gave her a quizzical look. "That is what I said."

Rachel giggled. "Let's try this again. It's—"

A mechanical squeal sounded over the console speaker.

"More noise?" Rachel eyed their coordinates, then glanced at the landscape.

"Nei." Mouth open in excitement, Larsen manipulated the rover's antenna. In seconds, she focused on the proper frequency. The squeal morphed into a consistent beep.

"That's a module transponder!" Rachel sped up. "Can you track it?"

"Five kilometers south of us. The sequence matches the one for *Bimini.*"

Rachel swerved past sinkholes and plowed over the dunes. Sand clouds erupted around the rover. She and Larsen shared excited glances and laughed.

After they crested the next dune, Rachel slowed down. There was nothing ahead of them but a blue…lake? The sun reflected off it like it was a faceted surface rather than liquid. Yet it possessed a watery appearance all the same. Like it was moving.

"It is what we saw yesterday." Larsen's joy evaporated as she studied the console. "The signal. It is coming from the center of…that."

Rachel stopped the rover thirty meters from the blue surface. "I don't see any wreckage. I don't even—hold on. There's something sticking up in the middle."

They put on their helmets and exited the vehicle.

With all of her EMU's sensor apps activated, Rachel approached the blue phenomenon as she would a cornered animal. It measured at least a kilometer in diameter, in a haphazard, oval configuration. Had *Centaurus* not exploded, they might've seen it from orbit. Its edges were dusted by the adjacent sands, proving it wasn't a liquid.

"Dosimeter dropped from 100 to 83 mSv," Larsen said.

Rachel knelt at the blue border. Her sensors detected electrical activity beneath it, to a depth of six meters. Even as she watched, the surface morphed and gleamed like a finely cut sapphire slowly rotated under a light. She extended a hand over it.

"Careful," Larsen said.

Rachel blinked as data on her HUD changed. "Hey, the temperature is lower. I'm reading 302 Kelvin." She leaned out over the blue vastness.

Loose sand under her boots collapsed. She fell forward.

"Rachel!" Larsen grabbed her by the waist, but both of them skidded over the blue surface. It felt sleek, glassy. They came to a halt after sliding a few meters.

Holding her breath, Rachel waited for the surface to break or envelop them. Nothing happened. It held their weight.

Rachel slowly stood, helping Larsen up with her. They both tapped the object gingerly with their boots, then walked around, hanging on to each other, testing the viability of the "lake." The thermometer on her HUD now read 291 Kelvin.

"My dosimeter," Larsen said in a breathless voice.

"I know." Rachel's app read their current radiation exposure at 59 millisieverts.

"Look there." Larsen rushed to the lake's epicenter.

"Now who's not being careful?" Rachel ran to catch up. The object, though it appeared faceted, was perfectly flat. The sun reflected off it, casting the "shore" and their suits in blue hues. By the time they reached the middle, where the transponder lay, radiation had fallen to 30 millisieverts, and the surface temperature had lowered to 260 Kelvin.

That was several degrees below freezing—an impossible difference.

The transponder stole their attention from such anomalies. It lay on its side, a meter-long cylinder sheathed in heat-resistant alloys. No other wreckage was visible.

One of the so-called vines was coiled around it, and several of the nodular, mud-like growths dotted its scorched casing. The vine was a lighter brown and appeared healthier than the ones Rachel had already seen. Plump, even.

Larsen paced around it, taking still images and video. "What do you think?"

"What I want to know is: Where's the rest of *Bimini*?" Rachel scanned the horizon all around, but other than their rover, nothing could be seen. No clues.

The same squeal as before filled Rachel's earbuds. She staggered around, instinctively trying to cover her ears—though it wouldn't do her any good while wearing a helmet. Scrambling on her hands and knees over the glassy lake, Larsen shouted something, but the keening wail of the radio transmission drowned her out.

Though the HUD showed she had plenty of oxygen, Rachel gasped for breath. Heaving, choking, wheezing. Dark shapes moved on the shore in her peripheral vision. She wheeled about, trying to breathe.

Several sinkholes had opened up around the blue lake.

Larsen quivered, eyes rolling back in her head. Trying to remove her helmet.

Rachel swatted Larsen's hands away and shook her head, trying to indicate that she would not allow Larsen to do such a thing. The noise continued.

The transponder vibrated, a motion Rachel felt through her boots. Still struggling to breathe, she tumbled over Larsen. She landed beside the transponder.

The vine had grown larger, fatter. Wrapping tighter and tighter around the device.

Whether born from desperation, terror, or anger, Rachel clawed at the vine. Her gloved fingers tore away at the pulpy mass. Yellow-green ichor splattered. She gasped—

Silence.

The merciless squeal ended. Rachel finally sucked in a breath.

The vine shriveled and coiled away from the transponder, then lay on the lake's surface like a dead weed. Nodules formed from the ichor's splash, hardening before her eyes into the brown, baked-clay shapes she'd stepped on outside the cockpit module.

"Rachel…"

Larsen's weak voice made Rachel hurry back to her side.

"Can you breathe?" Rachel knelt beside her, looking for any tears in Larsen's suit.

"Yes. I was frightened. There was no air. I thought if…"

"Maybe it was just a psychological reaction." Rachel scanned through all of her sensor apps. The queue rolled down her HUD in a parade of comforting green lights. "My suit wasn't compromised. All of my systems are working—"

Larsen grabbed Rachel's arm, her ice-blue gaze filled with skepticism. "Trying to take my helmet off was not a psychological reaction. Zentsov tried it when we first landed. You also reached for your helmet seal."

Rachel didn't recall doing that, but she trusted the fierce certainty in Larsen's face. "Something, or someone, is…I don't know, manipulating us? These vines?"

"We need to take the transponder, the vine, and these clay things back to camp," Larsen said. "A sample of this 'lake,' too."

"Were you still recording video when that noise sounded?"

"Or, can I decode it?" Larsen smirked. "This is in the area. The one matching the alien signal's images. We must return and investigate this further—"

"We almost suffocated, Vanja."

Larsen shrugged. "Only she who wanders finds new paths."

Rachel had to laugh. "Grandmamma Larsen never wandered this far."

"That is why we must. Else you would have stayed on your little red planet."

Though Larsen smiled, a flicker of annoyance sparked in Rachel's heart again. What did this woman know? The bigotry she'd endured, the machinations of her parents, never feeling truly at home on Mars, Luna, or Earth.

"You don't know me." Rachel blurted out the words before thinking.

"I was only—"

"No." Embarrassed, Rachel returned to the rover for storage cartons. Without waiting for Larsen, she used an entrenching tool to scoop the remnants of the vine and nodules into the containers. She dropped the next carton and fumbled for it.

"Damn it," Rachel muttered.

Larsen handed it to her. Her demeanor once again cool and neutral.

They gathered the transponder next, using straps and pulleys— careful not to touch the metal casing for long. Once all was loaded into the rover, Rachel got back in and radioed *Aloha*. A static-filled reply came back. She could tell it was Bakir's voice, but could understand nothing of what he said.

After driving away from the lake, they removed their helmets. Larsen gulped down water while Rachel kept trying the radio. She was still too ashamed to talk.

Rachel retraced their previous route, the nav app following the beacons. Though the mesa was still visible on the northwestern horizon, she was thankful for the aid. It would be far too easy to get lost in the dunes and blindingly white flatlands.

"*Nei,*" Larsen said at last. "I do not know you."

Rachel drove over a few tall dunes on purpose. Making the rover shake.

"But I want to," Larsen said.

After returning to the flatlands below the mesa, Rachel risked a glance at Larsen. Though concentrating on the rover's scanner suite, Larsen kept looking at her from the corner of her eye. Color filled her cheeks.

A kilometer from the *Aloha* campsite, Rachel stopped the rover beside a ridge. It was a good place for another beacon. She put her helmet on, looked Larsen in the eye. Then got out, climbed to the ridge's summit, and planted the device. She sat down.

Yes, she needed to get back to the others and report what had happened, show what they'd found, share her newfound hope and excitement. But she needed to know.

Her heart beat faster as Larsen climbed up after her. Ran her hands over the ridge's smooth green-and-red stone as Larsen sat beside her. They faced the sunset. The wind scattered over the sands below, creating dust devils, reshaping the land.

Staring at the vermilion sky, Rachel tentatively took Larsen's left hand. Squeezed.

Larsen gently squeezed back.

"I want to know you, too," Rachel said.

They studied each other, then shared a smile. Larsen scooted closer. Rachel leaned into her. Holding hands, they watched the sun descend beneath the horizon.

7

"A lake. Made out of blue glass." Bakir looked at Rachel and Larsen, then back at *Aloha*'s array of screens in the main chamber. "How can you expect us to believe this?"

Back in her IVA suit, Rachel stood before the others—Bakir, Larsen, Zentsov, Stevenson—while loading up a video conference with Kovac's camp. The reception was spotty, but nightfall had brought a lull in the wind and electrical noise. She was still ecstatic.

"Look, I know the images and video Larsen took got corrupted somehow," Rachel said. "But the audio component of her video still plays. There are the specimens in the cartons, and *Bimini*'s transponder. You have our suit link data. What else do you need?"

Bakir swiped, and the screens displayed Rachel and Larsen's link data. "Based on this, your EMUs recorded that both of you experienced near-asphyxiation. It also tallied changes in radiation exposure and temperature."

"Yes?" Rachel didn't like his tone.

"Isn't it possible, that while you both nearly ran out of air, you could have…well, hallucinated?" Bakir raised his hands in an apologetic gesture. "Please, hear me out. Yes, we have the audio that Larsen managed to get. Yet, once the 'sound' you described happened, her equipment corrupted the files. Like an electrical pulse ruined it."

Elation turned to humiliation as Rachel rubbed her forehead.

"Even the images?" Larsen swiped through the screens then glared. "*Jævla!*"

"Damning it will not make the information appear," Zentsov said. "But I am willing to give you two the benefit of the doubt. It needs study. I want to visit your lake."

Rachel smiled at Zentsov as the connection with *Seeker* finally came online.

"Kovac here."

He sat in *Seeker*'s main chamber. Li, Sakurai, and Burgess stood behind him, trying to look calm but unable to contain their excitement.

Rachel allowed Larsen to make the presentation but Kovac was less impressed with the lake itself than with the samples they'd brought back. Not even a minute into the discussion, he brought up Protocol Three.

"Terman, the science team should have those samples. All of your evidence. That is UEA policy." Kovac gave a humorless smile. "Besides, the proper labs for biological and biochemical analysis are here on *Seeker*. Let expertise take over from here."

"This mission is about more than your science team," Stevenson said.

"No," Li said. "It really isn't."

"We will accomplish nothing by arguing," Zentsov said.

"According to your last email, you're not accomplishing much over there anyway, Zentsov," Sakurai said. "Or are you refusing to share your findings?"

Several crew members spoke at once, and soon it became a chorus of yelling and shouting. Rachel raised her voice. "This would be easier if our teams worked together, side by side, rather than living apart in separate camps. Thirteen could accommodate—"

"I moved all of our supplies in there," Stevenson said. "They need the module's shielding from the moon's radiation. The shelters can't handle it."

"Aren't you looking for survivors?" Burgess asked.

"Yes." On the screen, Kovac leaned forward. "Where will you house them, if we all live in your camp? I'm beginning to wonder if you know how to handle this, Terman."

Larsen muttered in Norwegian and Bakir gave Rachel a slight shake of the head. Warning her not to botch what was already a tenuous partnership with the other camp.

Rachel didn't flinch. "I'm wondering when you'll set aside your ego and realize that we are here for each other now. Survival first, discovery second."

"Are you fucking kidding me?" Li glowered. "We actually found something—"

Kovac raised a hand and Li fell silent. "We will visit your camp tomorrow and talk it over. But discovery is priority. I hope you discover humility before morning."

The video connection ended.

"That's one arrogant son of a bitch." Stevenson cracked his knuckles.

"Finally, we agree on something." Rachel offered a slight smile.

Stevenson jabbed a finger at her. "You shouldn't have told Kovac anything."

"And act just like him?" Rachel asked. "I don't know who's worse, you or—"

"Please, we are professionals here," Bakir said.

"Some of us are." Stevenson shot Rachel a look.

Bakir raised his voice. "You are better than that, Jared."

"We'll see who's better, who has value. Kovac better stay the hell out of my way tomorrow." Stevenson went to his room and slammed the hatch shut.

Rachel rubbed her forehead. "Zentsov, you know Kovac. Is this normal?"

Sitting down, Zentsov opened a water bottle. "He's the most ambitious man I've ever met. He's also the best scientist I've worked with. We need him."

"We must return to the lake," Larsen said. "Beat them at their own game."

"This isn't a game." Bakir checked the apps on his tab, then handed Rachel two ibuprofen capsules. "For your headache."

"Thanks." Rachel swallowed the capsules and headed for her room. "You're right, it isn't a game. But we need to go back. The rest of *Bimini* has to be nearby, and I'm hoping we'll detect other transponders. There are still several kilometers of debris strewn westward and we need to examine all of it. I'm not giving up on our people."

"What about doing labs on these specimens?" Zentsov asked.

"I will compare what we heard today with the signal sent to Earth," Larsen said. "Might be something encoded within it."

Rachel met Larsen's eyes, then looked away. "Don't stay up too late. I want to head out at dawn—if you're coming, that is."

"It is best to search while the trail is new." Larsen slowly brushed past her and smiled. "Of course I am coming."

Cheeks burning, Rachel nodded and hurried off. After closing the hatch to their quarters, Rachel lay on her cot. She wasn't the shy type. In any other place or situation, she'd see how far these feelings might go. Now she was a commander breaking the rules.

UEA policy forbids inter-crew relationships. Such a bond might endanger their mission, summoning favoritism, jealousy, or impulsive behavior rather than logic.

Rachel tried to bury her yearnings. It was probably a result of her anxieties, seeking solace in the arms of yet another woman while facing death every day.

She kept telling herself that even as she stared at Larsen's empty cot.

Flight Recorder – *Maray* Crew Module
Sol 3 – 1115 hours
Orbiting Proxima Centauri C

CMP Worrel: Another crashed module? On fire?

MS Khandaar: That's what the imagery suggests, sir. There is increased rover activity around the first two crash sites. One went out alone and still hasn't returned to either site. If I had the apps on the satellite we were supposed to put in orbit—

CMP Worrel: But we don't, Khandaar. Do your best and keep looking. At least some survived and are working together. That's something to have a ripsnorter about.

MS Khandaar: A what?

CFE Moore: Think he means "party," honey.

MS Khandaar: Still not funny, Moore.

CFE Moore: Know what else isn't funny? Me not checking that scanner.

CMP Worrel: (sighs)

CFE Moore: Any other survivors need to know about us as much as we need to speak with them. That'd boost morale down there.

MS Khandaar: Up here, too…sir.

CMP Worrel: Okay, Moore. But any sign of debris, you get back inside.

CFE Moore: (laughs) I'm faster than those meteorites. I'll have us chatting to everyone within the hour. Suiting up now. See you in few.

MS Khandaar: Sir, how many do you think survived?

CMP Worrel: Five modules spotted so far, with four people per manned module, gives sixteen possible survivors other than us. But that's out of forty crew.

MS Khandaar: We lost some people. There's no doubt of that.

CMP Worrel: Stay positive. Don't focus on the negative.

MS Khandaar: It's a valid concern, sir. We only have supplies for a month.

CMP Worrel: Some of the supply modules should've landed. I'm more concerned by the bloody micro-g. Without the centrifuges, we have no source of artificial gravity. Not all of us were supposed to leave *Centaurus*.

MS Khandaar: I only have partial augmentation—gastrointestinal and cranial—so my bones will be affected before anyone else's.

CMP Worrel: My bones are the ones I was born with. I endured the appendectomy and cholecystectomy with the rest of you. (chuckles)

MS Khandaar: Yes. No appendix or gallbladder. Those of us from ISRO once joked that the UEA only did it to cut down on *Centaurus*'s weight.

CMP Worrel: Too right! (laughs)

CFE Moore: EMU is online, if *el capitán* is listening. Awaiting air-lock control.

CMP Worrel: (chuckles) Open the air lock.

MS Khandaar: Air lock is now open. Compression containment at 100 percent.

CFE Moore: Be right back, honey.

MS Khandaar: (groans) You better be. Air lock closed.

CMP Worrel: Stay on the tether. Don't get fancy and depend on the thrust pack.

CFE Moore: Yes, sir.

MS Khandaar: I'll be glad to get out of this chair once he's done. I need a stretch.

CMP Worrel: Stoked for that. I could use another low gravity workout.

MS Khandaar: So…What did you leave behind on Earth, sir? Wife? Kids?

CMP Worrel: I've been a widower since Carl died six years ago. No children.

MS Khandaar: Sorry, sir.

CMP Worrel: No worries, you didn't know. What about you?

MS Khandaar: No spouse or children, but I miss my parents. They did try to marry me off to a Cambridge professor, but I turned him down. I wasn't ready. When I get back, who knows? Maybe I'll call him up.

CMP Worrel: You'll have plenty of suitors, once we return. I mean…if we—

MS Khandaar: It's okay, sir. I know what you meant. Thanks.

CFE Moore: I've a visual on the antenna array. A little cooked, but if it's merely a wiring issue, I should be able to repair it.

CMP Worrel: Go ahead, but be careful.

MS Khandaar: Sir, I'm getting a yellow proximity warning.

CMP Worrel: Moore, you catch that? Do you have a visual on any debris?

CFE Moore: Negative. Opening the array now. Won't take but a minute.

MS Khandaar: Proximity warning upgraded to orange.

CFE Moore: Wait, I see the problem. It's—

CMP Worrel: Get back in, fix it later.

CFE Moore: It's right there. I got this.

MS Khandaar: Proximity red! Proximity red!

CMP Worrel: Moore, come inside right bloody now!

CFE Moore: Just a chunk of hull, and it just passed us. I'll be—
(static)

MS Khandaar: Sir, I'm closer to the air lock! Let me get him!

CFE Moore: (groans)

CMP Worrel: No, I need you working the thrusters. On my mark.

MS Khandaar: Damn it, sir—

CMP Worrel: That's an order! Open the air lock!

CFE Moore: (gasps, mumbles)

MS Khandaar: Air lock open.

CMP Worrel: Moore, if you can hear me, hit the tether wind button on your belt.

MS Khandaar: Proximity warning back to orange!

CMP Worrel: Damn it. No wonder he couldn't wind manually— it's cut. He's clinging to the bloody hull!

MS Khandaar: Oh my God.

CMP Worrel: Here, take my hand. Moore? Take my goddamn hand!

CFE Moore: (grunts) Tore…chest…

CMP Worrel: Khandaar, I have him but I'm using both hands. Wind in my tether.

MS Khandaar: Winding, sir. Proximity is back to red.

CMP Worrel: My boots are touching the air lock.

(scraping noises on hull)

MS Khandaar: We just brushed some debris! Sir? Sir, do you read me?

CMP Worrel: The tether is snagged on the framing. Khandaar, I need you to come to the air lock and pull us through.

MS Khandaar: Oh God. Oh God.

CMP Worrel: I need you to focus.

MS Khandaar: Sir, I can't—

CMP Worrel: Jivika. Do it. Now.

MS Khandaar: Oh my God. Is he dead?

CMP Worrel: Just keep tugging. Again. Okay, I'm in. Help me with him.

MS Khandaar: There. Compression normalizing. Air lock is closed.

CMP Worrel: Work the thrusters, raise our altitude. One more piss-up like that and *Maray* will come apart.

MS Khandaar: Will Kevin make it?

CMP Worrel: Good thing he's unconscious. His EMU links says a tiny meteorite burned right through his chest below the right lung. All I can do is patch the entrance and exit punctures. I've no idea how damaged his internals are without an MRI scan.

MS Khandaar: (sobs) Sir? I'm really scared now.

CMP Worrel: There's no time for blubbing now.

MS Khandaar: I don't…I can't…

CMP Worrel: Hey. Look at me. We're going to get through this. You hear? We'll make it. Now stabilize those thrusters and come over here and help me.

MS Khandaar: (sniffs) Yes, sir. I'm sorry.

CMP Worrel: You did great. So…that Cambridge professor have a nice arse?

MS Khandaar: What?

CMP Worrel: Well, did he?

MS Khandaar: (laughs) Yes, he certainly did. I know what you're trying to do.

CMP Worrel: Took your mind off of that bloody fear, didn't it?

MS Khandaar: Thanks, sir.

CMP Worrel: It's my privilege. Here, grab Moore's feet, I've got his arms.

8

Rachel laid awake the final hour before dawn. Larsen gently snored, sometimes murmuring in Norwegian. But the nightmares were the true thieves of Rachel's rest. They had been short, but they left a deeper impression this time.

Suffocating. Wandering across the flatlands outside, unable to breathe, even with her helmet on. Yet on the horizon, a blue glow. She knew if she could reach it, that she'd be able to breathe. That she'd be safe. Each time, though, she never made it to safety.

Which made her think about the glass lake, or whatever it was. The noise they'd heard there yesterday, coupled with the nightmares, planted a growing dread in Rachel's heart. Someone, or something, could be affecting their minds.

Worse, they had no defense against it.

"I woke you?" Larsen slipped off her cot, rubbing her face.

"I wish it had been you." Rachel gave a half-smile. "Shit, I want some coffee."

Larsen sat cross-legged beside Rachel's cot. "You are awake too much already."

"Well, usually it's your snoring." Lying on her side, Rachel inhaled the scent of Larsen's sweat. The light musk clashed with the vinyl odor of their IVA suits. She leaned closer to the edge and breathed in the aloe scents of Larsen's hair. They both used the same no-rinse shampoo, but Vanja's pheromones made it irresistible.

"You must get used to it." Larsen smirked.

"I'm sure I will." Unsure of Larsen's preference, Rachel wondered what to say.

A knock on the hatch made Rachel flinch.

Larsen rolled her eyes. "We are not decent." She gave Rachel's leg a squeeze.

"Forgive the intrusion, *damy*," Zentsov said on the other side of the hatch. "Our drone says a storm system may strike the region in four hours. If we are going…"

"Be right out." Rachel got up and they joined Zentsov in the main chamber to suit up. Though Bakir offered breakfast—soy chicken breast, spinach casserole, vanilla flan—Rachel wasn't hungry. Bakir tried his routine scan, but Rachel was pressed for time. Ten minutes later she, Larsen, and Zentsov left camp in the rover. Zentsov got in the back seat while Larsen sat beside Rachel, her field lab connected to the rover's sensors. The kilometers dragged by since they all were tired. Rachel decided to break the silence.

"Four hours isn't much. The first thing I'd like to do is return to that lake and search for the rest of *Bimini*."

Zentsov grunted. "Transponder or not, the probability that anyone from that module could be still alive is very low. You know this."

"Russians are so optimistic." A mischievous gleam entered Larsen's gaze.

Zentsov chuckled. "No, simply realistic. What I hope to find is how that transponder found its way to the center of your glass lake."

"Everybody keeps saying 'your lake' like I'm full of shit," Rachel said.

"With all due respect, Commander, I must see it for myself," Zentsov said. "Only a drunken scientist would take all of that at face value, without close examination."

"Drunk?" Rachel asked. "Don't you guys always bring vodka on every mission?"

"Yes, but we don't share." He smiled, and they laughed.

"We're not the ones who need a stiff drink around here," Rachel said.

Long moments passed in silence.

"Stevenson is…passionate." Zentsov looked out the window.

"Larsen, is that the Russian word for 'asshole'?" Rachel asked.

"*Nei.*" Larsen smirked. "It is '*drittsekk*' in my native *norsk.*"

"The UEA could have avoided controversy at home without creating it on this expedition," Zentsov said. "I am sorry, Terman, but that is true. The Martian people—"

Rachel sped up. "Have you ever been to Mars?"

Scratching his beard, Zentsov shook his head. "No."

"Then you've never seen the living conditions on the hydroponics farms," Rachel said. "The shanties they bulldozed outside New Paris. The rich Earthlings who come to adopt Martian orphans, ignorant that Earth's gravity might kill them at that early stage."

Zentsov frowned. "No, but I understand that your people want—"

"No, you don't." Rachel fought to keep her voice from shaking.

Larsen gently laid a hand on Rachel's shoulder.

"I have offended you," Zentsov murmured. "I am sorry."

"It's just…I didn't think I'd have to hear the same bigotry out here," Rachel said. "We're on limited supplies, there's not going to be a rescue in time, and everyone's on edge. Tomorrow we might be killing each other for a bottle of vodka."

"Unless it's Krupnik," Zentsov said. "That can take the paint off of this rover."

Larsen smiled, then chuckled. Rachel looked at her and finally laughed, too.

Zentsov's grin faded. "I agree, however, that we are in a precarious position. I suspect that some among us are hoping for a negative report on other crew members having survived, so that there will be more supplies available for them."

"Yes," Rachel said. "I'm worried about that, too."

"Rachel, several new craters ahead." Right after speaking, Larsen gave Rachel an apologetic look. "Our drone…sent the information."

If Zentsov noticed the slip in command etiquette, he didn't show it. "Something must have crashed last night. I am surprised it did not wake us."

Once they crested a few dunes, a series of fresh craters came into view on the western flatlands. The lips were blackened and still smoldering. Rachel drove closer for a better look. Nothing but small debris, judging from the crater sizes.

"It's not a crew or supply module," Rachel said.

"Unless one broke up before impact," Larsen said.

"It still serves as a reminder that we don't know what caused the fire in Centrifuge B." Rachel drove on.

"I was seated in *Vivaldi*," Zentsov said. "We heard the alarms, then everything was chaos. Stevenson was justified in trying to save us, but not in blaming you afterward. You did the right thing. Without you, we would all be dust in a crater like this one."

"Thank you," Rachel said. "But we need to look forward now."

The sun reached its zenith as they caught sight of the lake. The rover's nav system, following the coordinates Rachel entered the day before, had locked onto it a kilometer ago—which was miraculous, considering the moon's continued electrical interference. UEA had prepared such radar-based, terrain scanners for use without the aid of traditional GPS, but Modules Three and Seventeen had each contained a satellite meant to be deposited once *Centaurus* entered the moon's orbit. That would have made everything easier, even down to tracking each crew member's personal GPS tag, embedded in their right arm just beneath the skin.

Larsen leaned forward in her seat. *"Dette kan ikke være…"*

Rachel eyed the translation app on her HUD. "It cannot be… but there it is."

"And yet it is," Zentsov whispered.

The lake had shrunk to one-half its previous circumference. The sinkholes had filled in as if they'd never been. The sand around it didn't appear disturbed or flattened as it should have, if a huge glass lake had been resting atop it.

"Look there." Rachel snapped out of her shock and eased the rover forward.

Beyond the lake's southwestern edge was a crew module.

"It appears undamaged," Zentsov said in a hopeful tone.

As she drove closer, Rachel tensed. "How the hell did we not see that yesterday?"

"I do not like this." Larsen put her helmet on.

"I'm not a fan, either, but let's go." Rachel stopped and turned off the engine. They exited the rover and strode up to the downed module. The sand was so loose her steps wobbled. She surmised a windstorm could have cleared off the module, but she remembered what the landscape had looked like yesterday. The module would have been visible. She would've spotted it.

It all felt…wrong.

Getting closer, she spotted the words etched onto the module's side: *Bimini*. Its open hatch made a lump rise in Rachel's throat. Larsen and Zentsov let her enter first.

Bimini's aeroshell was scorched from reentry but the interior appeared in good order. No signs of fire, cracked hulls, breaches, or any other damage. Pristine, even. Which made the sight greeting them all the more horrific.

Three crew members sat in their seats, restraints still buckled. All still wore their IVA suits and helmets. The terrified expressions behind those faceplates made Rachel turn away. She'd never seen such fear in anyone's eyes, living or dead.

The recurring nightmare came back to Rachel and she forced herself to inhale. It took a second, like her body had forgotten how to breathe. She calmed herself before she started hyperventilating. "Did they…Did they asphyxiate?"

Zentsov checked the air supply dials on their suits' chest units. "Negative. In all three instances, their oxygen supply is nearly full."

"Any idea what happened?" Larsen shined her suit's flashlight into the crew quarters and storage lockers.

Studying the corpses' suit monitors, Zentsov paged through several screens until his eyes narrowed. "Each monitor says they entered cardiac arrest."

"Heart attacks?" Rachel looked at the small screens. "That doesn't make sense. Why didn't their suit links go off? I'd have seen that in the cockpit, on the roster displays. If someone had so much as farted, I—or Bakir—would have known about it."

"Unless it happened after *Centaurus* exploded," Larsen said.

Rachel paced around *Bimini's* main chamber, then stopped. There were four seats—and only three bodies. She hurried outside. Studied the sand around the module.

Following her, Zentsov shook his head. "Any footprints would be gone by now."

"You're right, but I have to try."

Zentsov sighed. "I am not happy to be. Contrary to popular belief, an astrobiologist doesn't always wish to be right."

"Try linguistics," Larsen said. "People only believe when I cross-reference theories in four dialects."

Rachel activated her suit's binocular app. Twin lenses slipped from either side of her helmet and covered her eyes. After a second of autofocus, she gazed around *Bimini.*

Despite her instincts, the landscape did indeed bear signs that a storm had disturbed nearby dunes. They were linear, with perhaps a kilometer between each, the troughs not as deep as yesterday. It still didn't explain how a crew module could simply not be there one day, and appear the next.

Sunlight glinted off an object in a trough, two hundred meters southwest.

"I see something!" Rachel hurried to the rover. The other two joined her. Minutes later, they reached the anomaly: the helmet from an IVA suit, faceplate intact.

"Damn it," Rachel said. There were no other pieces of the suit. No tracks in the sand, and though she stared around with the binocular app a few more minutes, the moon's surface was as devoid of life as ever.

"Crew from *Bimini's* manifest are inside except for Brent," Larsen said. "Think he sought help in the storm?"

"Or do you suppose he placed *Bimini's* transponder on the lake?" Zentsov asked. "Perhaps in an attempt to get a better signal? Your rover did detect it yesterday, correct?"

A chill spread through Rachel as she stared down at the abandoned helmet. Numerous explanations came to mind; all credible, all hypothetical. But she did remember Bakir telling her how he'd stopped Zentsov from removing his helmet. The same as she'd had to do yesterday with Larsen during the noise incident.

"Maybe that's what happened." Rachel spotted winds tearing across the reg fields to the southwest. Still many kilometers distant, but she would not risk it. "Let's leave."

There were many reasons she wanted to return to camp. The storm was the least of them.

It took them an hour to gather *Bimini*'s supplies, seal the corpses in body bags, and secure the hatch. Rachel swore to return and investigate.

No matter how much it scared the hell out of her.

Chief Medical Officer's journal. Mission date: Sol 4.

Terman, Larsen, and Zentsov left in the rover to examine the lake and scout for more crashed modules. Reception is much clearer today, with less electrical background noise, so they should have an excellent chance. Our Russian friend's demeanor brightened immediately; after the argument with Kovac last night, he has taken it upon himself to convince both camps to cooperate by making more discoveries. Larsen is rather cheerful as well. I heard her laugh and call Terman "Rachel" right before they exited Aloha's hatch. She's certainly not the typical, taciturn Norwegian I expected.

I cannot say the same for our commander, though her passion to succeed is admirable. Terman had dark circles under her eyes again, took no breakfast, and tried to avoid my routine morning checkup. I can only assume her nightmares are due to stress.

Which is how I feel now, after Kovac and his team practically raided our camp.

They came an hour after sunrise—conveniently, right after Terman's departure. Kovac was all jokes and smiles, and at first I was pleased to chat with him again. But when Burgess took our spare drone, and Li started carrying off the specimens Terman and Larsen brought back yesterday— without even asking—I protested.

Kovac tried to laugh it off, but Stevenson appeared—wrench in hand. Undeterred, Li accused us of inhibiting important work while Burgess activated the drone and ordered it to monitor a site they were working on to the southwest. Sakurai looked ashamed that she was affiliated with them.

That's when they turned to our equipment. Kovac claimed they needed our spare field lab and some of our fuel cells. Though both camps had already set up each module's solar panels, the cells powered the rovers, drones, and excavation tools.

I told them no. Kovac recited more subentries from Protocol Three as an excuse.

Li became taciturn, taking orders from Kovac only, ignoring anyone else. We started to argue, and I asked Stevenson to secure the fuel cells for our med equipment. This annoyed Kovac, saying the equipment belonged to everyone, not one person.

People talked louder until we were all shouting. Kovac said something in Croatian to Stevenson, and, before I could stop him, Stevenson punched him.

Kovac fell backward onto Santos, still bedridden. The cot flipped over, dumping Santos onto the floor. The respirator and intravenous fluid tubes were yanked from him. The life monitor screen cracked and Santos's wound ruptured.

Unable to control myself, I flung Kovac off of Santos and began bandaging the wound to stem the bleeding. Sakurai helped Kovac up even as she berated him. Burgess, wide-eyed, handed me more bandages, until Stevenson demanded she leave.

Li placed himself between Stevenson and the others. They would have fought, if I hadn't yelled at them, calling them children, fools, and other things I do not wish to repeat here. Like them, anger, fear, and frustration took hold of me. Allah forgive me.

Stevenson, already in his EMU, went outside and locked himself in Thirteen, which contained our food, water, spare oxygen, the extra rover, and basic tools. Via radio, he threatened any who would steal them, and appointed himself "quartermaster."

Wiping his bloodied lip, Kovac called us idiots, slammed his helmet back on, and stomped out of the hatch. The others followed—Burgess kept whispering "Je suis désolé"—and they all drove away. Not until later did I realize that was French for "I'm sorry."

So am I.

Once I had Santos stabilized, back on the cot, and connected to the respirator and nutrient drips, I activated my med sensors and swiped over his torso using my MRI app. The stupid, pointless fight had damaged the muscle fibers around his wound. The scan revealed a six centimeter diagonal rip across Santos's left pectoralis major. It was also two centimeters deep. Any deeper, and blood could have entered his left lung.

Unlike our first day on this world, I was better prepared. I pulled up the proper AMF specs for that specific muscle on the 3-D printer, cross-referenced it with the scan data of Santos's actual pectoral, and began printing him a new one. Four hours to completion. I paced around his cot, not daring to leave his side until I was finished.

What was happening to us? No one with previous psychological problems or issues becomes a UEA astronaut. I studied everyone's evaluations before leaving Earth; all forty crew members had been the best-prepared for such a mission. Yet now, all of that discipline and training is falling apart. I must discover the cause before things worsen.

I pray that Allah will have mercy on us.

Personal journal, Mission Specialist Li. Mission date: Sol 4.

Wow, what a bunch of assholes.

Even though we got the specimens and equipment we needed—equipment the UEA put on this mission for us to use—the treatment we received from Stevenson and Bakir was total bullshit. I mean, Kovac explained it so that even a five-year-old would have understood. But the doctor and his crony acted as if we were ransacking the place.

Kovac was cool about it all at first. Telling them why we needed to take the stuff, that Protocol Three gave us permission. This isn't some pissing contest, this is what we fucking came all this way for! But did Bakir and that big prick with the wrench care? No. They were more interested in hoarding equipment they aren't even trained to use, instead of aiding us like the team we're supposed to be.

I was impressed with Kovac's cool after we left. Me, I wanted to go back in there and kick their asses. It's not our fault Terman's out joyriding while we're doing real work. Even though Stevenson has the bulk of everyone's supplies now, I'm not going back. We have food and water, which won't last. But we're doing something for our species at least. Just waiting there for death, or whatever, is sheer stupidity.

On the drive back to Seeker, Kovac flirted with Sakurai and she actually blushed. Burgess was more reserved. I guess it bothered her that Centaurus's crew has split into factions. Well, to hell with them. I'm not focusing on it. With this equipment—another drone, a digger bot, and an extra field lab so that Sakurai and Burgess can conduct tests simultaneously—we're set.

Once we got back to our camp—I love how tribal we're becoming, like one of those old-fashioned reality shows—Kovac unveiled his plans. He thinks the sinkholes are artificial, instead of naturally occurring phenomena. He suspects—based on Sakurai's soil tests, and the soil data from the alien signal—that whoever sent that information to Earth had attempted to cultivate this moon. See, Sakurai's analysis revealed the presence of nitrogen, potassium, calcium, phosphorus, sodium, sulfur, and magnesium. You know, all of the macro nutrients needed to grow shit back on Earth.

A weird but exciting coincidence.

The "vines" might be evidence of this, Kovac says. Burgess wants to run tests on the samples ASAP. I mentioned revisiting those flatlands south of us—where Terman interrupted us last night. That's where the GPR scans showed possible ruins.

We spent the rest of the morning nibbling from IM food packets— intermediate moisture, meaning it wouldn't spoil immediately—and reading the samples. Kovac worked so fast and efficient, he almost ran the operation himself. I could only watch and learn, being an archaeologist. Using the new field lab, Sakurai did a deeper analysis of the soil samples she's taken the last four days. She became a little less forlorn since Kovac put us all at ease. Even Burgess lightened up, laughing with me at how bad the soy jerky tasted in comparison to the apricot crisps, which are fucking addictive.

Thirty minutes and a hundred of Kovac's jokes later, the tests were complete.

Biological cells still lived in the vine specimen Terman and Larsen found.

We stared in shock, then cheered and whooped. The previous samples Burgess—and Zentsov—had been studying were devoid of any cellular activity. They might as well have been fucking rocks. But this was different, right?

So, on this desolate moon, subjected to extreme heat, an apparent lack of water, and horrid radiation, this thing was alive.

Kovac stopped cheering and mentioned what Terman and Larsen had reported, and what audio they'd managed to record: The vine had been wrapped around Bimini's transponder. He suggested that it didn't require moisture, but energy.

I grinned, took the battery from the flashlight on my EMU's chest unit, and wrapped part of the vine around it. Burgess worried I might have ruined the sample, but I convinced them to wait and see. Then, right before our eyes, projected on the lab display, the vine's cells changed. They grew larger. More active.

Some even duplicated themselves.

We all grew quiet and stared at each other. Suddenly, the possibilities of this world changed. The message we'd received—it, too, changed in our minds, for now we had hard evidence to ponder. The theories started flying fast.

Sakurai posited that the signal is a request for help, since this world might be dying. I jokingly said the aliens wanted to see our capabilities and left the vines as a test. A little less enthusiastic, Burgess claimed that the vines might be remnants of a failed experiment and we shouldn't meddle with it. After we all spoke, we looked at Kovac.

All smiles, he said we all might be right, but he suggested an alternative. He wondered if the vines themselves weren't the aliens, or at least an extension of them.

After he said that, we all studied the lab display again. The vine's coloring had altered. Still a withered brown, but a little lighter in hue. It was also plumper.

This all matched Terman's description of what the vine had looked like, before she ripped it off the transponder.

A renewed drive and sense of purpose came over us. It alleviated any guilt we might've had regarding the argument with Bakir and Stevenson. We were on the cutting edge of discovery, and no one was going to stop us.

9

Driving across the moon's wastes reminded Rachel of her first job. She'd been a driver then, too. Ferrying supplies from the starport at Pathfinder Base to outlying farms and mining claims. There'd been an Earthling woman at the starport she'd developed a crush on. That height, those thicker arms and legs. Red hair and freckled skin.

The woman had seemed a goddess compared to Rachel's own frailty. Losing her virginity not only fulfilled Rachel's idea of love, but also hinted at a deeper fantasy: that she could be one of them. Respected, confident. She'd just turned twenty and felt she knew it all.

Until the woman left, her Martian tour complete. She'd laughed at Rachel when asked if they'd ever see each other again, if they could keep in touch via the Internet.

Rachel had been used. Now, seven years later, she wondered if she was being used again.

Zentsov watched the storm approach on the sensors while Larsen returned to her tab, studying the strange noise recorded at the lake. Rising winds tossed sand and pebbles against the rover, constituting the only sound inside the cramped vehicle.

Which ended as soon as Rachel drove up to their camp. Someone had built a barricade of supply crates and shelters in front of Thirteen's hatch.

"Bakir, this is Terman. Why is Thirteen's hatch blocked?"

"Stevenson's hoarded almost all of our supplies in there, and won't let anyone in. Where have you been? I've been trying to reach you."

"What the hell happened?" Rachel braked so hard that the others grunted.

"Please come to *Aloha*. I will tell you all everything."

The wind buffeted Rachel as she flung open the rover door and ran for *Aloha*. Bakir met her at the entrance, staring through the hatch's small window.

She banged on the hatch. "Let me in."

Bakir studied her for a moment, then looked at Zentsov behind her. "Have Zentsov watch the rover. We can't leave anything unguarded now."

"What?" Rachel's body temperature rose on her faceplate HUD.

"It wasn't just Stevenson," Bakir said.

She glared back at Thirteen, hoping that bastard Stevenson could see her. "Then we have much to discuss. Let me in."

Bakir hesitated and looked over his shoulder at something.

"That's an order," Rachel said.

"I'm waiting for the decompression chamber to load."

She looked at her feet and sighed. She really needed sleep. "Sorry."

Minutes later, she stood in main chamber with Bakir and Larsen. The cot housing Santos was in a different position. The med monitor had a cracked screen.

The vine specimens were gone.

"Okay, what happened?" she asked in a tight voice. "Where's the extra field lab?"

As Bakir related what Kovac and his team had done, Rachel's head ached. No one had a monopoly on *Centaurus*'s equipment, but simply coming in and taking it, causing an argument, was very dangerous out here. No wonder Stevenson had done what he did. He probably thought Kovac and the others would come for the food next.

"I'm going to go talk to Kovac," Rachel said, interrupting Bakir.

"Not alone," Larsen said. "We all must face them."

Bakir gestured at Santos, hitched to a respirator. "Do you see him lying there? We can't afford any more casualties. I printed a replacement muscle for him after that madness. I'd just finished implanting it when you arrived. Please reconsider. If we confront them, it will only cause more trouble."

"And if we don't, we might become their victims when the shit really hits the fan," Rachel said. "Plus, we need to deal with Stevenson, or we'll be starving while he binges for a few extra weeks. Fuck. We're supposed to be in this together!"

"Reacting with anger will ensure we all die together," Bakir said.

Rachel had to lean over *Aloha*'s computer console. "Then what do you suggest?"

"We stay in contact with Kovac and his team, asking if they require anything," Bakir said. "We invite them to any expeditions we make across this moon. We ask them how their research is coming along, and whether or not we can help."

"Like nothing is wrong?" Larsen asked. "The bear and the bear hunter are not of the same opinion. Next, Kovac will say Protocol Three means they eat first."

"They are still professionals," Bakir said. "They will realize their mistake."

"I'm still going out there," Rachel said. "I'm in charge of this expedition, whether anyone likes it or not. It's my duty to see that we remain a team, not disparate bands of vagabonds raiding each other like primitive tribes."

Bakir spread his hands. "Did you hear nothing that I—"

"We found *Bimini*." Rachel faced Bakir. "Beside the glass lake. They were all dead, except for Brent. We found his helmet hundreds of meters from the module."

Pinching the bridge of his nose, Bakir slowly sat. "How awful."

"That's why we need to go." Rachel headed for the hatch.

"Absolutely not." Bakir stood up. "The storm will hit us within the hour. You could get lost out there. With all the interference, none of your scanners will work."

"Then tomorrow." Rachel glared out the hatch. "No matter what comes."

"I am with you," Larsen said. "We wait until the storm has passed."

"All right, I'll wait," Rachel said. "But after we get Kovac straight, our only chance is to scrounge supplies from any crashed modules and build that temporary colony. For our continued survival, we're going to need everyone's help. Sakurai and Burgess must set up hydroponics. I also need to know how this planet is affecting us. That blood test you mentioned would be a great idea. If we get Kovac on board, we could pool our efforts and discover what unseen dangers we might be facing."

Bakir grudgingly nodded. "Very well, Commander. But I want you both to eat. No more skipping meals or checkups."

"Zentsov, we'll be out shortly to help you bring the rover and drone into *Aloha*'s supply berth. Terman out." She muted her radio. "I was hoping to save that space for survivors. And if the storm is bad, we'll have to clear the berth door before we can even drive the rover back out. But we dare not leave anything out there tonight."

While Larsen reheated the offerings from breakfast—the soy chicken breast still smelled good—Rachel spotted Bakir's prayer rug, rolled up in a corner.

"Any luck with that?" she said, suddenly drained of anger.

"Allah doesn't deal in luck," Bakir said. "I have been asking nonetheless."

"So…Stevenson hasn't answered you on the radio since the incident?"

"True." Bakir gathered a syringe and several vacutainer tubes. "I am not sure if he is embarrassed or angry. Probably both."

"He should be ashamed." Rachel accepted the food tray from Larsen and tried the chicken. A little too salty. At least the flan was firm and sweet.

"I made that myself." Bakir gave Rachel a slight grin.

The casserole was much better: lentils, spinach, and rice spiced with fiery masala.

"That is called *shola*," Bakir said. "It is not as good as my mother's."

"It's delicious." Rachel savored another bite. "Is the masala from your pantry?"

The UEA allowed each crew member a few personal selections in their overall food stores. Her own pantry contained hummus made from Martian soy beans.

"Yes." Bakir eyed her carefully. "Food brings people together, Commander. Perhaps we could convince Stevenson by inviting him to a meal?"

"We need to convince Stevenson that we aren't the enemy," Rachel said.

Bakir rolled Santos's sleeve up to the elbow and swabbed the skin in the crook of the man's arm. The stink of rubbing alcohol wafted through the room. "Let me try."

"Yes, we all know how much he likes me." Rachel blinked. She'd eaten everything. "Appeal to his sense of duty. Or dig up something from his psych evals."

"I have been reviewing everyone's since the crash." He inserted the needle into Santos's arm. The vacutainer went from clear and empty to maroon and full. "Including yours, Commander. Would you appreciate it if I used your personal data against you?"

"I'm not the one endangering everyone else." She hated sounding so defensive.

"Yet, I must be prepared for that eventuality." Bakir cleaned Santos's arm, bandaged it, then rolled the sleeve back down. "So, please. Tell me what ails you."

"She cannot sleep," Larsen said.

Rachel nudged Larsen's foot with her own. "Traitor."

"You might be right in keeping things like this from the crew," Bakir said. "Please do not keep such things from me. I cannot help you if you do."

"Has your bedside manner always been this condescending?"

"Only when I worked in the UEA's pediatric ward on Luna." Bakir grinned.

"Ha!" Larsen nudged Rachel's hip with her own.

Though Bakir smiled, he crossed his arms. "I am waiting."

"I've had nightmares every night," Rachel finally said.

"About the crash?"

"No. These are more personal. Like my worst phobia come true."

"Suffocating." Bakir at least appeared sympathetic.

Knowing that he knew her deepest fear set Rachel on edge. Medical necessity or not, she didn't like the idea of him having access to her background. He probably knew about her controlling parents, how she'd suffered on Earth, how much she'd undergone to get the proper surgeries for this voyage…

"Yes," she murmured.

"That incident at Ophir Chasma? When you were ten? It's in your medical records." The compassion in Bakir's tone embarrassed her further.

Rachel simply nodded.

"It might be just an anxiety, coming through your subconscious," Bakir said. "But I'm not trained for that. Chief Psychologist Higgs was on *Olduvai*. I could really use his help right now. I do have some medications that would alleviate—"

"Not yet." Rachel faked a smile. "Let's see how I sleep these next few nights."

"Of course, Commander." Bakir's smile combined sincerity with disappointment.

"A bath would be nice," Larsen said. "We stink."

Bakir cleared his throat. "We cannot waste water, but I understand. Hygiene is—"

"We know," Rachel said. "Stevenson didn't hoard all the tampons, did he?"

Bakir's mouth fell open. Larsen arched an eyebrow and crossed her arms.

"I…have already placed such items in your cabin." Bakir went to the lab table.

Only after shutting the hatch to their cabin did Rachel grin. "Did you see the look on his face? Poor guy."

"Poor us." Larsen held up a container of wet wipes.

"Ugh. I'd love a shower, too. But it's better than nothing." Rachel stripped and cleaned herself the best she could with the wipes. She was surprised some life-form hadn't started growing under her armpits since events had prevented everyone from bathing.

Larsen washed herself without shame, utilitarian in her movements.

Rachel did the same. Martians—well, the poorer ones—knew the value of water. Only the rich actually bathed in it on a regular basis.

Even though everyone on *Centaurus* wore Maximum Absorbency Garments in lieu of underwear, a clean pantyliner still made Rachel feel like a new woman. While Larsen washed her hair with rinseless shampoo, Rachel ogled her.

The Norwegian was tall, with an athletic build one would expect of a Scandinavian who'd grown up swimming in fjords. It made Rachel self-conscious of her own slim features and long limbs. She looked away and hurriedly put on fresh MAGs.

"Wash my back?" Larsen asked.

"Sure." Making slow swipes over Larsen's pale, blemish-free skin, Rachel swallowed. "No tattoos? I thought all you Nordic types liked those new nano-runes."

"No tattoos." Larsen turned. "Now you."

"Um…" Rachel swallowed again. "Okay."

While Larsen washed her back, Rachel tried to relax.

"Tattoos are an academic interest," Larsen said. "Last girlfriend had plenty."

Girlfriend. Rachel jumped at the particular word.

"Did I hurt you?" Larsen asked.

"No, that's all I needed. Thanks." While donning her IVA, Rachel didn't hide her glances at Larsen this time. Last girlfriend. The prospects excited her, though Rachel knew she had to remain focused on the mission. Still, her anxiety was now bearable.

Flight Recorder – *Maray* Crew Module
Sol 4 – 2000 hours
Orbiting Proxima Centauri C

CMP Worrel: Shit. Moore's stable, but we need a doctor. A real one.

MS Khandaar: The drone can only do so much, sir. It did patch him up.

CMP Worrel: Yes, but using a paramedic app for guidance? It's not programmed for serious injuries. Moore's lucky the meteorite burned through him in a straight line and cauterized everything. We'll keep him sedated for the rest of the day.

MS Khandaar: Sir, I think we should land. Imagery shows that could be *Aloha* on the mesa crash site. That's the module Dr. Bakir—

CMP Worrel: I know, Jivika, I know. But I can't trust our instruments under this much electrical noise from the moon. Once we begin reentry, any false reading would cark it for us. There's also another debris field in our orbit path.

MS Khandaar: Moore will die up here if we don't…sir.

CMP Worrel: He's stable for now. I say we use this time to study the noise. Didn't you say the emission spectrum varies?

MS Khandaar: Yes. I have taken spectrometer readings since Sol 1. The electromagnetic radiation around the moon is quite extraordinary.

CMP Worrel: How so?

MS Khandaar: It absorbs any other wave that comes into contact with it. Radio waves, X-rays, microwaves, infrared, ultraviolet. It's like a black hole in a way.

CMP Worrel: So information goes in, and none comes back out?

MS Khandaar: I'm not sure yet. If that's true, then our scanner is useless for contacting anyone on the moon below. Kevin—I mean, Moore—almost died for nothing.

CMP Worrel: Well, if that isn't the dog's bollocks. That means *Maray*'s sensors might not work if we attempt a landing. Not even simple radar.

101

MS Khandaar: We might not have a choice. Moore won't last like this.

CMP Worrel: If we could descend when the noise is at its lowest…maybe.

MS Khandaar. I'll get on it.

CMP Worrel: (sighs) Thanks heaps. I'll keep us away from that debris field.

10

The first piece of dried foliage that Etana sees reminds her of the vines in her Nigerian homeland. She has climbed them in the mangrove swamps of Bayelsa: playing as a child, courting as a teenager, and then stalking union leaders as a military contractor. Those vines had been an ally. She lifts it to her faceplate, rubs her gloved thumb over it.

It is dark brown. Like the soil of charred Yoruba farms she set aflame in Oyo. Even at nineteen years old, she'd had no illusions about her place in the "new" economies of the late twenty-first century. Her own tribe, the Igbo, rejected her for accepting money for blood. She never told her family of her refusal to blow up their hydroelectric business along the Niger's eastern banks in Anambra. The contract would have been lucrative.

Etana stares over the landscape. Spots the mesa, the smoke from the west. But she does not see it, for she relives the memory of watching her family's hydro business burn. Others had taken the contract and she did not stop them. Her tribe had known the consequences of accepting foreign money rather than operating under Nigeria's control. Some decried it as an assault on the global community, but the Igbo had already known slavery once. Etana helped ensure they need not know it again. The experience taught her a valuable lesson.

It takes fire and blood to become a great nation. Not dreams and ideals.

And in fire and blood, she will destroy the UEA's dreams. Its false ideals.

The memory fades. Etana tosses the vine back to the sandy ground and continues her trek southwest. To *Seeker*, according to her scanner. *Olduvai*'s rover follows her via the remote link in her EMU suit. She will drive it soon, but she has always acquainted herself with a battlefield before the battle. Using her own two feet.

Unlike the others, she isn't an employee of the UEA. Her employers are members of UEA's board, however, and forged her identity. Gained her a place on *Centaurus*'s crew roster. The manifest claims she is Mission Specialist Etana Okoye, a physician.

The only wounds she seeks to heal are her own.

Later in life, once Nigeria numbered among Earth's elite, Etana accepted lucrative contracts on Mars, policing the colonies there. Then on Luna, Ganymede. The dead were easier to hide on humanity's frontiers because everyone sees progress, not pain. In time, she forgot her own pain, and then only because she realized she no longer felt any.

Etana walks faster. The memories haunt her anyway.

She knows the alien signal is a lie. Not that it didn't happen, because it did. The message is a lie of the worst kind, one that brings misery. The kind of lie she has told, and retold, many times. The same lie she has whispered into ears, carved into flesh.

The lie history condemns, yet repeats all the same.

But Etana did not sleep four cold years to repeat herself. She did not undergo surgery—replacing her bones, her bowels, even her skull, so that her head will not swell in lower gravities—to spread the lie. Nor did she leave her family, tribe, and world behind, though they've all shunned her long ago. No one sacrifices so much for a lie, save fools.

She is here for the truth.

Chief Medical Officer's journal. Mission date: Sol 5.

Last night's storm continued well into this morning. Aloha's anemometer registered the wind speeds as high as 130 kilometers per hour, and never less than 85. That confined everyone inside, which annoyed Terman to no end. Larsen busied herself with deciphering the audio she recorded near the "lake." I took Terman's and Zentsov's blood for my upcoming test. But once the storm calmed, Terman asked Larsen to stay behind and continue her work. Larsen was very reluctant, but agreed. There is a bond between those two. I envy them, for it must offer some comfort on this perilous moon.

As soon as Terman and Zentsov left for Seeker, I put on my EMU suit and walked over to Thirteen. The barricade around its hatch had weathered the nocturnal gale, though I suspect Stevenson came out and repaired it once calm returned. He must have planned this, having the tools close at hand. It consisted mostly of storage bins and pre-fab shelter walls, fast-welded together with a heat gun. It wasn't an insurmountable barrier, but anyone trying to enter could be attacked by whoever waited at the hatch. And if the big man possessed more than just a heat gun and wrench, I fear any defense would result in someone's wounding, or even death.

Which is why I stood outside and hailed Stevenson on his personal channel. It was something Terman had attempted before she left, but she never received an answer.

Stevenson answered my third try, asking what I wanted. I implored him to listen to reason, that no one wanted to hurt him, that there was no threat from Kovac. But Stevenson barked a bitter laugh, saying that wasn't the only reason. He described a dream he'd had about something stealing our food in the middle of the night, then stealing all of our water. After some gentle interrogation, he admitted that the dream had bothered him since we crashed on this strange world.

I listened without interrupting—something I wish Terman would learn to do. Stevenson finally asked me if I thought he was crazy, to which I replied in the negative. One should never agree with such a statement when dealing with someone who is likely to be mentally unstable. Which is strange, because Stevenson had one of the best psychological evaluations before the voyage.

He ranted about Terman for several minutes. Saying that Martians never appreciated anything that others did for them. Blaming them for *their own miseries. Claiming that they all thought the rest of us owed them something.*

I said nothing, though his bigotry shamed me. The same accusations—and worse—were heaped on my grandparents, who moved to America decades ago. It is why my parents relocated back to Pakistan. It is also another reason I joined this expedition: to prove humanity could work together. And there I was, abetting racism with my silence.

We chatted about the moon for a few minutes, and what the signal could mean, now that we are actually here. I finally got around to asking if he could take a sample of his blood for me. He asked why, and I told him it was a precaution to ensure that the radiation had not damaged our bodies. That was when he asked me about Bimini.

He'd listened in on the crew's open channel, and knew Terman had found the module. I withheld nothing. Such honesty is the byproduct of being a doctor.

I heard him trying not to sob inside his little fortress, and I dared not mention it or patronize him. Yet, I did suggest the rest of us could avoid Bimini*'s fate if we worked together. Stevenson agreed but refused to join the rest of us yet, or to give up the supplies. He said he will dole out supplies as we need them, but he doesn't trust anyone else. So now we have a quarter-master. If it keeps the peace, so be it.*

After wishing him well I returned to Aloha. *While removing my EMU, I nonchalantly asked Larsen if I could draw her blood. I didn't want to bother her earlier, but she seemed to have reached a lull in her research. Focused on her lab screen, she rolled up her sleeve and accepted my needle. I placed hers and Santos's samples into the test receptacle. The bloodwork analysis took an hour. I prayed, snacked on cashews, and then looked through photos of Nasreen on my private drive. I miss her dearly.*

At the moment I had nothing but time. Or so I thought.

The first sample, Larsen's, showed a slight reduction in red blood cells. This was typical of astronauts. Low gravity affects the human body in so many ways. I had little doubt this was a side effect of our four year journey. Without Centaurus*'s centrifuges creating artificial gravity, our physiology would have suffered far more.*

Next was Santos's.

I had to look through the microscope a few times, then enlarge the plate on the field lab display, to convince myself of what I was seeing. There it was: a mutation. One unrelated to anything I have ever studied in hematology.

From what I could tell, the mutation was transforming adjacent cells, akin to a cancer. Rather than kill cells like that forgotten disease, this mutation left them alive. More active. The equivalent of a jumping bean under my microscope.

Already sweating, I made sure Larsen was occupied while I examined the remaining samples. Terman, Zentsov. Then, Larsen's again, now that I knew what to look for. Everyone possessed this mutation, but in lesser degrees. It was even in my own sample, which summoned chill bumps along my arms. My hands shook over the console.

It did not resemble radiation poisoning. The cells would be dying, not thriving. No one had shown signs of radiation sickness—nausea, vomiting, fever, skin discoloration, or diarrhea. Besides, we were shielded by the modules, and remained suited in either IVAs or EMUs at all times. That was no guarantee against minor exposure, but we had not experienced enough to justify my findings.

I wrangled with the moral implications of keeping this from the others. What would they do with Santos, if they found out? Quarantine him? Even kill him?

I immediately saved all my data and encrypted it, so that no one could access it. I will not share this appalling discovery until I know what this is. The last thing our crew needs is more stress. I cannot tell Stevenson. He will sink further into his paranoia.

I'm hesitant to tell Terman. She might overreact.

Kovac is the only one I can truly expect any positive results from. I need his expertise. I'll have to wait and see how Terman's meeting with him goes. Should she bungle it, I will contact the Croatian secretly—before we lose control of the situation.

The only thing I can do for the time being is to keep watch over Santos and ensure nothing else develops. I must also pay extra attention to everyone, even myself.

I fear we have made a big mistake in coming here.

11

Rachel drove away from *Aloha* as soon as the storm abated. "What if Kovac gets belligerent?" Zentsov asked.

"I'm not afraid." Rachel steered the rover clear of another grouping of sinkholes.

"He might be." Zentsov glanced at her. "They all might be."

"That's why I'm trying to keep everything together."

Driving southeast of the mesa, Rachel took note of the windstorm's effects. The landscape was changed, the flatlands covered in a fresh layer of sandy regolith. The linear dunes were fatter, the troughs between them shallower. Twice the rover spun out crossing them. If not for the onboard compass, she might have gotten lost.

"Should we plant a few waypoint beacons?" Zentsov asked.

"No," Rachel said. "The ones Larsen and I set up are likely buried now, and the electrical interference gets worse the farther east we go."

Once *Seeker* appeared ahead, Rachel stiffened. Regardless of what she'd told Zentsov, she was afraid—of bungling this meeting with Kovac, of angering him and the others further. She needed his expertise, and moreover, she needed to show everyone that she could negotiate.

Like *Aloha*'s campsite, the storm had dusted *Seeker* with several centimeters of loose sand. A rough trail had been swept from the module's door to a rectangular space. Wheeled tracks led away from it, further southeast. *Seeker*'s drone hovered in a haphazard pattern, fifty meters overhead. They must have just deployed it after the storm.

"Their rover is gone," Zentsov said.

"We'll wait a little while," Rachel said. "It'll be noon soon. Tell me…What do you make of this moon so far?"

Zentsov raised his brows and stared out the windshield. "I'm not certain what to make of it. I haven't witnessed a change in the physical laws of the universe. Atoms seem to be the same here as on Earth."

"That's not what I meant." Rachel gobbled the rest of her calorie block. Since they still hadn't found any crashed supply modules, she'd decided to eat what most of the others couldn't. Her artificial bowels churned mechanically.

"Oh…" He loosed a breath. "It's beautiful in its own way. One could become accustomed to it, much like the landscapes in the Karakum or the Sahara. I prefer the streets of Mumansk, where I can leave for the weekend and go skiing in the mountains, or sail over the Barents. I suspect that is not what you meant, either."

Rachel turned in her seat and faced him. "Have you had trouble sleeping?"

He eyed her for a moment. "Of course."

"Dreams?"

"I would not call them that." Sweat beaded his forehead.

"Bakir offered me some medication after I told him of my nightmares."

"I am sure he is doing his best to help," Zentsov said.

"And Kovac?" She chugged down a bottle of water, washing away the calorie block's taste-bud killing, canned-meat-and-natural-peanut-butter flavors.

"He is doing…what he thinks is best." Zentsov shrugged. "You disagree."

"He knows more than he's telling." Rachel got her helmet from the back seat. "I think the UEA briefed him on things the rest of us were left in the dark about."

"Like what?" Zentsov eyed her carefully. "There is nothing to keep secret. The whole human race knows about the signal and where it originated. We came here, blind almost, because we are too damn curious for our own good."

She realized he could be withholding information, too. And in the chain of command, Kovac was Zentsov's superior. Or maybe she was getting paranoid.

"Do you think Kovac would keep data from the rest of us?" Zentsov snorted. "Impossible. That man loves to share his discoveries. His victories. It feeds his ego, makes him popular. He is a driven man. That is why he charges into this mission. He knows our chances of survival are slim, and he wants to accumulate as much glory for himself as possible before they write his epitaph back on Earth."

"How macabre."

"It sounds better with vodka." He chuckled.

"Then he wouldn't mind if we take a look at what he's already found."

"If he catches us…it could feed their suspicions." Zentsov didn't look at her.

"I have nothing to hide." Rachel snapped her helmet on. "Neither should he."

They entered *Seeker* without trouble. Kovac hadn't even locked it with a code. She wasn't sure if that was arrogance or contempt, since both camps resented each other at the moment. The pressure chamber prepared them for entry, but when they exited it, the smell inside the main chamber made them gasp. It stunk worse than a compost heap.

Three open storage cartons lay on the lab table. Each contained a lengthy, plump vine. They were all fitted with small batteries. Brown coiled nodules had grown over the table, the lab screen, even the chair. A dozen empty water bottles lay on the floor, some in puddles where the water had spilled.

The carton containing the vine she and Larsen had taken from the lake was empty.

"Holy shit." Rachel glowered around the chamber. "Are they crazy?"

Zentsov's expression went from stony to terrified, then he composed himself. "This isn't like Kovac. That man is neater than my grandmother."

Seeker's 3-D printer beeped, and Rachel walked over to it. A custom AMF template had been drawn up, ready to be printed. The template was a vine.

"Did you know about this, Zentsov? Did your studies on Burgess's data—"

"Of course not. There could be any number of explanations for this."

"And I'd love to hear them. Why use batteries and water—things we can't spare—on these plants? It looks like Kovac is cultivating the damn things."

The unspoken point was if Kovac and his team were so free with their own supplies, it confirmed Stevenson's paranoia regarding *Aloha*'s supplies. Regardless, once word spread, the others would refuse to share anything with Kovac for fear he'd use it on experiments, rather than for survival.

"There has to be more to this." Rachel studied the files still open on *Seeker*'s main computer screens. Aerial photos and GPR data of a buried site to the southwest. Soil studies, with an emphasis on electrical conductivity. A detailed MRI of a vine.

"No more secrets," she said. "I'm going to hail Kovac on the radio again."

"He didn't answer any of your queries on the way here," Zentsov said.

"He might, once he realizes I'm using *Seeker*'s channel."

Personal journal, Mission Specialist Li. Mission date: Sol 5.

I think Sakurai is warming up to Kovac. They flirted with each other all morning while Burgess and I prepped for the day's work. I mean, good for them, but we still have a mission. I'm glad I didn't say anything. The look on Sakurai's face, after we found that burned foot…I guess that can make anyone seek affection just to forget all this crazy shit.

We all went for a quick drive to the northeast after picking up a transponder signal. Unlike Terman, we knew what we'd find. It was a supply run, not a rescue.

When we finally got there, Sakurai broke down. Burgess got angry, since she still hoped we'd find other crew members. Kovac just stared. I simply finished my breakfast.

There wasn't much left of Module Five. It must have crashed the same day we did, but we surmised that the storm uncovered enough of it so the transponder signal finally reached us. Even Kovac lost some of his humor when we spotted the busted hull. It looked like a cracked egg something had just shit out in the desert. The burned foot was the only remains we found, which Burgess promptly bagged and buried. It was weird, because Five was a supply module, with no crew on board. It's hard to tell how far Centaurus's debris scattered, especially with these constant storms fucking with us.

We uncovered a few supply crates that must have tumbled out of Five after it crashed, but all were busted, their contents irradiated after five days' exposure.

Kovac's somber mood broke like a flood through a dam. He drove back to camp while urging us to continue our work. Said we couldn't let this dampen our spirits, or our confidence in our mission. Sakurai was indifferent at first, but Kovac's smile won her over yet again. Burgess finally agreed. I was already all for it. We haven't even started reconstituting our own urine yet anyway. We can worry about supplies another day.

Back at Seeker, we noticed the vines had…changed. I mean, that's the best word I can find. The one I'd put a battery on was a different color, from brown to greenish-brown. Like grass after a spring rain. The others, though still in their cartons, had moved: Each had relocated the bulk of its mass to face the vine with the battery.

The clay-like nodules had sprouted smaller, newer vines. Replicating themselves.

Kovac grew excited and danced with Sakurai around the room. Burgess examined a sample of the "battery" vine beneath a microscope and recorded her findings into the lab computer. Its cells had undergone even more change. She said they now exhibited the characteristics of angiosperms—flowering plants. But the "seeds" didn't match the parent plant's DNA structure. Burgess compared it to an apple tree producing potatoes.

We all asked questions but Kovac said the only way to answer them was to keep exploring the moon. Starting with the sites discovered by GPR.

The only one who disagreed was Burgess.

She wanted to share our discovery with Terman's camp, and she recommended waiting to see what else developed with the vines before further exploration.

There was something else in her voice. Fear.

Kovac listened with respect, but I knew what his decision would be. There could be no sharing with the other camp while they hoarded supplies. He did suggest that Burgess wait in Seeker while the rest of us went to the buried site, maybe to placate her. She readily agreed. When we started to leave, I tried to fist bump her, but she hugged me instead. Mumbling something about a nightmare she'd had.

I hurried and left so she could wipe her eyes in private. The data had shaken her.

In contrast, Kovac was the first out the hatch, heading straight for the rover. You have to admire that kind of enthusiasm in the face of such awful odds. I know I keep saying that, but it's true. It's keeping us alive.

Leaving Burgess to her work, the three of us rode southeast. I sat in the back, ceding the passenger seat to Sakurai so she and Kovac could continue their little courtship. There was less cloud cover, so I checked our rad levels again. Still in the shitty triple-digit range. I told Kovac but he shrugged it off, saying we can become nocturnal, thereby cutting direct exposure to sunlight. But we both knew that, long-term, there would still be effects on us all.

Two kilometers out we passed some old craters, certainly not Centaurus wreckage. They were larger, six kilometers wide, indicating a hefty meteorite must have impacted the site. But the damage still stood out since we hadn't seen many signs of extraterrestrial bombardment on the moon so far. Sakurai convinced Kovac to stop the rover and we examined the craters. Though the constant storms covered up certain details—such as the crater's rays and ejecta blanket, according to Sakurai—we managed to acquire decent samples. The field drill's sensors detected metal in the sample cores. That's not unusual, considering the mineral compositions of meteorites. We drove on.

Kovac talked about the other camp and how we really should be working together. Though he made a few wisecracks about them—Terman's weird Martian accent, Bakir's fish-eye stare, Larsen's propensity to strip in front of anyone, even back at the UEA station on Earth—I could tell he really cared about their fate. I suppose we all do, but that's how it goes when one group has a plan, while the other wants to sit and wait while the supplies run out.

Using my helmet's binocular app I scanned the horizon, switching to infrared and X-rays at times, just in case our human eyes missed something. But I couldn't find shit because of the continuous electrical noise. The app allowed me to see it in waves.

Waves emanating from the ground.

Kovac hypothesized that it could be a result of the moon's magnetic field undergoing a geomagnetic reversal, or a shift in the moon's convection currents. Sakurai wasn't so sure, since the noise was so pervasive, without any variance. I mentioned that the UEA's initial observations of Promixa Centauri C hadn't revealed any such field. Kovac laughed and said the field existed whether we could explain it or not.

Sakurai tested some of the core samples with her field lab and cursed in Japanese. She told us the sample had to be tainted, since it contained a high metal content not present in meteorites as we know them on Earth. Kovac offered that it might be because we were in a different solar system, but Sakurai disagreed. I finally stopped listening and put on some music in my helmet. Some oldies from the mid-twenty-first century, stuff my parents raised me on. All I could think about was excavating that site up ahead.

That's when her voice came over the radio.

"Help me."

The horror in that familiar voice shook us out of our reverie. I turned off the music. Kovac yanked the rover back toward Seeker. We all leaned forward, fearing what we might see.

12

After hailing Kovac for two hours, Rachel was about to leave *Seeker*—until the voice came over the radio. There had been several blips on the open channel for the past thirty minutes. This time, there was no mistaking the frightened words.

"Help me!"

"This is Rachel Terman, do you copy?" She sighed and shook her head at Zentsov. "I repeat, this is Terman at *Seeker*, do you copy?"

"That sounded like Burgess," Zentsov said.

"She's in trouble." Rachel hurried for the hatch. "Maybe she's near the module."

Once outside, though, the only thing she saw was a dust cloud approaching from the southeast. There was no sign of Burgess.

Just like there was no sign of her own rover.

"What the hell?" Rachel cried as Kovac arrived with Li and Sakurai.

"How…?" was all Zentsov managed before Kovac shut off his rover and jumped out. He ignored Rachel and hurried into *Seeker*. Sakurai called for Burgess again and again on the open radio frequency.

"Where is she?" Li asked Rachel in a terse voice.

"Where the hell is my rover?" Rachel asked.

Kovac came back outside. "Burgess isn't here. What have you done with her?"

Zentsov raised his hands in a placating gesture. "Wait, my friends. When we arrived, *Seeker* was empty. We have been awaiting your return these two hours."

"That's impossible," Sakurai said.

"Yes." Kovac stomped up dust as he paced before Rachel. "I left Burgess behind to keep studying those vine samples. You claim that you didn't see her? That she stole your rover and simply drove the fuck off? Why?"

"Goddamnit, if I knew that, I wouldn't be asking you!" Rachel yelled.

"Why were you inside *Seeker?*" Li scowled at her.

"Why are you hiding these experiments from the rest of us?" Rachel stared right back at him. "I saw that mess in there. Are you all insane, exposing yourselves to an alien organism like that? You're endangering the entire crew!"

Kovac flinched as if she'd slapped him. "Endangering?"

Zentsov stepped between them. "Now, wait—"

"I don't need your fucking lecturing!" Kovac pushed Zentsov aside, maintaining eye contact with Rachel. "I don't take orders from someone who allows one man to endanger everyone by hoarding all of our supplies. I don't obey people who prowl around my lab, endangering the very work we were sent here to do. You think we left the lab in such a state? Burgess was working there when we left—"

"Help...me..."

The broken, anguished voice on the radio silenced them all.

"Burgess," Sakurai said. "Please, tell us where you are."

"Burgess?" Sweat rolled down Kovac's face. "This is Milo, talk to me."

Static was the reply.

"This is Terman, can you tell us if you are okay?" Rachel asked. "Copy?"

There was no answer for several moments, then a groan filled the connection.

Rachel glanced at Kovac. "Any idea where she might've gone?"

He simply studied the horizon as if he might spot her at any moment.

"What about the rover tracks?" Zentsov asked. "Might we follow them?"

"Which ones?" Li asked with sarcasm. "There are tracks all over the place here."

"You're not helping." Rachel stared at Li until he finally looked away.

Shaking his head, Kovac headed for the rover. "I must search for her. Standing here arguing accomplishes nothing, and she is in distress."

"I'm coming with you." Rachel ignored his frown and looked to Zentsov. "Keep trying the radio, use the binoculars to scan the flats around here. Radio me if you learn anything or if she turns up."

"Who put you in charge?" Li asked.

She glared at him. "The same people who thought you were good enough to be a scientist on this mission. Any more questions? Good."

As she slammed the rover door behind her, Kovac muttered in Croatian. Her translation app showed the words on her HUD: *This bitch might be crazy, but she's going to see this through until she finds Burgess. Start the damn engine already.*

Though he circled around the camp, it was several minutes before Kovac spoke. "I believe that you and Alexei did nothing to her. But I don't understand why she would have wrecked the lab like that, stolen your rover, and driven away."

"She was nowhere to be seen." Rachel adjusted her seat forward since Sakurai was taller. "Listen, this has to stop. We need to be a united crew again."

Kovac sped up, carving ruts across the flatlands.

"Want to tell me what that garden is supposed to be back there?"

He straightened in the seat. "The vines have proven responsive to electrical current, like that from a battery. When we left, all of the samples were still in their cartons. I'm as concerned as you, with what I saw in there."

"What else have you seen?" She fought to keep calm.

He looked her up and down, and she hated herself for blushing. It was something about his gaze: nonthreatening, nonjudgmental. The eyes of a hawk, combined with the intellect of one accustomed to long periods of observation, spotting the slightest detail.

"I see someone trying to prove herself," he said.

"Isn't that what you're doing?" she asked. "Charging recklessly into this mission, trying to prove…what, exactly? That you're the best scientist?"

Kovac smiled. "The difference is that I seek to prove something to others. You want self-validation, the most difficult prize of all. You came a long way to find it."

The rover bounced between a few sinkholes. She tapped a finger on the seat's armrest. "Were you going to tell the rest of us about the vines?"

"What you really mean is, when was I going to tell you?" He smirked.

"It's not like that."

He kept smirking, and she was ready to scratch a hole in the armrest. Another kilometer around *Seeker*. Then another. No sign of Burgess anywhere, even after Kovac activated the rover's infrared scanner.

"That means she didn't come this way, or whoever took the rover didn't," Rachel said. "Else the signature of heat exhaust would show up, however faint."

"Very good," he said. "Maybe she drove toward your little camp."

"Why would she do that?" Rachel eyed him closely. "Those vines are growing. They are alive. Could one have tried…?"

"To make a pass at her?" Though she sensed he meant it as a joke, Kovac's smirk vanished. "I'm not sure. Something made her leave. Something that frightened her."

"And what frightens you?" Rachel asked, hoping to find out what he really knew.

"Ignorance," he said without hesitation.

After a few more minutes she asked him to stop and turn around. The scanner still hadn't picked up any heat signatures and the radio remained a mute companion.

"And you, Terman?" He turned in the seat, watching her. "What frightens you?"

She stared out the windshield. "Suffocating."

"A valid fear in this place," Kovac said. "The only cure for it is to forge on."

"I get that," Rachel said. "But I was hoping—with your team's help—that we could find a way to grow food in this soil. To stay alive for months instead of weeks."

She was baiting him. Trying to see if he'd let anything slip.

"The UEA is not coming after us," he said. "I want to prolong our demise, too, but for different reasons. I have a goal: to educate the human species about this world, and maybe the sender of that signal, before we all perish. What do you want to accomplish?"

"To show whoever sent that signal that we are worth it. Worth the trouble. That we are ready to take the next step and spread out from our solar system. That we can handle dealing with others different from ourselves."

"Then you have already failed," Kovac said. "Look at our expedition."

Rachel turned away, flustered. "You're wrong."

"What you really want to know is: Are *you* worth it?"

"That's what you're doing out here, too," Rachel said. "Takes one to know one."

He smiled and kept driving.

They returned to *Seeker* without speaking. Still no further contact from Burgess, and the others had nothing new to report. Kovac's perpetual good cheer faded upon hearing that. He slowed down as they approached the module. The sun was setting.

"It is too dangerous to walk back to *Aloha* in the dark, and the rover must recharge," Kovac said. "There is plenty of room for you and Alexei in *Seeker*."

She considered contacting Larsen and Bakir, have them ask Stevenson for the spare rover in Thirteen. But it would show goodwill to accept Kovac's offer.

"There are sinkholes everywhere, and in the darkness, you will certainly fall into one." Kovac grunted. "I hope that Burgess hasn't suffered that fate."

"Fair enough," she said. "But tomorrow…we need to find Burgess."

Chief Medical Officer's journal. Mission date: Sol 6.

I am the one having nightmares now. Allah help me.

It started after I finished the radio conversation with Terman. She not only will be staying the night at Seeker _with Kovac and his team, but our rover was stolen. Burgess has gone missing. I practically interrogated Terman for details; but the connection was filled with so much noise, I was fortunate to learn even that much. Desperate, I checked their suit links—especially Burgess's—but they were out of range._

Once I told Larsen, she went berserk. She hailed Stevenson on the radio and demanded use of the spare rover he's stashed away in Thirteen. Stevenson made no reply. I told her that arguing with him accomplished nothing, but Larsen wouldn't listen. Irritated and tired, I watched her storm from Aloha _into the night._

She kept hailing Terman on the radio until I heard her breaking down in sobs. I wrangled with going out and convincing her to return. A few minutes later, Stevenson spoke on the open channel, telling Larsen that the rover awaited her outside Thirteen's lower berth hatch. She thanked him and sped off toward Seeker.

Yes, I could have done more. I might have coaxed her out of it, had I tried. Yet I have no cure for this foolishness. I cannot bandage this crew back together.

And now, I dare not go back to sleep after the hellish visions I saw in my dreams.

In the nightmare I was outside, walking the sands of this strange world. I was alone. I came across a stone arch, cracked and pitted. The civilization that made it, long dead. Beyond it was a beautiful, shimmering azure paradise. I wept upon seeing it.

It was Terman and Larsen's blue lake.

I passed through the arch and stepped onto the lake. I was crawling by then, though I know not why. From those glassy depths came Nasreen. She was wearing an EMU suit without the helmet. Her eyes were closed. I shouted that she would suffocate, that she would die, but she merely smiled and extended her hand. I reached for it, though my own hand was rotting. My fingers fell off my decrepit body. I cried out.

Nasreen smiled and opened her eyes. They were black pits.

I screamed. I screamed until I woke myself up, alone in Aloha *with Santos.*

I will not sleep again if I can help it. I have the proper eugeroics, such as Modafinil, to keep me awake. I cannot tell anyone. I must remain the pillar of decency and reason on this ruined expedition.

13

After a restless night—worrying about Burgess, another nightmare about suffocating, and irritated by the tension between the camps—Rachel ate the NF rations Kovac provided and suited up. She had no desire to stay longer than necessary in *Seeker.*

She munched the nuts and granola while Li and Sakurai finished cleaning the lab. They'd been at it all night. Despite their cold attitudes, Rachel had to admire their efficiency. The nodules and vines were placed back into cartons. A scan revealed no pathogens or microscopic remnants, but she still avoided that part of the chamber.

Zentsov busied himself with looking over Burgess's vine data. His frown grew heavier by the minute. "Since these organisms feed off of electrical energy, I must forbid any physical contact. Perhaps one of the drones should handle them from now on."

"Speaking of such." Kovac kept tapping his drone control tablet. "Damn it. Both are off-line. Terman, if you wish to help me search for Burgess…?"

She patted Zentsov's shoulder and followed Kovac to the hatch. "I'm coming."

Dawn rays from the red dwarf sun stabbed over the terrain. It gave the impression of a laser shearing between the ridges and arches. Occasional swirls of sand, aggravated by the breeze, resembled insect swarms as they passed through the beams.

She swiped her hand through the swirls and smiled sadly. Wishing the airborne grains were bees or dragonflies.

Back on Earth, Rachel had been fascinated with all the wildlife. At least, the species that hadn't gone extinct. Gaia First activists still blamed Martians for contributing to those environmental and biological disasters. Much had been spent—and wasted—to get humans to her homeworld. But Mars, like this moon, was a lifeless wasteland.

That first Earth landing was forever scorched into her memory.

"You skinny bitch!" the activist shouted in her face. "Go back to Mars!"

Dad shouldered the guy out of the way as Rachel continued down the shuttle ramp. Mom followed, taking tentative steps, already miserable under the heavier gravity.

A police barricade barely held back the Gaia First mob. They held placards proclaiming that Earth belonged only to them. One man even raised an antique War of the Worlds *cinema poster. Others displayed holograms of hairless, emaciated Martian children, a racist caricature she knew was false. Still she walked.*

As she reached the end of the ramp, Rachel flinched. A firefly circled around her head. Its bioluminescent abdomen flashed yellow-green. Smiling, she reached for it.

A handful of fecal matter splattered across her face.

"Earth is for humans, you mutant fuck!" someone yelled.

Half-blinded by shit, Rachel didn't see the blow coming. A club hammered her stomach. She fell to her knees as her family and the police fought back the protesters.

The firefly landed before her. It spread its wings and started to glow again.

Someone stepped on it as the press of bodies moved her forward.

"Terman?" Kovac waited by the rover, bearing a quizzical expression.

She jumped, blinked. Entered the rover. Fought the urge to wipe her face.

For thirty minutes Kovac made a circuit around *Seeker*. The rover's anemometer indicated light winds. He drove slowly to avoid creating large dust clouds. Visibility was excellent, at least eight kilometers in any direction. But even with that boon, and the aid of infrared scans, they found no trace of Burgess or *Aloha*'s rover.

"Goddamnit." Kovac drove toward *Seeker*. "Eduina remains lost out here. She joined the mission at my request. She can't be…I do not know what else to do."

"Her suit would've run out of oxygen by now," Rachel whispered.

Kovac punched the console. "You think I don't already know that—?"

The radio crackled to life as the rover's scanner picked up a transponder signal.

Several of them.

"Kovac, this is Sakurai. Did you get any of that?"

The signals were literally all over the map at first. A burst of white noise came over the radio, making Rachel wince. She fine-tuned the scanner until it focused on two strong signals: one to the southeast, and another southwest.

"One of those is near the site where GPR found buried objects," Kovac said.

"We should investigate," Li said over the connection. "The weather is damn-near perfect. We might find Burgess out there, too."

Rachel shook her head. "We've picked up no signs—"

"She might have driven there in your rover after all." Kovac sounded desperate and elated at the same time. "If she were scared, she would have come to find us, and that was our location last night."

"Aren't you taking Terman back to the other camp first?" Zentsov asked.

Kovac parked outside *Seeker*. "It could be Burgess, Alexei."

"Yes, you shouldn't ignore it," Rachel said. "But let me—"

"No more orders today," Kovac said. "I know what I have to do."

She tried to hide her scowl. "Wouldn't it be better if more went along? Another rover from my camp, with more people to help, like Zentsov?"

"Zentsov is the only scientist among your group," Kovac said. "With Burgess missing, he needs to finish her work in *Seeker*."

"I am sorry, Commander, but he is right," Zentsov said.

"Let me help you," Rachel said. "I can't just sit and wait here."

Kovac smiled at something on the western horizon. "You won't have to."

Larsen drove Thirteen's rover alongside them and stopped.

Though her heart soared, Rachel's joy was dowsed by the other rover's bent fender, dented hood, and the scratches on Larsen's faceplate.

"Now we both have things to occupy us." Kovac sounded all too smug.

Rachel left his rover and ran to Larsen's. As she reached the door, Li and Sakurai hurried from *Seeker* and got into Kovac's rover. Without a word, they sped southeast. Their egress flung a dust cloud over Rachel, angering her further.

"Came as quick as I could." Larsen grinned. "No time to make us breakfast. Maybe a picnic on the way back—"

Rachel slammed the door shut and glared. "What happened?"

Only then did Larsen seem to realize how angry Rachel was. "Stevenson let me use this rover. I left last night, but hurrying, hit a sinkhole. Got free only to ram into an outcropping of rock. One of—"

"And this?" She flicked Larsen's faceplate. Her entire body burned with fury.

Larsen's lips flattened. "One wheel was stuck. I got out and moved it. The autojack broke. I fell while pushing the bumper. Scuffed my faceplate on the rocks."

"What if you had busted it? What if you'd been unable to get back into the rover, and breathed the air? There was no one around to help you. Goddamnit, Vanja…"

"I am not a helpless child." Larsen turned the wheel and drove toward *Aloha.*

Before Rachel could say more, Zentsov's voice came over her private radio channel. "Commander, I should be able to do a walk-around every hour to scout out the immediate area with binoculars. If Burgess returns, we cannot risk no one being here. Plus, these vine samples must be monitored."

She couldn't disagree with that logic, but she was dying to argue. Everything felt wrong, as if she'd never get the expedition under control. Or herself.

"I would like everyone to have a video conference at nightfall, to assess where we are with supplies, personnel, and…objectives." She wrenched her helmet off.

"That is a good idea," Zentsov said. "Let us hope the noise will allow for a decent connection. Good luck, Commander."

"Thanks." Rachel tried Bakir's channel. "This is Terman, you read me?"

The radio popped and cracked a minute before Bakir finally answered. "Yes?"

"Did you oversleep?" She tried to sound nonchalant. Tried not looking at Larsen.

"I have been up all night. Did you find Burgess?" His tone indicated that he expected Burgess to be found dead rather than alive.

"Not yet." She studied the rover's scanner. The transponder signal from the southwest pulsed stronger and stronger. Rachel described her intent to investigate it.

Bakir made an exasperated sound. "That will leave us without any transport."

"Were you planning on going somewhere?" She sighed. "Look, I can't ignore this. Would you?"

His hesitation made her brow furrow.

"No, Commander," Bakir said. "I will deploy our drone to a higher altitude and see what it can pick up with its scanners and telescope."

"Careful, the wind is up. And thanks. I'll report as soon as I find anything."

Rachel shut off the connection. Her hands roved over the armrests. There were words she wanted to say. Words she feared she might say. Larsen stared ahead.

The ride continued in tense silence until they were two kilometers from the mesa. Larsen stopped the vehicle and slowly removed her helmet. Rachel swallowed.

"Never talk to me that way again," Larsen murmured.

"Don't you ever put yourself in danger like that again, either."

Larsen flung her hands in the air. "You cannot make that choice for me!"

"I order you not to, damn it." Rachel threw her helmet onto the back seat.

"That is Terman talking." Larsen jabbed a finger in Rachel's chest. "Not Rachel."

"I can't worry myself to death over you and keep this mission going." The rover's air now smelled like Larsen: sweat, aloe, musky hair. Rachel breathed deep. "I can't."

"*Min kjære,*" Larsen whispered, then shook her head. "Neither can I."

Rachel's app translated the words: "My dear." She wrung the armrests.

They searched each other's eyes. Larsen trembled but didn't look away.

Rachel unbuckled, climbed over the center armrest, and kissed her.

The contact was shy, slow. Then eager. Languorous. Rachel allowed Larsen to take her tongue while she tugged off her gloves. Naked palms traced the contours of Larsen's beauty while they shared a different, timeless beauty between them.

Hands cupping Larsen's face, Rachel gently pulled back. A smile passed from one to the other, lighting the private little world they'd just created.

"Then maybe together, we can," Rachel whispered.

Etana exits the rover outside what remains of *Persepolis*. The fires that gutted it have long since exhausted themselves, like fatigued spirits who wish only a return to the underworld. But Etana does not believe in such things. The ash-tainted sand beneath her boots is hell enough.

Two sets of footprints leading from *Persepolis* hint otherwise.

Their existence, despite last night's sandstorm, confirms that two crew members might yet live. Using her faceplate HUD, Etana checks the status of *Olduvai*'s 3-D printer, situated in her rover's back seat. It is creating bullets for the pneumatic pistol she printed yesterday. The gun, as well as a printed combat knife, rests in her EMU's side pouches.

The firearm is a self-pumping 11.43 millimeter caliber air gun that holds one round. With a barrel 127 millimeters long, she cannot reliably hit distance targets. Kills will be up close.

Another gift from her employer: outlawed additive manufacturing files on her personal drive. She has AMFs for a rifle and a crossbow should she need them.

Two burned skeletons, their suits melted to the seats, are all she finds inside *Persepolis*. The supply berth looks damaged, likely during reentry. She peeks inside. The rover, drone, and other equipment are nothing but misshapen blocks of slag.

She checks her chronometer, then tallies her supplies. As a cyborg she needs only to eat calorie blocks, and the lower gravity is unlikely to hamper her body. She has paced herself. In all probability she will outlive the others.

Probability also makes Etana question her mission. Sending her along with the crew, to guarantee their demise, implies that mere sabotage wasn't deemed enough by her employers. The expedition must fail in such spectacular fashion that none dare return.

She enters the rover, leans back in the seat. Takes deep breaths. Her mission hasn't been compromised, but it soon will be. The moon is small and things cannot remain hidden for long. In some ways, she doesn't want them to be. All her life she has kept her identity secret. From family, tribe, and nation. A mercenary relinquishes the right to a name once the first contract is taken. Forever after, their name is greed.

Here, at the end, she can be herself.

Personal journal, Mission Specialist Li. Mission date: Sol 6.

Kovac let me drive to the site this time. I needed something to burn my anger off. Terman is such a bitch. She's completely incompetent and doesn't understand why we were sent to this moon. Kovac says she's trying to prove something out here. For fuck's sake, she should've left the politics at home. No wonder Martians die so easily if they worry about petty stuff instead of the mission. Oh, but I'm racist if I say that out loud.

Good to see Zentsov finally come to his senses and do his damn job. Sad that it took Burgess's disappearance to nudge him in the right direction.

I hate being this angry. It wastes mental energy better used for science.

Still, I wonder what the hell happened to Burgess. She was always level-headed. I don't believe something as banal as wriggling vines would've sent her shrieking into the desert. Kovac is trying to keep our spirits up, but he's as worried as the rest of us.

But we have our mission, and a limited time to complete it. It's better that Terman spend all her pent-up energy searching for Burgess. That's her job, since she claims to be the commander. Take care of those who need it while letting the rest of us work.

On the way to the site, Kovac kept running the new signal through his computer. It had no analog we could compare it with. Too bad Larsen wasn't with us, this is her specialty. But the frequency strength is far greater than any of Centaurus's transponders, and those are intended for planetary-wide coverage.

After parking as close to the signal as possible, we left the rover and planted waypoint beacons into the ground. No chance in hell would we risk not finding this area again should the signal go dead, or another sandstorm cover the site.

Kovac got the extra drone working—the connection was shit earlier, but now it was functioning again—and ordered it to circle the area at a height of 1,500 meters. This way it could warn of us of incoming storms as well as provide a more concise GPR scan.

The site barely measured 1.2 hectares in area. Not large, but considering we only have one digger bot, this could take a while. The bot would've been the wet dream of the older archaeologists I studied under in college. Automated and capable of clearing topsoil at 125 square meters an hour—140 for *sand—it can clear the site in four days. But that's if it runs nonstop. It still should have the area cleared within a week. Its sensors know when to stop digging before damaging possible artifacts or buried structures.*

My uncle would've hated it. He did love his shovel and brush.

A few minutes later, the drone completed its GPR scan. There was definitely something beneath our feet. A rectangular object 11 meters beneath the surface that was 21 meters long and 4 meters wide. I ordered the drone to take a thermography scan. Since the radiation and electrical content of this moon is so high, I waited until now, rather than doing long-range scans. To ensure better accuracy, I lowered the drone's altitude to 300 meters.

Kovac and Sakurai crowded around me as the readings emerged on the tablet's screen. The thermogram coalesced into a bulbous shape, 40 by 40 centimeters. It looked like a jumble of cooled slag. Sakurai said it resembled hardened lava vesicles, or bubbles.

The object was located beneath—or inside—the larger, angular shape.

We had enough food, water, oxygen. We decided to dig with the excavator.

The first hour, all went well. The digger bot set to work, flinging sand into a pile south of the site. Sakurai drilled a few samples and sat in the rover, studying the cores with her field lab. Every now and then she smiled at Kovac. He had difficulty with the drone again. It crashed atop a dune at one point, though it had already hovered down to 12 meters. Still, the little bastard proved to be a liability. I focused on the bot, waiting.

The second hour was boring. Kovac finally stashed the drone for repairs when we returned to **Seeker**. *By then, the sun had reached its zenith. Still no radio contact with anyone or any word about Burgess. Sakurai frowned deeper and deeper at her field lab. What a fun day.*

The third hour…holy shit. The bot had traced an outline around the rectangular object. Its tiny movers had struck metal.

I rushed over and applied the tried and true method: I gently brushed and dug away the sand around the object's edge. After uncovering 60 centimeters of it, I sat back and motioned for the others to come and see. I couldn't stop smiling.

The metal appeared to be some sort of alloy, with what looked like reentry damage. Either that, or it had been through one hell of a fire. I even peeled off a few centimeters of it and stuck it in my sample carton.

We had discovered a buried structure. Maybe even a ship.

Our excitement exploded, suspending any sense of restraint. Burgess, Terman, the other camp—all was forgotten as we became lost in the euphoria of discovery.

Kovac was the first to calm down. He complained about still not having all of our equipment. There had been digger bots in Persepolis *and Module Seventeen, but none of us believed they survived* Centaurus's *explosion. Sakurai suggested that maybe we should work with Terman and her camp after all. Even they could help dig and excavate.*

I was lukewarm to the idea. But even I knew this could take days we didn't have. Another sandstorm could strike any time and our supplies wouldn't last for this project.

Kovac shook his head, which surprised me. I figured he'd make any compromise to get the job done. This perplexed Sakurai, too, but then it slowly dawned on me.

This could be the greatest discovery for humankind, after the alien signal itself. Terman and the others might get too excited, or even fearful. Though everyone had been trained to deal with a first-contact scenario, it was now obvious who could truly cope, and who couldn't. This was delicate territory. I respected Kovac even more for realizing it.

He wanted us to keep the day's find a secret. We'd return to Seeker *and come back later with the other drone. We had to know what lay beneath us.*

14

The signal pulsed on the console scanner again, interrupting Rachel and Larsen.

"I…" Burning with guilt, Rachel climbed back to her seat. "We've a job to do."

Larsen's joy became a frown, then she cleared her throat. "You are right."

"This is Flight Engineer Rachel Terman," Rachel said into the headset mic. "I am driving to your position in *Aloha*'s rover. Please acknowledge."

She waited. No reply.

Larsen drove southwest of the mesa. Above them, the floodlights around *Aloha* and Thirteen provided an erstwhile lighthouse in the growing darkness.

"Do you read me?" a voice finally asked. Rachel and Larsen grinned.

"This is Terman, do you copy?"

The connection went dead. Rachel tried a different frequency. Then another.

"Anybody hear me?" a male voice asked. "We…almost, and… running out of air."

Heart slamming in her chest, Rachel homed in on the frequency. "This is Terman, I read you. Where are you?" Her words came out too fast so she repeated them.

Static fizzled through the reply.

"This is Terman, over?"

The line crackled and the voice came back. "Oh, thank God! We survived but…*Luzinia* isn't…can't go much longer without…"

"Please, can you give me any clue as to your position?" Her voice shook.

A minute went by. Two. She hailed them again, throat dry, hands trembling.

"I have them on radar," Larsen said. "Less than a kilometer."

Rachel squeezed Larsen's arm. "We're coming. Just stay put, don't move."

"Thank God for you." the voice sounded raspy. "We thought those sinkholes…but we escaped, and…anemic, needs some meds."

Rachel muted the mic. "Oh shit."

Frowning, Larsen drove full speed across the wastes, wheels and axles protesting.

The next reply was static interspersed with words but Rachel knew she wasn't imagining things. The voice had mentioned the sinkholes. Her skin chilled as they drove across a darkening landscape, everything obscured by the setting of an alien sun.

"Those sinkholes cannot be natural," Larsen said. "Suppose it is a life-form? Remember those around the lake. They frightened me."

"You never act scared," Rachel said.

"Hidden away hardly means forgotten, grandmamma said."

"Would you hide it from me?"

"Yes." Larsen smirked. "Frightened you will never kiss me like that again."

"You're such a joker." Rachel wanted her more than anything now.

"Those sinkholes are no joke," Larsen said. "What do you think?"

"Kovac was taking those vines from the holes…I don't know." Rachel told her what she and Zentsov had found in *Seeker* the previous day. Larsen blanched.

"There must be an explanation. Burgess was nominated for a Nobel, but Kovac worries me. Caring more about mission than crew. Too sharp may be a burden, too, my—"

"Grandmamma said." Rachel smiled.

"Kiss me and finish my sentences?" Larsen asked. "You will want vows next."

Rachel laughed. "Whoa…Let's just do what we came here to do, all right?"

The banter eased their tension until they spotted the others.

A trio of shapes, stark against the featureless landscape, was revealed by the rover's headlights. They could have been ghosts in their white EMU suits. Rachel tried to scan their suit links but the moon's electrical noise garbled the data.

Each stared back at her, dumbfounded, then one figure waved both hands. The other two clasped each other, as if afraid or wounded. Rachel realized they needed to see another human being.

She exited the vehicle and ran to them. "I'm Rachel Terman, commander since Granger perished during the crash. Are you all okay?"

The tall one, a blond woman, stopped waving and shook Rachel's hand. "I'm Alisse Richter, chemical and nano engineer. We are so very glad to see you."

"I'm Luis Paredo," the one holding his fellow comrade said. It was his voice Rachel had heard on the radio. "Chief Engineering Officer. Thank God you found us!"

Rachel grinned; not only for finding them, but because they needed Richter's and Paredo's skills. "Hello. And you are?" She indicated the man Paredo was helping along.

"Kiano Jemutai, ecologist," the other man said, breathing hard.

Rachel helped Paredo shoulder Jemutai toward the rover. "What's the matter?"

"Seems to be some sort of anemia," Paredo said.

"I'm not anemic," Jemutai said in a tired voice. "I'm just thrilled to see you."

"Dr. Bakir is at our camp, he'll diagnose what's wrong." Rachel helped Jemutai into the back seat, where Paredo and Richter crowded in beside him. She couldn't blame them for their eagerness.

No doubt they'd expected to die out there, trillions of kilometers from home. If she could offer even a glimmer of hope, then it was all worth it.

As Larsen accelerated back to the mesa, Rachel radioed Bakir about their success, and that Jemutai would require medical attention. The lack of a reply embarrassed her, since some of the joy melted from the others' faces. She hated to admit all wasn't well with her camp, or Kovac's—or that there were two camps instead of one.

"The reception has remained poor since we arrived." Rachel tried to sound casual.

"We're simply glad you found us," Richter said. "Bellucci... he died when *Luzinia* touched down planetside. The module's aft thruster got bent in the first explosion..."

"When we fired it to slow our descent, it burned through the supply berth," Paredo said. "Bellucci's station was right above the damage. There was nothing we could do. We would have burned, too, if not for Jemutai's quick actions with the extinguisher."

"You stayed in *Luzinia* these last six sols?" Larsen asked.

"Until the ground gave way beneath us," Jemutai said. "Every day, *Luzinia* sank into the sand a few centimeters. Then, a few meters."

"Sinkholes?" Rachel asked.

"Yes," Paredo said. "We barely escaped before a large one opened up and swallowed the entire module."

Larsen's brow furrowed. "Your transponder was not detected until today."

"That is the unfortunate bit," Richter said. "The transponder, our radios—everything started working after *Luzinia* was lost in that sinkhole."

An uncomfortable silence filled the rover.

"Did you see any vine-like objects?" Rachel shared a look with Larsen.

"No," Jemutai said. "Then again, we stayed inside *Luzinia* as much as possible, due to the harsh radiation. Why, have you made some discoveries?"

"Yes…but there have been complications." Rachel quickly summed up the last few days' events, even the mess she and Zentsov found in *Seeker*. Even the lake, *Bimini*, and Brent's helmet. Bakir would've probably reprimanded her for divulging so much information—most of it confusing and negative—but she felt they deserved to know.

After she described the dual camp situation, the other three remained quiet the rest of the trip. Rachel couldn't blame them. To be rescued only to discover that their comrades had been arguing over petty issues, was harrowing at best.

The wind picked up. Sand and pebbles popped and cracked against the windshield. Like riding a gauntlet of shotguns in the dark. Finally, the floodlights outside *Aloha* and Thirteen were visible again, and the others' demeanors brightened.

Rachel and Paredo helped Jemutai into *Aloha*. Once everyone was inside, Bakir welcomed them with a tense smile. There were shadows under his eyes. Santos still lay on the cot in the main chamber, but was conscious now and grinned at everyone.

"About time you woke up." Rachel gripped Santos's hand.

"It seems just in time from all the doctor's told me." Santos's smile waned a bit. "You better have a damn good plan or I'm gonna go back to sleep."

She chuckled despite the anxiety such an offhand comment summoned.

"Anemia?" Bakir asked after Rachel explained Jemutai's condition. Jemutai himself was nearly unconscious by then. Richter and Paredo hurriedly unsuited and helped the Kenyan onto another cot. They'd not worn their IVA suits underneath, and were still attired in their maroon UEA uniforms. Bakir said nothing about radiation concerns. Rachel would bring it up later. Not now, in front of everyone.

"He said he's not anemic," Rachel said.

Bakir activated his stethoscope app and examined Jemutai. "You have all been in your EMUs since Sol 1? Everyone has been getting proper meals and rest?"

"Yes," Richter said. "We ate intermediates and rehydratables first, 1,700 calories."

"Same here," Larsen said. "Wish I had gone CYB after all."

"It's not all that," Rachel muttered.

"Any unusually strong, recurrent nightmares?" Sweat slid down Bakir's face.

"Yes." Paredo gave Rachel a curious sidelong glance. "All of us."

"Stand still, this won't take long." Bakir examined Richter and Paredo next. After a few swipes of the stethoscope, he rushed them into the Quick CT booth. It wasn't as accurate as *Aloha*'s MRI scanner, but a reading could be had within thirty seconds. After the scan's completion Bakir checked his tablet and offered a tight smile.

"You're cleared for duty," Bakir said. "I would like blood samples, and—"

Richter yawned. "We are very tired, Doctor. The gravity may be lighter, but that sand is murderous. May we continue this in the morning?"

Rachel nodded. "Of course. Please, eat and rest. Richter, you can share quarters with Larsen and me. Paredo and Jemutai should get Stevenson and Zentsov's room."

As the others gathered in *Aloha*'s galley, Rachel led Bakir aside and whispered in his ear. "So how are they? What's wrong with Jemutai?"

"Their cardiovascular, pulmonary, and metabolic/endocrine systems all check out," Bakir said. "Yet that CT wasn't in-depth. I'll have to run a blood test and a full MRI before I can be certain. Jemutai probably requires an ES injection."

"What's that?" Rachel asked.

"*Eleutherococcus senticosus.*" Bakir found a half-empty water bottle on his desk and emptied it in one gulp. "It's an immune system booster, older than the others I use. He might react to it better."

She pulled him into a corner as the others laughed at some joke. "How did the other blood tests go?"

Bakir's hesitation made her skin turn cold.

"Well?" She gently touched his shoulder. He was shaking.

"Nothing conclusive yet." He pulled away. "I need to run more tests, take more samples. Perhaps tomorrow, after everyone awakes, before eating breakfast."

"What's wrong?" Rachel searched his face, finding only polite reticence.

"My burdens must remain my own," he said.

"You've been a great help to us," she whispered. "Let me help you."

"I thank Allah you found more of our people, but we haven't recovered any more supplies. Neither has Kovac's team, to my knowledge. We could starve."

"I'm going to search every day in the rover," Rachel said. "For supplies and survivors. Remember, there's *Bimini* near that lake, and *Luzinia* might turn up. Something that large couldn't have sunk too far into the ground."

"Sounds good." Bakir returned to the medical station. There was a stiff fatalism in his voice and posture. A terminal evasiveness in his eyes.

She would talk to him again as soon as possible. In private.

A half hour later, Rachel shut the hatch to the women's quarters. Larsen and Richter were already present, making small talk but obviously waiting for her arrival. There were only two cots, and unless one of them slept on the floor…

"I'll share a cot with Larsen," Rachel said.

Richter shook her head. "*Nein.* I will be fine with a thermo blanket."

"Too late." Larsen lay on her cot and tugged Rachel backward.

"You are too kind. *Danke.*" Richter smiled and took the other cot.

As the room's lighting auto-dimmed, Rachel stretched out beside Larsen. Since those from *Luzinia* weren't wearing their IVAs, Bakir cleared everyone else to strip to their basic uniform as well. The skin-tight fabric made Rachel feel naked.

She turned on her side, facing away from Larsen.

Minutes passed. The closeness, the scent of her…Rachel couldn't sleep.

Larsen wrapped an arm around Rachel's waist.

There was nothing possessive about it. Nothing that might demand a reaction or hint at expectation. Seconds ticked by. Richter's placid snoring was a backdrop to the delightful anxiety enveloping Rachel. It was intoxicating.

Larsen's pinkie traced slow circles around Rachel's navel.

Rachel snuggled back into her, her rump in Larsen's crotch, her back pressed against Larsen's chest. She laid her hand over Larsen's as it tightened around her.

Breathing deeply, Larsen nuzzled her face against the back of Rachel's neck. Tension left their bodies as they settled into the embrace. Larsen's calm pulse created a comforting rhythm and Rachel closed her eyes.

Chief Medical Officer's journal. Mission date: Sol 7.

I know that Terman is suspicious of me. Withholding information from our expedition's commander betrays all I stand for, both as doctor and UEA astronaut. If I tell her now, it will only add to her burden. Finding the others from Luzinia *cheered her a little, but the blood test results would send them all into a panic.*

That's because I did not destroy the blood samples I took. I left the vacu-tainers in my field lab, for comparison studies once I drew new samples from everyone. Though the cells are still alive, that is all they should be. Yet these have mutated further.

Mutated without being in their parent body. These are cells no longer part of the circulatory system. They carry no oxygen, and yet they are under-going a form of erythropoiesis—the creation of red blood cells. It's like they have just come from the marrow, newly formed. It must be the mutation I observed in the samples two days ago.

Jemutai's ailment could be a result of this mutation. I still have no idea how we have been infected, exposed, or whatever the case may be. Those from Luzinia *weren't wearing their IVAs inside their module like the rest of us, but I cannot ascertain if that has affected the overall results. I need another blood test. I need Kovac's opinion.*

Exhausted, I sat at my station and ran a few diagnostics on the lab. I hoped it would occupy my mind enough to remain alert. I do not know when I finally fell asleep.

A banging on Aloha*'s hatch woke me right before dawn.*

I hurried to the hatch window and peered out. I spoke over the radio. No one answered. I saw nothing but blowing sand. Annoyed, I decided it must be fatigue and anxiety feeding my imagination. I rubbed the dull ache from my temples and yawned.

That's when I saw a shape walking from the burned ruin of Vivaldi *to* Thirteen.

It was only a glimpse, but I swear I spotted someone out there. A human being.

They weren't wearing a helmet.

As I hurried to wake the others, Stevenson shouted obscenities over the radio. I messaged him but he didn't reply. Scrabbling through Aloha*'s main* *chamber, I found the drone's control tablet. It should have pinpointed any intruder. The drone was off-line.*

Something heavy struck the ground outside.

I admit that I lost it. I screamed for the other crew members to wake up. I opened the cabin hatches and shouted at the dozing forms, I yelled for Terman to get out there.

Stevenson cursed over the radio again, then the line screamed with static. I ripped off my headset and massaged behind my ears. By then, Terman and the rest were awake. I explained what had happened, more tersely than I wanted, but I was terrified.

In my nightmare, Nasreen, too, had been without a helmet.

15

The nightmare left Rachel gasping for breath upon waking. The sensation of sand sliding down her throat made her cough. She started to rise but Larsen held her down.

"Shh," Larsen whispered. "It is okay."

"No, it's not." Rachel rolled over and faced her. "You think you can protect me?"

"*Nei,*" Larsen said. "You were keeping me warm."

The statement's bald honesty made Rachel chuckle. "Oh. Sorry. So do I use bilabial, whatever, in my sleep?"

"No, but I smell your morning breath," Larsen said.

Their snickering was cut short by someone flinging the hatch open.

Minutes later, after Bakir had finished yelling at them, everyone was awake. Hurriedly slipping into their EMU suits, asking questions. Rachel snapped on her helmet and exited *Aloha* first. Larsen followed right behind her. That comforted her more than she wanted to admit.

Sunlight peeked across the flatlands and stabbed over the mesa in harsh pink rays. Dust motes filled the air, as if something had just run circles around the module, disturbing the regolith. Rachel tried to connect her suit with *Aloha*'s drone for an aerial reconnaissance, then recalled it was off-line. If someone was out there, she wanted any advantage she could get.

"You saw only one figure, Bakir?" Rachel looked in all directions before settling her gaze on the wide tracks between *Vivaldi* and Thirteen. A large, heavy object had been dragged through the area.

"Yes, Commander," Bakir said. "It was still dark, the air was full of sand…"

"Something must have startled you to wake us like that," Paredo said. He was joined by Richter, while Jemutai remained inside.

"Stevenson, are you copying any of this?" Rachel walked around Thirteen and stopped. "Oh shit. Stevenson, answer me!"

Thirteen's supply berth was open. The maintenance hatch lay in the sand outside. It had been ripped free of its hinges. Metal scraps and scattered tools littered the ground.

"What is it?" Larsen hurried in Rachel's footsteps. Paredo and Richter came after.

"Someone sabotaged the power in Thirteen," Stevenson said on the radio.

Rachel took a deep breath. "What?"

"Yes. Sabotaged." Stevenson's voice took on a deadly edge. "I have no fucking idea who or why. The sounds of it woke me a few minutes ago. The reactor housing was ripped open. The power cells, stolen."

Paredo knelt before the supply berth and peered in. "I could attempt repairs."

"They took the goddamn power source, Luis!" Stevenson cried. "How do you plan on fixing that?"

"Your suit links are showing radiation exposure at 125 millisieverts," Bakir said over the connection. "Can any of you give me a video feed?"

"There." Rachel adjusted the focus on her suit's cam. "You seeing this?"

"It will be uninhabitable." Paredo rose and distanced himself from the module. "The saboteur exposed the deuterium capsule in the reactor. The result will eventually flood Thirteen with radiation. There is nothing inside it we can safely use now."

"What?" Stevenson's voice cracked.

"Damn it." Rachel paced around Thirteen. Though some supplies remained in *Aloha*, the bulk of their provisions had been stashed in the now-defunct module. They would starve within two weeks, even if she ordered rations cut to 1,000 calories per day.

"Kovac," Stevenson said. "That son of a bitch must have done this."

"Why take the power cells?" Larsen asked "They exposed themselves to the same radiation. Perhaps more."

"Correct," Richter said. "This amounted to suicide for the perpetrator."

"I'm telling you, that motherfucker had something to do with it," Stevenson said.

"Enough," Rachel said. "Stevenson, you need to come out and let Bakir examine you. Maybe we can salvage some goods before the radiation spreads. Let me help you."

"You're only here because of where you're from and what you are, Terman," Stevenson said. "Not what you can do."

Rachel kept her face blank. The others couldn't see her anger. Her pain.

Bakir circled the module. "Please, you must—"

"Forget it," Stevenson said. "I'm not coming out there."

"This is nonsense," Paredo said. "You are endangering all of our lives!"

Rachel approached Thirteen's barricaded hatch. "Open up. That's an order."

No answer came.

"Either open the hatch, or we will force it open," Rachel said in a flat tone, trying to keep her anger in check. "This ends right now."

"This is accomplishing nothing," Bakir said. "Jared, for your own safety, please."

"How stupid do you think I am?" Stevenson asked. "You'll let them have everything. Thinking there's plenty to go around."

"Who's 'them'?" Rachel asked.

Paredo and Richter took blow torches from the rover's tool kit. If another solution presented itself, she'd take it.

"Stop playing dumb," Stevenson said. "You know who I'm talking about."

"No, I don't." Rachel eyed her dosimeter: 130 millisieverts. "Kovac?"

"No." Stevenson emitted a bitter laugh. "The ones we came here to find."

"The aliens?" Rachel hated the word. It implied ignorance, which she possessed in abundance at the moment.

"Whoever they are," Stevenson said. "Ever since we crashed here—"

The connection popped and went dead.

"Damn him," Larsen said.

"Stevenson?" Rachel knocked on the hatch. "Stevenson, do you copy?"

Paredo pointed at *Vivaldi*. "If we cut this hatch off, we may be able to use the one from that module to replace it."

"How long will that take?" Rachel glared at the door.

"At least two hours," Paredo said.

"That is a bad idea," Bakir said over the connection.

"What do we wait for next?" Rachel asked. "For someone to sabotage our equipment, or the rover?"

Stevenson's voice crackled over the radio. "Check the security cams. You'll see."

Richter clambered up the side of Thirteen and shook her head. "The cam is gone."

"And *Vivaldi*'s?" Rachel hated the fear in her voice. In her heart.

Paredo checked it, answered in the negative.

"The cams are all enclosed in a heat-shielded array," Richter said. "Whoever stole them knew what they were doing. There's no sign of forced removal."

Rachel shined her wrist light at *Aloha*'s cam. "This one is still here."

"It will prove my innocence," Stevenson said.

Rachel stalked back toward Thirteen. "Why don't you prove it now by coming out and sharing the supplies—"

"I'm not on fucking trial here!" Stevenson cried. "Look at the camera feed."

Paredo and Richter paused at the hatch with torches in hand, looking at her expectantly. Larsen shrugged.

She had no idea what Stevenson was hiding or why she was even entertaining his request. But if further conflict could be avoided, then she would do it.

"Let's have a look then," Rachel said.

Still in their suits but helmetless, Rachel and the others waited in *Aloha*'s main chamber while Bakir loaded the cam's data onto the lab computer. Santos sat up on his cot to see the screen. He was stable at the moment, but Rachel wondered if Bakir was withholding information about him, too.

"We should have been checking these cams from day one," Rachel said.

"They're supposed to relay data to our drone," Santos said. "From what Bakir's told me, there's lots of crazy electronic noise preventing that."

The cam's feed began when *Centaurus*'s centrifuges blew. The footage showed debris and bodies flying past into the void. Lens flares, chaotic spins and turns. Brief flames. The others cleared their throats or fidgeted. Those moments came back to Rachel, churning her gut. An oppressive heat bore down on her. Could she have done better?

They watched in silence when the cam spiraled out of control, plowing straight into the moon's atmosphere. The fires of reentry licked around the footage's edges, teasing a taste of hell for those foolish enough to peer into its confines. More debris sped by. Glowing red-hot from the contest between velocity and atmospheric friction.

All of them gasped as another body darted by the cam. The crew member's suit went aflame as he or she became a living match, snuffed out a second later. Paredo mumbled a prayer and crossed himself. Richter wiped her eyes.

Finally, the cam showed *Aloha*'s crash, the initial camp set up by Bakir and Stevenson, and Rachel's arrival. Since little transpired of any consequence, Rachel asked Bakir to hit fast-forward. Until the feed showed Li and Burgess removing the cams from Thirteen and *Vivaldi*. The same day they took the specimens and other equipment.

"What the hell were they doing?" Rachel cried.

"Stevenson tried to tell us," Paredo said. "Maybe—"

"Damn that Kovac!" Rachel kicked a chair out of the way.

"Commander, please?" Bakir stared at her until Rachel sighed and nodded.

He slowed the feed when it approached the current day. The last storm blotted out the footage at times, the airborne dust being so thick. Bakir fast-forwarded again until the feed's time frame neared Rachel's return with the survivors from *Luzinia*. Within minutes of them entering *Aloha*, a figure crept past the cam.

"*Que diablos?*" Santos whispered.

The figure wore an IVA suit. No helmet. There was too much windblown sand in the feed to discern a name patch or any other identification. Bakir increased the image size, zoomed in, altered the contrast—still no way to tell who it might be.

A jolt shot through Rachel's heart as she leaned toward the screen. "Wait."

"Commander?" Bakir asked.

"Rewind and play that again,"

Bakir complied. The footage replayed.

"Pause." Rachel pointed at the screen. "That. Right there."

There was a vine wrapped around the figure's left arm.

"Is that thing…moving?" Richter asked.

Bakir replayed the segment again and zoomed in.

"Faen," Larsen murmured. "Stevenson was right."

"My God," Jemutai said. Richter cursed in German.

The vine was convulsing. Slithering around the figure's wrist and up the arm. It was bloated compared to the vine Rachel had found. Dark green rather than brown.

Bakir crossed his arms and looked away.

The figure walked around Thirteen, studying the module's surface. Then, for minutes at a time, the figure stood in place. The fingers of its left arm twitched. With its back to *Aloha*'s cam, Rachel couldn't see the person's face. After ten minutes of no activity, Rachel asked Bakir to fast-forward again. Skipping to an hour later, the figure finally jerked as if shocked. It pressed its left hand against Thirteen's wall for two minutes. Next, it walked around to the other side of Thirteen—out of the cam's line of sight. Bakir fast-forwarded a third time until the figure walked back into frame. He or she was stumbling. There were black marks on the suit. Scorch burns, perhaps.

The figure was dragging Thirteen's power cells.

No one looked at each other. No one moved. A breeze scratched sand across *Aloha*'s exterior, sounding like thousands of insects trying to get in.

"There's nothing here that incriminates Stevenson," Rachel said.

"So you will try to negotiate with him?" Bakir asked.

Popping her helmet back on, Rachel faced him. "I'm going to search around the camp. Anyone want to join me?"

"What do you hope to find?" Larsen put her helmet on.

"Anything we can." Rachel activated her radio channel. "Stevenson? We watched *Aloha*'s cam footage. It showed someone in an IVA suit with one of those vines. We believe you, but for your own safety, I suggest you rethink your situation."

Stevenson didn't answer.

"You're antagonizing him," Bakir said. "He is afraid something is after him, can't you see that? He will never leave Thirteen until we convince him otherwise."

"We're all afraid." Rachel neared the air lock. "That doesn't mean we endanger the rest. You defend him at every turn. Was stockpiling the supplies your idea?"

Bakir hesitated. The others tensed, looking from her to the doctor.

"No," Bakir finally said. "But I understand it in light of what has happened. What could still happen. So should you."

"And why is that?" Rachel scowled, annoyed he supported Stevenson.

"This mission is compromised," Bakir said. "Who is to say that *Centaurus* itself wasn't sabotaged? Why would anyone seek to ruin Thirteen like that, or steal your rover back at Kovac's camp? Where is Burgess? Is she the one doing all of these things?"

"Plus, we are dealing with an alien biology that we have no understanding of," Jemutai said. "You saw the vine-like thing on that person's arm."

"That's why we need to stick together," Rachel said in a terse voice. "That's why I'm trying to hold this mission together, so that we can survive longer than our comrades who didn't make it through the crash. That's why I need you to tell me what the hell you discovered in those blood tests, Bakir."

The other crew members stared at Bakir. More sweat dripped down his face.

"The matter should remain private," Bakir said in a low voice.

"Everyone deserves to know," Larsen said. The rest nodded.

Bakir swallowed and walked around the chamber, distancing himself.

"Bakir?" Rachel frowned with worry.

"This world has already started mutating our cellular structure," Bakir said. "It began early, perhaps our first day here. Santos, the most."

"Huh?" Santos scrabbled around on his cot. "How?"

"With what results?" Jemutai asked, wide-eyed as he studied his life monitor.

"It is similar to a cancer, but it doesn't kill cells," Bakir said. "It simply replicates itself. The resulting DNA isn't human. I do not know how it is happening. We are well-shielded from radiation inside the modules, in the EMUs—"

"Can it be cured?" Richter asked.

"Unknown," Bakir said.

"Christ save us," Paredo whispered.

"What?" Santos yelled. "You can't leave us hanging like that. Use your lab, figure this shit out! You're the fucking doctor!"

"I am trying!" Bakir shouted. He looked embarrassed, then left for the toilet.

"Commander, you gotta do something about this!" Santos cried.

"I will. Come on, Larsen." Rachel went back outside, away from their terrified faces and into a maelstrom of unanswered questions.

Etana gazes at the horizon, no sun visible as sand-filled clouds whip back and forth across the flatlands. There are others watching. Waiting. It is because of them that she will not disobey her orders. She continues walking, that stubborn impulse even the terminally ill still manage to obey. The rover follows, though the moon's signal noise has made her reset the vehicle's remote interface twice since dawn.

She keeps the pistol close.

The mesa housing Terman's camp is less than a kilometer away. Etana will have to scale it by hand if she wishes to maintain her cover. Even if she reveals herself as a friend, the others might expose her presence by excited radio chatter. She can't risk that.

Judging from the radio signals she intercepted last night, Terman found the survivors of *Luzinia*. Three more she will have to deal with. Already her enemies multiply while resources grow less by the day. Now her goals have been split: Terman's camp, which has gotten larger, or Kovac's.

She could make a report to one or the other.

She could reveal herself and what she knows.

What that would change, she cannot fathom. Everything has been set since she boarded *Centaurus*. Her orders are simple yet unmistakable.

Also simple to disobey, being so far from Earth.

Though she has taken other offworld contracts, it was not easy to accept this mission. Not because she will not be mourned. Because, like all beings of emotion, Etana possesses the flaw of vanity. She wants her family to know that this is for them.

A gleam catches her eye at the base of the mesa's northern side. Metal.

Etana activates her binocular app and adjusts the magnification. Bit by bit a blurred, moving shape comes into focus. She releases a slow breath, hand on the pistol.

It is a humanoid in an IVA suit dragging what appears to be a module's power cell. It is not wearing a helmet. The face is formless. Lacking discernable human features like eyes, nose, or mouth. Yet it feels familiar. A chill spreads through Etana's body.

A sinkhole opens in the sand before the figure. The figure walks right into it, power cell and all. The dark maw closes in a puff of dust. Leaving no trace.

Something shakes in her vision. Etana realizes she has drawn her gun. Pointing it at where the figure was standing. Something prevents her from keeping it steady.

It has been a long time since she has been afraid.

Etana stumbles toward her rover, then runs for it.

She makes her choice: She will kill the crew one at a time, when the opportunity arises. For all she knows, the others might have changed already. Her employers warned that this was why none could survive to bring such a danger back to Earth. She double-checks the status of her false appendix. What it contains.

They will not take her. Dead or alive.

Chief Medical Officer's journal. Mission date: Sol 10.

Two days have passed since Terman made her fruitless search around the camp. She and Larsen continued all day and into the night, even after a vicious windstorm struck the mesa. As I suspected, they found nothing in such conditions. And, as I suspected, this only made Terman more annoyed and increased the tension among our group. Though I sympathize with her, there is no way of finding out who the saboteur was. I don't think it is any among us. Nor do I think it's "aliens." And Kovac's people...

I don't want to believe they would do that.

Kovac hasn't retuned my private messages concerning the matter, though that could be the network going down again.

Terman ordered a constant watch be set over our camp. I immediately volunteered for the night hours to alleviate my nightmares. Jemutai and Paredo took the day watch.

Stevenson has remained locked in Thirteen. He's leaving supplies tethered outside the module. No one wants to eat or drink them. The radiation readings are too high—sometimes as much as 150 mSv on a single NF packet. Though Terman has devised a rationing system for our remaining foodstuffs, we will starve within two weeks.

Also, I'm fairly certain everyone is having stronger nightmares. The nocturnal data on their suit links proves it: less REM periods or gasping for breath as if they have sleep apnea, which was cured decades ago. Paredo and Richter reported theirs to me, but Jemutai is closemouthed about it. Santos says he can deal with them; his recovery is coming along, and he has spent the last day walking. Larsen laughs hers off, but I know that is her way of dealing with it. Terman refuses to discuss hers with me any longer.

I'm still taking meds to keep me awake, though I try to get at least three or four hours of sleep now. I usually catch that while the others are outside during the day, exploring. I refuse to sleep at night. The nightmares are worse then. Plus, I can keep an eye on the others, since Paredo sleepwalks. According to his UEA profile, he never did that on Earth. Santos's attitude is borderline abusive upon waking. He grows ever more demanding that I find a "cure" for our mutating cells. Jemutai has recovered, but he prefers solitary outings onto the mesa during his watch—against Terman's orders, who now forbids anyone leaving Aloha by themselves. I cannot blame either of them: She seeks safety, and he seeks solitude. Neither can be had on this moon.

That leads me back to Kovac's team. Zentsov has become our liaison to them, for lack of a better term. He says he will return to our camp, but he remains with his fellow scientists. His reports, about the growth of the vines when exposed to power sources, and of their connection with the sinkholes, troubles me. They view it as some big field trip, always driving farther and farther out into the wastes. Part of me envies them. Another part of me doesn't trust them. Everyone assumes Burgess is dead. No one says it.

Kovac refuses to file any medical reports—for himself or anyone on his team. They also refuse to give blood samples. Kovac told me simply to let them do their work while there was still time. We haven't had a sandstorm in a day, which he utilizes as an excuse to avoid my questions and tests because they are taking advantage of the lull and exploring. Terman has given up trying to issue orders to them.

The so-called "blue lake" that Terman and Larsen found has disappeared. The sands have also swallowed up Bimini. Terman is greatly troubled by this. I wonder if she isn't close to a psychological breakdown. I asked Larsen to always keep an eye on her. The only good news is that her right hand has healed well, requiring little care.

Most important, we haven't come into contact with those who sent the signal to Earth. No trace of alien equipment, dwellings, or even a probe that might have landed here from another system. It's as if we answered the call of a ghost. Now we are the haunted ones. Terman searches every day for the other modules whose transponders still broadcast a signal. These, too, are phantoms, often due to the constant signal noise.

Her drive to find other survivors, especially at this point, makes me admire and pity her. I sense it gives Terman something to occupy herself with, rather than argue with Stevenson or Kovac, debate religion with Paredo, or pester me for more test results.

Most of us eat in the cabins or even the toilet so no one else can see. Guarding our rations jealously. I have caught Santos and Richter searching the waste bin for the slightest crumb. Someone ate the rest of my halal processed food. Terman gave me the remainder of her vegetarian cuisine and now only eats calorie blocks.

It requires an effort to pray. I still perform wudu, *saying the* bismillah, *cleansing my hands, mouth, nostrils, face, and arms in the proper Sunni fashion. I still manage to say the* shahadah *with conviction. Last night, Paredo knelt beside me and murmured his own devotions. I am not offended, though it annoys Terman. Something to do with Catholic missionary work on Mars. It is easy to extrapolate from there.*

And what do I pray for? Nothing. I simply kneel facing Earth, the niche of my rug pointed to said homeworld. My daily observances are now mechanical and routine.

Allah forgive me.

The UEA thought we would come here, make contact with the signal's originators, and return home aboard Centaurus *after six months. Even if that had failed, we could always have reentered stasis and slept until a rescue mission came. Not now.*

There is a small amount of good news: The general radiation exposure outside has lowered to 85 mSv, and the surface temperature has lowered to 320 Kelvin. Zentsov says Kovac and the others assume it is due to the weather or other atmospheric conditions. There's also less hydrogen in the air and more nitrogen and oxygen.

Yet Aloha's seismometer detected a significant quake on the other side of the moon yesterday. The resulting seismograph revealed the tremor was 8.3 in magnitude.

In my last dream, Nasreen was leading me straight into a great fissure. Though I awoke weeping again, I cannot deny the peace that vision brought me. I need more meds.

Again, Rumi's words filled me with yearning:

When I am with you, we stay up all night.
When you're not here, I can't go to sleep.

Personal journal, Mission Specialist Li. Mission date: Sol 11.

The last few days have been depressing as fuck. Though we've kept digging around the buried structure, we can't make real progress due to the dust storms. The sand shifts around, and twice we had to use the rover to pull the digger bot out before it sank too deep. We've got both drones from Seeker and Thirteen scanning the area, but the data often gets corrupted. Zentsov bitched that he needs at least one drone to maintain the network with Terman's camp, but nobody cares. Kovac just mentions those vines, and that always sidetracks Zentsov until they change the subject.

We can't risk ruining any of our equipment. We can't let this opportunity pass. Kovac feels certain the object is the source of the signal sent to Earth. I mean, we haven't found anything else on this stupid moon so far. He's commended me on my doggedness. At least someone appreciates what I can do.

Kovac and Sakurai argue from time to time. Not shouting matches, but petty shit like who will drive the rover or who'll collect the next sample. But they always sit together at meals and she rarely speaks to me or Zentsov anymore. It's annoying because I thought we were a tight team, not like those following The Super-Duper Martian. They're still looking for survivors while completely ignoring our mission.

Dumbfucks.

Well, I hear Larsen has "translated" some of the signal Kovac detected the other day. I mean, c'mon. She talks more about elves and fairies than an Icelandic pop star.

Then there's that fucking Russian. Sure, I liked Zentsov initially. He made a few jokes, stayed out of our way, helped with the research. The guy knows his stuff, every bit as knowledgeable as Kovac. He snacks between meals while we're gone excavating, literally eating away at our supplies. He placed a vine outside without asking the rest of us—that was the team's specimen, not his. And then he lost the damn thing. He claimed it slithered into a sinkhole before he could catch it. Whatever. If the organism was alive, it's dead all over again now, and the resources used on it wasted.

He refuses to sleep. Sure, I keep having nightmares about excavating my parents from some moldy tomb. Only, they're alive, and I never get them out in time...anyway, Zentsov's dreams must be bad because the bastard's always *awake. He talks to himself. Once, I caught him staring into Sakurai's room while she slept, whispering nonsense. I yelled at him to stop. It scared the shit out of her, but Kovac smoothed the situation.*

After that I asked Kovac to send Zentsov back to Terman, but he refused. I think it's because Zentsov does all of Kovac's dirty work now. Tallying up things on the lab computer, using Jeong's data cache to help them understand the moon's weather patterns, stuff like that. Maybe it's for the best. He never wants to leave Seeker *after losing that vine. I bet he's afraid to go outside. Yeah, he'd probably shit his MAGs.*

Kovac got pissed when Terman asked us why we took the security cams from Vivaldi *and Thirteen. We're using them to help record our excavation. You could hear the accusation in her tone. Besides, why would we need a fuel cell? I swear, she's incompetent. Letting someone sabotage Thirteen like that. I suspect it's her, trying to create emergencies so the rest of us will become afraid and obey whatever she says. But that's biting her in the ass. Zentsov said that Bakir says she stays out in the rover all day because she can't get along with the others. At least she leaves us the hell alone now.*

Sakurai tossed some theories about who might have done it—Stevenson, or the aliens. She even mentioned Burgess! I laughed, but that pissed her off.

Now that the storms have gone for a day, we might have a chance to finally uncover the object buried out there. Kovac still hasn't told Terman. If there are saboteurs in her camp, we don't them need them destroying what could be the greatest find in human history. Kovac suggested we start camping out in the rover at the dig site in case the assholes try it. I agreed. Sakurai is lukewarm to it, but she'll play. So, back to work.

16

"We're not crazy." Rachel stopped the rover at the coordinates where the blue lake had been. It and *Bimini* were like mirages she was trying to recall with a few hours of sleep, scant food, and occasional dizziness. She assumed it was the moon's lower gravity taking its toll, though her augmented joints and bowels weren't aggravated by it.

"I know." Larsen ran a scan and sighed. "Bakir and the others think so."

"Can you blame them?" Rachel asked. "But we saw the lake eight days ago. Zentsov saw it. Saw *Bimini*. And now, it's all just vanished."

"*Ja,*" Larsen said. "It has stolen my peace of mind."

After her stomach rumbled, Rachel pulled a tube of toothpaste from beneath the seat. She needed a snack but couldn't spare the food. "Want some?"

They each squirted in a mouthful. The banana flavoring now tasted like ice cream after days of rationing. It dissolved quickly, leaving them no closer to satisfaction.

Rachel rubbed her temples and lay over the steering wheel. "This is the only time I can have some peace now. Inside *Aloha,* someone's always arguing. Paredo and that weird 'cleansing of the house' ritual. It reminds of me of the missionaries who came to Mars every summer season to convert us 'heathens.'"

"Richter stopped talking to me," Larsen said. "She saw me touching you—"

"I don't care." Rachel clasped her hand. "You'd better not care, either."

Larsen chuckled. "No fear. Without you here, I would go mad."

"Santos is the one driving me crazy," Rachel said. "I think he stole Bakir's food."

"The craziest speaks most truly." Larsen offered a slight smile.

"You and your Norwegian wisdom." Rachel stared out the windshield. "I wish it could help me figure out who the hell sabotaged Thirteen."

"As I said," Larsen said. "Elves. They are out here."

"So you believe Stevenson? That it was aliens?" Rachel snorted.

"Doubting your leadership does not make him wrong about this."

There was no rebuttal to that statement. The lack of a lake and a crashed module outside proved it. Nothing in her training—in her life—had prepared her for this. The urge to say that the mission was beyond her abilities, that someone else should take command, was so strong that Rachel had to bite her lip.

She remembered how confident she'd been upon leaving Earth for this mission.

The ramp leading to Centaurus's *cockpit hatch was for the media, the cameras. Rachel strode up it like all the other crew members, her IVA suit immaculate, helmet under the crook of her arm. They'd all been aboard for hours but played out this little ceremony for posterity. She was more nervous than she'd expected to be.*

Not because their departure from the solar system was imminent.

One by one her comrades waved at the crowd on the station's balcony. Many of their families stood there. Waving back, cheering, weeping. Rachel tried to look elsewhere. Fixed her expression into one of total neutrality, like all Martians learned once they'd lived among Earthlings long enough. A visage that advertised nothing could break her, nothing could bring her down.

All the while, she scanned the crowd. No sign of Mom or Dad. She'd told them not to bother coming. Not to bother pretending they cared anymore since she'd be out of their lives forever soon. But now, more than anything, she wanted to see them there.

It was Jeong's turn to wave. She was next. Still no sign of her family.

Out there she would be the ultimate expatriate. A renegade born of one world, shaped by another, yet belonging to neither. Earth and Mars were her true parents.

She could say how much she hated those worlds without crying. How both had promised so much while cruelly taking it away. But not about Mom and Dad.

The announcer said her name. In reflex, Rachel faked a smile and waved.

Her moist eyes searched the crowd. A sea of strangers.

As she lowered her hand, two figures pushed through those at the balcony's edge.

Mom and Dad. Waving.

Rachel shouted their names even though the Martian honorary anthem played over the station speakers, drowning her out. They grinned wide. Crying, shouting.

In that moment Rachel knew she could do anything. And now she finally knew that Mom and Dad believed it, too. She waved and waved and waved.

Now, threatened with starvation and worse, she felt powerless.

"Hey," Larsen whispered. "You were light-years away."

"Sorry." Rachel blinked and loosened her shoulders.

Smiling, Larsen smoothed Rachel's hair. "You needed it."

She needed more, but not yet. Not while she felt so low. Larsen deserved better.

"Did you get anything else from that signal we recorded when the lake was here?"

Larsen leaned back, propped her feet on the dash, and lifted her field lab into her lap. "It, and the one Kovac detected, match at the lower levels where humans cannot hear. Around 6 hertz. Nothing unusual until they reach 16 kilohertz at the same time. They correlate as if answering each other."

They studied the waveform on the lab screen. Larsen played both signals together for a few seconds. Though Rachel heard only teeth-grinding noise, the combined signal wavelength on the screen told a different story.

She lifted her head from the steering wheel. "Have you tried broadcasting that?"

"This?" Larsen giggled, then saw Rachel was serious. "No."

"Connect your lab to the rover's network." Rachel sat up and swiped commands on the console. "We'll send it out using the rover's transmitter."

Larsen stuck her tongue out as she completed the connection. "We are live."

They sat for a few minutes in comfortable silence. Rachel stretched and sipped from her flask. It contained Earl Grey tea whose leaves had been cultivated in the finest hydroponics domes in New Paris. One of the few food amenities the UEA allowed her, it was also something she'd never been able to afford.

"Got any more of that?" Larsen licked her lips.

"Sure. Best tea on Mars." Rachel handed her the flask. "Careful, though. Bakir will complain about the extra caffeine in your system."

Larsen drained the flask, burped, and gave a mischievous look. "Pardon me. Now I feel naughty. If you let me—"

The rover's scanner beeped with an incoming transmission.

They sat up straight and leaned over the console. The transmission matched the one Larsen had sent: in duration, pitch, and strength. It originated south of their position.

"We must investigate," Larsen said.

Rachel set the rover's nav app and followed the signal. "Naughty Mobile, away."

On the way, they jabbered about what it could be. Sent messages back to *Aloha* so Bakir and the rest knew. Giggled like two little girls hiding in a crater past their bedtime.

The nav app led them through eight kilometers' worth of reg fields, sandy escarpments, and steep ravines culminating in a basin of jagged buttes. They towered over the landscape, eroded to red-green spears threatening to disembowel the sky.

A blue gleam shone ahead.

"Oh my God," Rachel said.

An azure pillar stood in the center of the basin. It was at least twenty meters tall and eight meters in diameter. A rippling effect coursed over its surface, much like the lake they'd seen a few days ago. The glimmering, sleek surface should have shown a reflection of the surrounding terrain…but it didn't.

Rachel halted the vehicle. Unable to stop gazing at the structure, she felt around for her helmet. Larsen passed it to her, also staring out the windshield. "Okay. Let's go."

The ground around the pillar was hard-packed and spackled with fissures. An ancient lake bed, perhaps. Though Rachel wondered why the weather hadn't eroded it. They approached the blue anomaly as if it were a skittish animal that might flee.

"You getting these readings?" Rachel glanced at her HUD.

Larsen nodded. "Temperature has dropped since we came within thirty meters of it. Now reading 280 Kelvin."

Rachel's HUD showed the rest: Air pressure at 99 kilopascals. Atmospheric content 77 percent nitrogen, 20 percent oxygen, and 3 percent miscellaneous harmless gases. Radiation at 4 millisieverts.

"Cannot detect any bacteria or pathogens." Larsen gave her a questioning look.

"I know, but…" Rachel swallowed. "Remember what Bakir said about our cells mutating. What if this material is responsible?"

"See what happens?" Larsen reached for her helmet seal.

"No," Rachel said. "Our helmets stay on."

Larsen walked around the pillar. "The area around it is hospitable to our species. The transmission brought us here. These are not coincidences."

"I said no."

"This is what we came here for." Larsen removed her helmet.

"Goddamnit!" Rachel tackled her. They fell and rolled up against the pillar, Rachel on top. Larsen's helmet landed nearby.

The chill air around the pillar made Larsen's exhalations visible. She took deep breaths, closed her eyes, and smiled. "See, *elskling*?"

Rachel grabbed the helmet and gripped Larsen by the collar. "Put it on!"

"Kiss me first."

More curses came to Rachel's lips, but she hesitated. Her HUD readings hadn't changed. Larsen was alive. Joy and anger swept through Rachel's heart like a storm.

"I hate you." Rachel took off her helmet.

"Liar." Larsen pulled her down and they kissed.

So frightened and infuriated she could cry, Rachel kept kissing until the urge to weep morphed into laughter. She leaned back, holding Larsen's hands.

"You're going to drive me crazy. First you crashed the rover, now this—"

"I am high maintenance." Larsen patted Rachel's rump. "Let us explore."

They helped each other rise and gazed at the sapphire edifice. A few meters away, heat waves shimmered over the moon's surface where the temperature remained at the boiling point. They stood on a border of life and death.

Several thoughts occurred to Rachel. *Bimini* had been found near the lake, with everyone dead or missing. According to Bakir, Zentsov had tried taking off his helmet when *Aloha* first crashed.

"Let's leave." Rachel stepped back.

"We should study this." Larsen gestured at the pillar. "They are accommodating us. Breathable air at the right pressure. We may never get another chance."

"How do we know this—whatever it is—didn't kill *Bimini*'s crew?"

The pillar's surface stopped rippling. Shapes moved therein.

Larsen grabbed Rachel's arm. "Do not panic."

"I can take care of myself."

"Good, because you must save me, too," Larsen said.

"Now who's panicking—" Rachel's words died away as the forms beneath the pillar's surface took shape. A human-like profile. It was a figure in a UEA IVA suit.

Without a helmet.

"Dritt," Larsen murmured.

"Brent?" The name might have been spoken by someone else, since Rachel wasn't cognizant of anything other than the figure's face. It had Brent's features. Yet he was different. Something about the way he looked at them. No recognition. No human rapport that even people from different cultures and climes still shared.

The figure offered a hand.

"You're the communication expert," Rachel whispered. "Now what?"

"Accept it," Larsen said.

Rachel pressed against the pillar where the figure's hand was. A jolt shot through her. She convulsed and fell to her knees. Larsen shouted something but all sound warbled into a wall of distant noise. The figure's lips moved, then it vanished.

"I said, are you okay?" Larsen knelt beside her.

"I think so." Rachel grimaced as she stood on numb legs. "What happened?"

Sand clouds puffed in the basin around the pillar. Just outside the area where the temperature had changed. As the particles settled, the dark recesses of sinkholes became visible. The same thing had happened at the lake a week ago.

This time, the path back to their rover was blocked by the holes.

"Put your helmet on." Rachel snatched hers and donned it. For once, Larsen made no argument and obeyed. They stood close to each other. Not touching the pillar or venturing out among the holes.

Dust stirred in one of the pits to their right. The same figure she'd seen inside the pillar rose from it. Not climbed, not flew, just simply rose up from the hole's depths.

"Brent?" Larsen called.

"I don't think that's him," Rachel whispered.

Larsen stepped toward the figure. "You represent whoever sent the signal?"

The figure didn't speak. Didn't move. Its eyes, no longer the same brown shade as Brent's, glowed blue. Its gaze roved up and down. Studying them.

"Here." Larsen activated the holographic app on her wrist pad. "Where we are from." The pad displayed a three dimensional recreation of their solar system, the path they took to reach Alpha Centauri, and a breakdown of the original transmission sent to Earth. The figure kept looking at Rachel and Larsen instead.

"Is Brent dead?" Rachel asked. "Did you harm our friends?"

The figure smiled but the expression was crooked. Its cheeks quivered as if the muscles didn't know how to convey the most basic of visual communications. It gestured to its left. Rachel and Larsen looked in that direction. They both gasped and jumped back.

Bimini rested inside one of the ravines leading into the basin, perhaps two hundred meters away. It hadn't been there when they entered the area. Its hatch was open.

"Where are the others?" Rachel cried. "Do you have Burgess?"

"Stay calm," Larsen whispered. "Try again."

"You're the linguist," Rachel whispered back.

"It likes you."

Rachel swallowed and approached the figure. "Please. Where are our friends?"

The figure gestured to its right. A deep green object sat beneath one of the buttes. It was squat and oval with graceful curves. There was no mistaking it for anything else but a vessel. A starship of extraterrestrial design.

"Invitation or trophy display?" Larsen asked.

The figure pointed a third time. They walked around the pillar to see.

Centaurus's cockpit module lay on the other side of basin.

Before she knew it, Rachel was halfway there. Running. Heart pounding. Larsen hurried after, warning of sinkholes, but Rachel didn't care. She needed to know.

Her heart hammered against her rib cage. She dashed through the open hatch and stumbled around the burned seats, the smashed computer console. She finally was able to speak, though it felt like she was suffocating within the cockpit's ghastly confines.

"Granger!" Rachel backed away toward the breach. "Captain Granger!"

The body bag she'd secured Granger's corpse in—the same one she and Stevenson had buried him in atop the mesa—lay on the floor. Empty.

Dizziness savaged her equilibrium. Rachel collapsed.

Hands lifted under her armpits and pulled her from the cockpit module. All Rachel could do was stare at the crumpled body bag where the captain had been.

"Fuck. Oh fuck." Rachel's boots kicked at the sand outside, trying to put distance between her and the bag.

"Easy, *vakker*. Easy. I have you. It is okay. I have you."

Rachel clasped Larsen's hand without turning around. She took a deep breath, realized what she'd done, then released the hand. "Sorry."

Larsen helped her up and turned her so they could face each other. "You are fine. What happened?"

Having someone save her was a strange concept. It bothered and elated her at the same time. "The captain's body. It's gone. We buried him on the mesa in that same bag!"

Larsen gave her a funny look, then entered to see for herself. Moments later, she exited, face ashen. "Holy shit."

"I know." Rachel leaned over, bracing her hands against her knees. "I just—"

"He is gone," Larsen said. "Brent is gone!"

Rachel wheeled about. The figure had vanished. The sinkholes, *Bimini,* the strange vessel—all gone. The sparkling blue pillar remained.

"We're leaving," Rachel said. "We've got to warn the others."

As they ran back to the rover, Larsen spoke between breaths. "*Uff da!* Was this a threat or an offer?"

"I don't want to think, I just want to drive the hell out of here." Rachel felt herself blush. Let someone else call her actions cowardice. There were others buried on the mesa. Jeong, Nagel, Burgess, and Bellucci had yet to be found. Whatever the entity was that had taken over Brent, whatever its intentions, she had to ensure the crew's safety.

They got in and slammed the rover's doors. Ignited the engine, spun a wheel, and sped from the basin back toward the mesa. Rachel plowed over stones and dunes, jostling them around in the seats. Larsen buckled herself in, but Rachel spared no time for it.

"Think they took the others we buried?" Larsen stared around as if something might attack the rover at any moment. "If they did—"

"But why take Granger's body if they already have Brent?" Rachel asked. "If we're interacting with an advanced civilization, can't they communicate in a better way?"

"Their social mores concerning the dead might be different," Larsen said. "Sounds gross, but not a bad idea."

"It's gross as fuck, Vanja."

"That is because you are a pilot, not a scientist." Larsen chuckled.

"But…taking more than one body?" Rachel frowned, shook her head. "We still don't know if these beings killed Brent and the others in *Bimini*. And that other vessel."

"We are not the first ones here?" Larsen raised her brows and shrugged.

"I've been thinking about that," Rachel said. "We need more proof. We need everyone's input. Even Kovac and his team."

"Everyone will worry more." Larsen leaned back in her seat. "Nightmares worsened after we found the lake."

"What are yours about?" Rachel swerved around a crevice and made for the flatlands around the mesa. "If you don't mind telling me."

Larsen closed her eyes. "Meeting grandpapa at Nærøyfjord. In my dream its waters are like the blue lake. Grandpapa drags me across it and I cannot escape."

"I feel like I'm suffocating in mine," Rachel said.

Minutes passed. The sun was getting lower in the sky.

"It is okay to have been afraid back there, *vakker*," Larsen said.

Rachel grunted. "I was just shocked, that's all."

Larsen turned in her seat and regarded Rachel with those ever-curious eyes. "No. You were frightened. You keep it bottled inside."

"Are you the camp psychiatrist now?" Rachel slowed the rover a bit. Despite the subject matter, she liked talking to Larsen. Liked looking at her.

"No." Larsen sighed. "I am keeping my fears bottled up, too. Haven't felt safe on this moon since Burgess vanished. Still do not know why I am afraid."

Rachel slowed the rover even more, not wanting to return to camp just yet. Not wanting to spoil the small space of sanity and warmth between them. As soon as they left the rover at *Aloha*, the madness, the accusations—the fear—would begin anew.

"You hide all of those things well," Rachel said.

"Of course." Larsen smirked. "I am Norwegian."

"Hiding one's feelings is the first thing we Martians learn." The landscape passed outside like the moving backdrop in an old-fashioned puppet show. "From outsiders, offworlders—even each other."

"Yet you have a resolute passion," Larsen said.

"That's one reason I came out here. I want to let all that go. I'm tired of hiding."

Static came over the radio, then a voice.

"Coming for me."

Larsen adjusted the frequency. "This is Larsen. Say again?"

"Coming…"

Rachel couldn't discern the voice's gender. It didn't reply to Larsen's continued attempts at communication. Rachel sped back up. The vehicle raced over the flatlands.

A thin, dark column of smoke drifted into the sky ahead. From the direction of their camp.

Flight Recorder – *Maray* Crew Module
Sol 11 – 2200 hours
Orbiting Proxima Centauri C

CFE Moore: At least I can move now.

CMP Worrel: I'm not allowing you to make another bloody spacewalk, so stop asking. Jivika, any more image data today?

MS Khandaar: Same as yesterday. There's people down there, we're still up here.

CMP Worrel: How about a little protocol in here?

MS Khandaar: Sorry, sir. There's people down there, sir. We're still up here. Sir.

CMP Worrel: (sighs) Look, I'm bored shitless in this module too. But we used too much thruster fuel to avoid that debris. We don't have enough to make a safe landing.

CFE Moore: I say we chance it anyway. We're running low on supplies.

CMP Worrel: Did you not pay attention to the ration memo I sent two days ago?

CFE Moore: Memo? Sir, we live literally a few meters apart.

CMP Worrel: I want the UEA to know we did all in our power to survive. Now, Jivika, what about the changes in that blue anomaly you told me about yesterday?

MS Khandaar: (sighs) It was probably uncovered after another windstorm. I thought at first that vegetation might have grown—

CMP Worrel: Near that blue circular area, correct? There was what appeared to be brown algae and sinkholes. Next to those three derelicts?

MS Khandaar: Correct…sir. But these are taken from orbit. We could be misinterpreting every damn thing down there.

CMP Worrel: It looks like other vessels crashed down there. Not from Earth.

CFE Moore: Another reason we should land. They might've sent the signal.

MS Khandaar: They might be optical illusions due to lighting. I'm certain if Terman were here she could tell you the Face on Mars was the same thing.

CMP Worrel: We've better cameras than those probes did a century ago. I'm telling you, those're wrecked starships. Nonhuman derelicts.

MS Khandaar: We can't be certain without close inspection—

CMP Worrel: Stay on it. We need all the data we can get. If we do manage to land, we'll at least have a map with which to locate our mates.

CFE Moore: Andrew, I could talk you through the procedure. It's only a wiring issue. Twenty minutes, tops.

CMP Worrel: Hell. No.

CFE Moore: Play you a hand of poker for it.

MS Khandaar: (groans) Grow up.

CFE Moore: Never, honey.

CMP Worrel: Kevin, the scanner is off-line. You lost your tool kit in the debris field, and I'll be stuffed before I'll risk losing you— and more tools—just so we can yabber with whoever survived down there. We're serving the mission better by mapping the surface and imaging those anomalies. Now, Jivika. Tell me about that raised area south of the two camps. The place where the crew from *Seeker* are digging.

MS Khandaar: The windstorms haven't altered its shape. There's something large in that area. Something at odds with the rest of the terrain.

CFE Moore: Stop having us chase ghosts, Andrew. We need that scanner online! We need to land! Planetside, there'd be no danger of debris while trying to make repairs, and we might even get their help to fix—

CMP Worrel: Cark it, Moore. We remain in orbit a little longer.

CFE Moore: Why?

CMP Worrel: (clears throat)

CFE Moore: Damn it, why?

MS Khandaar: We deserve to know. You've mentioned it in your sleep.

CMP Worrel: We're all talking in our sleep now.

MS Khandaar: Stop gaslighting and have enough respect to tell us.

CMP Worrel: I dreamt that we crashed into that blue area. The lake.

CFE Moore: You're letting us rot up here because of some goddamn dream?

MS Khandaar: Shit.

CMP Worrel: Not just *Maray,* but other ships. Not parts of *Centaurus.*

MS Khandaar: You mean those things you think are derelicts?

CMP Worrel: Yes. I see them all crash in my dreams.

17

The smoke rising from *Aloha* became visible long before Rachel neared the camp. Her serenity with Larsen broken, she accelerated and slammed the radio button.

"Bakir! Paredo! Anyone copy? I'm seeing smoke coming from *Aloha*. Hello, does anyone have a copy?"

Sporadic static and broken words came back over the connection.

"Cannot see our drone." Larsen checked the scanner. "Network is down."

"Bakir, you copy? This is Terman. I'm driving into camp now. What happened?"

More words savaged by pops and crackles.

Rachel plowed through a sand drift and barely avoided a sinkhole as she neared the camp. Two suited figures were outside. One held a cylindrical object. Perhaps an extinguisher. *Aloha* was smoking from the underside, though no flames were visible.

"...no more, you son of a bitch! I know what...going down there!"

Stevenson's voice, on the radio.

"Stevenson, where are you?" Rachel practically shouted into the mic. "Stevenson? Answer me damn it!"

"*Aloha's* thrusters," Larsen said. "They are ruined."

As they got closer, Rachel realized it was Bakir directing Jemutai where to point an extinguisher. The barricade around Thirteen's hatch had been ripped apart but the hatch remained closed. Upon seeing their arrival, Bakir motioned for them to hurry.

Once out of the rover, Rachel ran to Bakir. "What the hell happened? Why didn't you radio me?"

"We just found out about this ourselves!" Bakir motioned at Jemutai. "Go check around the other side. We can't hit the fire from here."

Sitting on the ground, Santos looked tired. It was the first time he'd been outside in an EMU suit since they'd crashed. "We are so fucked right now."

Paredo rushed from around Thirteen. "Did someone provoke Stevenson? He was normal this morning when he offered those water bottles. No sign of him now."

"Whoever did this knew what they were about." Richter exited *Aloha,* her EMU darkened with soot. "The thruster couplings were crimped and then the thrusters were activated. We are fortunate the entire module didn't explode."

"'Activated'?" Larsen asked. "Without anyone inside knowing?"

Richter regarded everyone coolly. "By remotely hacking our network."

"Where's our drone?" Rachel's entire body felt numb and a painful chill spread through her stomach.

"Over there." Bakir pointed at *Vivaldi.* The drone lay outside it. Smoldering.

"It has been pierced." Larsen leaned over the drone. "A bullet hole?"

"That's impossible," Paredo said. "*Centaurus* wasn't stocked with small arms."

Jemutai ran from around *Aloha.* "I can't reach the fire from there, either. The smoke is coming from the exhaust duct. The only way to put it out is to get inside."

"Stevenson!" Rachel stormed up to Thirteen and yanked on the hatch.

It opened. Smoke billowed out.

"What the hell?" Santos asked.

"Be careful, we don't know what he might do!" Bakir cried.

"I know what I'm going to do." Rachel entered.

Thirteen's interior was filled with the black cloud, but with the hatch opened, enough was sucked out to show her the cause of it: the supply crates Stevenson had hoarded were stacked in the center of the module. They'd been burned to ashes and melted plastic containers. There was little flame left but she called in Jemutai anyway. He put out what remained. Paredo opened the vent releases. After twenty minutes, much of the smoke filtered out of the module.

What remained was a blackened, ash-filled reminder that Rachel had even less control of her situation than she'd thought.

"Stevenson?" Her voice was calm, contrasting the rage within her. Rachel ignored Bakir's chiding look and walked into *Aloha*. "Stevenson…this ends today."

Aloha's cabins were untouched but the main chamber suffered from smoke damage. The rest entered after Jemutai put out the fire and studied what had become their now-permanent home.

"No way *Aloha* can leave this moon now," Larsen said.

"Someone doesn't want us to leave," Rachel said.

"As if anyone could have survived for long in orbit," Bakir said.

"Jemutai, you were on watch," Rachel said. "Did you see anything?"

"Stevenson started shouting over the radio," Jemutai said. "I ran over to Thirteen to see what was wrong. That was when *Aloha* began smoking."

"A diversion?" Larsen asked.

"Why would Jared do that?" Bakir asked.

"Why do you continue defending Stevenson?" Rachel asked.

Bakir gave her an incredulous look. "Have you forgotten the figure we saw on the security cam footage? That is the best explanation. Not Stevenson."

"We need to find him." Rachel led them outside. After ten minutes they still hadn't discovered any trace of him on the mesa or in the camp. No footprints or tracks. She reentered Thirteen to double-check. Nothing useable remained, and it appeared Stevenson hadn't taken much, if anything, with him. The damaged reactor had irradiated the interior as Paredo had predicted. Her dosimeter read 175 millisieverts.

"He must have fled before you knew about the smoke, Bakir," Rachel said. "We'll have to search in a perimeter around the mesa with the rover."

Her boots crunched over a gritty substance.

Sand covered the floor near the module's generator room. Rachel knelt and cleared some of it away. It led to a maintenance hatch inset into the floor.

"You've got to be kidding," Jemutai said. The others gathered round.

Bakir gently pushed past Richter and Paredo. His face fell when he spotted the sand around the floor hatch.

"You don't think…" Bakir faced Rachel, real fear in his eyes.

She swallowed a curt reply and twisted the hatch release. Each *click* made her heart jump, but it opened without incident. What lay beneath it was shocking enough.

"Holy shit," Rachel whispered.

The others came around and stooped with her around the hatch. Where there should have been a few feet of hull and then the planet's surface, there was a deep, dark hole. It was a perfect square, three by three meters wide.

"He dug a hole and escaped?" Richter's tone dripped with disbelief.

Rachel turned on her wrist light. It shone down what she estimated to be a hole twenty meters in depth. At the bottom lay a few discarded food containers. It also appeared that the shaft branched off to the south ten meters down.

"Get me a rope," Rachel said. "The rest of you get away from this radiation."

"Commander?" Paredo gave her a worried look. "Why not use a cam drone?"

"Stevenson just burned whatever Kovac didn't take," Rachel said.

"That is far too deep, and there were no digger bots in Thirteen," Richter said.

"He has to be down there." Rachel didn't want to imagine the alternative. She had to check—not only to find Stevenson, but to ensure her own sanity.

"You have no idea what he might do," Bakir said. "Please be careful."

"Larsen?" Rachel asked. "Get in the rover with Jemutai, drive around, see if you can locate Stevenson. Do not engage with him. Just report back to me. Bakir, see if *Aloha*'s security cam caught anything. Richter, Paredo, wait for me outside."

"I'm not staying in *Aloha* alone!" Santos's shout over the radio made her cringe.

"Fine, go with the others in the rover," Rachel said. "Hold it together, Santos."

"Yeah, right," Santos muttered.

"Driving to you now, Santos," Larsen said.

Everyone did as she asked, and when she was given the rope, Rachel fastened it to a safety hook on the cabin wall. Thus secured, she descended the shaft, hand over hand on the rope, boots braced against the shaft wall. No one spoke over the radio. She wished they would, to hide her shuddering breaths.

Judging from the shaft's square, finely carved sides, something mechanical must have dug the hole. Yet burning the remaining food and water, the supplies, then trying to sabotage *Aloha*...it hinted at an extreme, dangerous paranoia. Bakir was right to be cautious: Stevenson might kill any of them on sight if they followed.

It still didn't explain how he'd created the shaft.

Rachel kept descending. The deeper she went, the more the hard-packed earth beneath the moon's sandy regolith changed. What was simply dirt and sediment gradually became red-and-green stone veined with sparkling blue deposits.

The same as the landscape appeared when she first crashed.

Sure enough, a second tunnel branched off to the south as she'd suspected. It was a meter in height. Stevenson would've had to crawl through. There was a hint of blue light which terminated in a dead end after fifteen meters.

There was no sign of Stevenson as she swept her light over the shaft.

"Larsen, do you see anything out there?" A sudden chill filled Rachel.

"Negative," Larsen said over the radio. "Trying my binocular app in infrared."

The walls shifted around her. A cerulean glow emanated from below.

"Bakir, there's another tunnel down here, but no sign of Stevenson. Maybe he dug—" Rachel gripped the rope and kicked off the shaft wall as vines bored from it.

Each was a pulsating, writhing tentacle. Their clay-like nodules all glowed blue. Beneath her, the shaft walls rippled then opened up to clusters of vines. The mineral veins in the stone flared like burning sapphires. A deep rumble sounded far below.

Rachel struggled back up the rope.

The ground quaked. Pebbles slid down past her. The blue glow blinded her.

"Commander, get out of there!" Bakir's voice was barely audible over the radio.

The vines gripped and slapped at her but Rachel kept ascending. She didn't dare leverage her boots against the shaft walls again. Using a basic wrap and lock technique, she tucked the rope between her knees, looped it beneath her right foot, and pressed down with her left. Rachel's biceps, lats, and deltoids burned as she pulled herself upward.

Every breath became more labored. The nightmare chewed at her psyche.

Suffocating…

With a primal cry she climbed back into Thirteen and kicked the hatch shut.

The quake stopped.

"Bakir?" Rachel caught her breath and made for the exit. "The drone?"

"Like Larsen said, there appears to be a bullet hole in the drone's protective shell," Bakir said, the connection clear again. "Right over where the CPU is located."

An hour later, Rachel stood with all the others in *Aloha*. Everyone had a helmet on, since oxygen was at critical levels and couldn't be spared to fill the module. Stevenson had burned the spare parts for the environmental system along with the food and water he'd stockpiled. At least this way, no one had to smell the ashy stink that surely permeated *Aloha*. It had been cleaned in a rush but soot stains still covered the walls.

Rachel stood in in the center of the main chamber while Bakir checked everyone's vital signs via their suit links. Larsen had found no trace of Stevenson, and *Aloha*'s security cam had been destroyed. The last footage it recorded was of a gloved hand smashing a rock into its lens.

"So we have a week's rations remaining," Rachel said. "We can make that last two weeks if we consume only 1,000 calories a day. The moisture reclamation tanks will allow our water supplies to last as long. But we will have to go easier on the oxygen now. No one leaves their EMU suit. That will preserve a lot."

"Two weeks?" Paredo crossed his arms. "That's it?"

"We're fucked," Santos muttered.

"What about Kovac and his team?" Jemutai asked.

"Not heard from them in two days," Larsen said.

"Do you think Stevenson is allied with them?" Richter asked.

Bakir frowned. "We are not enemies. Why would Kovac do something like this?"

"The same reason he came here and took our specimens and field labs," Santos said. "I say we head over there and make them split their supplies with us."

"That would only worsen our situation," Bakir said. "People might get hurt, even killed, if we take that route."

"I'm not starving while those arrogant assholes eat!" Santos yelled.

"Are you really prepared to start killing each other for supplies that will only prolong your existence here for a few more miserable days?" Bakir cried.

"No, we are not." Rachel stared Santos down. "That's why I'm going to continue seeking the other modules' transponders. If we can locate those that survived the crash, we can salvage supplies from them."

"To what end?" Jemutai asked. "We'll eventually run out of food anyway, no matter how much you find."

Larsen touched Rachel's arm. "Tell them."

"Tell us what?" Paredo asked.

Rachel stared into Larsen's eyes, then sighed. "We transmitted a signal earlier today that Larsen has been piecing together. We received an answer out in the rover. It led to a blue pillar in a basin that resembled the lake we found—"

"For fuck's sake," Santos said.

"Let her speak." Jemutai gave Santos a harsh look.

"*Bimini* was there," Rachel said. "Along with other wrecked starships."

Everyone gaped at her.

"The signal matches the one UEA received on Earth," Larsen said.

"We also found Captain Granger's body bag there—inside *Centaurus*'s cockpit module. Both had been moved to that basin. Both were empty."

She made no mention of Brent. Considering their reactions, Rachel knew that piece of information would only complicate matters. Right now she needed to keep the team together. If that meant omitting things for the moment, so be it.

"What are you saying?" Bakir's voice was ice calm.

"Whoever sent that original signal is claiming our wreckage, our equipment—even our dead," Rachel said. "We need to report this to the UEA, convince Kovac to help us, and try to survive as long as we can."

"Help us with what?" Richter asked. "You saw that drone. The security cam. Those thrusters. If these 'aliens' are hostile, what do we do? We've no weapons!"

"Whoever shot *Aloha*'s drone sure as hell does," Santos said.

"We 3-D print some," Rachel said. "Even if it's only a blade."

"That is the last thing anyone needs right now," Bakir said.

"You got any better ideas?" Santos asked. Bakir rolled his eyes and turned away.

Paredo shrugged. "It might work. Though it'd be much easier—"

"Can you do it or not?" Rachel asked.

Sighing, Paredo uncrossed his arms and nodded. "I'll do my best."

"After we explain this to Kovac and his team, I'm sure they'll help us," Rachel said. "This is for their survival, too, not just ours. We need to drop the 'us vs. them' bullshit. We are still a team. We are still a UEA expedition."

"That also means telling us the truth," Jemutai said.

"What do you mean?" Rachel tried to rein in her annoyance.

"Someone wants this mission to fail," Jemutai said.

Larsen shifted on her feet. Bakir shook his head. Richter studied everyone else. Santos narrowed his eyes at Rachel. Paredo looked from Rachel to Bakir.

"Considering all that's happened to us, I strongly suspect *Centaurus* exploded due to sabotage, not malfunction." Jemutai arched his eyebrows. "And it started right before Granger was going to give us a briefing not even mentioned in the mission parameters."

Rachel stared at her feet. "I also think there might be a connection. Bit by bit, our supplies, living quarters, and now our morale have been either attacked or—"

"You're both grasping at straws," Bakir said.

"Was the person who sabotaged *Aloha* grasping at straws?" Rachel asked. "Besides, you've always cautioned us against taking any action against Stevenson. Why is that? Because you knew he was armed? Did he make a gun and shoot that drone?"

"If he had a gun, I never knew about it," Bakir said as everyone stared at him. "I always pressed for caution because of the delicate situation we are all in. We are supposed to be comrades, not ene-mies. Yet everyone has been seeking an enemy since the first day we crashed onto this world. Someone to blame, someone to hate. I agree, Stevenson and these other phenomena present a danger. Who's to say your style of leadership didn't drive him to this?"

"My leadership?" Rachel glared. "I have been fair with everyone."

"Fair in your disposal of knee-jerk decisions," Bakir said. "You antagonized Stevenson, you alienated Kovac, and you keep making fantastical claims without any evidence, such as that lake and now a pillar."

"I was with her, we are not lying!" Larsen cried.

"We know why you would lie for her," Richter said.

Rachel glowered. "Go in Thirteen and look down into that hatch—"

"I did," Bakir said in a low voice. "While you all cleaned up *Aloha.*"

"And?" Rachel stepped toward him.

"There is a hole, but no shaft," Bakir said. "None of the things you described. No vines, no glowing blue mineral veins—"

"What?" Dizziness overcame Rachel. She leaned on the lab table.

"There is no 'passage' beneath Thirteen," Bakir said. "There was a small quake."

"Where did Stevenson go?" Larsen asked.

"Thirteen's hatch was unlocked," Paredo said. "Perhaps he fled while we all were focused on the fire."

"I know what I saw," Rachel mumbled.

Bakir sighed. "Commander—"

"I know what I saw!" Rachel shouted.

"We are all suffering from sleep deprivation and stress." Bakir's tone was condescending. "You need rest. Perhaps the moon's gravity is having a more adverse effect on your psychological state due to your Martian physiology. It is 0.4 higher—"

"I'm more prepared for this gravity than anyone here—so I know where this is going." Rachel turned in a slow circle, making eye contact with everyone. "Who else feels I'm not equipped to handle this?"

"None of us are." Paredo absently fidgeted with his rosary.

"Bakir disagrees," Rachel said.

Bakir rolled his eyes. "I never said—"

"Who else?" Rachel asked.

"Not me." Larsen moved to Rachel's side.

No one else answered. Some looked away.

"Or is it that none you have the guts to take charge, to accept this responsibility?" Rachel stepped toward Bakir. "It's easy to criticize when you're not making the 'knee-jerk' decisions. Larsen and I risk our lives daily against sinkholes, or getting lost in sandstorms when signal noise disrupts the scanners. All for the chance to find another comrade or a little food. A little hope."

Still no one spoke.

Rachel snorted. "From now on, I'll be staying in the rover to ensure no one steals it while the rest of you sleep. That should keep me out of your way."

"This isn't helping," Bakir said. "Please, we can talk about Thirteen—"

"I know what the hell I saw." She left *Aloha* and leaned against the rover. Smoke continued drifting from Thirteen, fading into the night sky.

Chief Medical Officer's journal. Mission date: Sol 13.

Santos is driving me mad. All he does is complain about what the rest of us are doing, and how he would do it better, if only he wasn't so weak from the surgery and lack of food. I know he wants to do something, rather than feel helpless inside Aloha _all day, but his attitude is making the better side of my nature turn a cold shoulder to him._

I think all of our better natures have died, and we are but the remnant.

Our blood has mutated further. Everyone tries to act too busy for a test, but Terman is always the first to volunteer, shaming the rest into doing it. She says nothing about our argument two days ago. I am embarrassed for her. I wonder if she is mad.

Perhaps we all are at this point.

I do have one blood sample that I dare not tell the others about: Stevenson's.

I discovered the vials hidden under the bunk Stevenson used in Thirteen. He sent me a text the day before the sabotage to Aloha, _telling me he had some vials ready. The DNA doesn't match his sample that is in the UEA database. It has mutated far beyond that. Beyond even that of Santos's. Perhaps this is why he refused to leave Thirteen and show himself. I wonder what Stevenson looks like now, or if he is even alive. He wasn't as crazy as Terman and the others think. I wonder what he knew or saw. What he wasn't telling the rest of us. I still do not believe Terman saw a pit beneath Thirteen._

There has been an earthquake every day. The seismmometer indicates they are hundreds of kilometers away. I have noticed that the electrical noise plaguing us always spikes in strength for the duration of each quake.

Allah prepare me for what is coming. Grant me strength.

This planet is changing us at the cellular level. It has to be more than the radiation. I examined our dwindling food and water supplies. There doesn't seem to be anything out of the ordinary, no extra ingredients that would prove suspect. The oxygen supply, and the scrubbed air we have recycled is also free of foreign agents. I have no hypothesis as to what is causing these mutations.

Last evening, Larsen confronted me about the lake and the pillar. Her sincerity in defending Terman, and trying to convince me of their claims, *was touching. I do not think she is lying, but I wonder at her state of mind. I know my own hangs by a slender thread.*

No one has seen or come into contact with these phenomena again but those two. They are inseparable now. Larsen asked me to ride out with them, but I refused. I cannot abandon my duties here at Aloha, as Terman has apparently done.

Paredo said his nightmares were worse and asked for meds to help him stay awake. I declined, since I am saving those for myself and they are in short supply. I hated to refuse him—I can only imagine what terrorizes his mind at night—but I must remain sane so that I can take care of the rest. If I lose control, then I fear we are all doomed.

I yearn for slumber like one yearns for a lover. Sometimes I stare out Aloha's hatch window at the parked rover where Terman and Larsen sleep. And I hate them for it.

Santos trusts them less each day. They hardly even enter Aloha now, staying in the rover as much as possible. Richter worries they may be setting up stasis pods for themselves at an undisclosed location, and then leave the rest of us to die while they await rescue. Paredo thinks they're hiding something, too. Jemutai talks to no one.

Perhaps I am falling victim to their paranoia.

But I trust my instincts. It is the same thing I would consider, were I in command of a crew who detested me.

Contact with Kovac's team has been sporadic. I managed to receive a few emails from Zentsov after the last storm ended. He remains alone inside Maray while the others have extended their stay in the flatlands. That Russian says they have found something magnificent but won't give details. I didn't tell the others, because why get their hopes up? Until Kovac sees fit to share it with us, I will focus on our more pressing problems.

Zentsov didn't reply when I told him about our latest horrors and Stevenson's disappearance. He also won't say whether he saw that blue lake when he went out with Terman and Larsen. I'm hoping it is the lack of a stable network rather than any coldness on his part. I told him to remain alert and stay safe.

I didn't pray at all yesterday. I rolled out the rug a few times but could not bring myself to kneel on it. Right after my watch started at sunset, I found Paredo with my rug.

He was kneeling and praying on it.

I lost all self-control. Without warning I kicked Paredo off of the rug. While he screamed at me, and the others left their cabins to see what the commotion was, I snatched up the fabric, shook any dirt from it, and proceeded to roll it back up.

Paredo lunged at me but I avoided him. I neared my surgical instruments on the lab table. Like a demon he came at me again, accusing me of heresy. I grabbed a scalpel from the table and brandished it. Before the situation worsened, Jemutai and Santos manhandled Paredo back to his cabin. I kept the scalpel in hand while fumbling with the rug. It had been ripped in the scuffle. After calming down, I wept but could not pray.

Does Allah even answer one's prayers, this far from Earth? I speak blasphemy and do not even fear the consequences. That is what this moon has done to me. I fear the djinn outside as the wind howls at night, as that ugly red sun sets, and stare at pictures of my beautiful Nasreen on my tablet. Her mother sewed that rug for me, utilizing a few strands of my wife's hair. It had been a gift on my wedding day.

I dreamed a little yesterday after I stupidly nodded off while doing the blood tests. Nasreen was coming for me again. She wore a UEA space suit without the helmet. Hair blowing in the breeze of this horrendous world. A smile rivaling any sunrise.

She showed me a crashed ship on a crystalline azure lake. One not of Earth.

I know it cannot be her. I know it is merely my subconscious playing tricks on me. Terman's mention of derelicts and that cursed lake planted this nonsense in my mind. It is a phantom of my psyche. Nothing more. Yet I kept recalling a passage of Rumi's:

**I have lived on the lip
of insanity, wanting to know reasons
knocking on a door. It opens.**

Personal journal, Mission Specialist Li. Mission date: Sol 13.

I saw Kovac and Sakurai fucking in the rover again.

I didn't say anything. They didn't see me, anyway. I was climbing out of the new pit our digger bot excavated. I must have been down there longer than I'd thought, because he had her bent over the front seat, banging her like there was no tomorrow.

That might have been true yesterday, but not now. Not after what I've found.

Right above the structure's metal surface, the bot had stopped working. I checked the diagnostics, ran a troubleshooting check, and finally had to clamber down into the hole and examine the damn thing. The rappel cords are stout, and I'm an experienced climber, but the sand was loose. So my unlucky ass fell. I landed in a sand drift from the last storm. Four meters down and I don't think I was even bruised.

I started to radio Kovac so they'd know I wasn't dead.

The bot had stopped, yes—right above a clump of what looked like more of those vines. As I crawled closer, I realized I was wrong.

My breath caught. I remember it, because shit like that never happens to me. But this actually took my breath. I stared at it for a while; I'm not sure how long. No wonder Kovac and Sakurai had time to get it on. An eternity might have passed, and I'd not have been the wiser for it.

The object was the size of a helmet. Round and hard as steel. But it was light. I had picked it up before I even realized it. Breaking all scientific protocols like a rookie.

It was dark blue in hue with golden tints, and it gleamed like metal. It resembled a cluster of the vines Zentsov has fallen in love with back at Seeker. Glad he wasn't there with me at the dig site, or he'd have lost his shit over something like this.

I stuffed it into my field bag and sealed it. After I climbed out of the pit, I headed for the rover. Saw them fucking, walked back to the pit so they could finish. I wasn't about to interrupt them. Besides, what I had was far more important than a piece of ass.

It did make me wonder at how they felt about each other. How that could present problems in the future since we're running low on supplies. They'd *favor each other over the rest of us. Over the mission. I had to keep that in mind.*

When I came back, they were suited up. Exiting the rover, trying not to look at each other. I didn't bother hiding my smile. I showed Kovac the field bag and he stopped dead in his tracks. Like he was afraid for a moment. Then he snatched it from me, peered inside, and whooped for joy. We cheered and danced around the rover like primitives from our ancient past. After we calmed down, Kovac asked me a thousand questions, maybe four of which I was able to answer. We immediately started the digger bot again.

That was when sparks flew from the bot. It stopped. Smoke rose from it. Fucking hell.

We climbed back down into the pit and checked the bot. Its system was fried. I removed the maintenance cover. The little bastard's circuits had melted together.

Having the blue object in hand, Kovac wanted to go back to Seeker *and examine it. Since the bot was ruined, I saw no reason to disagree, but worried about another sandstorm erasing the progress we'd made. But Kovac and Sakurai were far more interested in the object—and each other—than in anything I had to say. I get it, this was a big discovery. But I felt left out. Kovac took all the credit. Like he knew it was there.*

Back at Seeker, *Zentsov told us that Terman's camp had experienced a fire. Then some craziness about a crew member running off into the wastes, but we simply nodded and showed him the object. Being a scientist, of course he forgot about the other camp's drama. We cleared off the lab table and lay the object on it. Then we just stood there, silently staring at the thing.*

In Seeker's *better lighting, I realized it had an organic look, with tubes snaking across it. Corded like the vines we'd found on this moon.*

Sakurai said it looked like a coiled snake. Grinning, Kovac said we could dub it draco centaurus. *I like it.*

Zentsov wanted to seal it up and run tests. Only then did I pay attention to his appearance. His IVA suit was stained with food and…other things. He'd not shaved. His eyes were bloodshot and he stunk. And he never moved far from the vine specimens.

We all agreed with him. Soon we were bent over the lab computer screen as Kovac keyed in commands. Draco lay in the sample area, closed off and vacuum-sealed. A battery of tests showed that it wasn't metal or even mineral.

Zentsov asked if it was organic and licked his lips.

Leaning back in the lab chair, Kovac reported it was emanating a form of energy the lab couldn't identify. Not radiation or electrical.

Sakurai half-joked it could be one of the "aliens."

We all looked at each other.

Zentsov read the results. There were no signs of respiration or heartbeat but there was cellular activity: a strange mixture of eukaryotic and prokaryotic cells. Within those, the lysosomes, mitochondria, and Golgi apparatus appeared…artificial. Mechanical.

My suggestion that it was biomechanical was met with silence, since no one could really answer it. It made them uncomfortable.

We tried to use a nano blade to skim a piece of material off the artifact's surface. To our shock, it snapped the blade. We replaced it, tried again. The same thing happened. I've never seen or heard of anything, not even diamonds, resisting the tiny blade's edge.

X-rays revealed a very fine interior structure akin to bird's bones. There were various chambers inside, perhaps organs of some sort. Even Zentsov, an astrobiologist, wasn't sure what to make of them.

Zentsov demanded we radio Commander Terman about our find. I hated to admit it, but he was right. This was just too fucking big.

Kovac slowly backed from the screen and shook his head. Saying it was best we keep it to ourselves for the moment. Something in his eyes, his tone, pissed me off.

I said the discovery might even get Terman to see the big picture and create unity between our camps. Take everyone's minds off of surviving this hellish place for a while.

Kovac gave me that condescending smirk. He said it might cause the saboteur from Terman's camp to come here and steal our prize. Or worse, destroy it. Said it needs to remain a secret until we know who our friends are on this planet.

Sakurai grudgingly agreed and studied her field lab.

I mean, I was shocked. Sure, Terman's annoying, but she did find survivors from Luzinia. Even I can't be smart-ass about that. But Kovac wouldn't budge on the subject.

I cleared my throat and asked Zentsov if he'd seen any sign of Burgess.

Retrieving a bottle of water from the galley, Kovac snorted and said we all know that she is dead by now. She didn't have a week's worth of oxygen in her suit, after all.

Red-faced, Zentsov asked why he was so callous. I was getting angry, too.

Kovac said he was being realistic. We haven't seen her anywhere for several kilometers. By now, the storms would have already covered her body with sand.

Zentsov got all huffy and went to his cabin, but I didn't back down. Then Kovac got all smarmy. Saying now we'd found something that justified our coming here. Draco was a different life-form, not just vines in sinkholes, but something else. And he claimed that the metal object buried beneath it was connected to it somehow.

I said it might be a starship. The tests I ran on that flake of metal hinted at it.

He mulled that over and sipped some water. Said it's not a bad idea, then went into his cabin. By then, Sakurai sat slumped at her field lab. Said nothing made any sense.

I asked why. She'd been obsessing over her soil samples for days.

Sakurai measured me with narrowed eyes, then sighed and told me. The soil samples she'd taken from the dig site showed metallic contamination. Minerals we hadn't come across on this miserable asshole of a moon so far.

I said they could have been meteorites, or even ejecta from Proxima B itself.

Sakurai regarded me with annoyance; she'd obviously had this argument with Kovac. Her data showed that the samples contained refined minerals. Not the sort of thing one finds in meteors, comets, or asteroids.

I asked her if she also thought a ship had crashed here.

She simply stared back at me.

Then I asked her to coax Kovac into telling the other camp about the artifact. Oh, did she get mad. Told me that she wasn't his plaything and I should mind my business.

We played cards and chess the rest of the evening. Zentsov, who usually destroys me at chess, was so off his game that I captured both of his bishops before he even knew what was going on. All he could do was keep staring at the artifact and the vines.

Kovac and Sakurai snuggled in her cabin to watch some Japanese comedy film in her personal data cache. I left them alone and paced around the main chamber. Like Zentsov, though, I couldn't stop looking at the artifact. I studied the object's contours, how it sparkled as if it had been forged for some ancient dynasty.

Holy fuck.

As I stared at it, it looked a little different. I knew it hadn't moved—the lab had a motion sensor and we'd have heard the alarm if anything had happened—but it still looked like it had been…I don't know. Rearranged. Hell, I was tired. I needed sleep.

I went to my cabin. Kovac and Sakurai were still watching that stupid movie. I dreaded sleep, since we'd all been having weird nightmares. Nothing major, but after Zentsov reported that Terman's bunch were having bad ones, too, I worried that we might have contracted something on the moon that affected our sleeping patterns.

Maybe it was the six-hour day, six-hour night cycles. My circadian rhythms were playing a different beat I guess. Plus, I hated that nightmare I'd been having: digging my own parents from the excavation site. It's got to be the stress and excitement.

Regardless, that night I slept great. At first.

I heard a clatter. I opened my cabin's hatch as the sample cartons fell off the lab table. Rubbing my eyes, I yawned. Said something to Zentsov, whose cabin was open. I figured he was up screwing around. Son of bitch probably woke me up for nothing.

He called my name in a feeble voice, like a frightened old geezer.

I asked what he wanted and started to go back into my cabin.

Until I spotted a vine slithering off of the lab table.

Zentsov cried out and hid behind a chair, but I stood still and watched. The vine writhed back and forth as if it were searching for something. Then it crawled up the wall and wrapped around the base of the ceiling's light fixture. There it coiled tight, pulsating.

Terrified, Zentsov said we must contain it.

I said it might be communicating. Either with us, or the artifact. I reminded him of how the other one absorbed power from that battery. I felt like we were in no danger. Scientists don't cower behind chairs and cast knowledge back into the shadows. We'd come here to bring such things to light.

Zentsov cursed in Russian and suggested this was what drove Burgess away.

I have to admit, that bothered me. Burgess had guts. So I waited.

After a few minutes the vine stopped pulsing. Zentsov calmed a little, but I could tell he wanted nothing to do with the thing. I took video and still images while making sure the lab computer was recording any changes in the artifact. Zentsov should have helped, but he ran back to his cabin and locked the hatch. What a fucking wimp.

The vine stopped pulsing around the light fixture but stayed there. The other vines had slid over to the receptacle containing the artifact. A strong bleach-like scent made me take shallow breaths. Enough was enough. Progress takes courage.

When I sat back down at the lab computer, I discovered that the artifact's appearance had shifted again. I wasn't crazy after all. There had to be some sort of link between it and the vines. Let Kovac get his dick wet and claim all the glory, let Zentsov hide in his room. I'm going to find out what this thing really is.

18

While Larsen went into *Aloha* to replenish their food supplies, Rachel leaned against the rover. The moon's twelve-hour day still disrupted her circadian rhythms. She'd not felt so fatigued since her first Earth trip. It didn't help that she and Larsen had spent yet another day without finding any survivors. The time had come to face facts.

They were the only crew members who'd made it. The ones who would perish much more slowly and painfully. But they were still picking up transponder signals.

Like the moon was teasing them.

Jemutai passed her on his way to *Aloha*, quiet as usual, finishing his watch shift. He made eye contact for a second but kept walking.

"Hey," Rachel said over the radio.

Though he stopped, Jemutai stared off across the mesa. "Commander."

Rachel walked over to him. "See anything interesting out there?"

He squinted at the setting sun. "This place is unnatural."

"How so?"

Jemutai started toward *Aloha*.

"Please." Rachel touched his arm.

"Why?"

"I know why you keep to yourself. Why you stay out here."

Jemutai faced her. Some of his detached reserve faded.

"It's the nightmares, isn't it?" Rachel asked. "Mine are horrible, too."

"You will say I'm losing my sanity," Jemutai said.

Rachel snorted. "I've seen a blue lake, remember? Tell me."

Crouching, he once again gazed at the wastelands around them. "I see my father. In my dreams, and out here. He still wears the UEA suit he died in."

"Wow, I didn't know your father was an astronaut," Rachel sad. "My dad was a farmer his whole life. Growing crusty plants in bio domes."

He studied her with narrowed eyes. "There is honor and sincerity in the soil."

"Wish I'd told him that," Rachel murmured. Jemutai nodded and smiled.

"Our surnames are different, due to my mother divorcing him. I did not want the celebrity attached to him. I wanted to make this journey without promotion."

"Do you know what he wants?" She crouched beside him, keen on every word.

Jemutai took a handful of sand and studied the grains. "He wants me to go with him. I cannot, since he wears no helmet. Are you getting me? I know it isn't him."

"You think it's those who sent the message to Earth?"

"This moon…it is unnatural." Jemutai dumped the sand onto the ground. "I showed Bakir my soil tests, but I don't think he relayed them to Kovac's camp."

"What were the results?" Rachel asked.

"It has trace amounts of carbon, hydrogen, nitrogen, oxygen, sulfur, and phosphorus. There is silica, sandstone, and feldspar, which sand is typically made of. The sizes aren't unusual: 0.2 to 1 millimeter, fine to coarse. But these other elements? Atypical."

"I thought the UEA's instruments showed the soil was the most accommodating they'd ever seen on an observed exoplanet?" Rachel asked.

Jemutai grinned. "So you do know your stuff. I would love to study the regolith of your homeworld someday. But yes. Accommodating indeed. Isn't it?"

Rachel frowned. "You're saying it's too perfect?"

He tapped a finger on her faceplate. "Exactly. These are the basic elements required for life as we know it back on Earth."

"You're not a believer in coincidences, are you?"

"No more than I believe that is my late father out there." He scowled at the desert.

"I wonder what Commander Granger knew. What he was going to tell us."

He raised his brows. "I wonder who wanted to keep it from the rest of us."

Though she loathed entertaining such paranoia, Rachel sensed Jemutai was correct. Mentally she ticked off suspects: Stevenson, Li, Kovac. Then she realized that she'd had negative interactions with all three. Finding the truth required objectivity, which the moon and all its hardships had drained from her.

Rachel stood and offered a hand. "Will you tell me if you see anything else?"

He took it and rose. "Yes. Though I fear when I do, it will be too late."

The next day Rachel drove the rover between two ridges north of their camp after Larsen had detected radio activity in the area. They'd ventured this far only twice; now she just wanted to get away from the depressing situation back at *Aloha.*

It'd been fifteen days since *Centaurus*'s explosion. Everything had fallen apart in such a short time. Their expedition had been prepared for a six-month stay, possible colonization. Now those plans seemed the dreams of a madman.

"There's more sinkholes out here than there were yesterday," Rachel said.

"Yes," Larsen said absently, checking their oxygen supply for the third time that morning. She'd not spoken much the past two days. Last night she had cried out Rachel's name during a nightmare. The fear in it still made Rachel feel cold all over.

Maybe she wanted too much. She should put those ideas out of her mind and focus on the mission. But ever since Larsen started sleeping with her in the rover, both of them suited up and ready to go at a moment's notice, Rachel had found it difficult.

It was even more difficult to forget the last time she'd cared so much for another.

The apartment was a prison of bare austerity after Rachel's last girlfriend moved out. The walls were empty of picture frames and holos. The couch was gone, as well as the kitchen table and chairs. Rachel stared at the emptiness, arms crossed as much to warm the chill within her as to embrace herself. No one else would do either for her now.

Growing up on Mars had been a utilitarian experience. No one moved furniture around there like they did here on Earth. It was another level of possessiveness. Rachel had liked it at first, for she had possessed someone else as they had her. Like she could finally give and take without fear. Without boundaries.

Rachel had been in some of those pictures. Those holos. Had helped pay for that rare walnut table. Taking them had stripped away a part of her she never realized could be taken away. It wasn't the material items themselves.

It was a reminder that she was no longer part of someone else's world.

The rover shook and slid to the left.

"Huh?" Rachel jumped.

Its wheels spun so fast they spat sand into the air. The vehicle dipped left thirty degrees. Larsen braced herself and gaped at Rachel.

They'd hit a sinkhole while she'd been daydreaming.

"Shit." Rachel checked her door. If she opened it, she would unbalance the vehicle and send them into the opening, which had grown larger in the last second. Sand and stones slid into it at an alarming rate.

"Do not move!" Larsen opened her door, leaned out on the safety step, and shook the rover by gripping the railing on the roof. The vehicle titled to a sixty-degree angle.

"It's getting bigger!" Rachel gaped as the sinkhole spread apart like the maw of an antediluvian creature. Light reflected off the sand grains spilling into it, which in turn gave her a glimpse of a curved surface. Something blue and engorged, coming out.

"When I press down, accelerate!" Larsen shouted over the radio.

But the wheels continued spinning, creating a rut. The rover leaned over worse than before. Sand splashed up against the window on Rachel's door.

"It's not working!" Rachel laid off the accelerator and tried the rover's gyro system. Usually, it could force the vehicle to right itself, but this time it simply sank into the sand.

Another sinkhole opened behind them.

"Get out of there!" Larsen offered her hand.

Rachel stretched and reached out. Larsen was too far away.

She couldn't breathe. The rover's display console lit up red with warnings as the wheels spun faster, grinding the axle. She tried the gyro again, but the movement caused Larsen to lose her footing and slip off of the rover. She hit the ground, screaming Rachel's name.

Others had screamed for her, too. Screamed in vain.

"Rachel!" Mom yelled, holding her hand in the emergency room.

The pills Rachel had taken made her mother look like a fleshy blur. Her voice sounded sluggish as it bombarded her ears.

"Rachel, please, don't give up."

A doctor motioned another nurse over. "We have an overdose victim here!"

It had been so easy after that last breakup. The pills hadn't even tasted bad.

"Rachel, stop doing this to yourself." Dad sobbed, then contained himself. "Please, honey. You are not alone."

The rover tilted further. Putting Rachel closer to the sinkhole.

"Rachel? Just stop."

Push. Must push her way out of it. Push out, thrust, escape. Live.

Dad's and Larsen's voices blended in her mind. Calling her name.

"Rachel!"

Thrust.

Rachel turned in the seat, slammed the rover door release, and activated her suit's thrust jets. The concentrated air, though not as effective planetside as it would be in vacuum, still pushed the vehicle over enough. Rachel slammed the accelerator at the same time, allowing her to drive away from the holes. The rover sputtered, teetered as one side struck the ground then the other, and finally fell still.

She remembered how to breathe as she reached for the open driver's side door, her gloved hand an infinity away from stabilizing herself.

"Rachel? Herregud!"

That beautiful voice in her earbud gave life back to Rachel's reality. She sucked in air so hard her chest hurt. She coughed and slumped in the driver's seat. Dizziness made her swoon. A rainbow of lights crackled and melted in her vision.

"Hey."

Rachel coughed again, blinked.

"Hey!"

"What?" Rachel scrambled up in the seat, then stopped as her faceplate banged into Larsen's. Larsen leaned over her, adjusting Rachel's oxygen supply manually. Boosting the oxygen content, getting it into her lungs and brain. Rachel gripped Larsen's arm while the air filled her, afraid that if she let go, the sinkhole might still claim her.

Coming all the way out here to Proxima Centauri, she was supposed to know what she wanted by now. Dad had warned her that nothing would be different. That she couldn't run from her problems. As she stared out the windshield at the desert moon, she was no closer to that knowledge than if she had remained on Earth. A billion light-years she might travel, and she doubted she would find it even then.

"Hey," Larsen whispered, clasping Rachel's hand. "I have you, *kjære*."

"Shit." Rachel leaned over the console.

Larsen laughed. "Quick thinking. Thought I had lost you."

"I'm not going anywhere," Rachel murmured, exhaustion deflating her adrenaline rush. "Who will pester Bakir and the rest?"

Larsen reached across her and shut the driver's door, then shut her own door. "I am glad. I would have jumped in after you."

Rachel glanced at her. Saw the look she hungered for, but started the rover. "We'd better head back, fix our mapping. Try another route to that signal."

She drove around the ridge to their right, heading west. As she gripped the wheel, it was hard not to look at Larsen. Hard not to acknowledge the undercurrent in her words. If she gave in to it, she would endanger not only herself, but all the others. A leader couldn't develop emotional ties to those under her command. She would place Larsen above the others in importance. Favoritism, petty discretions, and greedy risks would follow. That would betray her training, her crew. Herself.

"There is a problem with the oxygen," Larsen said.

"What is it?" Rachel still didn't face her.

Larsen activated the rover's life support. Oxygen gushed into the compartment.

"What are you doing?" Rachel stopped driving and reached for the off button.

Larsen's jaw firmed, then she removed her helmet.

"No, wait!" Rachel was on top of her, trying to put the helmet back on, but Larsen let it drop to the floor. She inhaled slowly. The compartment was safe.

"Are you crazy?" Rachel sat back down and wrenched her own helmet off. "We can't waste air like this!"

Larsen stared at Rachel for a long moment. "Who is wasting it?"

Their inhalations were the only sounds as Rachel gazed at her, bewildered. Larsen started removing her gloves, but Rachel yanked her own off, straddled Larsen's lap, and cupped her face.

"Why haven't you been talking to me?" Rachel whispered.

"You have been in my dreams." Larsen gripped Rachel's thighs. "Grandpapa dragged you into Nærøyfjord. Could not stop him. I tried, Rachel!"

She smoothed Larsen's blond locks. "Vanja…I'm right here." She swallowed.

"You almost died back there." Larsen held Rachel tighter. "Like my nightmare, I could not help you."

"I'm sick of being afraid," Rachel said.

Larsen wiped Rachel's cheeks. "Me, too."

Rachel licked her lips. Her body was electrified with need.

Larsen pulled her down closer.

She kissed Larsen hungrily, demanding everything from her. In contrast, her fingers traced tender circles on Larsen's face. Then down her neck. Then her breasts.

Larsen returned the passion in kind, just as voracious. Just as daring.

They removed their suits. Their inhibitions.

The dashboard lights reflected off Larsen's smooth skin, gleamed in her eyes. Her fingers slid across Rachel's stomach, thighs. Gently prying at her crotch.

Spreading her legs, Rachel helped Larsen find what she was looking for. She moaned louder and louder as Larsen rubbed circles of ever-deepening pressure. The fire of her orgasm, the pungent scent of its wet-hot gush, sent Rachel into a frenzy.

"Lie down." Rachel kissed her. "I'm not waiting anymore."

Shaking with excitement, Larsen obeyed.

Rachel tugged off Larsen's underwear and tasted paradise.

They kissed and touched for a half hour afterward. Promising each other things they knew they couldn't make come true. Not as long as the moon held them prisoner.

But in that moment, Rachel felt complete for the first time in her life.

Etana parks her rover behind the ridge north of Terman's camp and opens her binocular app. Terman herself and that Norwegian linguist have left on yet another excursion. Their rover should be Etana's next target. She senses that tensions within the camp are near a breaking point, and keeping them all boxed in will make her job easier.

Stevenson's madness has served her mission well. What he has done with the fuel cell from Thirteen is beyond her. The fool destroyed much of their supplies, raising the level of paranoia among the survivors. Though they remain alert and on edge, they are also getting little real rest.

Like herself.

She is having nightmares each night. Every time Etana sees that jungle outside Calabar, near the border with Cameroon. Cutting that little boy's throat before he could give away her position to the rival mercenaries. He'd begged her not to. Promised he'd be quiet. But snitching on patrols for money was common. She could still hear his gurgling, still feel his hot blood splashing her cheek. Staining the blue lake beneath her feet.

There never was a lake like that, of course. Only in the dream.

None had ever discovered her deed. One among many. She is a silencer of men and women, of boys and girls. Of kingdoms and governments, politicians and scientists.

Shooting the drone was more for the erosion of morale than to sever communication with the other camp. But *Aloha*'s thrusters had to be rendered useless. Etana will not risk anyone departing the surface. If even one crew member survives, she will have failed. She has done the same to all the other modules she's found.

But her mission is stalled. This moon tricks her.

Yesterday she sat trapped in a windstorm. After it ended, the landscape was changed. Dunes were replaced with stony buttes and deep fissures, as if she'd been transported to another region. None of her rover's scanners work now. Etana spent hours simply finding the mesa again. It has altered its shape. Nothing is the same on the moon.

The same goes for her mission.

Stevenson fled Thirteen after she sabotaged *Aloha*. She had been waiting, pistol aimed, hiding behind *Vivaldi*'s burned-out shell. Then a sinkhole engulfed him. Etana glimpsed the look on his face as the opening claimed him. It wasn't one of fear.

It was relief.

The sinkholes have tried to take her, too. The last two nights she parked the rover atop rocky ridges to avoid the treacherous chasms. After dark she has spotted diffuse blue glows over the horizon. Flaring in brightness and vanishing. An earthquake caused her to crash into a stone arch two days ago. Two of the rover's six wheels don't work now.

Her next move will be tonight, before anything else happens.

As her binocular app closes, a blue gleam appears in her peripheral vision.

Etana spins around, pistol in hand.

The area behind her rover is now coated in a glass-like azure surface.

The blue lake from her dream.

Brent stands in the center of it. Not wearing a helmet. His pristine IVA suit looks as if it was just pulled from his locker. His visage is kind, appeasing. The eyes lack humanity. Both of his hands are wriggling vines.

Etana aims the pistol at him. Tries to control her nervous breaths. She has heard of these vines, and of Brent's appearance, by listening to the radio chatter from both camps. It all seemed like the rantings of overtaxed astronauts going mad. Not now. It confirms her employers' fears of what the aliens on the moon would do to humans.

She will not allow her people to be enslaved a second time. Colonizers, whether alien or European, economic or religious, will never own what she has sacrificed to save.

"You should go."

The language is Ibibio. It is one of the many tribal dialects she learned in Nigeria.

"Please," a familiar voice says from behind her. "Go."

Etana half turns, trying to keep both Brent and the one behind her in sight. Environmental readings change on her HUD, but she ignores them.

The boy from Calabar stands a few meters behind her. His neck is whole, uncut.

"Please go with him." The boy's voice comes over her earbuds—though he is neither equipped with a radio, nor does he wear a suit and helmet.

Etana takes a deep breath. Taps her wrist pad for a Modafinil injection to help her focus. None of it makes the boy disappear, nor Brent and the lake to vanish.

"Please," the boy says. "This is why you were asked to come here."

Her HUD indicates that the atmosphere has changed. More nitrogen and oxygen. The dosimeter shows radiation exposure down to the single digits.

"You will be comfortable. You will be whole." The boy smiles.

Etana backs toward her rover. Sinkholes open across the landscape.

Movement on her right. Brent is gone. The lake gleams brighter.

"Go." The boy is right there beside her. Reaching for her.

She fires the gun. But the boy is gone.

Etana wheels about. Scans the landscape. No lake. Breathing so fast her lungs hurt. Sweat glides down her cheek. She aims at rocks, shadows cast by dwarf buttes.

There is nothing but her fear.

The dry, dead silence makes her hurry into the rover. Slams the door. Takes off her helmet. Stares at her shaking hands. Touches her face.

It is not sweat. It is a tear.

Chief Medical Officer's journal. Mission date: Sol 15.

I didn't eat my rations today.

This moon, my situation, and those around me, all rob me of appetite. I can't seem to get enough water, and have imbibed double my ration for the last two days. I hope Terman doesn't find out because it is her ration I have been stealing from.

Yes, I am committing a sin. A crime. A form of mutiny, perhaps even murder, since I am ultimately depriving our commander of what is due to her to survive.

What is survival now but delaying the inevitable?

Paredo has taken to blessing Aloha _every day now, which grows insulting. His Latin prayers are slaps to my face after his desecration of my prayer rug. I feel he is doing this to demonstrate some sort of dominance. I find it petty and unlike him. He is not even a priest! He counts his rosary aloud now. It is never out of his grasp._

Santos busies himself with finding gossip on the rest of us. When he's not arguing with someone, that is. I've been tempted to leave him locked outside, since he can never remember the hatch code. Terman has started ignoring his questions—meant more to start an argument than to learn anything— which simply angers him more. Richter threatened to kill him after she caught him masturbating in her cabin—while she slept. He's also taken to soiling his MAGs multiple times without changing them.

At first, Richter was a great help. Her engineering expertise helped us repair Aloha _and she has the endurance of a horse. But she's angry that Terman and Larsen stay away in the rover all of the time. I think she wants to get out and explore, too, but her paranoia grows. She claims they have supplies stashed elsewhere while we starve. That they are filthy people who must have murdered Stevenson and Burgess._

Someone 3-D printed a few blades like Terman suggested, then wrecked the printer beyond repair. I suspect it was Richter. She watches our every move like a killer.

Jemutai is faring better than the rest of us. Perhaps that is based on his training in the Kalahari, Gobi, and Sahara. Unlike the others, he never offers an opinion on anything, and is always the first to go outside, the last to come back in. Though what he does on foot, I've no idea. He has supplied *much data about the soil, weather, and a possible water table—though we've not seen any rain since our arrival. I envy his calm.*

I did finally receive a radio message from Zentsov. He sounded frightened. Crazed, even. He told me they were coming and there was nothing any of us could do. Then something about Li releasing an abomination, and the connection died. I have kept this to myself. What is a warning from one lunatic to another? We are all growing mad.

I am running low on Modafinil. I think the others grow suspicious of how I am able to remain awake while they sleep. Their suit links show me their nocturnal distress, their troubled mutterings. Their screams and sobs. But they simply do not comprehend the terror I face each night. As the doctor I must ensure my own survival or we all die.

In my last dream, Nasreen was waiting for me inside Aloha *itself. She was naked save for one of those vines wrapped around her waist. I tried to cover her, but each time, instead of hiding her shame, I pushed her into a lake of shimmering beauty. She sinks into it. Dragging me down with her. Suffocating until I scream myself awake.*

More than once I've glanced at my morphine stock since then. I have been saving it for myself, I will now admit. The others communicate on their private frequencies, leaving me out of all conversation. Someone has eaten my remaining food.

I must ponder my options.

Flight Recorder – *Maray* Crew Module
Sol 15 – 0925 hours
Orbiting Proxima Centauri C

CFE Moore: Fuck this. We're losing altitude by the hour.

CMP Worrel: I'm sick of your attitude. Once we stop showing respect for each other, the whole bloody mission will—

CFE Moore: By the fucking hour, Andrew! You want *Maray* to go into reentry while we're asleep?

CMP Worrel: That's why we take shifts.

CFE Moore: Sure, those of us who can sleep.

CMP Worrel: We can't use the thrusters yet. Not until our orbit deteriorates further. Even then, it's a fair chance that we'll crash. *Maray* wasn't built to operate long-term without support of *Centaurus.*

MS Khandaar: You're an idiot.

CMP Worrel: Cut the rubbish. We use that fuel now, then we're guaranteed a shit landing. If we wait until this module begins reentry—we might have a chance.

MS Khandaar: That's no—

CMP Worrel: Do the calculations. You know I'm right.

CFE Moore: We've been up here for two weeks now. We've seen two, maybe three camps established below by other survivors. We've seen modules catch fire, and, if Khandaar is right, we've spotted corpses left out in the goddamn desert. If we wait much longer… sir…there won't anything down there to reunite with. And we're starving.

CMP Worrel: You think I don't know this? You think I enjoy floating up here, listening to you both constantly berating me, eating bloody NF rations? Should I sleep with one eye open now, fearing a disconnect in my sleep?

CFE Moore: Are you shitting me?

MS Khandaar: (groans, mutters)

CMP Worrel: I've seen you, Kevin, checking the oxygen supply every other hour.

CFE Moore: How dare you—

MS Khandaar: Shut up. The aft camera just picked up an explosion down below.

CMP Worrel: Where?

MS Khandaar: That large dig site. Look, after I zoomed in. There's a small fire.

CMP Worrel: Is that a rover?

MS Khandaar: Oh God.

CFE Moore: Who the hell keeps destroying things down there?

MS Khandaar: This is crazy.

CMP Worrel: We don't have enough information to make snap judgments.

MS Khandaar: This is just so crazy.

CFE Moore: Not enough information? Did you not see those photos Khandaar snapped of those two bodies near *Persepolis*? It looked like—

CMP Worrel: I know what it looked like.

MS Khandaar: So crazy…

CFE Moore: It looked like they were murdered, Andrew. Murdered.

CMP Worrel: (sigh) I'm as worried as you are. But—

CFE Moore: Fucking murdered!

CMP Worrel: The bloody hell you want me to do about it? Even if we land, we might be next!

MS Khandaar: What about that object?

CFE Moore: Yeah, honey. That blue object that keeps turning up on the cameras. Funny how the damned thing shows up whenever calamity strikes on the moon below, huh? Is it the same one you got all dreamy about?

CMP Worrel: I don't…What are you saying?

MS Khandaar: Do you know something we don't, sir?

CMP Worrel: Don't be absurd.

CFE Moore: Us staying up here, that's what absurd.

CMP Worrel: Stop blaming me like everything's my fault.

CFE Moore: Then do something!

MS Khandaar: Oh my God.

CMP Worrel: What is it?

MS Khandaar: Portside camera just caught a flare down below!

CFE Moore: No shit?

CMP Worrel: Location?

MS Khandaar: Northeast of that mesa. Where that last quake opened the ground.

Personal journal, Mission Specialist Li. Mission date: Sol 15.

Our rover blew up as soon as we reached the dig site.

We are lucky to be alive.

When it happened, my helmet's aural sensors almost fried my brain with the explosion's noise. A second later I heard Kovac and Sakurai cry out over the radio.

The force of it knocked me into the excavation pit. My elbow cracked on the buried object. The bone was broken, my HUD said. I managed to climb out. Sakurai just crumpled to the ground, clasping her right knee. Shrapnel from the blast had slammed into her without piercing her suit. Kovac was unscathed, save for his temper.

Here we were, thirty kilometers from our module with no vehicle. Our EMU suits had three hours of oxygen, max. Two of us were injured. We were good as dead.

Kovac kicked at the sand, cursed in three different languages. I was angry, too. It had to be an act of sabotage. The rover had never overheated or broken down. It was built to withstand pyroclastic flows from a volcano, and survived multiple tests across Antarctica, the Sahara, and Mars. No way in hell this was an accident.

The perpetrator's identity? That motherfucker Zentsov.

He'd been the one afraid to leave Seeker. _Afraid of the vine specimens. Acting all crazy. Plus, he never sleeps, so he could've rigged the vehicle to blow while we slept._

Kovac wouldn't listen to me. He got on the radio and argued with Bakir for five minutes, cursing, accusing, demanding. The doctor finally cut the connection, which only pissed Kovac off more. I suggested we get moving back to Seeker _as soon as possible. If Terman really gave a shit about the crew, she'd come out here in her rover and save us._

Sakurai said nothing the whole time. Just kept staring at the excavation pit.

After stomping around the site for a minute or two, Kovac finally listened to me and hailed Zentsov on the radio. There were no storms. A clear day. Good reception.

But no answer.

Something changed in me after that. The disappearance of Burgess still bothered me, and the laziness in Terman's camp pissed me off severe, but once Zentsov didn't reply, I'd had it. It finally sank in, I guess. We were really going to die on this moon.

Now, Kovac…I never saw him joke or smile again. At least he became more focused, which I didn't think was possible. Like a razor getting even sharper.

Kovac found the remains of the tool carriage in the rover's smoldering ruin. There wasn't much left, but four entrenching tools had survived.

He wanted us to dig up the object.

Sakurai and I shared a glance. She was lame and I was essentially one-armed.

Glaring at us, Kovac shoved the tools into our grasp. Said it was an order.

There was nothing else to do. So we dug.

Shoveling like a madman, Kovac refused to rest. His grunts and gasps over the radio were the only sounds between us. I did the best I could with my left arm while Sakurai cleaned away the object's edges. After twenty minutes my broken elbow hurt so bad that I cried out and had to stop. I had my suit inject me with mild painkillers. The recent windstorms had covered much of the digger bot's work. By noon, though, my shovel finally struck the metal surface.

There was a dull, hollow echo underneath us. We all looked at each other.

Kovac also struck the surface. The same echo resulted.

Too excited to stop, we pushed aside the last swaths of sand by hand. It felt visceral, like we were about to touch the face of God or something. Despite all the shit that had happened, despite how we'd treated one another, we all smiled at that moment. I think it might have been the happiest moment of my life.

The next moment will no doubt scar me for the rest of it.

My glove revealed what we had been digging for. It was dull gray metal. The more we uncovered, the more became apparent: black and brown burn marks, scarring from reentry. A few bolts that had fused inside their holes along the hull. Tight weld seams hinted it had been crafted in a vacuum rather than a terrestrial environment.

But that color…that fucking gray-white hull…

Kovac whispered in Croatian, nodding. Sakurai's eyes went so wide they bulged.

We cleared off more of the surface. The dimensions were familiar. Sakurai blanched and jerked back as if afraid to touch it anymore.

My gloved fingers traced three letters inset into the hull.

UEA.

My whole body went numb. I doubled over, shaking my head. Not until Kovac nudged me did I realize I'd been laughing. Cold reality erased my hysteria.

Sakurai theorized it could be part of Centaurus, *but no. My shock turned into anger. Holy fuck, you have to understand what it was like to uncover something like that. Were we lied to by the UEA? Had others come before us? Had we somehow shifted forward in time and this was Seeker, years later? All sorts of crazy thoughts hammered at my mind. I was on my knees, questioning my own sanity.*

Kovac was the first to get his shit together after we kept staring at the hull like idiots. The wind rose, casting sand back over the vessel. Erasing hours of work.

Theorizing that since it was a UEA design, there must a hatch nearby, Kovac cleared away more sand. He said it resembled our own modules.

How he could tell that from the small amount we'd uncovered mystified me, but the sand was hitting us and we had to act fast. I helped him with Sakurai as we walked along the craft's hull, desperate to get out of the storm, as well as to see if Kovac was right. With all the loose sand still surrounding us, we could've gotten buried there.

Sakurai stumbled. Her tight gasp hinted at how much her leg must really hurt. I helped her along while Kovac ignored her. The hurt on her face made me angry again.

Kovac found what he was looking for, lucky bastard. He lifted a small cover, turned and pulled the emergency release that's on top of all UEA crew modules. A meter-wide hatch opened up. We slipped inside, along with generous amounts of sand.

The hatch closed behind us. The windstorm became a distant thrum.

Darkness surrounded us for a moment before we activated our suit lights. The sounds of the storm muted altogether, but we were even more silent after that discovery.

The module interior, save for the sand we'd let in, was clean. And I mean fucking spotless. No dust, nothing. Farther in, there was a cabin converted into a garden where dozens of the vines grew. They snaked all over the walls, even up to the ceiling. The soil looked moist. We found a water reclamation tank that was still—albeit slowly—dripping its contents into the soil. My HUD indicated that a current of 16.5 amperes ran through it. The water wasn't nourishing the vines—it was conducting power to them.

Sakurai wanted to leave.

Kovac refused to take our chances in the storm. Said it was just vines.

Wow, was that the wrong answer. Sakurai went into a tirade, how all of this was wrong, and why weren't we told about this, and did the UEA send another expedition. How long has this thing been here and where was the crew.

I didn't blame her.

Kovac shined his light here and there, saying we wouldn't find any answers if we left. There was something in his tone. Like he wasn't as surprised as we were.

We continued through the module, only to find it connected to another one. And another. Kovac was right. It was just like Centaurus *in configuration. Eight modules altogether. The cockpit module, centrifuges, and engines were missing.*

I didn't like it. They'd landed like we were supposed to. Then vanished.

The second module contained more plants, but these were from Earth. A hydroponics lab. All were long dead in dry tanks. In a corner lay a pile of tablets and computer drives—burned, melted to junk.

The third module wasn't as clean as the first one, with empty food packages tossed about, and a collection of water bottles fused together into a weird sculpture of a humanoid. There was a dried-up vine wrapped around its neck.

Sakurai repeated that she wanted to leave.

Kovac just smiled and asked her to wait there. Leaving her behind, we continued on. The fourth and fifth modules were totally shitcanned, with bunks thrown around, space suits cast about, and a supply crate used as a fire pit. There was graffiti on the walls, though not in any alphabet we could recognize. It was more pictorial than letters, with what I took to be representations of vines, UEA crew members, and even a rover. Then there were dozens of lines crossed out on one wall showing where someone had tried tallying the number of days they'd been there.

I asked what he knew about this. How long he'd known.

Ignoring me, Kovac searched until he found a field lab folded and tucked in a corner. It was an older model than the ones we have. Kovac booted it up.

A log-in screen appeared. Kovac knew the fucking password.

I shook inside my suit. I forgot how much my elbow hurt. How hungry I was from eating only 1,200 calories a day. All I could think about was how badly I wanted to beat the shit out of him. I'd looked up to Kovac, defended him, done all this work for him.

And he'd been lying to us all along.

The screen displayed a collection of videos and docs recorded by the captain of UEA Chiron, *dispatched to Proxima Centauri eight years before our own crew left Earth.*

Eight fucking years.

I wanted to shout. To grab Kovac and choke the truth from him. But I watched.

Kovac accessed some of the video journals. These detailed the arrival of Chiron *in this solar system. The various crew modules detaching from the parent ship and landing on this moon. Lots of cheering, smiling, parties. The kind of shit we should've experienced rather than this hell. But the journals took a darker turn. People went missing. Everyone reported disturbing dreams, suffered equipment and power failures.*

There were some docs about how the moon came from somewhere else. That it wasn't native to the Alpha Centauri system.

Kovac said that was the reason the UEA sent Chiron. *Because the moon kept changing places in the UEA's telescope observation data back home.*

I demanded to know why we'd really *been sent here. Kovac raised a hand for silence. The next journal was the medical report from* Chiron's *crew. Mutating blood cells, an urge to breathe the atmosphere outside. Some crew members found those vines and were reprimanded for tampering with them. Wearing them. Sleeping with them.*

The last few journals showed only a few crew members, always wearing their EMUs, even indoors. There were reports of infighting. People changing. Worsening nightmares that always featured a deceased relative trying to get crew members to breathe the moon's air. A couple of suicides. Even a murder.

I saw us there on that screen. I saw our fate.

Sakurai walked into the chamber. She must've heard the lab's speakers. Her shocked expression degraded into one of heartache and anger. Kovac hadn't told her, either. We stood behind him, pissed off and staring at the screen.

Some of the entries got all crazy. Crew members talking to themselves or even speaking to the vines. One featured a woman staring into the camera, shaking her head in the negative for an hour. Kovac fast-forwarded to the end, where she fainted. The next entry showed everyone burning their food, pouring out their water, and burning their tablets and drives. Shouting things about keeping a secret from the moon.

Then the journals simply ended. They were followed by a distress signal, which I realized was a broadcast intended for anyone to receive, not just Earth. Only the signal was corrupted. Fragments of images, words, video, and other information.

The same signal that reached Earth. The same one we were sent to investigate.

I shoved Kovac against the wall and yelled at him. I pounded him again and again against the hull until Sakurai pushed me away. But Kovac, that bastard didn't even try to defend himself. He hung his head and leaned on his knees.

Sharp pain shot through my broken arm, but I calmed down. Sakurai cursed Kovac, her finger jabbing at his faceplate. She started crying. I glared at him.

Then he took his helmet off.

Sakurai jerked away from him. I thought him a coward, taking an easy way out.

The bastard was still breathing.

I finally paid attention to my HUD stats. The modules had filled with breathable atmosphere with 100 kilopascals pressure. Radiation was two millisieverts. Almost like being back home.

Kovac revealed that the systems came online when we entered the modular complex. That he knew what was buried here, and hoped some life support would still be functioning. He'd saved our asses, but I wanted to kick his.

After Sakurai and I pressured him—hell, I threatened to kill him— Kovac told us that the UEA wanted to know why the last expedition failed, but didn't want to cause a public outcry. Chiron's *mission had been kept secret, launched from the UEA station orbiting Ganymede. The UEA thought the moon must be an alien object, possibly a starship, since no celestial body can actually change its location like that. He said the moon was spotted orbiting the other planets in the Alpha Centauri system—all within the same year.*

But since Chiron's *crew sent that signal out—distress call, warning, whatever the hell it was—the UEA had to investigate. One, to discover what went wrong; and two, to maintain public confidence and allay fears, since there was no way to prevent the rest of Earth, Mars, and other colonies from receiving the same interstellar message.*

I demanded to know if he knew what Granger's briefing was going to be about.

Wearing a rueful smile, Kovac told us that Granger also knew this information, and had been instructed to allow only one or two modules to land on the moon at a time—in order to prevent the entire crew from suffering the fate of the previous one, should something fuck up. So that none of us would know beforehand, Granger was supposed to relay this stuff only when we entered the moon's orbit.

I wanted to call him a liar. Call bullshit on this whole enterprise. Kovac sank to the floor as if telling the truth drained him. He laughed sadly, saying he'd really wanted to find something that changed humanity's place in the universe. Even he had not expected all of this, despite being briefed by the UEA beforehand. The mishaps and sabotage had made him keep it a secret from everyone.

For the first time, there was fear in his eyes.

I accused him of keeping these secrets just so that he could have all the glory to himself, if he survived. That was when Kovac slowly looked up at me and blamed me for wanting the same thing. Shaking again, my teeth gritted, my fists clenched.

Goddamnit, but he was right.

Finally I looked away. A coldness swept over me. This wasn't why I'd worked so hard for this career, this opportunity. This wasn't who my uncle had taught me to be.

Sakurai pulled her helmet off, wiped her eyes, and knelt beside Kovac. They held each other. He whispered in her ear, calling her his beautiful Yuki. She cried again.

Anger seeped from me like water from a cracked dam. I also sat and removed my helmet. The air tasted stale. I wondered how long it'd been since the life-support system had been used. Who the last person was who'd inhaled this air. How fast they'd breathed it, if they'd been as frightened as we were.

After a few minutes I stood and explored the rest of the connected modules. Kovac and Sakurai kept holding each other. I didn't resent them for it. I didn't even hate Kovac. I'm a scientist, a trained astronaut. I was going to finish what I came here to do.

The sixth module contained a suited-up body lying on a lab table. Its hands were crossed over its chest like it was in a mortuary or something. I edged closer, my suit's light scattering shadows, real or imagined, over the bulkheads.

The suit was empty save for a bunch of desiccated vines. There were words scrawled over the faceplate in black marker: NO REST, NO PEACE.

Damn.

Whoever put vines in that suit and arranged it like that was obviously crazy. An adjoining crew cabin had another suit set up on the bunk in similar fashion. There were vines inside of it as well, and the message on the faceplate read: SHE DIED BEAUTIFUL.

That one gave me chills. Whoever did this cared about the deceased.

But, I mean, they're dead, so what did it matter? I respect things that teach me something, can kill me, or can help me. The dead can't do any of those things. In being dead, they failed to learn something, or they'd still be alive. I couldn't get careless now.

The seventh module looked to have been the main living area for Chiron's survivors. Tablets still lay on the tables. The bunks had been slept in. There were supply crates filled with empty packaging and bottles. I found a large cache of oxygen canisters, perhaps two supply modules' worth. At least our breathing troubles were over.

The eighth module's contents eroded my slight relief.

There were two bodies, not in suits, lying beside the module's exit hatch. It looked like they'd stabbed each another with silverware sharpened into deadly weapons. They were mere bones now. And the hatch had sand at the foot of it.

I opened it. Instead of leading right into solid earth, or flooding the module with loose sand, it revealed a tunnel. My suit's light shone down it. I couldn't spot its end.

19

The night sky is filled with stars. Each another version of Chukwu the creator, according to her tribe's ancient beliefs. Beautiful motes harboring miniature universes. Though Etana stares at them, she doesn't see them. Instead, she sees the faces of those she has killed. They glow in her sight like those distant suns. Twinkling wraiths illuminating all the misdeeds of her life, all the things she has tried to consign to the shadows of her consciousness.

She knows that boy wasn't really there yesterday. The data sent back to the UEA by *Chiron* had indicated the previous expedition also suffered from such illusory visitations. That does not change how it bothers her. Etana had never told anyone about the boy.

The inhabitants of this moon are using her mind against her.

The UEA has augmented her body, but the best cyborg technology offers no cure for the ailments of the biological mind. No mental block against these faces even now filling her sight. The easiest way to remove them has always been to kill again. Replacing the old faces with new ones. Although that has never worked for long.

She closes her eyes. Trembles.

It is now her fifteenth night on this miserable satellite of Promixa Centauri B. Fifteen days of wasted opportunities. Etana knows she could have finished her duties days ago. Had she ignored her mental phantoms, the survivors of *Centaurus* would all be dead. Her superiors had dictated that none can escape, but the moon's inhabitants are ruthless. Using one's greatest fears against them.

Etana has used those tactics all of her life. Even as a child she learned to trust only herself. As a woman she learned how to destroy the self-trust of others.

Now she doesn't trust reality.

She has never considered this trek a suicide mission. Saving Earth and its people will ease her guilt, redeem her ill-spent life. Etana told herself that when she took this final contract. Seeing that boy changed everything. There is no redemption for her.

The final beacon she's been tracking has made her realize this.

It had not been easy, despite her training, her stealth. All life, regardless of species, will always fight back when death is imminent. Whether it is a fish gasping for air while writhing on the shore, or a human gasping after his helmet has been compromised to poisonous atmosphere, there is no difference. Both struggle as if there will be another breath, another day of life, another chance. But that is a lie Etana learned long ago. Once one no longer believes the lies, they have no hold over the mind.

And everything on this moon is a lie. *Bimini*'s beacon has changed positions multiple times over the last several days. Etana has tracked it since it is the last module she hasn't sabotaged. All of the rest—*Aloha, Olduvai, Persepolis, Seeker*—will never use their thrusters again. She sabotaged them all, even while the Russian locked himself away from her predations. But *Bimini* eludes her. Brent cannot be alive. Yet he beckons.

It is the moon. Playing with her, with its prey, before the kill.

Sitting atop *Olduvai*'s rover, Etana studies her pistol. It helped kill the two who escaped *Persepolis*: Võsu and Zaoui. They ran. Begged. She made it quick.

Etana will not run. She will not beg.

She aims the gun at her head. Her helmet's faceplate cannot stop the bullet. Lying back over the vehicle, she once again gazes up at the stars.

One of them is moving.

She sits up. Double-checks her astronav app. Gets down, starts the rover. Drives.

The star grows brighter. Falling from heaven into hell.

"Straight ahead." Excitement grew in Larsen's voice.

Rachel drove over a steep ridge and into an alluvial valley. It was the rockiest region they'd seen on the moon so far. A few days ago she might have worried about throwing the rover's wheels out of alignment or breaking an axle. Not now.

They'd sighted the flares yesterday but the rover had to recharge before they could set out. She and Larsen had laughed, cried. Made love again despite their dwindling oxygen supply. A flare meant another survivor, for nothing on board *Centaurus* automatically fired such pyrotechnics. Rachel had told the others inside *Aloha*.

None of them seemed to care.

Their apathy hadn't dampened her and Larsen's joy. Now it made her tremble inside her suit: Dead ahead, the rover's scanner indicated they'd homed in on a beacon.

"Definitely a UEA signal." Larsen chuckled and patted Rachel's leg. "The fair wind blows even if the sailor does not see it."

Rachel smirked. "Thank you, Grandmamma Larsen. There were winds that swept down Ares Vallis that could knock you on your ass. Couldn't help but see that."

"I can see what matters." Larsen rubbed Rachel's shoulder. Though they both wore their EMU suits again, the contact felt wonderful. "You have proven the others wrong. Without you, we would all be dead."

Though she kept her eyes forward, Rachel smiled and gripped Larsen's hand.

Twilight stole over the landscape since it'd taken most of the day to reach the site. Rachel radioed Bakir but he sounded disinterested, which had become his typical behavior for the last several days. Perhaps he didn't want a larger workload if any survivors needed medical attention. No doubt he was still sore at her over how the situation with Stevenson had played out. Like Burgess, Stevenson had still not been found.

Not for lack of trying. She and Larsen had circled the camp, the mesa, and the flatlands several times. Even braved the canyon north of the mesa. Like the blue lake and the pillar, their comrades had vanished without traces.

Rachel wondered if she wasn't going insane.

But now, with the prospect of finding more survivors so near, she wasn't about to let any of that bring her down. Her mind was clear.

The wheels bumped over the valley's reg, akin to hard-packed pavement. Rachel shifted into a lower gear. "Think this might have been a riverbed or glacier?"

"A million years ago," Larsen said. "Wish this would convince Kovac to lend us Sakurai. She would love examining this."

Rachel sighed. "What we find here could change their minds."

Larsen rolled her eyes. "You say the glass is half full. I say there is no glass."

"Ah, there's that Norwegian reticence." Rachel smiled. "Right?"

"No more than your stubborn positivity is so Martian." Larsen winked.

"It's not that as much as it is a refusal to roll over and die," Rachel said. "This universe has never been kind to me."

"Do not let it make you bitter. I like my Rachel sweet."

"It's a lesson I've had to learn twice," Rachel said. "Once on Mars with all its harshness, then on Earth with all its tempting beauty not meant for me. Now this place."

"Third time is the charm," Larsen said.

Moments later the rover reached a break in the reg. Despite the failing light, Rachel made out a module's round outline against the horizon. It was lying on its side. As they got closer, it appeared that a ring of sand had mushroomed around it.

"They crash-landed," Larsen murmured, her good humor gone.

"It looks intact." Rachel linked her suit with the rover's radio. "This is Commander Terman. Does anyone copy?"

They got closer. Rachel stopped the rover eighteen meters from the module.

"Scanner shows a disproportionate amount of potassium nitrate and magnesium coating the module and the sand around it," Larsen said.

"Given off by the flares," Rachel said. "That has to be it."

Larsen smirked. "You are an aggressive optimist."

Rachel smirked back. "That's the nicest thing I've been called in days."

Leaving the vehicle, they activated their suit lights. Their boots crunched over the alluvial pavement. Circling the module, Rachel frowned. The craft's heat shield was deeply blackened. As if it had made more than one reentry. Which was impossible.

"We still getting that beacon signal?" Rachel asked.

"Yes." Larsen's voice was tainted with uncertainty.

"What's wrong?" Rachel checked the main hatch. Sand had been pushed away from it. Boot prints trailed off into the stony wastes.

"This is Commander Terman." Rachel swallowed. "Do you copy, over?"

"*Herregud,*" Larsen murmured from the other side of the module.

Rachel hurried over. "What is it?"

"Look." Larsen aimed her light and pointed.

The name on the module was *Ilios.*

Cold sweat slid down Rachel's back. There had been no module with that designation on board *Centaurus.* Another impossibility.

Rachel hurried back around the craft and tried the hatch. It opened too easily. No passcode necessary, no validation of her UEA credentials. A blue light blinked within.

She shone her light inside.

Ilios's interior walls were covered in the strange vines. Some quivered with the barest semblance of life. The lab station had been overturned but the command console was in sleep mode, as if it'd been used mere hours ago. Two crew members were strapped into their seats, wearing EMUs. Their helmets had been busted open; one was missing a faceplate. Whoever they were, they were skeletons now. Two skulls grinning at her.

The blinking blue light was a message screen on a tablet lying beside one of the stasis pods—showing a queue of Rachel's radio queries. Waiting to be answered.

A chill radiated through Rachel: the frigid mockery of depression, of loss. The beacon had been a siren after all. Calling them to what was just another grave.

"Someone was here!" Larsen cried. "Why did they not answer?"

"I don't…" Rachel forgot whatever she'd been about to say.

The pod's life monitor indicated an occupant had been woken from stasis fifteen hours ago. Yesterday, when she and Larsen had first spotted the flares.

A sob built in Rachel's throat. Not only for the dead, but for her dashed hopes.

"Fuck," Rachel whispered. She was shaking.

Larsen examined the corpses. "They fought with one another?"

"That doesn't matter now." Rachel walked between the stiff forms. "I want to know where the hell they came from. What ship *Ilios* was assigned to."

"*Faen.*" Larsen waved Rachel over. "These suits have the old UEA logo. Unused for over five years."

"Fuck," Rachel muttered again.

"That is all you can say?" Anguish rose in Larsen's voice.

"What am I supposed to say?" Rachel tried to wipe her eyes but her gloved hand bumped into her faceplate. "Some bullshit prayer?"

"Calm down," Larsen said.

"I'm tired of everyone telling me to calm down." Rachel grabbed the tablet. It, too, was an older design. She swiped the screen but the security lock activated. A log-in appeared, asking for a password. A ship's title graced the log-in border.

UEA *Chiron.*

"This is insane," Larsen said. "There is no ship by that—"

"We were lied to," Rachel said.

They stared around at the vines, the corpses, the blinking tablet. All of which caused Rachel to infer a grisly tale she wanted no part of—but she had to know.

"They sent a ship here before us?" Larsen asked.

"Yes."

Larsen's nostrils flared. "Why did we not see it when *Centaurus* arrived?"

"With all the signal noise around this moon?" Rachel asked. "*Chiron* could have been right in front of us and we'd not have known."

"Not liking this, Rachel."

"Occam's razor," Rachel said. "The easiest explanation is usually the right one."

Scowling, Larsen shook her head. "There is no reason for this. Unless they tried to cover up something?"

"Judging by the state of this module, that mission failed." Rachel laid the tablet on the stasis pod. "But we weren't sent to rescue or look for the crew of *Chiron*. I bet that was what Granger was going to tell us. He must have known. A secret this big wouldn't have been mentioned in any logs or data caches."

Larsen slowly shook her head. "But...such risk..."

"The UEA expected us to encounter the same things. These vines, the blue lake."

"The UEA could not have expected us to succeed." Larsen peeked in the crew cabins. "There are supplies remaining. We at least have that."

"Unless someone else knew. One who was briefed before *Centaurus* left Earth."

They shared a glance and spoke simultaneously. "Kovac."

Rachel wanted to scream, to run around and kick the rocks outside, to find whoever was responsible and beat the truth from them. But Larsen tugged crate after supply crate toward the main hatch. She faced Rachel and waited.

"Every little bit helps," Larsen said.

"You're right." Rachel helped her load the crates onto the rover. "At least now we won't starve or asphyxiate before the week's out."

"What about whoever was in that stasis pod?" Larsen shined her light all around *Ilios*'s landing site. The blue-white beam cast jagged spectres over the alluvial valley.

Rachel secured the last crate to their vehicle. "Try your infrared app in case they're close by. Look for any tracks in the sand."

Larsen prodded the prints they'd spotted earlier with her boot. "Recent. No older than a day. Suppose they fled before we arrived? To hide?"

"If this module landed here yesterday, but was sent to this solar system that long ago, then that means *Chiron* is still in orbit," Rachel said. "There's no other way it could have been up there this many years. That would also explain *Ilios*'s scarred heat shield."

"Rachel." Larsen raised her brows. "Answer me. Think they are hiding?"

"I don't know." Rachel shivered. "But something got out of that pod. I want answers, too, but I'm not searching this valley at night. Plus, the others need to know."

"Crazy enough as it is," Larsen said.

"If *Chiron* is up there…then we might have a way home." Rachel studied the sky. "Once everyone realizes that, we have a chance. It might be the only thing that will get everyone to can the bullshit and work together."

"We cannot use this module." Larsen shined her light at the crimped thrusters and cracked hull near the mushroomed sand at *Ilios*'s base.

Rachel smacked Larsen's rump. "Then you better hope there's another module up there that we can bring down by remote. Let's get this stuff back to *Aloha*."

Something crunched over the reg behind them.

They both spun around.

A figure in a dirty IVA suit stood there. The mission patch read *Chiron*.

"Who are you?" Rachel asked.

Larsen greeted the figure in English, Norwegian, Spanish, and Mandarin.

The figure shifted on its feet. Something was written on its faceplate in marker.

Larsen tried sign language. She traced glyphs in the sand. Showed a hologram of their solar system with her wrist tab, like she'd done with Brent. Still no response.

"What do you want from us?" Rachel asked.

The figure approached them with unsteady steps.

Rachel focused her light on the figure's helmet. The words ESCAPE TO A WARMER PLACE covered the faceplate in jagged black letters. As the figure drew near, she jumped.

Inside the helmet, vines wriggled around a human head with green-brown skin. It had no face. The same nodules she'd seen on the other vines covered the sides of its cranium. Blue light glittered from tiny holes in the nodules.

"Oh shit," Rachel whispered, backing into Larsen.

"Wait." Larsen extended her hand.

"Don't!" Rachel knocked Larsen's hand aside, only to have the figure grasp hers.

A flash of memories and sensations passed through Rachel's mind.

Growing up on Pathfinder Base as an only child. Her parents, putting her through school and college while struggling with poverty. The bigotry of humans at the spaceports. Moving to Earth, then suffering under its gravity. Nine years training to be a UEA astronaut, but always getting passed up for other candidates. Coming here in search of something greater.

Suffocating...

Rachel jerked her hand away.

The figure backed up. The vines inside the helmet wriggled faster and the nodules glowed bright blue. The reg split apart at its feet into a sinkhole.

"Stay back!" Rachel shielded Larsen, unsure whether she meant her or the figure.

Without a sound, the figure vanished into the sinkhole. The reg resumed its shape.

"Let's get out of here," Rachel said.

"What if it was trying to communicate?" Larsen asked.

"I don't care, we need to go!" They ran to the rover.

Rachel drove as fast as she could from the valley. Twilight deepened into night. Once the rover made it back to the flatlands around the mesa, she accelerated to top speed. The vehicle shook and a few red warning lights lit up the console.

Though Larsen gave her a few concerned looks, she kept radioing *Aloha* rather than admonish Rachel's driving. Bakir and the others didn't reply. On any other day that wouldn't have been unusual, but there'd been less signal noise for hours. Nevertheless, seeing *Aloha*'s lights in the distance evoked relief in Rachel for the first time in days. She drove up the western face of the mesa and rolled into camp.

"Bakir? Richter? We're going to need some help out here unloading the rover. And there's something we have to tell you. Right now."

No one answered Rachel. She looked at Larsen, who shrugged. They got out.

"Paredo? Jemutai?" Rachel didn't ask for Santos. He'd want to argue again.

Once they entered *Aloha*, Rachel frowned. No one was about. The cabin where Richter slept was open, and Santos lay on the cot.

"Santos, do you—" Larsen's jaw dropped.

Santos's suit link indicated he was dead. Eyes shut, mouth open.

"Bakir!" Rachel hurried to the cabin she and Larsen had shared with Richter. The German engineer lay on her bunk, arm dangling off the side. Richter was dead.

"Goddamnit!" Rachel checked the other cabins. All were empty, but the one Paredo and Jemutai slept in was locked shut. She banged on it. "Anybody in there?"

Larsen found Bakir's personal tablet on the lab table. Blood covered it and the surrounding floor. It showed everyone's medical data in real time via their suit links. The more she studied it, the deeper her frown became. "Rachel…"

As Rachel ceased banging on the hatch, a voice filled her earbud. "Go to hell!"

"Paredo?" Rachel knocked on the hatch again. "What happened out here?"

"He said it was out of mercy," Paredo said in a whimper.

"Who?" Rachel asked.

"Bakir." Larsen glowered at the tablet then showed it to her. "Look."

The screen revealed that a lethal morphine dose had been administered to Richter and Santos a half hour earlier. While they slept.

Rachel paced *Aloha*, frowning so hard her face hurt. "What. Happened."

"I caught him doing it." Paredo sobbed over the connection. "I caught that heretic injecting Santos. Richter must have already been…already been…"

"Where are Bakir and Jemutai?" Rachel stopped before the locked hatch.

Paredo kept sobbing and mumbled a prayer in Spanish.

"Paredo." Rachel glared at the hatch. "Where are they?"

"Jemutai tried to stop him," Paredo said. "With those printed blades. He stabbed him, but…Bakir fought him off…ran out of *Aloha*, with Jemutai following after."

Larsen stood beside Rachel. "Why are you still in there? You can come out."

"I will not," Paredo said.

Fighting anguish and rage, Rachel tried to calm down. "Please, we—"

"No!" Paredo yelled so loud that Rachel flinched from the pain in her ear. "He met them outside. Bakir. He met them. Jemutai is likely dead, too. Don't you see?"

"What do you mean, 'them'?" Even speaking the word gave Rachel chills.

"The ones from my dream," Paredo said. "They have been coming for us. They came for Bakir. They are…Oh God, please forgive me. I will not go. I will not."

"Paredo?" Rachel started to knock when a concussive *thud* came from the locked chamber. The hatch bulged outward. The floor shook. Alarms sounded over her earbud and lit up her HUD. There'd been an explosion inside Paredo's cabin.

"Paredo!" Rachel tried the hatch as Larsen grabbed the fire extinguisher, but it was too late. *Aloha*'s system reported that the hull was breached on that side due to an interior blast. The hatch, even if it could be opened, had to remain closed. *Aloha* had detected the release of pure oxygen and the presence of an open flame right before the blast. Paredo had used a welding torch to ignite his air supply.

Rachel tuned her radio to Larsen's private channel. "We'll only speak on this frequency from now on. We can't advertise our location anymore."

"And we cannot stay here." Larsen grimaced at Santos's body.

"Bakir and Jemutai—and whoever or whatever else—might come back," Rachel said. "Let's grab what we can and get away from here. We have food, water, and air aplenty on the rover now. We've been living in it anyway. Now we must stay mobile."

"What will we do now?" Larsen loaded up Bakir's field lab and tablet.

"We find Kovac and save everyone we can," Rachel said.

Chief Medical Officer's journal. Mission date: Sol 16.

I am one of the damned.

My only regret is that I failed to release Paredo and Jemutai from this awful place. I tried to wait until everyone was asleep, but then she came. I had to do it.

Beforehand, I'd been studying everyone's blood test results again. The mutations have continued unabated. I noticed a correlation in the severity of one's nightmares and how much their cells had already changed. Santos was the worst. I took care of him first, to put him out of his misery. I fear that, had I waited any longer, he might have become something inured to pain. Even death.

It is what I saw in my own dreams.

This world is taking us for its own. Transforming us into something of its own design. I compared everyone's nightmares—those who were willing to discuss them—and the most common element is that we've all dreamt of this moon affecting us in some way.

Richter said she dreamed of peeling away her skin, only to discover she was an automaton built of those vines. Paredo claimed Mother Mary was coming to deliver us all in a shaft of blue light. Though he refused to talk about his own dreams, Santos yelled in his sleep enough for me to discern that his nightmares involved his family forcing him into one of the sinkholes. Jemutai dodged my questions by simply stating that the past wasn't going to affect his future. I later learned he dreamt of his father, who was the first Kenyan to visit Europa but died on the same mission due to equipment failure.

Stevenson never told me his. I suspect they were truly horrible, given his paranoia. I still resent Terman for driving him to that point.

I never got word of Kovac's dreams, nor the members of his camp. Zentsov would repeat that "they" were coming. His last messages were more paranoid than Stevenson's.

As I already knew, Terman dreamed of suffocating in the deserts and sinkholes of this moon. Larsen readily told me she kept seeing her Grandpapa rising from a fjord she liked to visit in her native Norway. Except, the fjord's waters were a gleaming blue.

I kept seeing my Nasreen, wrapped in those vines, gorgeous and vibrant, leading me to a fissure of blue light. Or a blue lake. Once she took me to a crater coated in blue.

Now that she has found me at last, I might know why.

You see…I thought I was dreaming when I saw Nasreen outside Aloha, *through the main hatch's window. She was naked save for a few vines dangling from her limbs.*

Just like I had been dreaming these many agonizing nights, she had come for me.

I had no choice but to go with her. I wanted to know if it was truly her. If she still loved me. Whether or not I could save my comrades from what was coming.

I tried. Allah knows that I did. But Jemutai confronted me. I don't know why I swung the scalpel at him, for I was so afraid. Jemutai stabbed me and Paredo locked himself in his cabin. Bleeding, I fled outside to where she waited. It wasn't until I felt the wind on my face that I realized I had removed my helmet.

Jemutai yelled something. I don't know how I heard him without the radio inside my helmet. He spotted Nasreen and ran from the camp. She paid him no mind. My lovely wife only had eyes for me. Eyes of gleaming blue. She offered her hand. It was a vine.

Allah forgive me, but I took it.

We've been walking south from the mesa for two hours now. Though leaving a trail of blood, I have been able to type this into my journal via my wrist tab.

I shouldn't even be alive. Yet I am.

Which is why I must see what they want of us. I sacrifice myself, though I cannot deny the selfishness of this act, since I am reunited with Nasreen. She is even more beautiful that I remember. Here is where I shall stay. This is my fate, by Allah's will.

I hope the others will understand.

Flight Recorder – *Maray* Crew Module
Sol 16 – 0241 hours
Orbiting Proxima Centauri C

CFE Worrel: No, I don't want it.

MS Khandaar: Stop being a stubborn asshole, sir, and eat it.

CMP Worrel: You two need it more. I'm fine.

CFE Moore: You've a better chance of making it. (coughs)

CMP Worrel: We're all going to make it. Now eat your rations.

CFE Moore: (laughs) Yeah. Sure. At least we're too weak to argue now.

CMP Worrel: I'm sorry.

(various coughs, sobs)

MS Khandaar: Sir. Please don't.

CMP Worrel: My husband used to tell me I cried too bloody much.

CFE Moore: C'mon. We all lost our shit. I'm sorry, too, for what it's worth.

MS Khandaar: After what the cameras have shown us, I'd rather be up here now.

CFE Moore: You were trying to do what you thought best. I'm over it, okay?

CMP Worrel: (sighs) How much longer do we have?

MS Khandaar: The hull is slowly heating. We'll be in reentry within the day.

CFE Moore: Yay.

CMP Worrel: (chuckles) Then you two can finally stop bugging me.

CFE Moore: Not a chance.

MS Khandaar: Sir…How did your husband die?

CMP Worrel: (clears throat)

CFE Moore: Not sure if now's the time, honey.

MS Khandaar: Got somewhere you need to be, Kevin? Now is perfect.

CMP Worrel: He bought it during the UEA's first crewed mission to Charon.

MS Khandaar: Aboard *Persephone?*

CMP Worrel: Yes. He was the captain. It was an unusually strong solar flare. That was before the UEA upgraded that bodgy shielding on their spacefaring tinnys. The cancer killed him before *Persephone* reached Charon.

MS Khandaar: Sorry, sir.

CFE Moore: Yeah (heavy breathing)…Sorry to hear that.

CMP Worrel: I keep dreaming that he's down there on the moon. He rises from this blue lake and wants me to follow him, like it's all spiffy. But I don't want to.

(various murmurs, coughs)

CMP Worrel: We need to talk about it. Jivika, what'd you dream?

MS Khandaar: I dreamt about Moore again—

CFE Moore: Call me Kevin. Since you're dreaming about me and all that.

MS Khandaar: Um, anyway. Oh God. I was being dragged into the sand by vines. You were screaming my name and I wanted to answer so bad—

CFE Moore: The vines again? Yeah. I had the same nightmare. I almost had you.

MS Khandaar: Just stop. It felt way too real.

CMP Worrel: These aren't normal dreams. Something wants us to land.

CFE Moore: No shit. I wish that… (grunts). Damn. Give me a sec.

MS Khandaar: Hold on, Kevin, I'll get the syringe.

CMP Worrel: We're out of painkillers. The med drone did its best.

MS Khandaar: But he's in agony! He keeps running a fever—

CFE Moore: I'm good, honey.

MS Khandaar: (laughs) I can't believe I've gotten used to you calling me that.

CFE Moore: Well, I am better looking than that Cambridge professor. How could you be ready to marry a guy like that?

MS Khandaar: I suppose it should be a stubborn ass like yourself that flirts at the most awkward times? (laughs)

CFE Moore: Hell yes.

CMP Worrel: If you two are having a naughty, I'm going to my cabin. (laughter)

CMP Worrel: Kevin, what about you? Jivika and I've told our stories.

CFE Moore: Do I have to?

MS Khandaar: Yes, "honey."

CFE Moore: (chuckles) Here goes. I'm twice divorced. Both of them worked for NASA, like me. Two daughters, one by each. Neither of my girls will speak to me.

CMP Worrel: Why?

CFE Moore: They didn't want me to come on this expedition. Even though they've shut me out of their lives otherwise. Teenagers, right? That's what I get for being a pigheaded space cowboy. (coughs) They didn't even show up at *Centaurus*'s launch.

MS Khandaar: No, there were two young women there, in your booth at the pad.

CFE Moore: Really?

MS Khandaar: Yes. They looked very proud.

CFE Moore: Yeah? (laughs) Yeah. I hope they are.

CMP Worrel: I know they are, mate.

CFE Moore: Hey…you feel that?

CMP Worrel: Status report?

MS Khandaar: Proximity level at orange.

CMP Worrel: It should be red, the way the hull is vibrating.

MS Khandaar: Holding at orange.

CMP Worrel: Check the aft camera—

MS Khandaar: Oh my God!

CFE Moore: (coughs) What?

CMP Worrel: What is it, Jivika?

MS Khandaar: It's a ship trying to dock with us!

20

The radio woke Rachel. She'd cuddled with Larsen in the rover a few kilometers east of the mesa. Their nightmare-induced sleep deprivation had finally taken its toll. Both needed rest, and Rachel needed distance from the tragedy they'd found at *Aloha*. She should have stayed. If she'd been there, Bakir wouldn't have been able to…

Static popped from the console speaker.

Rachel sat up and rubbed her chest. "Vanja, what do you make of that?"

Rising with a groan, Larsen squinted at the console. "We cannot answer it. Remember what you said." She reached for her helmet.

"Yes, I know." Rachel put her helmet on. "Let's—"

A knock rapped on the driver's side door.

Rachel jerked in her seat and hit the accelerator. The rover plowed into a dune. The motion thrust Larsen into the dashboard and Rachel's helmet into the steering wheel.

Her faceplate cracked open.

"Damn!" Rachel tried to put the vehicle into reverse. A second knock hit her door.

Grasping a wrench, Larsen sat up and scowled out the window. "Look!"

A figure outside Rachel's door waved its arms. A voice crackled over the radio.

"Terman, it's me! Mission Specialist Kiano Jemutai!"

Though it was his voice, Rachel kept staring out the glass into the darkness—wanting to believe it was him, but suspicious of anyone finding them this far from camp.

"I will go out and see." Before Rachel could protest, Larsen exited the rover. The short release of air made Rachel squirm in her seat. One poisonous breath and she'd die.

"Are you getting me?" Jemutai asked. "Let me in so we can get out of here!"

Rachel watched as Larsen walked around the vehicle and shined her light on the figure. It was Jemutai, his EMU suit filthy from his trek across the desert.

It was also covered in blood.

"Vanja, be careful," Rachel said over the radio. "Jemutai, where's Bakir?"

"How the hell should I know?" Jemutai looked over his shoulder in the direction of the mesa. "I hope he is dead. Him and Burgess. It's his blood I am wearing."

"*Hva?*" Larsen's question was laced with horror.

Jemutai spread his hands. "Let me inside and I'll explain. I've barely made it through all of the sinkholes opening across this terrible place. They cannot be natural."

Rachel looked him up and down from inside the rover. Did a quick scan for contaminants or anything unusual on his person.

"We must trust each other," he said. "Please, Commander. Stop wasting time."

"Get in." Rachel held her breath.

"Try to hurt us and I will kill you." Larsen got in first.

"You might be one of those things, too, for all I know." Jemutai clambered in, saw Rachel's busted faceplate, and quickly shut the door.

Rachel waited for the rover to normalize the interior atmosphere before she took another breath. "Now…about Burgess."

Jemutai reclined in the back seat and removed his helmet. Sweat beads peppered his forehead. "When Paredo shouted, I ran from my cabin and saw what Bakir had done. I drew a knife that I'd printed out earlier, right before Santos ruined the printer."

"Why'd he do that?" Rachel asked.

"Santos was talking crazy things by then, so who knows," Jemutai said. "I stabbed Bakir in the side after he tried to kill me with his scalpel. He fled outside, so I chased after him. Only—" He wiped his face.

"Here." Larsen handed him a water bottle.

"Thanks." After draining half the bottle, Jemutai continued. "Only Bakir, he wasn't wearing a helmet. The atmosphere did not affect him. He was breathing it. The stab wound didn't affect him. Burgess was outside waiting for him."

"How is that possible?" Rachel backed the rover from the dune.

"She wasn't wearing a helmet, either." Jemutai took another drink. "Her eyes glowed blue, and her hands…Oh damn. Her hands were like those vines."

Rachel stared out the windshield. Trying to understand what was happening. Jemutai could be addled by lack of sleep himself, eating less food like the rest of them. It could be stress or even madness given their situation. Maybe he thought he saw Burgess.

"I'm not insane," Jemutai said.

Buzzes emitted from the console radio speaker. Larsen turned it down.

"I believe you." Rachel turned in her seat and told him all that she and Larsen had discovered in the alluvial valley. *Ilios*, the dead bodies, *Chiron*. The extra supplies. Someone waking from stasis. Or rather, something.

"And you think Kovac knew about all of this?" Jemutai asked.

"Some of it," Larsen said.

A voice on the radio made chill bumps pop out along Rachel's flesh.

"Commander, repeat, this is Zentsov in *Seeker*. Please answer."

They all focused on the console speaker. Rachel didn't breathe.

The connection grew fuzzy, then cleared up. "Kovac and the others found something out there. They have sworn to keep everything secret, fearing someone in your camp is the saboteur, but you must know this: Kovac uncovered the remains of—"

Rachel hit the mic button on the dashboard. "Zentsov?"

No reply.

"We have to go out there," Rachel said.

Larsen shook her head. "Why reach out to you now? After what has happened?"

"Does he even know?" Rachel started driving southeast to *Seeker*.

"Bakir used to email Zentsov, or so Paredo told me," Jemutai said. "I doubt he would've told the Russian about this."

"I do not like it," Larsen said.

The nightmare came back to Rachel. Of her running across the desert. Suffocating. This time, the ground was collapsing under her feet. Full of sinkholes, vines.

"We have to." Rachel drove on through the night, not slowing down.

Airborne sand made the floodlights outside *Seeker* seem to flicker and brighten as the fine grains shifted with the rising winds. The airflow shook the rover as its anemometer detected gales up to 120 kilometers per hour. The vehicle creaked from the buffeting forces, but Rachel was more concerned with the supply crates strapped to its back. Their addition disrupted the vehicle's streamlined shape, which was intended to reduce wind shear and drag. She parked it on *Seeker*'s northern side, shielding it from the rougher southern winds.

"Wait this out or go inside?" Larsen asked.

"Leaving the rover now would be insanity." Jemutai stared out the windshield and shook his head. "These idiots didn't even set up a tether for use in whiteouts like this."

Rachel shut off the engine and cued *Seeker*'s radio frequency.

"Don't tell him we're with you." Jemutai clasped one of his printed blades.

"Zentsov? This is Terman. I'm outside in the rover."

They waited thirty seconds. A minute. Larsen peered through the windshield and sighed. Jemutai gathered rope from the tool cache behind the back seat.

No reply came from *Seeker*.

Rachel spoke again. Two more minutes passed.

Wind battered the rover, tearing one of the supply crates loose. It tumbled away into the darkness. Sand piled up on the windshield then was scattered by another gale.

Three minutes. Still no answer.

"I'm going in," Rachel said.

"The hell you are," Larsen said. "Your faceplate is busted and you will get lost—"

"I'm not sending either of you in there," Rachel said. "Don't even try to—"

"No." Larsen gripped her arm.

It'd be easy, driving away. Staying in the rover until their supplies ran out. Letting the moon win while Larsen held her until the end. It'd be peaceful, gradually expelling oxygen from the rover until they asphyxiated in warm, blissful slumber. Beautiful, even.

Until she finally allowed herself to remember.

Rachel sat on the precipice's edge, overlooking Ophir Chasma. Her legs dangled above an eight kilometer drop. A vastness too small to hold the pain crushing her heart. But Mars's unforgiving environment was a brutality to which she was accustomed. An unintentional, amoral cruelty. One she could quantify, understand, and prepare for.

Unlike the cruelty of others.

Her helmet's aural sensors detected footsteps behind her. She knew who it was without turning around. "I'm not going back there, Mom."

Mom sat beside her on the ledge, which made Rachel gape. Just the other day, Mom had admonished her yet again for walking too close to the chasma's edge. The fear of heights, of uncertain footing, always kept Mom from such places. But there she was.

"What are you doing?" Rachel hated that a sob escaped her throat after the words.

"Why, I'm enjoying the view." Mom's fake grin was obvious.

"I'm ten now." Rachel scowled. "I don't need you to lie to me anymore—"

Mom gripped her hand. She was trembling. Frightened by the nightmarish drop mere centimeters away. She stared forward, the setting sun gleaming off her faceplate.

"The teacher told me what happened," Mom said. "You have to go back."

"So the other kids can make fun of me?" Rachel sobbed. "I won't!"

"They fear what they don't understand," Mom said.

"That I'm smaller than other Martians? That the Earth kids think I'm an alien?"

They'd shoved her from the school's exterior air lock without a helmet. Teased her that she could breathe the air since she wasn't really a human. She'd pounded on the hatch, trying to hold her breath, Mars's frigid air chapping her flesh. Feeling her tears boil off her cheeks due to the planet's lower atmospheric pressure.

The teacher had opened the hatch right before the pressure difference boiled the moisture from her skin. Before it started boiling her blood. And even then, while she writhed and screamed on the air-lock floor, while the medics rushed to her aid, and the teacher shouted at the perpetrators, the other kids laughed.

Laughed while she suffocated in more ways than one.

Though the culprits had been expelled, the others hated her even more for it.

Mom's eyes glistened with tears. "Please, dear—"

"They were going to watch me die!" Rachel cried.

Mom slowly turned and met her eyes. Released her hand. Set her jaw.

Then stood up on the chasma's edge. Sand and pebbles tumbled into the abyss.

"Mom!" Rachel scrambled to her feet.

"I'm scared to death right now," Mom whispered over the radio.

"Then why are you doing this?" Rachel didn't hold back her tears. "Get down!"

"I'm facing my fear." Mom spread her arms and shuddered. "I'm not going to let it beat me. I'm not letting it tell me what I can and can't do."

"This isn't the same thing," Rachel said.

"No," Mom said. "But you can face it, and deal with it, like I am right now."

"Get down!" Rachel yelled.

"Promise me." Mom closed her eyes, her fear stabbing into Rachel's heart.

"I…I promise. Just please come down."

Mom left the precipice and fell to her knees. The fear in her eyes turned to embarrassment, but she tried to hide it with another smile. All of it for Rachel.

Rachel engulfed her in a hug. Mom returned it. They knelt beside the chasma like that for a long time.

Never again would Rachel let fear stop her.

The memory faded, along with her fear of it.

"I have to." Rachel smiled at Larsen. "Now give me your helmet."

"No—"

"Vanja," Rachel said in a low voice. "That's an order."

Larsen's lips trembled, then she yanked off her helmet.

"If I don't come back…" Rachel hesitated and faced them. "Then get far away."

Outside, the wind pressed against her like an iron wall. She had to tuck her head down and force her way through the merciless tempest. Another supply crate blew past, nearly taking her head off. Her steps wobbled in the sand drifts. She fell twice.

"Zentsov, this is Terman. I'm coming in."

Sand and gravels pounded her body. She tried not worrying about her suit's integrity. The faceplate HUD flashed warnings but she trudged on.

Rachel finally reached *Seeker*'s hatch by clinging to its walls and feeling her way around. Pebbles snapped against her faceplate so much she feared it might crack. The squall's raw noise forced her aural sensors to automatically switch off. Clasping the handrail in one hand, she tugged on the hatch's lever release with the other.

It refused to open.

"Zentsov? Let me in."

Ten seconds. Twenty seconds. Still no answer.

"Zentsov! Open the door!"

After applying all her strength, the lever finally moved. She fell forward into *Seeker*. Sand blew into the module's exterior air lock as she crawled all the way inside. It took her three attempts to shut the hatch, the winds were so strong. She leaned against it, caught her breath. The storm's fury muted to a dull roar as her aural sensors reactivated.

"Larsen?" Rachel coughed. "Jemutai? Either of you read me?"

A warbled voice replied but the frequency contained too much signal noise.

"Anybody copy?" Rachel entered the interior air lock. A rush of air announced her arrival into *Seeker*'s main chamber. The view made her stumble backward.

Fat, throbbing vines covered the interior walls. Her HUD indicated an overabundance of static electricity in the thinning air. The greenish-brown pseudo-flora was attached to a dark blue, metallic object lying on the lab table. Its glow coated everything in wintry cobalt hues. The cabin hatches were open. Burned food containers still smoldered in a corner. A puddle lay under dozens of punctured water bottles.

"Vanja?" Rachel whispered as she walked about. "Please answer me."

Something brushed her shoulder.

Rachel whirled around.

A body dangled above her, stripped to its underwear. A knotted sheet was wrapped around its neck and tied to an air vent. The bloated corpse was covered in small tears as the skin's top layer was beginning to loosen with decay. The face was so swollen that it took Rachel a few seconds to recognize it as Zentsov.

Her sanity threatened to rend apart like his dead skin. She'd just heard him on the radio outside. Nausea squeezed her guts until she quivered. Its taste seared her throat.

"Damn it, Vanja or Kiano, answer me!" She crossed the chamber to where a tablet lay on the floor. She swiped the screen and was able to enter a security override since the device came from *Centaurus*. A document was open. Zentsov's suicide note.

It was in Cyrillic but her translation app rendered it into English.

"*I cannot take it any longer,*" Rachel read aloud. "*By now Kovac and the others are dead. I saw the smoke drifting from the south. The rover exploded as I intended. Now I must take care of myself before my resistance to them is gone. They are all connected. They know us. They want us. There is no escape.*"

Shivering, Rachel stared at the vines, the blue object. It resembled a coiled serpent without head or tail. She swiped through a collection of still images and videos on Zentsov's tablet. There, apparently laid out for her to see, were his experiments on the vines and the blue object Li had found. It resembled something from her nightmares.

It was in the sinkholes from her dreams. Drawing her in.

One of the videos started playing though she hadn't touched the screen.

"The damned thing changes shape when you're not looking." Zentsov was standing over the lab table. The timer indicated the recording was made three days ago. Sure enough, the object did possess slight differences from the one a few meters away. Even as she glanced at it, the object—dubbed *draco centaurus* by Kovac— had changed. Like the coils rearranged themselves whenever she looked away.

The video stopped and another played. Again, Rachel did nothing to the tablet.

"Once you've been around it..." The video showed Zentsov staring off into space. "It shows you things. It visits you in your dreams. All of my tests indicate that this is the result of an energy field within the moon itself. There are no countermeasures against it."

Rachel shook so much that she dropped the tablet. It kept playing.

"What do you mean?" Kovac asked on the video.

She scowled. So Kovac had known a great deal—and never warned her.

"It tells you things." Zentsov's voice sounded as if he was undergoing hypnosis.

"What does it tell you?" Kovac asked.

"That we are almost there," Zentsov said.

"You are worrying me, Alexei." Kovac backed away from him.

"We are beyond worry," Zentsov said. "Beyond food and water."

"You simply need rest, old friend." Kovac tried to smile.

"They will provide whatever we need." A slow smile parted Zentsov's stubbled face. "They have even changed this moon for us. We no longer need our suits."

Kovac neared *Seeker*'s hatch. "You are mad."

Zentsov laughed. "They are coming to—"

The tablet shut off.

"Shit." Rachel nudged the device with her boot. "Vanja? Kiano?"

A low rumble sounded. It shook *Seeker*.

"Do either of you copy me out there?" She ran toward the exit hatch.

Another rumble. Louder than a thundercloud. *Seeker* tossed to and fro. Scattered equipment and tools rolled from one side of the module to the other. Zentsov's distended body swayed until its rotten neck ripped apart. The corpse splattered on the floor.

Rachel pounded the interior air-lock release button. "Come on, goddamnit!"

Seeker shook, then tilted thirty-five degrees eastward. Its walls creaked. The sudden jerk slammed Rachel into an EMU suit locker. Her left shoulder flared in pain. The rumbling continued, preventing her from standing or gaining a handhold.

"Rachel!" Larsen's voice burst from Rachel's helmet speaker. "Are you—"

The connection fizzled into static. The rumbling stopped.

Seeker's main console blinked on, displaying warnings in bright red. A moment later, a seismograph chart appeared on-screen. The module's seismometer indicated the region had suffered a magnitude 7.2 earthquake.

"Vanja?" Rachel coughed, tasting bile. It burned her mouth, stomach.

The console screen flashed off, then back on. It showed Brent in the butte basin.

Extending his hand to her.

Rachel lurched to her feet and tried the interior air lock again. Still stuck.

The image on the console panned out, revealing crashed starships around Brent. The basin became a blue lake, and the buttes, azure pillars. Brent beckoned her.

She punched the air-lock release, then kicked it. The hatch finally opened in a shower of sparks. After she leapt through, it didn't shut back.

The exterior air lock was cracked but not compromised. Yet the sight outside made her sob, made her guts shrivel, made her chest throb until she thought her heart would claw itself free of her body. As soon as her HUD indicated it was safe, she flung open the exit hatch and stumbled from the module into the first rays of dawn.

They illuminated a hellish world. The earthquake had ripped open a great ravine fifty meters to the south. Fissures and sinkholes now fractured the landscape. On the westward horizon, the mesa had vanished. The southern flatlands were jagged and crackled like a giant, dry lakebed.

The rover was gone. In its place was a yawning crevice.

Rachel staggered over the uneven ground until she reached the crevice's edge. She knelt but soon found herself on her knees and elbows, crying. Each breath came fast and hard. Her gloved hands raked through the sand, trying to find stability, only to have it slip between her quivering fingers.

A red light blinked in the chasm's depths.

"Vanja, Kiano!" she shouted over the radio.

The light blinked again: the rover's emergency strobe. In that split second of crimson radiance Rachel spotted a cracked windshield. A crushed wheel.

"I'm coming! Anyone read me?"

A rumble, followed by a suctioning noise, made Rachel spin around.

Seeker disappeared into a massive sinkhole. A dust plume jetted into the air.

Rachel looked from the sinkhole to the crevice. She stood, judged the fissure's depth. Checked her thrustpack's fuel. Calculated her rate of fall in 0.7 G at her body mass of 48 kilograms in an EMU suit weighing 20 kilograms.

As she leapt into the crevice, Zentsov's final missive came back to her:

They know us. They want us. There is no escape.

Chief Medical Officer's journal. Mission date: Sol 17.

I kept telling Nasreen how much I loved her. Her only answer was that enigmatic smile, followed by a gesture indicating she wanted me to follow. After she touched me with a vine, I stopped bleeding. I must have lost a liter or more. Why wasn't I dead?

I was so thirsty. So fatigued that my feet were numb, my steps those of a bumbling, blind fool. Perhaps that is what I am. Yet Nasreen was no longer there. It was Burgess. Helmetless, healthy, and possessing all the humanity of a marionette. Her eyes glowed blue and her hands were vines, like Nasreen.

Nasreen. Who had never been here after all. Who was dead and buried on Earth.

I refused to follow Burgess at first. As she walked toward me, I scrambled to inject myself with a final morphine dose I'd saved for myself. The needle pierced my side.

Burgess ripped through my EMU suit and yanked out the embedded syringe. I screamed for her to let me die. She answered by shoving one of those vines over the tiny perforation the needle had made on my skin. It dug through my flesh and wrapped around my torso. The morphine's initial insensate euphoria faded. She'd saved me.

Weeping, I punched her. Shoved her. Begged for death, for mercy.

Then the ground split open all around us.

We must have been kilometers away from the camp when the earthquake struck. Dawn's sunlight crept over the turbulent landscape. The seismic juggernaut knocked me down but Burgess lifted me in her arms. As I watched in speechless horror, the mesa fell apart and collapsed. I hated myself all over again for not getting Paredo and Jemutai in time. Now they had perished in a far worse manner than I would have honored them with.

Worse, I felt used. These aliens, demons, djinn—whatever they are— had lured me out here with a trick. It's as if they know what I desire most and have shamed me with it by using Nasreen's form against me. The quake reminded me all over again of how she died. Of how I had volunteered to dig through the rubble in order to find her.

I cursed and attacked Burgess all over again. A flea challenging a camel.

Carrying me over her shoulders, Burgess never tired in her pace. I had no idea where she was taking me. Why I was spared. How I was even alive, breathing this air.

After a while she bore me into a newly opened crevice filled with those vines. They weren't dried or desiccated, like the samples Terman and Larsen had found. These were alive, for that is the only way I can describe them. I tried talking to Burgess again. I asked where we were going, what had happened to her. Each query was ignored.

Where she took me replaced my curiosity with terrified wonder.

The vine-choked opening gave way to a wide, flat expanse. Ruptured, torn ledges towered over it, as if the earthquake had birthed this anomaly. A blue lake, exactly like the one Terman and Larsen described, lay in the center. It was surrounded by a virtual forest of the vines. Here and there a pillar of the same sapphire-like material stood.

Scattered amidst this impossible vista were countless starships. Wrecked, burned, torn, or even whole, they varied in design and coloration.

None were of Earth, save for one.

Bimini. *Brent stood outside it, his eyes glowing, his vine-like hands beckoning.*

Burgess set me down and walked into the forest of vines. Minutes passed.

I should have knelt and begged Allah's mercy, but I was through with prayers.

As I waited, I noticed that the flat area's rounded borders appeared unnatural. Precise, as if machined down to certain specifications. Especially with the ripped cliffs above it, mangled by the quake. I stood and paced its perimeter, and soon noticed a faint design within the stone: a coiled, serpentine shape. Like a labyrinth from humanity's mythological past. From the dark, primitive reaches of the subconscious.

I walked that circle, over and over, until I realized I was standing on the blue lake. I wasn't exhausted. Wasn't hungry or thirsty. I felt safe within the lake's confines.

It was the way I felt whenever I was around Nasreen.

It was love.

It bothers me to be so selfish, and not respond with fear, or even anger, at all the people we have lost on this mission. Those I have murdered. Perhaps I have lost all empathy; the very quintessence of what it means to be a doctor.

But what else do I have to look forward to? I will never return to Earth. I'm not sure I would even if I were given the chance. Things have changed. I am changed.

Something stirs in the vine forest. The lake vibrates beneath my feet.

They are here.

Personal journal, Mission Specialist Li. Mission date: Sol 17.

Kovac wouldn't stop screaming.

I tried to coax him into calming down. Which was crazy, since a huge wall of dirt and stone had just filled in the tunnel behind us. Kovac had stood the closest to it. One more meter and he'd have been dead. Not sure if I would've cared. Though the earthquake had spared us, it cut off any return to Chiron's modules. Shit, shit, shit.

The screaming continued. Sakurai shook Kovac, shouted at him.

I finally punched him in the stomach, ending that fucking noise. Kovac fell to the tunnel floor while Sakurai shoved me away from him. We argued for a few minutes, but Sakurai shut up after I reminded her that Kovac had kept this from us all along. The bastard didn't say a word, just stared down the tunnel with some sick hope.

I hated him all over again.

Sakurai said we'd be okay since we'd replenished our oxygen supplies with whatever the previous crew left behind in that weird-ass place. Though it was obvious she was changing the subject, it summoned all of those questions again.

Why were the modules buried? Where was Chiron itself? All day yesterday we'd spent searching the eight modules and accessing more data from that one tablet. These people had believed the moon could give them something. Something from their dreams.

While the dust cleared, I shined my light forward. Kovac was excited that the tunnel ahead of us hadn't collapsed as well. So was I, but for different reasons. I wanted out of there. I think he still wanted to find whatever the UEA had really sent us here for.

Despite the quake, and sand leaking into the tunnel from cracks overhead, we continued. After twenty meters or so the tunnel went deeper at a thirty-degree decline.

Kovac became even more enthused. Said something about an energy field emitting from within the moon's interior. That Zentsov had surmised the same thing. Yes, I was interested, but it pissed me off even more. Then he started talking about draco centaurus _and why the artifact had been buried with the modules. Though Sakurai was still limping, my elbow was_ *throbbing, and we might be walking to our deaths, I realized that even then, after all this bullshit, only the mission mattered to Kovac.*

I'd been so stupid in following him.

After twenty minutes we spotted a light far below. At least six hundred more meters down. The pedometer on my HUD indicated we'd already walked four hundred since descending. The tunnel remained a perfect square though a few cracks showed.

No digger bot had made this. It had to be the beings we were searching for. Of course it scared me. I walked on anyway. I needed to see.

At the bottom the tunnel branched westward, then terminated in a grotto filled with wreckage. Damaged crew modules. A rover with Aloha *painted on the doors.*

Persepolis. Olduvai. Luzinia. *The cockpit module from* Centaurus. Seeker, *lying on its side.*

My suit's scanner told me all of it was real. Not a hallucination from pain, hunger, or stress. Far above, a sinkhole opened up, allowing in a brief flash of daylight. We all shined our lights skyward as it closed. Then the damn thing moved. Moved! The sinkhole crawled across the grotto's ceiling like a desert tarantula navigating the Gobi wastes.

Sakurai gasped and I gazed forward. Vines slithered over the wreckages, plump and giving off an occasional electrical spark. Blue light leaked through an opening on the other side of the grotto. But that wasn't what she started pointing at.

Someone knelt outside Seeker's *hatch. Their EMU was dirty, grungy, like they'd been working in the desert for days. The figure wasn't wearing a helmet.*

I stopped a few meters away, but Kovac kept walking over to it. The person in the suit didn't turn around, and I wasn't about to break radio silence. Sakurai shook her head.

Seeker's *hatch opened. A bright blue glow spilled from it.*

Whimpering, Sakurai shook her head more vehemently. Like she was angry.

Kovac was all smiles, hands extended as if to receive something.

The figure turned and asked me to help.

It was my uncle.

Using a brush, he cleared away the remains of my parents at his feet. They weren't there before. He urged me to join him, the smile I remembered so fondly crinkling the crow's-feet around his eyes. Even though I was still wearing my helmet, I smelled the earthy aroma I recalled from his clothes after we'd been excavating all day in my childhood. My anger with Kovac melted away. I stepped forward, feeling a peace I'd not experienced since leaving Earth. My uncle kept grinning. Offered me my old brush.

Sakurai charged forward and kicked my uncle in the back. He fell over.

Kovac shouted in anger and flung Sakurai aside. I, too, rushed forward, ready to pummel her. Until I saw the figure's face. It wasn't my uncle. It was Stevenson. Or, it had been him. Most of his face was gone, bordered with gleaming blue nodules.

Crying, Sakurai cursed her father for beating her and her sisters, swearing she would kill him if he ever touched them again. But when I held her back, and she realized it was Stevenson instead of her father, she, too, relented.

Not Kovac. Mumbling something about his wife, he stepped into Seeker *and came out carrying the artifact,* draco centaurus. *Vines from within the module slithered around him. I yelled a warning, Sakurai screamed at him, but he looked down at Stevenson. Thanked him for the forgiveness. It dawned on me that he still believed Stevenson was his wife. Like I'd seen my uncle, and Sakurai her father.*

The things from our nightmares, used to fool us, to draw us in.

Sakurai and I kept yelling at Kovac that it wasn't his wife. He ignored us as the vines opened the seals of his suit and entered. Coiling inside his faceplate.

The artifact glowed brighter.

Other figures blocked any retreat back up the tunnel. One was Burgess. Some wore suits with Chiron *under the name patch. The rest were…Well, they weren't human. That's all I can say because, at that point, Sakurai grabbed my hand and we ran.*

We reached the opening across the grotto. I'm not sure what worried me more: seeing people that I knew were dead, seemingly controlled by those vines, or the fact that the assholes didn't bother chasing after us. I stopped short as we neared the opening.

Sakurai tugged me on, yelling like crazy, but I looked over my shoulder.

Kovac held the artifact aloft like a prize. Laughing like the selfish bastard he was.

Something zipped past me from the opening. I felt the wind off of it, heard a sharp crack through my aural sensors. Kovac jerked and tumbled backward. When the artifact hit the ground the dead—whatever the hell they were—all flinched.

A hole smoked in Kovac's chest. He was still smiling.

I turned and spotted a figure in an EMU suit—complete with helmet— running away. More curious than angry, I raced after it. Sakurai tried to follow. After I went ten meters or so, I remembered and went back for her. No way would I leave her to them.

We hobbled from the grotto into an open area coated in a gleaming blue, crystalline vastness. Like reality suddenly morphed from that subterranean shithole to this grandiose edifice. It felt like walking on the sky and the ocean at the same time.

The figure who'd shot Kovac was still running up ahead.

I didn't waste breath hailing them on the radio. My elbow smarted even worse and Sakurai's steps were slowing. Shapes moved beneath the blue surface, then formed into pillars, pyramids, spheres, and other objects. At the area's edges I spotted distant cliffs. Surrounding us on all sides. Judging from the exposed sediment layers, I assumed it was damage from the earthquake.

Until things clicked and snapped together within those layers. Glowing blue collections of objects that could only be described as machinery. Thousands of vines knotted together in pulsing clumps, moving earth, sand, and stone. They clasped other wreckages. Other vessels and derelicts. And no way in hell did any of it come from Earth.

The readings on my HUD were just as improbable: surface temperature of 295 Kelvin. Air pressure steady at 100 kilopascals. No radiation. Gravity was 1 g.

It would've been a perfect day back on Earth.

The figure wheeled around and aimed a pistol. Despite the distance, I recognized the face. It was Etana Okoye. A mission specialist assigned to crew module *Olduvai. Presumed dead with all the others we lost when* Centaurus *blew up.*

Sakurai yelled, but I pushed her down. The increased gravity made it easier.

Okoye fired. The bullet pierced my torso just below the sternum.

The next moment I was on my back. Sakurai tried to help me but I waved her on. Blood was already pooling around my body. I felt an awful chill. Numbness stole sensation from my toes, fingers. My elbow hurt less.

Something flashed ahead.

Sakurai looked forward, her jaw shaking, then she gazed at me. I saw fear mixing with apology in her eyes. I told her to go. That I'd be okay. She finally ran on.

Even as my life drained away, I felt movement on the ground behind me.

Bakir was there. Holding the artifact. My draco centaurus.

When I looked back up, Okoye was still running across the blue expanse. Sakurai fled between the starships as more figures followed her.

Bakir knelt and lay the artifact on my chest. He was also without a helmet and had glowing blue eyes. His voice came over my radio, telling me I was ready.

The blue lake opened beneath me. I fell right in, landing on a bed of vines. They wrapped around me, binding my legs and arms. I couldn't move, couldn't even scratch my ass. But now I clutched the artifact. It was throbbing.

Oddly enough, I wasn't scared. This was the reason I'd joined the UEA, the reason I'd given up eight years with my friends and family to come here. So I laid still.

A vine wrapped around my neck. It removed my helmet. The air was perfect.

Other vines latched on to my flesh. Within seconds I entered a different state of…well, consciousness, I guess. Like I could see, hear, and feel everything of the others who'd been taken by the vines. Some were dead, like Stevenson and Burgess, whereas Bakir was still alive. Sort of. They were glad I'd come. They'd been waiting for the right species, with a populated world, to continue their mission.

The moon's mission.

Flight Recorder – *Maray* Crew Module
Sol 17 – 0822 hours
Orbiting Proxima Centauri C

CMP Worrel: I told you not to open *Maray*'s hatch!

MS Khandaar: It wasn't me!

CFE Moore: You're saying it opened all by itself?

CMP Worrel: Or whatever's flying that vessel opened it. Shit.

CFE Moore: But they've been docked with us for hours. (gasps) No attempt at communication—that we can tell—and no change in course. It's orbiting the moon, too.

MS Khandaar: Sir, what are you doing?

CMP Worrel: This ship docks with us, forces our hatch open, and a bloody earthquake has just rocked the moon below. I'm not waiting for more coincidences.

CFE Moore: You're going in there?

MS Khandaar: Oh my God, sir, are you crazy?

CMP Worrel: I guess we'll find out.

CFE Moore: Hell with this, I'm coming, too. (coughs)

CMP Worrel: Not in your condition. We've barely kept you stable.

CFE Moore: Damn it, Andrew—

CMP Worrel: Kevin? I'm ordering you to stay here. Please.

MS Khandaar: I'm going.

CMP Worrel: I just gave him an order and now you're lairing it up?

MS Khandaar: Kevin can take *Maray*'s controls. You need me. Going in there alone is insanity. Look through that hatch. Nothing on *Centaurus* gave off a blue light.

CMP Worrel: (sighs) No drama, then. But stay behind me. If something happens to me, you'll at least have the chance to shoot through back into *Maray*.

CFE Moore: You trying to be a hero, sir?

CMP Worrel: No. I'm doing what an officer's supposed to bloody do. How's your EMU setup, Jivika? Hopefully Kevin didn't use all of our air while bragging about that last poker game. Do you know what the odds are of drawing three aces?

CFE Moore: (laughs) Oh, you're funny. Listen, I'm not sure what I can do to help from here. (groans) No radio transmitter, and no way to disable their docking locks.

CMP Worrel: If something happens, or we're not back in ten minutes, fire *Maray*'s thrusters. Use all of the fuel to push that other vessel into reentry. Maybe that will warn any of our mates down below.

CFE Moore: Got it. Good luck, you two.

MS Khandaar: Take care of yourself, honey.

CFE Moore: (laughs) Yeah. You, too.

CMP Worrel: Ready? Let's do this.

MS Khandaar: Look here. This can't...Oh shit, this can't be possible.

CFE Moore: What is it? You okay?

CMP Worrel: This dock has the same configuration as the one on *Centaurus*.

CFE Moore: What?

CMP Worrel: It's like a sister ship to *Centaurus*. There's a title over the air lock.

MS Khandaar: *Chiron?*

CFE Moore: You've gotta be shitting me.

CMP Worrel: Wait, here's...

(static, garbled voices)

MS Khandaar: Sir! Get away from it!

(static, shouts)

CMP Worrel: It's as mad as a cut snake! Don't let it touch you!

CFE Moore: Get back in *Maray*. Do you copy?

MS Khandaar: (sobs) Oh shit. Oh my God, what is that? Oh my—

CMP Worrel: Some kind of vine all over these stasis pods. I don't—

(static)

MS Khandaar: (gasps) Who are you?

CMP Worrel: She's not replying.

MS Khandaar: Her eyes are glowing blue. That's the light we saw.

CFE Moore: Damn it. (groans) Do either of you copy? What's happening?

MS Khandaar: She's also not wearing a helmet. I'm not detecting any oxygen, sir.

CMP Worrel: Jivika, stay back.

MS Khandaar: (screams) Get it off! Get it off!

CMP Worrel: Kevin, shut the damn hatch! Hit the thrusters!

CFE Moore: Tell me what's going on!

CMP Worrel: We're not alone up here.

21

As she hides behind a blue pillar, Etana regrets not printing a spare pistol. Trying to dispatch her comrades with only one shot at a time cannot succeed. She had hoped to keep one bullet for herself. Now she might not even get that. Her oxygen is running out.

Etana trailed Terman's rover to this location, and was in the process of sneaking up on the vehicle while Terman was inside *Seeker*. Then the earthquake struck.

At first Etana hoped the disaster had done her work for her, but no. Since her own rover has been swallowed by a fissure, and Terman entered one to find her friends, Etana followed. The sights she sees down here are beyond anything she has imagined. Her superiors never mentioned any of it. It is likely they did not know. Will never know.

Finding Kovac and Li was a surprise she took advantage of. Sakurai is next.

Burgess steps out from behind a nearby pillar. Stevenson and Higgs. Santos.

The sight of those she has already killed makes Etana freeze. It is worse than her superiors thought. The moon is using the dead and the living.

She shoots Burgess in the chest. Reloads, sends a round through Santos's skull.

The vines on their bodies pulsate and cover the bloodless injuries. Out of instinct and reflex, Etana loads again. Fires. The futility of it makes her cry out in rage.

As one, they stop coming. Her HUD flashes red as her air decays into CO_2.

The vines along the cliffs sway but there is no wind. A low hum permeates the area, vibrating in her chest. Her HUD indicates acceptable environmental conditions.

Etana removes her helmet. Breathes in the fresh air. Reloads her gun.

Brent stares at her from across the lake as another figure walks up behind him.

She aims.

The boy stops beside Brent. Smiling at her with enticement.

It has come down to this. Etana slowly lowers the pistol. The gun is more symbol than weapon at this point. An emblem that rejects life, compromise, and peace. Just as she rejects what they offer. Rejects it for all of Earth. The only way to pay for her crimes.

The boy comes closer. Etana trembles. It has always been so easy to pull the trigger. To draw blood for a cause not her own. Yet now she hates herself for it.

He offers his hand. Brent, Stevenson, and others. They all wait. There is no hatred in their eyes. No judgment.

It would be easy to simply hand the boy her gun.

His smile is that of a much older person. A visage of pure contentment.

She has another choice. One final, declarative act. That decision would also be easy, were it not for the pain in her heart. Now at the end it betrays her.

"I did it," a voice croaks behind her.

She whirls around. Aims.

Kovac stands there, holding a strange serpentine object that gleams like a sapphire aflame. Vines slowly crawl over his body. Burrowing into his flesh.

"I did it," he says. "I found it. This makes everything worth it, Etana. Our suffering. But I can feel them…taking me over. Help me get this…back to Earth…"

Even with a bullet and alien organisms invading his body, Kovac remains driven. Etana has felt such conviction in moments of great pain and sorrow. Now she knows that drive was an attempt to silence her conscience before guilt and remorse drove her mad.

"I cannot," Etana murmurs, then her voice strengthens. "I will not."

"You're a fool…like all the rest." Face wracked with the effort of resisting the vines, Kovac stumbles toward her. She moves aside, but he grabs hold of her gun.

They wrestle for it. As he screams at her, Etana knees him in the stomach. Punches his face repeatedly with her other hand. Yet the vines grant him vigor.

"You won't stop me!" Kovac wrenches the gun away. Points it at her.

Etana manages to push the barrel down as Kovac fires.

The bullet pierces her where she wants it. Her false appendix ruptures, discharging its contents. The bioterminator, meant to make the moon uninhabitable for humans, gushes from her in a yellow cloud. It surrounds her and Kovac. It kills him first.

Her lungs burn. Sores tear open along her flesh. Convulsions force her to kneel.

Blue energy arcs from the lake, zipping over the cliffs. The hum strengthens. The resulting vibration sends Etana onto her back. A reanimated Kovac stands straight as the other absorbed crew members gather round. Blood pools around her. It hurts to breathe.

"I am sorry," Etana whispers. "For everything."

The boy again offers his hand. She accepts it. His grin is the last thing she sees.

Three meters still separated Rachel and the crevice's bottom when her thrustpack depleted its fuel. She tucked and rolled as her feet connected with the ground. A jolt shot through her body. If her bones weren't titanium polymer, she'd surely have broken some.

"Vanja?" Rachel removed the pack from her suit and stood.

The rover lay fifteen meters up ahead, pitched on its side. The driver's-side door was mashed inward, the windshield cracked, and both front wheels crushed.

"Kiano? Anybody read me?"

She clambered over boulders and chunks of fractured sediment layers. Tiny blue gleams popped across these layers, as well as the crevice's sides towering above her. Here and there a vine burrowed through the stone, as if the material merely parted itself for the pulpy tentacles. Rachel walked and climbed faster.

The rover was empty. Huge gouges marred it. The passenger door was open. It was smeared with blood.

"Does anyone copy?" Rachel jumped atop the rover and continued along the crevice floor. The exposed earth led down dozens of meters into an even larger fissure. A blue light emanated from far below.

She wondered who was wounded. How Larsen was breathing without a helmet.

A manic, fiery energy filled her.

"Someone answer me." Rachel slid, climbed, and skidded down into the fissure. Sharp stones ripped holes in her EMU's outer layer. The inner layer sealed itself against her flesh as a safety measure. Her HUD glowed red with warnings.

Loose pebbles and sediment crumbled beneath her. Rachel tumbled to the bottom and landed on her back. Her left shoulder blazed anew with pain. As she carefully stood, it required more effort. As if someone had loaded her with fifteen or twenty extra kilos.

Her aural sensors detected a shrill, tinny noise.

A light flashed orange, then red, on her HUD. She was losing oxygen.

With desperate, feverish movements Rachel managed to reach around and touch her air supply. Her fingers encountered a hole spouting gas.

The fall had punctured her oxygen tank.

"Please, answer me!" she shouted. The radio's silence mocked her.

She ran on. Jumped over fallen stones. Tripped on loose sand.

"Vanja!" She cried, already getting short of breath. "Kiano? Anybody? I pierced my oxygen tank in a fall, and—"

Loose sediment collapsed from the fissure walls on both sides. Stone slabs larger than the rover crashed into the crevice behind her. Pebbles and dust slammed into her.

She dove forward.

Gasping for air as her oxygen ran ever lower, Rachel crawled through a crude tunnel created by the falling slabs. Her gloves scraped through sand and dirt until her left shoulder ached so much she screamed. A meter later she had to stop altogether. Most of her air was gone, robbing her of energy. The noise of the cave-in muted until the only sounds were her weakening breaths and hammering heartbeats.

"Vanja...Jemutai..." She swallowed. "This is Terman...please respond."

Onward she crawled, her suit lights winking in and out as she fumbled through the cramped confines. The tunnel collapsed behind her. Each breath became hotter from inhaling more carbon dioxide than oxygen. Her lungs hurt, her throat constricted. Still she wriggled until open sky shone above her. The sight elicited laughter that turned into sobs.

The radio was an empty well she poured her emotions into, asking for Larsen, for Jemutai, even for Bakir to put her out of her misery. She giggled, she prayed to gods she'd never believed in, she told stories to herself. This was what it was like to go mad.

A voice on the radio made Rachel fall still.

"Repeat, this is Andrew Worrel, orbiting above you in UEA *Chiron*. We have its scanners online and we're detecting a module transponder near you. There might—"

Rachel shut her eyes, opened them again.

"Commander Terman, please respond. This is Worrel—"

"I'm not her anymore," Rachel muttered, her words slurred. "She's dead."

The outlines of a sinkhole formed around her. Vines slithered close.

Suffocating, claimed by the moon, her nightmare had come true.

Something tugged on her hand.

Rachel raised her head. Mom stood a few meters away, balancing herself on a boulder like she'd done that day at Ophir Chasma.

"What are you doing?" Rachel whispered.

"I'm facing my fear." Mom spread her arms and shuddered. "I'm not going to let it beat me. I'm not letting it tell me what I can and can't do."

"You're not Mom," Rachel said. "You're not…"

Colors swirled in her vision. Rachel forced herself to focus. It was her HUD.

Updates blinked on it. The moon's air quality and pressure were now safe. No radiation, but the gravity had increased. That explained why everything felt heavier.

She gazed across the fissure again. Though Mom was gone, her words weren't.

Hope surged in Rachel as she took off her helmet. She'd not tasted air this fresh since her last visit to Earth. Larsen and Jemutai might be alive. The helmet clattered on stone as she raced through the fissure. Her voice echoed as she called for her friends.

The crevice's ledges grew taller as she traveled deeper into the massive declivity. More vines wiggled and pulsed along the exposed layers. The farther she went, the more Rachel realized none of it could be natural. Glowing blue devices burrowed, reshaped, and spread through stone and earth faster than any human-made analog.

She halted at a blockage in the chasm. A pile of rubble and boulders.

Before she could climb over it, the rubble cleared away of its own volition. The ground morphed into a flat, sparkling blue surface. Vines bordered it like trees flanking a boulevard or walkway. Though she quivered in terror, Rachel forced herself to continue.

The fissure gave way to a wide, circular area bounded by ragged cliffs created by the earthquake. The area was covered in the blue material. Sleek, nonreflective—just like the lake she and Larsen had found. Pillars and other structures dotted the lake, formed of the same substance. For all her worries and aches, Rachel could only stare in amazement. Though she'd ascended Olympus Mons, walked the Sea of Tranquility, and swam in the Bahamas, her eyes had never beheld such beauty. It was like a sapphire temple to some forgotten goddess. A sense of harmony overcame her. She didn't hurt any longer.

Forests of vines surrounded the lake. They swayed and scintillated with green, brown, and yellow hues. Derelict spacecraft that defied the imagination lay all around. Some were tiny capsules akin to humanity's early forays into the void. Others were kilometers in length, shaped like titanic biomorphs of violet and black metal.

She spotted *Aloha*'s rover, the one that had vanished days ago outside *Seeker*. Next she gaped at *Seeker* itself, still lying on its side. *Persepolis, Luzinia, Olduvai,* and even *Centaurus*'s cockpit module were present. In the center of them stood *Bimini*.

Its transponder had been reattached, swathed in vines.

Brent waited there. Larsen lay at his feet, clasping a bloodied right arm. Jemutai knelt a meter away, his helmet beside him on the azure expanse.

"Don't you touch her!" Rachel rushed toward them.

"*Kjære*, wait," Larsen said. "He means no harm."

"What?" Rachel circled Brent, ready to pounce. "Look at him. They've taken him, changed him. He's no longer human!"

"It is not like that," Larsen said.

"You better be right," Jemutai said. "Because here comes more of them."

Others walked toward them across the blue lake. A few she recognized as fellow crew members, including the three dead astronauts from *Bimini*. Some were humans in older UEA suits: the *Chiron* expedition. Most, however, were what could only be called aliens. Hovering rhomboids with tentacles, insect-like quadrupeds, robotic spheres with pincers, even a collection of glistening organs that reshaped itself with each step. Each had a vine attached to them.

Rachel knelt at Larsen's side, still eyeing Brent with suspicion. "Are you okay?"

"The rover struck sharp stones on the way down into that crevice," Larsen said. "One pierced the door and got me. Jemutai bandaged it."

She kissed Larsen's cheek. "What do they want? Why are they doing this?"

"Whatever this moon is, it uses these bodies to communicate." Larsen leaned into her. "Brent was taken so they can talk to us."

"But…he's not talking." Jemutai held a knife at his side, ready to defend them.

"Maybe they do not understand how the human body works yet," Larsen said. "Also explains the nightmares. Thought Brent was my Grandpapa and this lake, the Nærøyfjord. Then I saw you, Rachel. All was from my dream."

Rachel slowly nodded, recalling what had replayed earlier from her own dreams. "Maybe. But for what? Why have they taken all of these ships and vehicles?"

Larsen's smile faded. "That is what bothers me."

A gunshot rang out. Then another.

The former crew members and nonhumans faced eastward. The lake gleamed so bright that Rachel closed her eyes. She clasped Larsen to her chest. Waiting for the end.

Personal journal, Mission Specialist Li. Mission date: Sol 17.

Kovac gave me a pat of assurance, as if everything would be all right—even as the vines slid through my suit's seals. It was weird, interacting with a man I knew was dead. I mean…he had to be dead, right? Okoye had shot him, after all.

I was no longer beneath the blue lake, but sliding through earth and stone to a great mass of vines. Kovac wouldn't answer any questions. I stopped asking after the vines parted for him. And I don't mean he pushed them aside. They literally fucking moved, creating a path for him. What he showed me was both terrifying and…wonderful.

It was other dark blue artifacts. Coiled and metallic like the one I'd found.

Kovac smiled and extended his hand. A vine snaked from it and sank into my chest. Like the dirt and rocks, my flesh spread apart for what I thought was the end.

This…I can't…It was too much, you know? It was like this:

I was blind before, but after they opened my eyes, I could truly see—through all of their eyes. Hear and feel what they experienced. A biomechanical network.

My body was free of pain. Of hunger, anxiety, jealousy, and anger. Since I felt complete, there was no need for those things. Now I could focus on the moon's mission.

Each "artifact" was a world unto itself, in comparison to what my species has encountered. A driver, an intelligence and nerve center, for what the moon does. Chiron's crew had discovered it, but they failed to comprehend it. Thus, it absorbed them.

Its network allowed me some free will. I guess because I didn't resist.

The ground opened for me and I was once again on what Terman had called the blue lake. I walked through the forest of vines. They parted for me now, the chosen one who could bridge our species. I touched them, feeling the stems and leaves with my naked hands. Each had a name, a face. But not from this world. From countless worlds.

I know why the moon had lured us here. Like it has lured so many others over its long existence. The assimilation of data from Centaurus's cockpit module is complete. That's why Chiron's crew burned everything, even their supplies, in a desperate attempt to stop this damn thing from finding the route back to Earth. It's why the moon took vehicles, ships, devices, and finally people. To find a way—any way—to obey its directives.

Even now, I sense through this network that Chiron *has been sent to intercept a module still orbiting us. Those aboard* Chiron *will install themselves, and their vines, into that module. Extending the network, you know? And the more people it absorbs, the easier the moon thinks it'll be to convince the rest of our species to accept it.*

It thinks it needs Earth to complete its mission. It cannot be stopped.

Etana tried. She used all the faculties allowed our species by evolution, all of our technology. She can't be faulted for that. But she still made the wrong decisions.

She kept watching the boy as I walked up beside him. I felt pride at the courage in my former teammate's eyes. We humans express so much with our ocular organs, and Etana delivered a command performance in that moment before the moon took her.

Flight Recorder – *Maray* Crew Module
Sol 17 – 0952 hours
Orbiting Proxima Centauri C

CMP Worrel: Terman's not answering her radio. Damn it.

MS Khandaar: Sir, what do we do with…with these things?

CMP Worrel: Jettison them out the air lock.

MS Khandaar: But they're still moving! They might still be human!

CFE Moore: You said you conked one in the head with an air canister.

CMP Worrel: I did. The woman it used to be is still…alive. Her face has merged with these nodules full of blue light. She doesn't even have eyes, nose, or a mouth.

CFE Moore: Yeah, fuck that. I say air lock.

MS Khandaar: We should at least study them. Did you see their eyes?

CMP Worrel: Yes, like some form of bloody psychosis. Perhaps they were all exposed to something on this moon. These cranky vines.

CFE Moore: Yep. Air lock. (coughs)

MS Khandaar: Kevin, don't be an asshole.

CMP Worrel: How soon until *Chiron*'s above that lake?

MS Khandaar: Sir, we're reading *Bimini*'s beacon, but—

CMP Worrel: This is the first time since we've arrived that all that signal noise has gone quiet. We'll not get another chance to save them.

MS Khandaar: How? We hear Terman crying and talking craziness over the radio, and then she doesn't answer us?

CMP Worrel: I'm not leaving her. How soon till we're above the lake?

MS Khandaar: Five minutes.

CMP Worrel: Hey, what's that noise?

MS Khandaar: Wait, that thing is getting up—(gasps)—sir!

CFE Moore: Shit. I told you.

CMP Worrel: Close the hatch to the cockpit module!

(hatch closes, pounding on the door)

MS Khandaar: We can't rescue anyone with those things on board.

CMP Worrel: Open the air lock in the adjoining modules.

MS Khandaar: Shit.

CFE Moore: (coughs) Well?

MS Khandaar: The air locks. They're not responding.

CMP Worrel: Keep trying.

MS Khandaar: Oh God. Sir, those vines. Power has rerouted through them.

CMP Worrel: Damn it. Moore, how are you doing in *Maray*?

CFE Moore: I'm… (gasps) almost there.

CMP Worrel: What? Stay in *Maray*, there's nothing you can do.

CFE Moore: I can open that one air lock manually. (gasps) Those bodies and vines are in Centrifuge A, right?

CMP Worrel: Kevin, get your ass back into *Maray*!

MS Khandaar: Please, you can't stop them!

CFE Moore: Someone down there has hope now. A chance to (coughs) make it out of here. I'm going to make sure you all get that chance.

CMP Worrel: Kevin, please! Tether yourself to something and we'll—

CFE Moore: Too late. They're onto me. But I'm (gasps) almost there.

MS Khandaar: The release of atmosphere will take you, too! Please. (sobs)

CFE Moore: Shh, honey. Tell that Cambridge professor he's a lucky guy.

MS Khandaar: No! Don't do this!

CMP Worrel: Damn it, I'm bloody ordering you—

CFE Moore: Good luck, you two. It's been an honor.

(sounds of depressurization)

<h1 style="text-align:center">22</h1>

Rachel flinched as the area shifted. Some of the pillars and spheres changed position. The ground shook. Deep blue objects rose in the far distance. So tall she could see them above the lake's surrounding cliffs, which were themselves a kilometer away.

"What is happening?" Jemutai asked.

Larsen shook her head. "This is not for our benefit. Feels like preparation."

A figure in an IVA now stood beside Brent. The same one that had landed in *Ilios.*

The others all stared at a prone figure twenty meters away.

"Etana Okoye?" Rachel murmured.

A yellow gas hovered over Etana, lying in her own blood. Brent and the others simply watched, making no move.

A yell pierced the air as Sakurai leapt onto Etana. They rolled around on the blue surface, trading blows until Etana flung Sakurai away. Sakurai slammed into *Bimini,* slid down onto her rump, and coughed. Etana stood. The gas was leaking from a bullet hole in her abdomen. Her eyes glowed blue.

"The hell?" Jemutai jumped to his feet, knife brandished.

Rachel shielded Larsen. "What are you doing?"

"She killed…Kovac." Sakurai held both hands over her stomach.

"Why?" Rachel shouted.

The lake opened up. Vines parted. A bright glow presaged the arrival of Li. Though still in his EMU, his hands and feet were now vines, and several had bored into his body. He paused and stared at Etana, then Sakurai.

"Li?" Rachel asked. Speaking was an instinctual response, an inquiry if it was really him. To see if he would answer like any normal human would. It was as much a test of her own sanity as it was a reflection of the insanity he now represented.

The gas stopped spreading from Etana's body as vines absorbed it. Each pulpy tip acted as a voracious, suctioning maw. A vine slid from Li's body and wound around Sakurai's stomach. She gasped and wriggled, but color returned to her ashen features.

"What do you want from us?" Rachel asked.

Bakir stepped from among the others. "It only wishes us peace. It can give us what we have always wanted, Commander Terman."

"What the moon has always wanted," Li said. "What it was created for."

His voice was calm, calculating. Lacking its typical conceit.

As Li drew close, Rachel helped Larsen to her feet. With Jemutai, they formed a wall of resistance. Li paced around, staring at the tall structures far away.

"And what is that?" Rachel asked. "Why have you joined them?"

Li shrugged. "I didn't join them. They accepted me into their biomechanical system, you know? Like they have all of these others. Even the ones who died."

"They don't look alive," Jemutai said.

"They're not." Li regarded Stevenson, Burgess, and the rest sadly. "The moon's trying to understand us. Larsen was right—they've tried to communicate with us from the very beginning. Via our dead, our gear, and our dreams. They don't wish to cause harm, which is why these interactions have remained benevolent. The moon isn't a murderer."

"You believe that?" Rachel asked.

"The first expedition misunderstood this moon and sent a message to Earth, asking for help," Li said. "Etana was sent by others who also misunderstood. She detonated the bomb on *Centaurus*, though she was not the one who planted it. Her benefactors got her placed in *Olduvai*, at the extreme rear of the ship, as far from the bomb as possible."

"So she could survive the blast and eliminate us," Jemutai said.

"But why?" Rachel's question turned into a wrathful sob.

"There are those within the UEA who fear that humanity will be enslaved," Li said. "The bioterminator inside her appendix would've made the moon uninhabitable to organic beings, ending its mission."

"Damn," Jemutai said. "So she was going to kill herself and us, too."

Li glanced at Etana as a vine slid around her shoulders. "She is at peace now."

"What was the moon created for?" Larsen asked.

Vines passed a coiled object to Li. "This is all that remains of the race who crafted this moon. All of their knowledge, culture, even their DNA—it's all inside this artifact, and others like it. The moon is tasked with finding other life-forms it can use to re-create its original masters. Changing other beings at the cellular level until they finally become the species who built this moon. Like a form of immortality, right? It's traveled from star to star, planet to planet, carrying out this duty. That's why it appeared to move in the UEA's telescope observation data—because it was relocating in this star system."

"The moon is transforming us into them," Rachel said. "That's why our blood cells have mutated—"

"Yes," Li said. "It's studied us in every way. Its network—the vines, the bodies—have taken what it needed for examination. Thirteen's fuel cell, *Aloha*'s rover, these modules and starships. Even *Chiron* in orbit above us. All added to its knowledge. Its energy field facilitates this transformation, as well as absorbs any waves it comes into contact with. This same energy creates all of the signal noise we've dealt with. Sometimes it used that to reach out to us, like sending fake transponder signals."

Rachel shared a look with Larsen. Recalling all the signals they'd chased.

"What do you mean, it 'absorbs'?" Jemutai asked. "Why us?"

"The moon's curious about humans," Li said. "It thinks our species might provide an acceptable foundation for the rebirth of its creators. It seeks more of us."

After activating the astronav app on her wrist pad, Larsen gasped. It showed their native solar system—and thus Earth—in a different position.

The moon was moving again.

"So it plans to invade Earth?" Rachel held Larsen tight. "Turn us all into this?"

"That's its intention." Li studied Rachel for a moment. "It captures and absorbs everything it encounters. All of these ships and nonhumans you see here. It's taken over entire civilizations, for billions of years, across millions of star systems."

"Its task still is not complete?" Larsen asked.

"No," Li said. "Candidates usually don't survive the process. But humans…"

Rachel shook her head. "Then it's a destroyer. Not a creator. Not a preserver of whatever its makers were."

"Etana, and those who sponsored her, suspected as much," Li said.

"Then we failed, whether we survive or not," Larsen said.

"Yes," Jemutai said. "The moon brought out the worst in us."

"No," Rachel said. "The moon screwed up. It used our obsessions and fears in an effort to converse with us. It used our dead. Our friends. It doesn't understand us any more than we understand it. Its makers created an imperfect machine."

"It was fed imperfect data," Li said. "Every human reaction to its attempts at communication were grounded in fear. So that's all it knew about us, and the moon used that. Fear was a useful survival mechanism earlier in our history, yet now it hinders us. The moon thought that, only through fear, could we understand and converse with it."

"Only so it can make us into something we're not," Rachel said.

Li stared at the azure brilliance under his vine-like feet, then faced them. "Look, I didn't come here to fail. I came here to explore and discover, you know? I came here to prove I'm more than just another asshole taking up space."

"Then let us go," Rachel said. "Let Earth and all its people live on."

Li lifted one of his vine appendages and stared at it. "You're assuming I can control it. It's absorbing me, too. It's trying so hard to understand. To find a home."

"So am I." Rachel stepped forward and clasped Li's vine-like hand.

Memories flooded her mind. Some were hers. Many more were not. The recollections of a million beings, from as many worlds, passed through her psyche like a horde of fireflies at midnight. Countless suns flaring in her consciousness. Each of them had been a thinking, feeling being. Taken by the moon in its lonely quest. A failed effort to satisfy the vanity of a long-dead race. The moon was indeed guileless. Innocent, even.

Aimless in its endeavors. Much like herself.

Larsen called out to her. Li regarded her with bewilderment.

Eyes closed, Rachel could sense the moon's network waiting, via her physical contact with Li's hand. Anticipating her input with the patience of eons.

Taking a deep breath, Rachel concentrated. She focused on all the trials she'd faced in her life. All the hardships, the heartaches. But the triumphs as well. The elation of accomplishment, laughter, contentment. Then love—for Mom and Dad, and Larsen. All the things that had made her who she was, and what she still could be. She showed the moon that she, too, had absorbed, had taken and borrowed. But only to learn and grow.

Never to replace or destroy.

Shuddering with emotion, Rachel opened her eyes.

Li stared at her with newfound respect. The other beings all faced her and extended a hand, a tentacle, a pincer, a vine. Connected to the network, they all felt what she'd imparted. The pillars, spheres, pyramids, and other structures flared brilliant blue.

"And home?" Li whispered.

"We carry it with us," Rachel said. "No matter where we go."

Gently withdrawing his hand, Li studied her for a long moment.

"Your bodies have already been exposed to the moon's energy," Li finally said. "I don't know how leaving will affect you."

"No one's ever escaped?" Jemutai asked. "None of these other species?"

"No," Li said.

"We'll risk it," Rachel said. "Isn't that what exploration is about? Risk?"

Li frowned. "I—"

"You want to prove something?" Rachel asked. "If the moon's accepted you, then convince it to choose a different mission. Share what its masters knew with the future, instead of trying to re-create the past. You're an archaeologist. That's what you do."

Brent, Kovac, Bakir, and the other beings all stared at Li. The rumbling stopped.

"That's what my uncle thought, too," Li said.

"Please," Rachel said.

"I'll try. But I can't make promises." Li closed his eyes.

The other beings cleared a path to *Bimini*.

"Sakurai?" Rachel asked as Larsen and Jemutai carefully backed toward *Bimini*.

"No." Sakurai rose and walked to Kovac. "I want to stay. I want to see, too."

Rachel gaped at her. "You're sure?"

"Yes." Sakurai leaned into Kovac and stared at the horizon.

"Go, while I can still influence it." Li's voice was tight. Sweat beaded his face.

Rachel wanted to say thanks, but Larsen grabbed her hand. They stumbled into *Bimini* as Jemutai activated its launch system. She turned for one last look.

Li, Sakurai, the other beings, the derelicts—all slowly sank into the blue vastness.

"Buckle yourselves in!" Jemutai shouted.

Rachel fastened Larsen into a seat, then sat and buckled her own restraints as the thrusters came to life. The view outside the hatch window blurred from gleaming blue to clouds to starry void. G-forces mashed her to the seat, then *Bimini* stopped shaking.

The thrusters went silent.

But they'd escaped. They were free.

The microgravity made Larsen's hair stand up. Rachel laughed.

"Oh no." Jemutai stared at the flight console. "Brace yourselves!"

Rachel glimpsed the proximity warning. A large object was coming at them.

The radio buzzed. "Commander Terman, is that you?"

Rachel frowned until she recognized the voice. "Worrel?"

"Your module is at the wrong angle to dock with *Chiron*," a female voice said. Rachel knew it had to be Mission Specialist Khandaar. "Use your thrusters and see if you can turn your yaw thirty degrees counterclockwise."

"Jemutai here, *Chiron*. We blew through all of our fuel."

"Think of something fast or we're going to shear right through you," Worrel said.

"Thirty seconds," Khandaar said.

Rachel stared around, sweat sliding down her neck. There was nothing to do.

"Twenty seconds," Khandaar said.

"Come on!" Jemutai tried the thrusters to no avail.

"Think, damn it, think!" Rachel turned to and fro in her seat. Desperate.

"Fifteen seconds." Khandaar's voice shook.

Larsen slowly grinned. "Good wind in the back is best." She indicated the hatch.

"Are you insane?" Jemutai cried.

"Do it!" Rachel yelled.

Jemutai slammed the release button. *Bimini*'s hatch opened. A maelstrom of air swirled out the opening with such force that the entire module shuddered. Rachel's breath went along with it. Loose tools and a few remaining vines darted out into the blackness.

But there was no way to control their direction. None of them wore a helmet.

Rachel caught Jemutai's attention amid the earsplitting chaos. She pointed at the service hatch on her left. He nodded, hit the release. The slimmer entrance slid open, competing with the main hatch for atmospheric release. *Bimini* spun round and round.

Jemutai watched Rachel until she made a cutting gesture across her neck. He shut the smaller hatch just as the last of their air gusted out. *Bimini* was no longer pressurized.

That meant they had ninety seconds until exposure to the vacuum killed them.

Larsen was the first out of her restraints. She pointed at her thrustpack and reached for them. Jemutai unbuckled and took her hand.

Holding her breath, Rachel tried to ignore a slight burning as the lower pressure started boiling the moisture in her flesh. Childhood memories held her back as much as the seat restraints. Larsen beckoned. Jemutai reached out. Still she struggled.

Until she glimpsed the moon below.

It was spackled with blue lines as massive fissures opened up. An azure halo appeared around it, then it zipped to another star system. Far away from Earth.

Li had done it. So could she.

Rachel unbuckled and flung herself from the chair. She drifted a painful second until they both grabbed her. The next moment Larsen jetted her thrustpack. They flew from *Bimini* as its main hatch aligned with *Chiron*'s air lock.

They were in.

Chiron's air lock clanged shut.

As their bodies acclimated with proper air pressure and breathable atmosphere, Rachel floated with Larsen further into the ship.

Drifting in the microgravity, Jemutai placed his hands behind his head and smiled. The hatch to the cockpit module opened. Worrel and Khandaar smiled with immense relief.

"Permission to come aboard?" Rachel grinned.

"Permission granted, Commander." Worrel grinned back.

"You have really let this place go," Jemutai said. The others laughed.

Larsen chuckled. "Better a whole ship than a—"

Rachel kissed her.

"Broken one," Larsen whispered.

They all laughed, hugged, and cried.

"You sure you want to do this?" Worrel asked.

Rachel nodded. "I'm sure."

Khandaar activated the main air lock. The remaining vines—gathered from *Chiron* and *Bimini* and now just rotten stalks—were jettisoned into space. Crowded into the cockpit module, they all watched it recede into the vastness, backlit by Proxima Centauri.

"The UEA might prosecute us," Jemutai said. "We just dumped one of the greatest finds in human history."

Larsen rolled her eyes and nudged him with her hip. "You wanted to keep it?"

"Hell no." Jemutai smiled.

Worrel sighed and leaned over the flight engineer's station. "Kiano's right, though. The UEA will sue us. We'll never get another mission, or even be astronauts after this. Our careers are gone. Like so many of our mates."

Rachel rose from the commander's seat. "*Chiron*'s databanks have everything that was recorded on that moon. Even Bakir and Li's journals, since it was all connected to the moon's network. They'll scapegoat us publicly, but privately they'll study us. Make us comfortable. Hoping we can provide something to satisfy their scientists."

"Li must have done that," Jemutai said. "Uploading all of that to this ship. That's incredible and….scary. You getting me?"

"Is he even human now?" Khandaar asked. "Or Bakir? Or Sakurai?"

Rachel gazed out the viewport. "That's not for us to say, but for them to discover. We still are, according to the blood test we just took."

"Leaving the moon eliminated the mutations and returned us to normal," Jemutai said. "Makes me wonder if that would have happened to those aliens, had they left, too."

"Wondering what will happen if I do not get something to eat," Larsen said.

They laughed and shared a meal in the galley. Though everyone ate their fill and made the occasional joke, there was no avoiding the cost: out of forty, only five survived.

The med drone checked their injuries again: Rachel's left deltoid had been bruised when she'd hit the locker inside *Seeker* and would heal. The cut on Larsen's right arm was a superficial one, but it would leave a scar.

Afterward, Worrel held a small ceremony to honor those they'd lost. Some muttered prayers or simply bowed their head. Rachel did neither, finding faith in herself and her friends. The whole time, she never let go of Larsen's hand.

The time came for them to enter stasis. Worrel had already set *Chiron*'s course for Earth. Four years. They'd spent hours checking the ship to ensure it could make the journey. The others gave Rachel and Larsen knowing glances and got into their pods first.

"When we get back…I want to show you Mars." Rachel deactivated *Chiron*'s centrifuges. "The places where I grew up. The sunset over Ophir Chasma."

They slowly rose from the deck as the artificial gravity ceased. Promixa Centauri was already a tiny dot outside the viewport.

"My little Martian girl will freeze after I dunk her in the Nærøyfjord in winter. I will have to keep her warm." Larsen kissed her. "Alone, with you all to myself."

Rachel glanced out the viewport, smiling. Millions of stars shone back at her.

She and Larsen—humanity itself—would never be alone again.

About the Author

Tony Peak is an Active Member of SFWA and an Affiliate Member of HWA. He is represented by Ethan Ellenberg of the Ethan Ellenberg Literary Agency. His debut novel INHERIT THE STARS was published by Penguin Random House in November 2015. His interests include progressive thinking, transhumanism, and planetary exploration. Residing in southwest Virginia, he has a wonderful view of New River.

About the Publisher

This book is published on behalf of the author by the Ethan Ellenberg Literary Agency.

https://ethanellenberg.com
Email: agent@ethanellenberg.com

www.ingramcontent.com/pod-product-compliance
Lightning Source LLC
Chambersburg PA
CBHW070623100726
47907CB00007B/1842